Little Lady, Big Apple

By the same author

The Little Lady Agency

About the author

Hester Browne bakes a perfect sponge, collects bright red lipsticks and etiquette books, and divides her time between the King's Road and Waitrose in Great Malvern.

HESTER BROWNE

Little Lady,
Big Apple

HODDER

For Isabella Cooper, the most charming little lady I know.

I

My name is Melissa Romney-Jones, but between the hours of nine and five you can call me Honey.

That's when I'm at work, running the Little Lady Agency, London's premier freelance girlfriend service – and during office hours I'm Honey Blennerhesket, queen of scruffy bachelors and scourge of slacking domestics. The Little Lady Agency, my very own business, is the first port of call for hopeless single chaps who need to borrow a woman's expertise for the afternoon, and you'd be astounded at how many of them there are.

It's not, I should stress, as racy as it sounds, but it's completely changed my outlook on men, in more ways than one.

As it says on my business cards, I offer – or, rather, Honey offers – every girlfriend service a man could need, except sex and laundry. Aside from that, I'll tackle anything, no matter how random or daunting, and it certainly keeps me busy. In the last year, for instance, I've advised on the purchase of hundreds of suits; frightened tens of broody would-be grannies into leaving well alone; helped break off five engagements and assisted nine proposals; salvaged three flats after three wild parties; bought stacks of godparental gifts; sent thousands of roses to spouses, secretaries, sisters and secret girlfriends; and generally acted as the invisible woman most men need to keep them on the straight and narrow.

You're probably wondering why I can't just do all this as Melissa. Well, there are several very good reasons for that.

First of all, if the name Romney-Jones seems familiar it's because my father, Martin, is the only MP to have survived no fewer than four separate political scandals (two tax, one sex, and something murky involving an EU cheese producer in Luxembourg that I've never quite got to the bottom of). When I started my business, I didn't want him to find out what I was up to, and now things are working out rather well I don't want him cashing in.

Second, if I'm being honest, in real life I'm a complete pushover – ground down by years of merciless advantage-taking by Daddy and the rest of my horrendously selfish family. So I found that creating bossy, super-groomed Honey sort of gives me permission to put my foot down where I'd normally fear to tread. Honey has much better shoes than me, for a start. Most of them are stilettos, to go with the fitted pencil skirts and devastating bombshell jumpers I wear for work, and Honey's not afraid to stamp those stilettos when she needs to get results. Rather hard, too, if the situation demands. Sometimes I don't even notice the blisters till I get home.

Plus, to be honest, there's something kind of sexy about being Honey. She never rounds her shoulders to hide her ample cleavage, or worries about how she looks from behind. And I never realised that wearing stockings for work would have such startling knock-on effects . . .

Ahem. Anyway . . .

Third? Well, everyone likes to be able to clock off at the end of the day, don't they? When you've spent hours ironing out endless male problems, it's nice to be able to walk away from them. And I do walk away. In dress-down Melissa's comfortable flatties.

Quite apart from the delicious wardrobe, I absolutely love my work. Up until I started the agency, I'd been an unthanked, frequently sacked PA, but now I positively look forward to going to work each morning. There's something so satisfying about taking shambolic bachelors and revealing their inner fox – rather like tarting up derelict houses that no one can bear to move into, only to see them besieged with buyers the next week. Some of my clients do need an element of structural repair, as well as cosmetic improvement, but that's even more satisfying to sort out, and the results sometimes bring a tear to my eye.

For a while I didn't think Melissa would ever be able to compete with Honey. She was just so much more . . . colourful than me. More confident, more dynamic, more everything, really.

But then the weirdest thing happened. We met – I mean, *I* met – someone. Jonathan was tall, charming, courteous, with perfect American teeth and a very handy foxtrot: in short, a proper old-fashioned gentleman.

The fact that he was a client made things a little complicated, but just as I was sure he was falling for Honey, he told me he'd fallen for me. Melissa! Not Honey! When I'd got over being amazed, I was very, very happy.

And I still am. Very, *very* happy.

However, being practically perfect during working hours didn't mean I wasn't still prone to lateness and laddered tights in the mornings. I was already seventeen minutes behind schedule, and since my best friend Gabi was meant to be helping me out on my first job of the day, I had no doubt those seventeen minutes were about to double.

I was running late because my flatmate, Nelson, had phoned LBC to add his twopenn'orth to a heated debate about recycling, and had insisted on my hanging around to record his contribution on the kitchen radio.

Gabi was running late because there was some sample sale on in Hampstead, for which the doors opened at 7 a.m.

At 8.33 a.m. we were both scuttling down the street towards the agency, knowing full well that Tristram Hart-Mossop would be waiting for us outside Selfridges at 9 a.m. on the dot, and I wasn't anywhere near ready for that.

'I don't see why we can't just go straight to Oxford Street!' panted Gabi.

'Because I need to get changed! Come on, we're nearly here now.' I walked briskly down Ebury Street. I went to the kind of school that encouraged brisk walking.

'Jesus, Mel, you move fast for a big girl. What kept you, anyway?' she gasped. 'A morning quickie with Dr No?'

'Certainly not!' I should explain that Gabi worked part-time in the estate agency that Jonathan managed and she had great trouble seeing him in a non-managerial role. He had a rather 'result-focused' management style. While Nelson tended to refer to him sarcastically as Remington Steele, on account of his all-American clean-cut jawline, the girls in the office – *apparently* – liked to call him Dr No.

Jonathan, I might add, rarely said no to me.

'He likes to get off quickly in the mornings,' I added. 'He's usually ready to go by seven.'

Gabi snorted dirtily. 'That's what I meant.'

I looked at her, baffled. 'No, I thought you were asking me if we'd—'

'Forget it,' she said. 'Get back in your Enid Blyton box.'

Gabi and Nelson were always baiting me with double entendres. I never got them. With a family like mine, one grows up habitually looking the other way.

'Nothing wrong with having an innocent mind,' I said, unlocking the door and pushing it open.

There was the usual stack of interesting-looking post, but I didn't have time to check through it. Instead, we bounded up the stairs two at a time, past the very discreet beauty salon on the ground floor, where Chelsea wives snuck off for their Botox and electro-whatsits, and into my office.

I threw my huge handbag on the leather sofa, and handed Gabi the bunch of ranunculas I'd bought on the way.

'Right,' I said, peeling off my cardigan. 'I'm going to get changed. Stick these flowers in water, would you?'

'OK,' said Gabi, looking round for a vase. 'God, this place is comfy. I'm surprised half your clients don't try moving in.'

'That's the point.'

My office was a little second-floor flat: the main room was my lilac-walled, calming consultation space, with a tiny bathroom, an even tinier kitchen alcove and a small second room, in which I kept spare clothes, supplies and a fold-out bed, in case of emergency.

Leaving the door open so I could chat to Gabi, I slipped out of my floaty summer skirt, and hunted about for my suspender belt. There weren't that many businesses where you could spend hundreds of pounds on

Agent Provocateur underwear and charge it to office furniture. As I slid the first crisp new stocking over my toes, and carefully smoothed it up and over my leg, I started to feel, as I always did, that little bit more confident. More put together. More in charge.

'Do you want a coffee?' yelled Gabi.

'Please!' I fixed the stocking in place, and quickly rolled on the other. I'd got quite adept at this. There was a knack to it, a little flick of the finger and thumb, which was really rather satisfying to acquire. I could imagine Jane Russell doing it. After my stockings came the black pencil skirt, which skimmed over the curve of my tummy. It was a high suspender belt, with a decent flattening capacity, but it could only do so much.

Something about stockings made me stand up straighter. I hunted through the rails to find a clean blouse.

'Biscuits?' yelled Gabi.

'In the barrel. Home-made. Nelson knocked some up for me.'

Gabi let out a gusty sigh of admiration for Nelson's shortbread.

I slipped into a fresh black shirt, and buttoned it over my rose satin balconette bra. Not that clients ever got to see my spectacularly glam underpinnings, obviously, but it made *me* feel better, knowing they were there. My fingers hesitated over the third button, parting precariously close to the delicate lace of my bra. I left it undone.

It promised to be a warm day, after all.

Finally, I wriggled my stockinged feet into a pair of high-heeled court shoes and I was ready.

Honey Blennerhesket. Five feet eleven inches of woman.

Out of habit, my hand reached for the finishing touch,

the final piece of the Melissa to Honey transformation: Honey's long blonde wig, currently sitting on top of the filing cabinet like a religious icon, its caramel curls spooling lusciously around the antique porcelain head.

I stopped. No. That was the one thing that Jonathan *had* said no to. No more wearing the wig, as part of the 'stand-in girlfriend' service. The wig had only been a disguise, but somehow it had unleashed a whole side of me that I'd never really known was there.

Still, it was so lovely. And it made me look so glamorous. Quite spectacular, in fact.

I took a step nearer, and stroked the real hair.

I never felt as gorgeous as I did when I was a slinky blonde. Would it hurt, just to try it on for a moment, just to get me in the—

'Here you go, milk, no sugar . . . Jesus Christ!' blurted Gabi as she stepped into the room with the coffees.

I sprang back from the wig guiltily.

'I never get used to how different you look in the whole Honey get-up,' she marvelled. 'Look at that tiny waist! You sex bomb, you.'

I flapped my hand. 'It's all tailoring. You should—'

'Yeah, yeah.' Gabi preferred a lower-maintenance style. She nodded towards the wig. 'So, you going to put that on?'

'No,' I said firmly. 'I don't wear this any more.'

'Ever?'

'No. Jonathan and I agreed that I wouldn't.'

'Not even at home?' Gabi twinkled naughtily. She was shameless sometimes. If you asked me, she got away with a good deal under the guise of straight talking. 'He doesn't ask you to do any . . . role-playing?'

I blushed. '*No.*'

Between you and me, I still liked to put it on now and again. When no one was around. Just swishing all that hair about was so sexy and confidence-inspiring. Nelson, who never tires of taking the mickey out of me, claimed it had voodoo powers like something out of a spooky novel. The Wig That Flounced on Its Own.

Actually, in my middle-of-the-night panic moments I sometimes wondered if Jonathan secretly preferred me when I was Honey the blonde. He was a very successful estate agent. He drove a Mercedes that cost more than Nelson paid for his flat. And his ex-wife Cindy was a real blonde, who probably wasn't drummed out of the Pony Club for over-feeding her horse (out of love, not carelessness).

There was something about the thought of Cindy that put the fear of God in me, on many levels. I suppressed a shudder.

I reminded myself that I hadn't actually met her, and so probably shouldn't be drawing unfair conclusions. Of course if I had met her then maybe I wouldn't be haunted by my vivid imagination.

'No,' I said, more firmly. 'He doesn't like me wearing it full stop. Says he's had his fill of blondes for now.'

'More fool him then,' said Gabi, offering me the mug and gulping from her own. 'Come on! We've got three minutes and that's if we can find a cab.' She blew on her coffee, then added, 'Mind, dressed like that, I doubt you'll have a problem on that front. Not that you ever do.'

'Don't rush,' I said. 'No point in scalding yourself.'

She thrust her watch in my face. 'Look!'

A strange calm had descended over me. 'Tristram can just wait. We'll get there when we get there.'

Gabi looked at me with something approaching admiration. 'Blimey. What a difference a dress makes.'

'I think better in high heels,' I said serenely. 'You've got the camcorder?'

'Check.'

'Wonderful.'

We made it to Selfridges by five minutes past. That was the beauty of Honey: she was never exactly late, but she knew the value in keeping men waiting for a minute or two.

Tristram Hart-Mossop looked less than thrilled to see us, nonetheless, and I hurried him up to the menswear department as fast as possible, trying to keep Gabi away from the lure of the perfume hall. With the benefit of hindsight, she might not have been the ideal choice of sidekick for this particular job.

When the three of us were safely upstairs, I took a deep breath, marshalled my thoughts like a midget gymnast about to perform a complicated series of flick-flacks and piked what-nots, and launched into full Honey mode.

'So, you see, Tristram,' I trilled, with an expansive wave of the hand, 'you've got one thousand pounds to spend on clothes, and I'm going to help you spend it!'

Then I turned to Gabi, who was filming me on my office camcorder, and added, with a smile so broad it made my cheeks hurt, 'Because I'm Honey Blennerhesket and I'm "Making You Over"!'

Gabi, to give her credit, didn't laugh when I said this. Which was good of her, because I heard some passing shopper snigger behind me and someone else say, quite distinctly, 'Who?'

'Tristram,' hissed Gabi. 'Say something!'

Tristram Hart-Mossop, the textbook illustration of 'awkward teenager', shuffled self-consciously, but with the camera readiness of an adolescent brought up on *Big Brother* and *Wife Swap*. 'That's great!' he managed, in response to my discreet prodding. 'Um, Honey. Um, yuh, cheers.'

'So,' I finished, with another chuckling smile, 'without further ado, let's get on and *make you over*!'

'And cut!' said Gabi. 'That was great. You're very good on camera, you know, Tristram.'

I gave her a quick 'don't build your part up' warning look and she raised her eyebrows in fake innocence. It wasn't, I must say, very convincing. Innocence wasn't one of Gabi's natural expressions.

'Still don't remember entering this competition,' Tristram mumbled poshly as I strode into the lambswool sweaters, hustling him ahead of me like a sheepdog. 'And, y'know, I don't remember seeing this programme on MTV, like you said . . .'

'That's because your mum entered you, as a surprise!' I carolled gaily, and slid my arm into his. 'And you won't have seen it before, because this is a pilot. Isn't that exciting? You're the first one! Now, let's go and find you some new clothes . . .'

Tristram I don't think even considered that I might not really be called Honey. The good thing about sounding quite posh is that you can have the most ridiculous name and no one seems to bat an eyelid. I mean, I know a Bobsy, a Troll and a Muffet, all from one year at school. Muffet, come to think of it, was actually *christened* Muffet.

We weren't really filming a makeover show for MTV,

needless to say. I was using stealth means to get the shop-a-phobic Tristram into a new set of clothes that wouldn't make him look like he'd covered himself in glue and cart-wheeled round the back room of an Oxfam shop. His mother, Olympia, had tottered up the stairs to my office in a state of utter despair, having heard about Honey from a friend of hers whose son I'd cured of nail-biting. (Seventeen surprise phone calls a day soon shocked him out of it.)

'Tristram simply refuses to buy new clothes. Refuses!' she'd wailed. 'He's so self-conscious about his height, but also, I think, it's because he has dreadfully shaped *knees*.' She stopped herself. 'Not that I've ever told him that. But he takes any comment about his appearance as a personal criticism, for some reason, and just slobs around in the same two T-shirts all the time. He won't listen to a word I say. I mean, he's got university interviews coming up and they're going to think he's some kind of drug addict!'

Looking at Tristram now, towering uncertainly over a display of boxer shorts as if he wasn't quite sure what his gangling limbs might do next, the only drug he seemed to be on was some kind of growth hormone.

I'd calmed Mrs Hart-Mossop down as best I could with a plate of shortbread, and promised to smarten up Tristram to the point where his own father wouldn't recognise him.

'You'll have a job,' she'd said, forgetting herself suffi-ciently to start dunking her biscuit. 'He simply refuses to spend money on clothes, even when it's *my* money. Insists he'd rather have it in cash to spend on his computer.'

That made my heart sink. Computers and fashion weren't easy bedfellows. Still, I'd had much worse cases in the past. Some of my clients, it turned out, had actual *infestations*.

'Don't you worry about a thing,' I'd said with a beaming smile, offering Mrs Hart-Mossop a top-up of tea from the family silver teapot. 'I pride myself on being a lateral thinker.'

'You'll have to be a bloody hypnotist,' she'd said bitterly, and took a second biscuit.

And so here we were in Selfridges, pandering sneakily to Tristram's obsession with reality TV and, in the process, introducing him to the world of linen.

Gabi really was filming too. Even though I'd asked her to pretend and keep the camera turned off. I could already imagine the hilarity that would ensue when she played it back at home to the amusement of Nelson, who never missed a chance to have a good laugh at my expense, particularly when it involved me having to fib. Given my family background, I am an incomprehensibly bad liar. Nelson has an annoying habit of shouting 'Ding!' whenever he spots me telling a porkie.

'Turn it off!' I hissed, while Tristram toyed curiously with cufflinks, as if he'd never seen them before.

Gabi shook her head and stepped out of my reach, just as Tristram turned back to me.

'Are these, like, fabric nose-studs?' he asked, holding up a cufflink to study it more closely.

'No.' I took it off him and replaced it in the huge bowl. 'That's advanced dressing. We'll get to that later.' I upped my encouraging smile. 'So, Tristram, where would you like to start?'

His face went dark with reluctance. 'The computer department.'

'No!' I laughed, rather grimly now I could see what an uphill battle this would be. 'I mean, shall we start with a smart suit, or with casual wear?'

He looked at me like a giraffe peering down on a brush-wielding zoo keeper, then swung his gaze towards Gabi, who had stopped filming long enough to inspect a very lifelike dummy modelling tight jersey briefs.

'Is that thing off?' he demanded.

'If you want it to be,' I said soothingly. 'Gabi? Could you give us a moment?'

With the camera off, Tristram sounded dejected, rather than sullen. 'Look, can't I just have the money? Nothing's going to fit. Nothing ever does. Even when Mum pretends it looks OK, I just look like a big freak.'

'No, you don't,' I said bracingly. 'You just need the right clothes!'

'I like the ones I've got.' He flicked balefully at a row of ties, then stared at his shoes. 'Poppy Bridewell, um . . . This . . . girl I met at a party said I looked artistic in T-shirts.'

There was a fine line between artistic and autistic. I wondered if it had been a loud party.

'Is she your girlfriend?'

He shook his head, scattering dandruff on the cashmere jumpers. 'Don't have one. Never meet girls.'

'Well, Tristram, just think how many girls will be watching this!' I said conspiratorially. 'And when they see you looking great in new clothes, clothes that really make the most of those lovely shoulders you have . . .' I lifted my eyebrows. 'I'm sure you'll soon be *fighting* them off!'

I could hear Nelson 'ding'ing in my head, but I crossed my fingers. Nothing enhanced a man's confidence like

knowing his shirt was working for him. He'd get more
attention, one way or another.

'You think?' grunted Tristram, but his face looked more
hopeful.

'Just come with me,' I said, and propelled him towards
the changing rooms. I'd phoned ahead and asked the
personal shopper to put aside some bits and pieces just
to get us started. 'You're already very good with layers,
Tristram,' I said, nudging him into a cubicle with some
buttery-soft cotton T-shirts and a cashmere jumper. 'You
just need to upgrade them a little. Now pop these on,
and let's see what they look like.'

Gabi reappeared, viewfinder to her eye, and Tristram
shuffled compliantly behind the curtain.

'It's amazing what people'll do if they think they're
going to be on telly, isn't it?' whispered Gabi, as if she
herself wouldn't do exactly the same thing. 'I was in
Brent Cross Shopping Centre at the weekend, just
looking for sale bargains, you know, and this camera crew
were there, and I . . . What?'

'You said you'd cut up your credit cards.'

Gabi shuffled. 'Yeah, well. You'll never understand
about me and my credit cards. They're like you and your
wig.'

'Let's drop the wig, shall we?' I said breezily.

Gabi's generous mouth twisted into a naughty grin.
'You can't Honey me, Mel,' she said. 'I work with women
much posher and much arsier than you.'

Technically, Gabi and I didn't have much in common
– what with me being what she generically termed a
'Chalet Girl Princess' and her being the Queen of the
North London Shopping Centres – but since my first day
at the Dean & Daniels estate agency, where she'd ripped

her skirt doing a very cruel impression of our office manager Carolyn mounting her Vespa, and I'd stitched it back up for her with the sewing kit I always kept in my bag, we'd been bosom buddies. The best friendships are like mobile phones, I think: you can't explain exactly *how* they work, but you're just relieved they do.

'Shh!' she said, before I could say anything, and pointed at the cubicle. 'Clothes are appearing!'

I looked over to the cubicle and saw reject clothes being tossed petulantly over the curtain. Oh no. If Tristram thought he could just run through the lot in five minutes and pretend nothing fitted, he was sadly mistaken. I glanced about for the nice tailoring man to pop in and get his measurements for a decent suit. Tailoring made all the difference with these scruffy Sloane lads: once they were out of some awful inherited-from-Dad tweed Huntsman number and into something that *fitted*, they started to walk better, stand up straighter, preen themselves a little more.

Well, in most cases.

Tristram slunk out of the changing room with the T-shirt riding at half-mast, revealing some not-unattractive stomach, and the jumper concertina'd around his elbows. He looked like the Incredible Hulk mid-transformation, but still about ten times better than when he'd gone in. He even managed a shy smile for the imaginary massed audience of single girls waiting for him behind Gabi's lens.

'See?' I said to the camera. 'Fabulous! With shoulders like those you can carry off practically anything. Now, try on these jackets!' I pushed some jackets at him and made a mental note to find a sales assistant to ask discreetly if they had some in longer lengths.

'Are you in for dinner tonight then?' asked Gabi dreamily. 'Nelson says he's making something with fresh trout. He's a really excellent cook, you know.'

I gave her a level look. I *knew* Nelson was an excellent cook. I'd known he was an excellent cook for the best part of the twenty-odd years I'd known *him*.

When I'd moved in to Nelson's slightly shabby-chic flat behind Victoria Coach Station, five years ago, it had just been me and him, and we'd been very cosy, in that way that only old, *old* friends can be. Our fathers were at school together, and Nelson and I had grown up fighting over endless rounds of Monopoly, and squabbling over bunk beds. I'd rather got used to our unmarried, marital lifestyle – him bossing me about, criticising my parking but helping me with my accounts, while I generally added some female fragrance to his lifestyle. Nelson sailed a lot at weekends with his mate Roger. Now summer was coming on, the flat was beginning to smell like a marina, but without the champagne and suntan lotion.

However, since my sister Emery's wedding at Christmas, Gabi had been sort of seeing Nelson, and much as I wanted both of them to be happy, I couldn't help feeling what Jonathan would call *conflicted*. (He's an American estate agent. He specialises in euphemisms.) Gabi was my best friend and Nelson – well, Nelson was like my brother. The first night Gabi stayed over without giving me time to make myself scarce I gobbled three Nytol and slept with my head wrapped in the duvet, just in case I heard something I shouldn't.

Nelson made a point of leaning over the breakfast table the next morning, before Gabi got up, and intoning, 'Nothing happened,' at me as if I were some dreadful maiden aunt – which was ironic, since 'maiden aunt' is his own default behaviour setting – but unfortunately the Nytol had made me too groggy to yell at him, so I had to settle for a glare which he huffily interpreted as prurient interest.

So, yes. It was all getting rather awkward. I loved them both, wildly unsuited as they were, but the whole thing was just a little bit . . . Urgh.

Still, that was the beauty of being Honey, I thought, checking my list of must-buys for Tristram as a retrospective blush rose into my cheeks. At work Honey always knew what she was doing and wasn't afraid of speaking her mind. And she wasn't shy either. Not like Melissa.

'So, are you in tonight or what?' asked Gabi again, examining some silk briefs that I sincerely hoped she wasn't planning to buy for Nelson.

'Um, yes,' I stammered. 'Actually, no. No. I'll, er . . .'

'You think Nelson would wear these?' she asked, holding up a pair of red silk pants.

'Definitely not!' I said, without thinking. 'He's always going on about how he hates that swinging free feeling and how he's constantly thinking he's about to catch himself on something . . .'

We stared at each other in mutual horror.

Fortunately, at that moment, there was a yelp and Tristram's head reappeared round the curtain, looking both panicked and affronted. I snapped back into Honey mode without even thinking.

'This chap's just told me to take off my trousers!' he howled.

'He's only measuring you for a suit, Tristram,' I said briskly. 'Nothing to worry about. Let the nice man get the measurements, and then all you have to do is choose a colour!'

The head disappeared.

'Blimey,' said Gabi, impressed. 'I've never really seen you doing this Honey thing before. It's quite scary, isn't it?'

'Is it?' I wasn't sure what to make of that.

'Are you wearing stockings?' asked Gabi, casting a sideways glance at my skirt.

'What?' I shifted from foot to foot. I didn't normally have anyone around when I was working, and I was beginning to wish I hadn't asked Gabi to help me out. It was putting me off my stride. Or rather, I couldn't get into my stride as Honey when she was there to remind me I was really Melissa.

'Are you wearing stockings?' Gabi did a suggestive shimmy, and I blanched. 'Or did Jonathan knock that on the head too?' she enquired. 'I know he's not happy about you carrying on with the agency, not now you're meant to be a respectable estate agent's girlfriend and all that.'

I looked suspiciously at the camcorder. Did that red light mean it was on or off? Things had also gone very still inside the cubicle, so I dropped my voice discreetly. 'Jonathan's fine about the agency, for your information. He just doesn't want me to pretend to be anyone's *girl-friend* any more. What I do with the rest of my time is my own business. If you must know, he's very proud of me for being so entrepreneurial. End of topic.'

'Oooooooh,' said Gabi. 'Touch-eeeee.'

'Not in the least. I'm going to get Tristram into a suit,' I announced, to change the subject. 'It's like getting a suit of armour. Gives you bulges in the right places and hides everything else.'

Gabi looked unconvinced. 'You'd know best. And I wouldn't want to argue with you, not in this sort of mood. Still, you know you could be getting all this a *lot* cheaper elsewhere? You ever thought about using me in an advisory capacity? I could be saving you a lot of money.'

'It's not the money his mother cares about,' I said, my attention caught by the twitching of the cubicle curtain. Gabi's shopping expertise went without saying. 'It's the fact that he's going to be persuaded into wearing adult clothes.'

As I said this, Tristram stepped out of the changing room, in a black jacket and a really cool pair of dark jeans. He looked pretty good, if I said so myself.

'Oh, wow!' I swooned, clapping one hand to my bosom. 'Tristram! Look at *you*! Don't you look fabulous?'

The beginnings of a shy smile began to tug at the corners of his mouth, despite his best efforts to look cool and don't-care-ish. The clothes made a difference, but what really finished it off was a touch of confidence.

I went over and put my arm around him so we were both facing Gabi's camera. I hoped she had it on steadicam, because her shoulders were twitching with barely suppressed laughter.

I, on the other hand, was taking it very seriously, because Tristram obviously was. I felt him flinch, then, as I cuddled him tighter, he relaxed into me and even put a gangling arm round my shoulder.

'So, how do you feel, Tristram?' I cooed. 'That jacket really brings out the blue in your eyes! You've got such lovely eyes, you know!'

'Um, yeah, um, I . . . cool,' he mumbled. That was about as articulate as most public schoolboys got, but from the way he was sufficiently emboldened to start some tentative groping, I chalked that up as a win and subtly removed his paw from my rear.

Tristram, Gabi and I had a very nice cup of tea downstairs in Selfridges, next to the computer department, before we sent him on his way, promising to let him know the moment we had a broadcast date. I thought I saw the salesgirl wink at him on the way out, and realised that enlisting similar encouragement might be a good confidence-boosting strategy to employ in the future.

'You realise that Tristram had his nose practically down your cleavage at the end?' said Gabi, peering at the flickering playback screen.

'Did he?' I blushed and poured myself some more tea.

'Any closer and he'd have been talking to your navel. You want to see?' she offered.

'God, no!' I shied away. I hated seeing myself in pictures. It never quite matched the vision I had in my head. The one in which I was played by Elizabeth Taylor, circa 1959.

'You know, we should so send this tape into MTV,' said Gabi, through a mouthful of raspberry cheesecake. 'You could get your own programme. Mel's Munters. Geek to Chic. You think?'

'No, I don't think.' I looked on enviously. I only had to breathe near cheesecake and I put on about half a stone. 'Shouldn't you be saving yourself for supper?'

'Not a problem.' She squished the last few crumbs down on the back of her fork and popped them in her mouth. 'Got the fastest metabolism in London, me.' A broad smile illuminated her face. 'S'why I think me and Nelson are just fated to be together. Fast as he cooks it, I eat it!'

Funny. Gabi's last boyfriend, Aaron, hadn't had time to make a Pot Noodle, but he'd made money as fast as she could spend it – almost – and she'd nearly married him.

I pushed aside these unworthy thoughts. It was the end of a very long week, and frankly I was looking forward to spending the rest of the evening in a soap-opera-related trance, ideally with Nelson rubbing my feet. He was so good at foot rubs that I even forgave him the accompanying drone about learning the techniques while doing gap year charity work in Thailand.

Then I remembered that it was dinner for two and gooseberries for one at our house that evening, and the blissful image abruptly shattered. I supposed I could go round to Jonathan's, but he had tennis coaching on Friday nights, and, in any case, we hadn't quite reached the stage of our relationship where I was happy for him to see me dribbling onto a pillow as I fell asleep watching *Coronation Street*.

Oh, don't be such a misery-guts, I told myself sternly. Pull yourself together!

I looked up at Gabi. She was a good friend, and I should be thrilled she'd found someone as decent as Nelson. 'Thanks for giving up your day off to help me out,' I said. 'It was really sweet of you.'

'No problemo.' Gabi finished off the last of the tea. ''Sides, it's not my day off. Carolyn thinks I'm having a root canal. She's not expecting me in till Monday at the earliest.'

'Gabi . . .' I said reproachfully.

She cut me a cheeky look. 'Oh, come on. Let someone else make the tea for a change! Anyway, it was an education. For me and for Tristram. I bet you ten quid he'll be back for new jeans and another crack at your cleavage next week. Listen, what time's supper tonight?' Her dark eyes went all dreamy. 'God, Nelson. There's something about him that just makes me want to warm his slippers. He's so big, and sensible. I feel like a heroine in an old-fashioned novel when I'm with him.'

I stared at her disbelievingly. Since when had Jane Austen run to small, cynical north London shopaholics?

'Well, he certainly makes a change from Aaron,' I said tactfully.

Gabi tossed her head dismissively. 'I am so over Aaron,' she said. 'Him and his ridiculous quarter-life crisis. Nelson's much more focused. He wouldn't chuck everything in to go back to college at his age.'

'You know, I don't think giving up a stressful job to study pathology is necessarily a bad thing,' I tried. 'I mean, OK, he should have discussed it with you first, but maybe he wanted to follow a dream.'

'Honestly, Mel, you and your benefit of the doubt! Jesus!' She gave me her best 'dur!' look. 'If he's so interested in dead bodies, why couldn't he have just bought himself a *CSI* box-set?'

'Maybe it's just a phase?' I suggested. I wasn't so sure *she* wasn't going through a phase.

'Yeah,' she snorted. 'A phase of *singleness*.'

I was saved from having to continue this now-familiar discussion by my phone ringing in my bag. I have two: a normal one for myself, and a swanky black one for work.

But this was my own line, and the number displayed made my heart sink, right into the pit of my corseted stomach.

'Hello?' I said, as brightly as I could nonetheless.

'Melissa!' barked Daddy. 'Get yourself home at once. There's a family crisis. Your mother needs you.'

Then he hung up.

Well, I thought, trying to look on the bright side, that sorted out one of my immediate problems, at least. There was little or no chance of having to avoid public displays of affection at my parents' house.

'Congratulations,' I said to Gabi. 'You and Nelson have got the place to yourselves this evening!'

'Thanks, Mel,' she said with a wink, and I felt pleased, guilty and slightly sick, all at the same time.

2

I drove to my parents' house in a state of some consternation, not helped by the stream of messages arriving on both phones.

Even if Nelson wasn't such a home-made policeman, lecturing me incessantly about hands-free car kits, I wasn't sure I wanted to check the messages anyway, in case they contained even more pleas to fit appointments into my bursting schedule and/or updates about whatever this emergency was at home. When it came to my father, ignorance was usually bliss. Which was just as well, because as far as he was concerned, 'the truth, the whole truth and nothing but the truth' were three entirely separate levels of information.

The others weren't much better. My family rarely bothered to explain their crises in advance, on the basis, I think, that if I had any inkling of what I'd be letting myself in for, I'd simply drive in the opposite direction.

I pulled a reflective face in the mirror. That said, things had been quite peaceful in the eight months since my younger sister Emery's wedding at Christmas to William, a sports-mad, ultra-competitive, thrice-married solicitor. Peaceful by Romney-Jones standards, at least, since they'd spent most of those eight months moving to Chicago and therefore removing themselves from immediate contact. Although Emery was so vague she could easily be on the verge of childbirth by now and not thought to mention it.

There had been nothing in the paper about my father for months – although Parliament was out of session at the moment.

My mother was, the last time I called home, resident in the marital manor house and not shacked up in some seaweed spa in the west of Ireland, or, worse, in some discreet ranch called Serendipity in Arizona having her liver holistically massaged. Though that, again, may have been connected in some way with Parliament being out of session.

My other sister Allegra was in Sweden, where she lived with her husband Lars, an art and antiquities dealer specialising in prehistoric arrowheads and other more arcane stuff that I didn't like to ask about.

And Granny . . . I turned up my Julie London CD, which reminded me of her. Granny was the one redeeming feature of my family: she was glamorous, amusing, and the only person I knew with sufficient self-confidence to rattle my father. She had friends in higher places than him, coupled with a mysterious private income which meant that he couldn't crack the financial whip at her either.

I loved Granny more than anyone, but if there was some crisis afoot at home she was almost certainly on a camel tour of Egypt or similar, charming all and sundry from beneath a diaphanous veil.

I made it back to the family pile in a very decent two hours, and when I pulled up in the drive there was a full complement of cars outside. That never boded well. Family crises seemed to escalate exponentially the more

Romney-Joneses joined in. And from the chewed-up state of the gravel, all the cars had been parked with some rage. Mummy's mud-splattered Merc estate still had a dog in the back that she'd obviously forgotten to let out in her haste to get in. Daddy's Jag was blocking in Emery's old lime-green Beetle, left there since her wedding, and an enormous black BMW X5 was halfway across the ornamental flowerbed in the centre, looking not so much parked as stalled and abandoned.

I peered at it. It was brand-new. God knew who that belonged to.

I parked my own Subaru well out of the way, next to an ancient hydrangea, and checked my face in the rear-view mirror, taking three slow deep breaths to prepare myself for the onslaught. When that failed, I had a couple of squirts of Rescue Remedy. Even so, my hand joggled rather as I was freshening up my lipstick.

The gardens were looking deceptively calm in the warm August evening, and I could smell the tall box hedges that ran around the perimeter of the house mingling with the musky roses climbing up the front wall. Jenkins, Mummy's oldest basset hound, leaped up at the window of her car as I approached, barking his head off with excitement, and I helped him out. He was getting on a bit and sometimes needed a hand over the dog shelf, as his back legs were somewhat arthritic and his undercarriage tended to ground him on obstacles like a barge.

'Hello, old man!' I said, wobbling his big ears, and trying not to get my face within reach of his toxic breath.

He snuffled gratefully at my bag as I made my way inside. Already the echoes of a family row were bouncing off the parquet tiles like so much distant cannon fire. I adjudged, from the level of shrieking and bellowing, that the row was taking place not in the kitchen, as usual, but in the drawing room, which indicated that it was quite a high-level argument. In the intimidatingly formal drawing room, my father could take full advantage of the uncomfortable antique sofas, which he liked to stalk around then lean over, aggressively, without warning, to bellow in the ear of the occupant. My mother much preferred to argue in the kitchen, where she had improved access to plates and knives, not to mention 'cooking sherry'.

'Have you taken leave of your senses entirely?' Daddy was yelling at some unfortunate – my mother, I guessed, since he asked her this question more often than anything else. 'Do you think the world revolves entirely around you?'

I paused at the door, temporarily paralysed by the sheer hypocrisy of this comment, coming from a man who refused to read the morning paper if someone else had got there first and 'spoiled the pages'.

'No,' said a low, but equally piercing voice. 'I imagine the world revolves around art. Which is better than imagining it revolves around money, like you do.'

Oh, God. Allegra. What was she doing here?

Jenkins whimpered, turned tail with the grace of an oil tanker, and skittered across the parquet and down to the kitchen, out of harm's way. I was tempted to join him, especially since it was village fete time, and I knew Mummy would have cleaned out the cake stalls with her usual inability to stop at four fruit scones.

'Don't be so bloody precious!' roared my father, who had no time for Allegra's artistic nature, or, indeed, Lars's art gallery, oddly profitable though it was. 'Even Melissa doesn't come out with claptrap like that and she doesn't know the difference between shorthand and street-walking!'

Charming. The 'real' nature of my agency, as understood by Daddy, was something of a running joke. Or it would be, if it had been funny.

'Martin!' screeched my mother. 'Do not use my Meissen dish as an ashtray!'

I gave Mummy or Allegra ten seconds to leap to my defence, then, when no one did, I barged in before they actively joined in with slurs of their own.

'Oh, Christ, what now?' Daddy bellowed, by way of paternal greeting. He had apparently forgotten that it was in fact him who had summoned me there in the first place.

'Hello, Melissa,' said my mother, through tight lips. I mean they were tight lips, literally. She seemed oddly lifted and was wearing her shimmery blonde hair much more forward than usual. 'I'm so glad you're here. I know you can talk some sense into everyone, darling. You always do.'

'Hello, Mummy. Hello, Daddy,' I said, reverting, like Alice in Wonderland, to my nine-year-old self. 'Hello, Allegra, how lovely to see you at home! I thought you were in Stockholm at the moment.'

Allegra was quite something to behold in the chintz of the drawing room. She seemed taller than ever, in a long black kaftan-type thing that would have made me look like a funeral parlour sofa but it draped over her willowy frame like couture. It may well have been couture, come to that. Her long dark hair – about the only thing we had in common – rippled down her back, and her face was unmade-up, apart from her lips, which were a bright matte scarlet. I couldn't take my eyes off them.

'I've left Lars,' she announced, red lips moving in a hypnotic fashion amidst all the black and white. 'I have Come Home.'

'God alone knows why you have to come back to this one,' interrupted my father. 'You've got a perfectly good home of your own on Ham Common.'

She shot him a poisonous glare in reply and turned back to me with a pained expression. 'It's over. All over, Melissa.'

'Oh, no!' I said, feeling terrible for her. 'You poor thing!' Allegra and Lars were notoriously tempestuous, as befitted artists, but she'd never actually left him before. That was, she explained, the whole point of having two houses in separate countries. It cut down nicely on the togetherness. 'What's happened?'

A dark look crossed Allegra's pale face. 'I can't talk about it.'

'Is it too painful? Give it time,' I urged. 'When Gabi split up with Aaron, she couldn't—'

'No,' said Allegra. 'I mean I really can't talk about it. I have to speak to my solicitor first.'

'A solicitor?' My hand flew to my mouth. Was it that bad? 'Oh, Allegra! I'm so sorry!'

She nodded. 'I know. He's on his way over now.'

Now? I frowned. 'But surely it can wait until you've had a chance to sleep on things a little, you know, calm down?'

Allegra made a zipping gesture over her lips.

My mother let out an impatient sigh, but Daddy shushed her with his raised hand. 'That's my girl,' he said, with a ghastly smile of pride. 'Always make sure you're on firm legal ground before you get the kicking brogues laced up. Aren't you glad now that I made the pre-nup in England and not in Stockholm? Hmm?'

Allegra tossed her head scornfully.

'I always think there's a touch of *art* in a really clever contract,' he concluded.

'But, darling, why can't you go back to Ham?' asked my mother. Her hands twitched automatically for her cigarettes, but she was obviously on one of her annual giving-up kicks, because I couldn't see her familiar gold cigarette case around. Instead, she reached underneath the sofa and pulled out an embroidered bag with a kitten on the front. To my astonishment, she withdrew a shapeless hank of knitting and started clicking away, lips pressed firmly together where her cigarette would normally have gone.

Daddy tapped the ash from his cigar ostentatiously into the fireplace.

'I wonder what will kill you first, Martin?' she said, shutting her eyes. 'Tobacco or me?'

'You, I'd hope, my darling,' replied my father easily. 'I'm on the board of at least two tobacco importers – shame to cast a shadow on business.'

He whipped back round to Allegra. 'Answer your mother's question, Allegra: why can't you go back to Ham? Perfectly good house you've got there. What's happened? Lars changed the locks?'

'Lars has not changed the locks,' snorted Allegra, flapping her long black sleeves huffily. She and Daddy were practically nose-to-nose on the carpet now. 'That's *my* house!'

'So why can't you go and boil with rage there, instead of cluttering up my home?' he demanded. 'Your mother and I have been through this when you were a teenager. We don't need to have another round of midnight phone calls and dead cats in the garden.'

Dead cats? No one told me anything, even then.

'Not that we don't love to see you at home, darling,' added my mother, clicking furiously. 'It's lovely to see you.'

My father wheeled round on his heel. 'Are you off your head, Belinda? Of *course* we mind her turning up here! Not only am I a busy MP, I am now serving on no fewer than two Olympic sub-committees!'

'Are you?' I asked, temporarily distracted. 'I didn't know that.'

'Yes, well, I've been invited to join a couple of select committees for the London 2012 business. Taking up a lot of my time, involves a tiresome amount of meeting and greeting and so on . . .' He sighed as if he didn't spend half his life trying to find junkets to skive off on.

'Really?' I said, impressed all the same. My father, involved with the Olympic spirit! 'Congratulations!'

He brushed it away, but was unable to hide his preening. 'Well, lots of opportunities floating around right now. For the right people . . . If you know what I mean.'

Unfortunately, I did.

'So what sort of committee are you on?' I asked, intrigued.

'Oh, this and that. I can't really talk about it,' he said. 'Very hush-hush just at the minute, but it's very high-level. Very high-level.' This seemed to bring him back to reality, because he swung back to glare at Allegra, who had arranged herself along a sofa like a militant end-of-the-pier crystal-ball reader.

'So you'll appreciate that I don't need all these amateur theatricals going on when I have work to do. If I want to see *Phantom of the Opera* I'll have a night out in the West End. You're welcome to stay here tonight, Allegra, but you can't just land up here and treat this place like a hotel. You have no idea what plans your mother and I have for entertaining this week, for one thing.'

A look of dread passed across Mummy's face, and she knitted faster. She spent most of her time organising dinners and cocktail parties for Daddy's constituents and contacts, and what time was left writing notes of apology and explanation to cover any untoward consequences.

'I can't go back to Ham because it's covered in "Police Line Do Not Cross" tape!' Allegra roared.

'What?' I gasped, but no one was listening to me.

Daddy tutted. 'All the more reason to get back there, I'd have thought.'

I stared at her, my skin crawling with panic. Mummy looked less concerned by this news than she had done about Daddy's weekend plans, and as for Daddy and Allegra, they seemed to be positively revelling in the drama.

'There are forensic policemen from three different countries swarming all over my beautiful home, and I am not *allowed* to go back, all right?' Allegra spat, with no small relish. 'You don't think I'd put a foot over your godforsaken threshold unless I absolutely had to? I've left my husband, not had some kind of mental collapse, for Christ's sake!'

Mummy made a choking sound and scrabbled around in her knitting bag. I wondered if she had a whole other set of knitting patterns for serious stress, but instead she pulled out a medicine bottle, wrenched off the cap, shook out a handful of pills and swallowed them.

'Valerian,' she lied unconvincingly, seeing my shocked face.

'Valerian, Vicodin, Valium,' mused Daddy, puffing on

his cigar. 'What's a couple of letters between friends when you're working your way through the narcotic alphabet?'

'Right up to Viagra,' spiked Allegra.

'Enough!' roared Daddy. 'I will be in my study. Working. At the job that twenty-three thousand sentient voters have elected me to do.' And with that, he hurled his cigar butt in the fireplace and stalked out.

Allegra, who had momentarily risen to her feet, threw herself back on the sofa, and glowered at the open door. 'I thought age was meant to mellow bastards like him.'

'It doesn't,' said Mummy, who was suddenly much more serene now Daddy was out of the room. Her knitting, however, remained jerky. 'It just intensifies them. Like those really stinky cheeses.'

Since no one was going to offer me any, I helped myself to a cup of stewed tea from the tray on the mahogany side table. There were many questions I was burning to ask Allegra, but I fished around for an easy, non-confrontational opener. Which wasn't as easy as it sounded, believe me.

'So, how long are you planning on staying, Allegra?' I asked. 'In England, I mean.'

'God knows.' She let out a theatrical sigh and kicked off her shoes so she could tuck her bare feet underneath her on the chaise-longue. She had enviably red toenails. 'Until I'm deported, I guess.'

'Oh, darling, it won't come to that, will it?' murmured my mother. She paused, then asked more seriously, 'I mean, will it?'

I looked on, aghast.

'That depends what that little shit Lars has been up to,' Allegra hissed. 'And believe me, when I find out, it won't just be Scotland Yard he'll be scuttling away from.'

I sipped my tea and thanked God that I, at least, had a morally upstanding and thoroughly responsible boyfriend in Jonathan. The dodgiest thing he was liable to do was send his secretary out to feed his parking meter.

'Allegra,' I began carefully. 'Why *have* the police taped up your house? No one's been . . . hurt, have they?'

She cast an imperious look towards the door to check that Daddy wasn't lurking. Clearly she was hoping to keep him out of the picture for as long as possible – why, I didn't know. Power games, presumably. 'Lars has been implicated in some international smuggling ring. I don't know what. Cocaine, I assume,' she added airily, 'and there was some mention of rhino horn.' She paused and twisted the large gold rings on her right hand. 'And antiquities. Such an *idiot*.'

'Gosh,' I said, shocked. 'I never thought Lars—'

'And arms,' she went on, with a flick of her long white fingers. 'Some other type of drug too, but I can't remember what . . .'

'Allegra!'

'. . . and possibly money laundering, but for God's sake! Is there any need to be searching *my* house for evidence?'

As there was no polite sisterly response to this we sat in silence for a moment while Mummy's needles clicked hysterically. I couldn't work out what she was meant to be making: it looked like it could be anything from a matinee jacket for Jenkins to some kind of ceremonial hat.

'Mummy, why are you knitting?' I asked, because I had to know, imminent Interpol raid or not. 'Emery isn't pregnant, is she?'

'Not as far as I know, darling,' she said. 'I just enjoy it. It gives me something to do with my hands. Some lady at one of the WI fairs recommended it for giving up smoking. She was on forty a day, she said, and now she knits entire kingsize blankets in under a week. Plus,' she added, 'I can fantasise about shoving these needles up your father's ghastly nose at times of stress.'

'No plans for your wedding anniversary yet then?' asked Allegra. 'Thirty-five years in September, isn't it?'

Mummy knitted faster. 'That's weeks away. Don't buy a card just yet.'

'So what are you going to do?' I asked Allegra, to change the subject. 'Have you, er . . .' It was delicate, talking about money. I hated it. 'The police haven't done anything awful, like freeze your bank accounts, have they?'

Allegra's head swivelled over to me, sending her curtain of jet-black hair swinging. 'How the hell did you know that?'

'Oh, just a guess.' I wasn't stupid. It had happened to Daddy twice.

She sighed. 'Well, yes. That has happened. And I refuse to ask that bastard for a loan.'

'Which one? Lars or Daddy?'

'Daddy. Lars owes *me*.'

'Just as well, darling,' murmured Mummy, 'because I don't think Daddy'd give you one.'

'No,' I agreed. 'And there are always conditions.'

I knew that from personal experience. Daddy's loans made Mafia money-lending look like some form of charity hand-out. What you didn't pay in interest, you paid in favours owed.

'I can give you enough to tide you over,' offered Mummy, 'but—'

'No, no,' said Allegra, placing her hands firmly on her

knees. 'I'll just have to get a job. That's what you did, wasn't it, Melissa? When you couldn't find a rich husband?'

I stared at her in shock. On so many levels.

'Just joking,' Allegra said. 'I mean, how hard can it be? I don't need that much to live on in London. I reckon about fifty thousand would be enough. Where's *The Times*? Don't they have an Appointments section?'

I narrowed my eyes slightly. I sincerely hoped *this* wasn't what Mummy had wanted me to come and sort out. I was a problem-solver, not a white witch. 'Allegra,' I began, 'have you thought about, er, what skills you'd be able to offer? Because there really aren't that many jobs that pay that sort of money for so little experience.'

The phone rang on the side table. Mummy stared at it for a second, as if trying to place the sound, then picked it up. 'Hello?'

'Your lipstick is smudged,' Allegra informed me. 'You should either wear lipstick with panache or not at all.' She paused to let this information sink in while I fiddled self-consciously with my compact, then added, 'Have you thought about plain lip gloss?'

Mummy put the receiver to her chest and looked at me sympathetically. 'It's your father, calling from his study. He says can you pop in to see him, please? He'd like a word.'

'And that word will doubtless be *cash*,' snorted Allegra.

'Allegra,' said my mother weakly.

I got up, startled by the novelty of actually wanting to escape to my father's Study of Doom.

I only had to get within ten feet – yelling distance – of my father's study to feel my stomach begin to knot, and

my palms begin to dampen: virtually every difficult conversation of my childhood had taken place within its
book-lined walls. Most of those difficult conversations
had been about the cost-effectiveness of educating me
at a series of very expensive schools – I'm afraid my
results made Princess Diana look like Stephen Hawking
– but there had been some other corkers thrown in for
variation, like the time he explained we'd all have to go
and live in France to avoid a tax scandal, and then there
was the one about our au pair's horrendous court case
in which my Snoopy pyjama case played an embarrassingly central role, and . . .

Well, I could go on, but I won't. The only minor satis-
faction came from a detail gleaned from my mother about
two years previously: that Daddy was in no position to
lecture me about my glaring lack of academic garlands,
since he'd bought every single book on the oak shelves
behind him at a house clearance in Gloucestershire,
including the leather-bound set of Jilly Cooper's collected
works which were the only ones that looked as if they'd
ever been opened.

However, when in situ in his oak-panelled study, Daddy
still had the ability to reduce me to jelly, even after a year
of asserting myself through Honey's no-nonsense persona. These days I could just about tell Emery to buy her
own curtains rather than have me 'run some up' for her
on my sewing machine, but Daddy was a whole other
kettle of fish.

The decanter was already on his desk and he'd poured
himself a large Scotch by the time I'd walked down the
corridors that led to his bit of the house. When he heard
me knock, he swung round in his chair like a Bond vil-
lain and steepled his fingers. I hated it when he did that.

It usually meant he knew something I didn't, and wasn't going to tell me straight away.

'Ah, Melissa,' he said, gesturing towards the chair as if I'd turned up for an interview. 'Do sit down. Take the weight off your feet.'

I tried not to take that personally.

'It's a while since we've had a little chat, isn't it?' he mused, sipping his Scotch. 'I think the last time, if I remember rightly, was at your sister's wedding. When you told me all about your escort agency.'

The wedding I'd organised, I might add. All by myself.

'It's not an escort agency,' I replied hotly, rising to the bait despite myself. 'It's—'

'Yes, yes.' He flapped a hand at me. 'So you say. Anyway, how is business? Booming? Hmm?'

'It's going well,' I said cautiously.

'Making lots of contacts?'

I eyed him, not sure where this was going, but certain it was going somewhere. Somewhere I would almost certainly not want to end up. 'Ye-e-e-es.'

He frowned in what I think he imagined was an understanding manner. 'Or is that awfully dull boyfriend of yours laying down the law about what you can and can't get up to? Hmm? I imagine he's got some pretty strong views about, ah, a few of your sidelines, eh?'

How did he know that? Did he have some kind of telepathic hot wire into my deepest secrets? I went hot and cold.

'No,' I insisted, for what felt like the millionth time. 'Jonathan's very happy for me to carry on the agency. I mean, I'm mainly sorting out people's wardrobes and arranging their parties these days, but I'm sure if I wanted to take on a client who needed me to . . .' I slowed down, realising the untruth of what I was saying. But I was committed now. 'Deal with more lifestyle issues, he'd understand.'

'Ding!' went Nelson in my head.

Damn.

Daddy tipped his head to one side, and smiled at me, as if I were a very stupid little girl. 'Well, that's nice. It would be a shame to let such a clever business idea go to waste.'

I was thrown by this unexpected turn of events. Last time we'd discussed the Little Lady Agency he'd accused me of working as a hooker, and dragging the family name into disrepute.

'Anyway, Melissa, since you're doing so well, you must be run off those great big feet of yours, no?'

'Well . . .'

'Come, come, either you're doing well, or you're not?'

'I'm doing well.'

'So you can give Allegra something to do.' He pushed himself away from the desk with the air of a job well done and started flicking through his Rolodex of cronies by the phone. 'Keep her busy. Out of our hair.'

I stared at him. 'You *are* joking now, aren't you?'

Daddy looked up from his address book. 'Does Allegra's divorce strike you as anything to joke about?'

'Well, no, but . . .'

'You do seem to be remarkably uncaring about your sisters,' he observed reproachfully. 'I practically had to twist your arm to help out with Emery's wedding. Is it because you're feeling the call of the old maid's apron, eh? There's always voluntary work, you know. Spinsterhood isn't the end of the world any more, my dear girl.'

'But I can't *give* Allegra a job!' I wailed. 'There isn't enough for her to do, even if I wanted to help out. Which I do. Of course I do. But wouldn't she be better working in an art gallery, or something like that? She's got lots of experience of . . . um, art.'

I didn't want to say that Allegra could clear my client list in about seven phone calls. She had the interpersonal skills of a grave robber, and most of my clients were ridiculously sensitive.

Daddy peered at me patiently. 'I realise that, Melissa. Allegra would be an asset to any gallery.'

We both knew he was lying here.

'But, thinking as a protective father,' he went on smoothly, 'it would be quite stressful for Allegra to re-enter the job market at—'

'*Enter* the job market,' I corrected him. 'She's never actually had a proper job.'

'Quite so,' agreed Daddy. 'Even more reason why this isn't the time to open herself up to the strain of inter-views and possible rejection.'

'And she's also under investigation by the police,' I added.

'I *know*,' said Daddy. 'And, well . . .' His voice trailed off discreetly. 'The press are ghastly, prying creatures. And I know you girls have always suffered the pressures of being the children of a prominent politician.'

He looked at me beadily over his fingers, and the penny dropped. With a clang, right in my eye.

'You want me to give Allegra a job at *my* office because you don't want her showing you up in someone else's!' I said.

'Right first time,' said Daddy, shuffling some papers on his desk, as if the interview were nearing a close. 'We don't want some nosey HR woman poking around in our business, and I don't want Allegra getting on the front page of the *Sun* for downloading porn or taking drugs in the loo or whatever else she's liable to do.'

'But I can't afford to pay her anywhere near what she wants,' I protested, thinking of Allegra's exorbitant ideas about salary. 'I don't even pay myself that sort of money!'

'Oh, I don't expect *her* to scratch around on nothing,' said Daddy. 'I'm happy to, how can I put it, supplement her income?'

I stared at him, trying to see where the scam was. There had to be one. Daddy was not a 'free money' sort of businessman.

'And I can put a little something your way too,' he said generously. 'I'm going to need some guidance on international etiquette, with so many meetings with dignitaries in my Olympic diary, and who better to guide me than London's premier etiquette expert?'

If I was reeling before, I was seriously wrong-footed by this, and Daddy seized on my uncertainty like a hawk spotting a fieldmouse with a gammy leg.

'Wouldn't that be *wonderful*, Melissa?' he demanded. 'Not only working on an internationally significant project, but helping your father at the same time! And promoting your business! And getting paid! And,' he added as an afterthought, 'maybe meeting some nice young man!'

'I have a nice young man, thank you.'

Daddy sniffed. 'Well, an American one, yes. So, can we agree on this? Between us? Hmm?'

I knew there was something I was missing here, but I couldn't put my finger on what it could be. 'And what if I say no?' I hazarded bravely.

Daddy picked up the phone. 'Don't make me answer that, Melissa. Bottom line is she can't hang around here like some kind of very high-maintenance vampire bat, and that's the long and short of it. I have things to be getting on with. I'd be most upset if I had to add Allegra – and you – to that list.'

'Er, I'll think about it,' I said. What option did I have? 'I'll do my best.'

'Good, good . . .'

He gave me a ghastly smile, showing all his teeth, old and new.

I excused myself and went down to the kitchen for something to calm my nerves.

3

After a testy Sunday, most of which I spent out walking the dogs to escape the fierce legal drama taking place in the drawing room, I drove home in a state of exhaustion, my brain teeming with all manner of crushing things I could have said to my father had I only been able to get my brain in gear.

He was right, I thought remorsefully, crawling through a contraflow on the M25. I should maybe think about how I could help Allegra out in her moment of need. She was my sister, after all, and much water had passed under the bridge since we were children. We might have things in common now, if only I looked hard enough.

I focused on conjuring up three positive things about Allegra while I sat in the traffic. I'm a firm believer in trying to find three positives in any gloomy situation. It distracts you from the negatives for a while, if nothing else.

One, she was my sister.

Two, she could speak fluent Swedish – which would be helpful for, er, all the stubborn IKEA self-assembly units my bachelor clients seemed so keen on – as well as Russian, colloquial Norwegian and a smattering of Icelandic, mainly swear words. And that would be handy for . . . au pairs?

Three . . .

My brow furrowed. There had to be *something* else.

Three . . .

Three, she wouldn't take any nonsense from anyone, and that was really what I was aiming for as Honey, wasn't it?

A chink of light appeared in the general Allegra gloom. Maybe I *could* find some way of her helping me out in the office? She'd be more than happy to negotiate with tough customers, and she did have a certain artistic bent . . .

She was also utterly amoral, self-righteous, loud-mouthed and bloody-minded. If she wasn't my sister, I'd swear she had a kleptomaniac streak too. Not exactly prime office manager material, even in London.

A vision of Allegra in the middle of Selfridges, screeching at Tristram Hart-Mossop to 'pull yourself together and just get laid!' blazed across my mind, and I nearly swerved into the side of an articulated lorry as chilly beads of sweat touched my armpits.

I'd have to think about it. Hard.

The moment I opened the door to our house and breathed in the mouth-watering aroma of a full roast chicken dinner, my heart swelled with gratitude for the little things in life, like having a flatmate who made his own gravy.

Nelson knew me well enough to rustle up a comforting evening meal on the weekends when I'd been home, and this smelled like the works: apple sauce as well as chicken, and roast potatoes. I sniffed the air. Was that bread and butter pudding? I inhaled like a Bisto kid while my stomach rumbled gleefully. My favourite. And he usually insisted I lavish it all with home-made custard too. My curve-enhancing lingerie wouldn't be half so tight if Nelson wasn't such an ace cook.

God, I was jolly lucky to have a flatmate like Nelson, I thought, for the millionth time. It was like being married, but with none of the worries about not 'communicating properly' or letting your leg hair grow over your ankles.

'Hi, honey, I'm home!' I yelled, dumping my bag in the hall. I couldn't help noticing that none of Gabi's designer belongings were hanging on the coat pegs, and my mood lifted a little further.

'Hi, Mel.' Nelson appeared at the kitchen door, wiping his hands on his blue-and-white-striped professional home chef's apron.

We might have behaved like brother and sister, but we didn't look alike. Whereas I was brunette and, um, *well-built*, like a water spaniel, say, Nelson was tall and dark blond and reminded me, in many ways, of a golden retriever. Reliable, handsome, happy to help blind people and children. Slightly smug.

Actually, that's not fair. Nelson never made a big deal about helping people; he worked in fundraising, but never forced me to buy Fairtrade chocolate or lectured me about driving the sort of car that single-handedly destroyed seventeen trees a year, or some such. He was just one of those naturally good chaps.

I know, sickening.

He had a dreadful singing voice, though, which took the edge off the perfection, thank God, especially at Christmas.

'Smells like a big dinner?' I said, popping a sprout in my mouth and hunting around for the corkscrew. 'I am so ready for a night in.' I bestowed a broad smile on him. 'And if you want to watch that *Onedin Line* DVD, I promise I won't talk through it. Just as long as you do my feet at the same time.'

Nelson didn't respond to this generous offer with the

enthusiasm I'd hoped, and I paused, wine bottle in hand, to examine the confusing mass of emotions playing across his normally very simple-to-read face.

'Um, that's really kind of you, Mel,' he said. 'But you don't have to. Did you have a good time at home? How were your parents?' he asked, oddly.

'Oh, still alive,' I said.

'Even your mum?'

'Er . . . she seemed OK. In the circumstances.' I poured Nelson a glass of wine, then a large one for myself to fortify my spirits, and sank down at the kitchen table. The relief at being home trickled through me like melting butter.

'Which circumstances are they?' He turned back to the stove and carried on stirring. 'The being married to Teflon Martin circumstances, or the being an alcoholic retail-junkie circumstances?'

'Nelson!' Honestly, if he didn't know my parents so well, I'd be forced to contradict him. 'No, she's in a bit of a tizz, actually. And for once Daddy isn't the reason. Do you want to guess?'

'Melissa, I really couldn't,' said Nelson heavily.

'Oh, go on,' I urged. It was funny how much easier it was to deal with the Romney-Joneses when I didn't actually have to see them in front of me.

He sighed. 'Whatever I guess isn't going to be insane enough. Er . . . Your mother's seduced the gardener.'

'Don't be silly!' I hooted. 'He's *bald*!'

'Your granny's admitted that the unnamed gentleman she lived with in the 1950s was the Duke of Edinburgh.'

'No!'

Although I really wouldn't want to rule anything out.

'No, come on, Mel. Just tell me.'

I was rather surprised that Nelson gave up so easily; normally he was happy to bait me about my family for hours. Still, maybe he was tired.

I pushed away the reasons why Nelson might be feeling worn out.

'Allegra's left Lars,' I said, topping up our glasses. 'He's been busted for drug-smuggling. She's moved back home, and isn't allowed to go to Ham because there are forensic teams dusting her house for evidence.'

'No!' said Nelson. He didn't sound very surprised.

'I know! Isn't it awful!' I sipped at my wine. 'I never did understand what it was that Lars actually did.'

'To be honest, I think you were the only one who didn't, Mel.'

'Well, yes. Thinking about it, they did seem to have an awful lot of money for a pair of artists,' I mused. 'When I got there, there was a great big BMW in the drive and we argued for ten minutes about who it belonged to before Allegra remembered it was hers. She'd bought it when she flew in. With *cash*.'

Nelson grunted.

'Anyway, apart from the BMW, she says she's completely skint, back at home, driving them up the wall, and now Daddy wants me to give her a job,' I went on, less cheerfully. 'He's on an Olympic committee, you know. Isn't that a turn-up for the books? Daddy, doing something sporty?'

'Tell me he's not running the ladies' beach volleyball team.'

'Gosh, no! I think it's administrative.'

Nelson goggled at me, as though I'd missed a joke, so I added, 'It's all above board, you know. He wants me to help him, actually, with some research into local etiquette and that sort of thing. I expect he'll be meeting lots of people, you know, with the committees and so on.'

Nelson gave me his Grade Three Big Brother look, the one that despaired of my naïvety. It was very familiar to both of us.

'And is he paying you for this?'

I nodded. 'Of course he is! I'm not stupid!'

'Out of his own money?'

I hesitated. 'That's not the point. He needs my advice!'

I didn't add that the unusual glow of pride at actually being able to assist my father legitimately would almost have persuaded me to do it for nothing.

Nelson narrowed his eyes, then seemed to relent. 'Well, OK. I just hope he's not sitting on the committee handing out the tenders. It would be mortifying, and yet entirely predictable, if your father, the man with stickier fingers than Nigella Lawson, was caught with his nose in the five-ringed trough.' Then a funny look passed across his face. 'Still, if he's out and about on Olympic business, your mum will be lonely, won't she? All on her own in that big house. No one to talk to.'

I got the feeling he was driving at something here, but I couldn't see what.

'Nelson, let's not talk about my family.' I got up and started to help him transfer the supper to the table before I could start picking at it. 'Let's talk about, um . . .'

Our eyes met over the hob, and we both looked down. I didn't really want to talk about Gabi, and I could tell he didn't either.

There was an awkward pause, and then I said, 'Sailing!' at the same time as he said, 'Shoes!' In the same bright, 'making an effort!' voice.

'Ah, well, yes, I'm glad you mentioned sailing, actually,' he said rapidly. 'Because there's something I need to talk to you about.'

'Go ahead,' I said, as he heaped up my plate with food. 'I'm all ears.'

'Um, don't wait for me,' said Nelson, gesturing towards my plate. 'Tuck in. I made all your favourites.'

'I know,' I said happily, loading up my fork. 'I can see.'

'So,' said Nelson. 'I, er, do have something we need to discuss.'

Then the mists started to clear. This was an elaborate supper beyond a mere weekend home. This was cupboard love at another level. The butter-roasted sprout turned to ashes in my mouth.

'What?' I mumbled, trying not to look concerned as my mind raced through a series of unworthy horrors, each of which made me feel more guilty than the last: Gabi was moving in. Nelson was selling the flat. Gabi and Nelson were getting married.

I swallowed the sprout with some difficulty and had to chase it down with an unwise mouthful of wine.

'Are you OK?' asked Nelson solicitously.

I nodded and spluttered. He was being a bit too nice now.

'You sure you don't want me to punch you in the back?'

'Quite sure,' I gasped.

'OK, well,' he said, picking up his knife and fork with studied casualness. 'The thing is that I've finally got a place on a training tall ship.'

'A what?' Relief returned, along with the feeling in my throat. If it was just sailing . . .

'A tall ship, you know, an old-fashioned sailing ship.'

I must have looked blank, because he sighed impatiently. 'You know, masts, sails, crow's nests, ar, Jim lad . . .'

'Crow's nests?' I coughed away the last flake of sprout. 'I thought they were wrinkles.'

Nelson rolled his eyes pedantically. 'No. They're the lookouts on top of the masts. Yo ho ho, and a bottle of rum? That sort of ship. Anyway, it's a charity that teaches young people how to crew and run the ship, and I've got a place on the volunteer staff. You know it's something I've wanted to do for ages.'

Indeed I did. The opportunity to sail while ordering people around *and* doing good was something Nelson couldn't possibly turn down.

'And I've got some time off work to go and do it. They let us do that, you see,' he added. 'Take time off to pursue charitable projects. The young people on the ship come from very different backgrounds. Some are disabled.'

'There's no need to look so smug,' I protested, riled by his sanctimonious expression. 'You're not the only one helping the less fortunate. Only this week I saved a teenager from five years of enforced celibacy, just by getting rid of his trousers.'

'That was very generous of you,' said Nelson seriously. 'Did you charge him extra?' Then he suppressed a snigger and spoiled the trendy vicar effect.

I studied his face for clues. I assumed this was some kind of rude joke. Straightening up my back, I looked him in the eye, to show I wasn't going to rise to whatever bait he was dangling.

'I charged him the normal wardrobe consultation fee, and knocked a bit off because he took us out for tea afterwards. If you must know. So how long are you going to be away playing Captain Pugwash, then?' I asked, getting back to the matter in hand. 'Do you want me to use the time to redecorate your room?'

Nelson helped himself to the remaining chicken leg. 'Ah, well, that's the second part of my, er, news. You know I had that builder over to check the damp for the house insurance?'

I nodded.

'Well, we need the damp fixed. And also the whole flat needs rewiring and the bathroom needs moving. Apparently, it's a death-trap.' He looked cross, as if he'd have been rewiring it himself had he known – not, I might add, because I'd been risking electrocution every time I plugged my straighteners in. 'So I thought, if we're going to have the plumbing done, I might as well have it repainted. And if it's going to be repainted, then I might as well look into new carpets, and—'

'Ah, I get it!' I said, pointing a fork at him. 'Don't tell me. Finally, you're going to admit that I might have a point after all, and you're going to hire Honey to charm your builders into meeting their deadlines!'

Nelson gave me a funny look. 'Melissa, since you've been seeing that American, you've turned very "Apprentice-esque", you know that?'

'I have no idea what you're talking about, darling,' I said, relieved that the news hadn't been of a marital nature. 'I can knock something off my rent for my foreman's fee, can't I? About fifty per cent, say? Just think of all that dust . . .'

'Ah, well,' said Nelson. 'That's the thing. The dust and so on. I'm going to have to ask you to find your own accommodation for a while, I'm afraid.'

My face froze.

'I'm going to be away for three months, you see, until

end of October-ish, and the place will be like a building site, and I'm not sure what the insurance situation would be, so . . . Mel?'

I wasn't listening. I was a couple of steps ahead of him.

'Where am I going to live?' I demanded.

Nelson had the nerve to look disapproving.

'Oh, no,' I said, cottoning on. So that's why he'd been so concerned about my poor mother's lonely existence! He was hoping I'd move in there for the interim! 'Oh no, Nelson, I know what you're thinking and the answer is categorically no. Weren't you listening? Allegra's in residence, and she's making the place look like Dracula's castle. She and Daddy are already at loggerheads, and I absolutely don't want to get involved.'

Nelson threw his hands in the air. 'But, Melissa, you honestly can't stay here. I'm really sorry. It just makes more sense to get everything done at once. It's not going to be for long.'

'How long?' I was really trying to be brave now, but the mere thought of going home . . .

'A month?' he tried.

We both knew this was a complete guess.

'Right,' I said, bravely stabbing three sprouts onto my fork and larding it up with apple sauce. 'Well, if that's the way it is.'

'Can't you move in with Jonathan for a while?' he asked. 'You've been going out for six months, and you're always going on about how great it is, dating someone with two spare bedrooms and a guest bathroom.'

I bit my lip. As usual, Nelson had hit straight on my weakest point. 'I don't want to pressure him. I mean, Jonathan's divorce only came through at Christmas. I don't want him to think I'm pushing him into anything . . .'

'For God's sake, Melissa, he's an estate agent! Ask him if you can arrange a sub-let on one of his spare rooms. He'll cut you a deal, I'm sure.'

I chewed miserably on my sprouts. What were my options, after all? Home? Moving into Gabi's titchy studio in Mill Hill?

There was always the tiny spare room at my office. But that was full of boxes and dry-cleaning bags and about ninety pairs of shoes. And I spent enough time there as it was.

'I don't know why you're making such a big deal about it,' he huffed. 'I thought you were meant to be Miss Dynamism these days. I thought wimpy old Boo Hoo Melissa was a thing of the past. I thought—'

'OK, OK,' I snapped. He was quite right. I needed to pull myself together. It wasn't like he was moving out with Gabi, for ever. 'I'm just concerned about, um, how it'll affect my work.'

Nelson smiled smugly. 'That's more like it.'

I glared, annoyed at myself for falling straight into his trap.

'Three months at sea,' I said, suddenly realising how much I'd miss his company. 'That's ages.' I could always find somewhere to sleep for a month, but without Nelson's solid presence around the place, roaring in disgust at the news, it wouldn't be the same.

'Well, yes,' he said. 'But I'll have access to text and email and stuff. Come on, I'll be back before Bonfire Night.'

We looked at each other over the roast chicken.

I swallowed. Nelson was going to sea!

'You'll text me, won't you?' he said. 'And you'll let me know if anything, um, untoward happens?'

'What? Like me and Jonathan getting married?' I asked, trying to be jolly.

'I was thinking more of any blackmail or legal actions arising from your business, really,' said Nelson, helping himself to more roast potatoes. 'But that sort of thing too.'

I was touched, although I didn't let it show. Nelson and I had an unspoken agreement that at moments of high emotion, all affection was to be demonstrated only by rudeness. So instead, I said, 'You'll text me too if you sink the boat, won't you? Or if the disabled kids get so sick of you patronising them that they make you walk the plank? I'd like to get a good photo of you ready for showing on the Ten O'Clock News.'

'Cheers. I've put Roger in charge of distributing my effects,' he said drily. 'So don't think you're getting the DVD player.'

We munched through our heaped plates in companionable silence for a moment or two.

'How's Gabi taken it?' I asked.

Nelson had the grace to look a little uncomfortable. 'I haven't told her yet. I thought I should tell you first, so you wouldn't hear about your impending homelessness from someone other than your landlord.'

'Thoughtful of you.' Homelessness. I sighed again, so hard that the red bills on the table all lifted and fluttered back down again.

'Tell you what, I'll pay the phone bill this month,' offered Nelson. 'Gesture of goodwill.'

'Thank you,' I said, and mentally put the money aside for spending on earplugs – if I had to go home – or, failing that, a very cheap hotel room.

Still, I let him watch his *Onedin Line* DVD, and he rubbed my feet until I fell asleep.

4

On Monday morning, I arrived in the office and was pleased to see four new messages on the answering machine already. Weekends could be trying times for my clients. Families, as I knew myself, presented all kinds of problems.

I made a pot of coffee and settled in behind my big desk, kicking off my stilettos for comfort, and allowing myself a long, heart-warming gaze at the framed photograph of me and Jonathan, positioned next to the phone where I'd see it the most. It was my favourite photograph: me and him in black tie, taken at a dinner-dance at the Dorchester the previous November when I'd still been pretending to be his girlfriend and he was still pretending to be hiring me for convenience. The night I really fell in love with him, I think. I hadn't realised that beneath the starchy exterior was a man who could dance like Gene Kelly, and make me glide like Cyd Charisse.

Even now, remembering the way he'd moved his hand only slightly on the small of my back as he'd swept me round the floor, just enough to make me want him to hold me tighter . . . My skin tingled deliciously at the memory.

Sometimes, looking back over the oily parade of lounge lizards and Sloane Square no-hopers that made up my romantic past, I wonder if they were just some kind of trial I had to undergo so I could end up with Jonathan Riley. Like the *Krypton Factor* assault course, only with three times as many mud-slides, and an estate agent at the end of it.

Jonathan was so far out of my league that since we'd started going out officially I'd got into the habit of taking lots of pictures of us together, just so I'd believe it was true. He was thirty-nine, worked as a CEO or COO or something at Kyrle & Pope, the big international estate agency that now owned Dean & Daniels, and he had a real old-fashioned film-star *gorgeousness*. Gabi disagreed, on account of his red hair ('Basil Brush's more ginger cousin'), but he did something to me that I can't really explain.

I'm a sucker for men in well-cut suits, but there was something going on underneath Jonathan's business-like exterior, a sort of naughtiness that melted my insides whenever I caught a glimpse of it. The exterior itself was pretty charming: all-American cheekbones, grey eyes, and perfect square white teeth. But it was the little, private things that swept me off my feet: he stood up when I came in, and noticed my clothes, and murmured things in my ear that made me blush, while looking utterly impeccable. And he never, ever needed to be told what kind of socks to wear.

Obviously, I didn't want to jeopardise this dream relationship by moving my stuff into his plush pad in Barnes prematurely. I still wasn't convinced that Jonathan knew exactly what he was going out with. He might have thought he'd stopped paying for Honey's professional perfection in favour of my own more ramshackle charms, but the reality was that I was spending just as much time and effort on being a super-groomed, super-organised version of Melissa as I'd ever done tarting myself up into Honey's Hollywood glamour. If you see what I mean.

Sometimes I wondered nervously just how long I could afford to keep up this level of waxing.

Then the phone rang. Composing myself into a more professional frame of mind, I picked up the heavy Bakelite receiver. 'The Little Lady Agency. How can I help you?'

There was an infinitesimal pause on the other end. 'Mmm,' said Jonathan appreciatively. 'Say that again?'

Butterflies fluttered up inside my stomach. He had the sexiest upmarket American accent, the kind you hear on legal dramas where the lawyers are impassioned and terribly expensive. Luckily he thought my posh English accent was equally sexy, so we spent quite a lot of time just talking to each other about total rubbish, then falling into passionate embraces.

'I could say, "Hello, it's Honey"?' I suggested huskily.

Jonathan spluttered something I didn't catch, then said, in a very grown-up voice, 'Listen, let's not go there right now. I'm wondering if you're free for some lunch?'

'Absolutely!' I said, my accent intensifying into cut-glass precision. 'What time?'

'I'll meet you at one, at Boisdale on Ecclestone Street.'

Oooh. Scottish steak.

'That would be delightful,' I said. 'I'll look forward to it!'

'Mmm, just one more time? The delightful bit?' he said, but fortunately his PA Patrice came in with some papers before we could get into trickier waters.

I went back to work with a much lighter heart, and skimmed through a list I was making of suitable presents

for all ages of children. It was one of those ironies that
the more unmarried the bachelors on my client list were,
the most suitable their friends seemed to deem them as
godparents, despite their having no experience of children whatsoever. It was all to do with available cashflow,
Nelson informed me: the more puking, howling babies
they saw, the less likely they were to want any of their
own and therefore the more cash they had to spend on
the godchildren.

As I was checking the Hamleys website for teddy bear
prices, the phone rang again, and when I picked it up I
knew it was Nelson's mate Roger even before he spoke.
He had a distinctive way of breathing.

'Roger Trumpet!' I said cheerily. 'How's tricks?'

There was a surprised squelch, as Roger cleared his
sizeable nose. 'Shouldn't I be asking you that? Eh? Eh?'

That sounded like a dig. I ignored it.

'If this is about Nelson's trip, I'm afraid I can't talk
him out of it,' I went on, sending my list to print. 'Anchors
aweigh, and all that.'

'I wasn't ringing about Nelson, actually,' said Roger,
though I could tell by the sulky tone that had entered
his voice that I'd struck a nerve. 'I need to book your
services. Your professional services.'

'Oh good!' I said, pulling my appointments book
nearer. I liked a challenge, and since Roger combined
astonishing assets *on paper*, with some of the worst social
graces I'd seen outside a monkey house, he was a big
one. 'What for?'

'Well, you remember that party of my mother's where
you pretended to be my girlfriend?' he began.

'Mmm,' I said sympathetically. It had been memorable,
for many reasons, not least the unexpected rush of female

attention Roger had enjoyed afterwards. 'Is she still trying to set you up with your cousin Celia?'

'Yeah.' Another wrenching nose clearance. Honestly. I made a note to mention it tactfully at a later date. 'Only this time it's the Hunt Ball, and Celia's running the show, and won't take no for an answer. She's taken up women's rugby recently, and, you know, I don't like to, er, let her down . . .'

'Roger, have you considered telling your mother that we're in the twenty-first century now, and that it isn't compulsory to get married by the age of thirty any more?'

'I have, but she's making her *will*. I'm getting the grandchildren guilt trip thing. Who's going to get the cider interests? What will happen after she's gone? I keep telling her that she didn't marry my dad until he was forty-three, but what can you do?'

'I know. Parents can be a trial.'

'Yeah, well, I knew you'd understand. So if you wouldn't mind popping along in one of your nice tight dresses to the old Hunt Ball next month, that would be splendid. Third Saturday in September, Hereford. No funny business, obviously, but just let her know that it's all back on with you and me. Wear the wig if it helps.'

My pen hovered over the date, then sadly I clicked the cap back on.

'I'm really sorry, Roger, but I can't. I don't do those girlfriend dates any more.'

'What?' The panic in his voice was audible. 'But, Melissa, I *need* you to do it!'

'Roger, I'm awfully sorry. Um, I can try to find you a nice girl to meet, though – maybe take her out for dinner beforehand, and ask her if—'

'No, no, no,' Roger interrupted impatiently. 'No, that's

not the same thing! I need someone temporary or not at all. What do you take me for? Some kind of sleaze-bag?'

'I'm sure we can work something out,' I soothed. 'Leave it with me.'

Roger harrumphed and hung up.

I looked at the clock. It was twenty-five past twelve. That seemed like as good a point as any to call it a morning and walk slowly to lunch with my real boyfriend before any of the other needy males in my life phoned the office.

As Roger would have twigged, had he been sensitive in any way, the fact that Jonathan and I had met while I was pretending to be his girlfriend was a major reason why I'd discreetly removed it from my advertised services.

The funny thing being, of course, that Jonathan was the only client I ever had who didn't actually need my services at all – an irony that occurred to me yet again when I saw him sitting at our table in the elegant surroundings of the Boisdale's courtyard garden. He was pretty much perfect as he was.

Jonathan's working wardrobe comprised lots of smart suits and sober ties, but today he was dressed down, and it made my heart skip. He was wearing a pair of navy trousers and a soft periwinkle shirt that brought out the silvery grey in his eyes. The sunlight bounced off his hair, making the waves gleam like licks of flame, and I noticed that his ears were turning pink where he'd forgotten to put sun cream on them.

The casual effect was slightly undermined by the fact that he was busy making notes about something into his Dictaphone, but he always did that, even for grocery shopping, so I forgave him.

I allowed myself a tingly moment to enjoy the novelty of ogling my own boyfriend, then made my way over, rather self-consciously.

'Hello,' I said, almost shyly, as he leaped to his feet with a smile.

'Hello, yourself.' Jonathan leaned over the table, put one hand lightly on my arm, and kissed my cheek. It was a warm day and I could smell the cologne rising off his skin, which sent a shiver running through me. He wore Creed, like Errol Flynn. Jonathan wasn't a PD⹂ type of man, which suited me fine, and I found the polite restraint he showed in public actually rather sexy. Knowing his private displays of affection as I did, if you know what I mean.

'You look lovely,' he said.

I swatted away the compliment modestly, but I had put some effort into my outfit: a neat 1950s-style print sundress with a little vintage cardigan, pinned together with one of Granny's old diamanté brooches. And some stiletto sandals that I'd slipped on outside the restaurant, while my flatties went into the enormous bag I toted everywhere.

Looking lovely in London in the summer took some effort, especially since I wasn't what you'd call a summer person.

'Thank you,' I said, examining the menu. 'You're looking rather fresh yourself.'

'I can get fresher if you want.'

I looked up. 'No, honestly, there's no need. You smell fine.'

Jonathan let a little laughing breath out through his nose. 'That wasn't what I meant, but . . . OK.'

The waiter approached to take our drinks order and Jonathan smiled at me, then looked up and said, 'Two glasses of champagne, please. No, you know what? Bring us a bottle.'

I beamed. 'Are we celebrating?'

'Yes, we are. On several counts.'

'One, it's a beautiful day?' I suggested.

'Two, I have beautiful company.'

I beamed, inside and out.

'Three,' he went on, 'I have good news.'

'Oooh,' I said. 'What?'

'All in good time,' he said playfully. 'Four . . .'

My stomach lurched as he arched his eyebrow.

'Four?'

'Four, this morning, I brokered a deal on the most enormous house you've ever seen,' he finished, as the frosty champagne flutes arrived. 'It had a carport you could fit three Range Rovers in.'

'Oh.' I'd have preferred something more romantic, but that was Jonathan – very work-focused. Which wasn't unattractive.

'And how about you?' he asked, letting the waiter pour the champagne, then raising his glass in a silent toast. 'How was your weekend in the country?'

'Awful,' I said, chinking his glass. Jonathan had met my parents on more than one occasion now, so there was no point pretending they weren't nightmarish. 'And I had some bad news at home too. *Home* home, I mean.'

'I'm sorry to hear that,' said Jonathan. 'Nothing too bad, I hope?'

I sighed. 'Well . . . It depends. Tell me your good news first.'

'OK.' He coughed, stroked his tie unconsciously, and said, 'They're restructuring at work and I found out this morning that I've been promoted to CEO in charge of

International Sales and Relocation.' He widened his eyes, as if this should mean something to me.

'Oh, wow!' I said. 'Well done! That's great news!'

'Yeah. Yes, it is.'

'You're such an international man of mystery, Jonathan,' I teased, only half joking. 'I didn't know you were going for a promotion?'

'Well, I didn't, really.' He moved the salt and pepper around the table. 'I had a few conversations . . . you know . . .' He paused. 'Thing is, it's going to mean more travelling, and . . .'

'What?' My stomach was rumbling as I perused the menu. I fully intended to stick to steak and a salad, but I'd heard such good things about their haggis that it seemed bad business sense not to try it out for future recommendations. I was, after all, supposed to be an authority on date restaurants.

'It'll mean I'll have to travel more,' he repeated slowly. 'And spend more time in New York. Starting from very soon.'

I looked up, as I realised what he was saying. 'Oh.'

We were both silent for a moment. My appetite shrank.

'So go on, what's your bad news?' he asked. 'We can package it up with my having to travel more, and make one bad news bundle.'

I bit my lip. Suddenly it was more of a stack than a bundle. 'Oh, Nelson's going on some sailing expedition, and he's getting the builders in to overhaul the flat. I have to move out for a month while they pull the place to pieces.'

'He's getting someone reputable, right?' queried Jonathan, looking concerned.

'I think so.'

'Because you know what some of these cowboys are

like. You end up spending twice as much fixing the damage they do. Listen, I have a great contractor . . .' He reached into his jacket pocket for his Dictaphone.

'That's kind of you,' I said faintly. Priorities! 'But I still have to move out.'

Jonathan's hand froze. 'I know, honey. But I was just thinking, how can we make this as painless as possible?' He reached over and took my hand. 'So where are you going to go?'

'Well, actually, I was wondering,' I began hesitantly. Then I stopped as a new awful thought struck me. What if 'I'll have to travel' really meant, 'We should cool things down'?

I stared, panic-stricken, into his grey eyes, and wished I could tell the difference between amusement and seriousness in Jonathan's expression. Sometimes he played his cards a little *too* close to his chest.

'Come on,' he said, 'where are you going? I need to know where I can get hold of you. You don't get away that easily!'

He stretched his other hand across the table and circled my wrist. 'Not when you were so hard to get hold of in the first place,' he added in a soft undertone.

'I don't know *where* I'm going,' I admitted, trying to keep my voice level as Jonathan discreetly stroked the inside of my wrist with his thumb. 'I really don't want to go home – I mean, I couldn't, it's too far to commute into my office – Daddy won't let me have the keys to his London flat because he reckons he needs it, Gabi doesn't have enough space for all her shoes, let alone me.' I looked up and met his eyes. 'I don't suppose you've got a room in your house you could sub-let?'

I tried to sound jokey. But I wasn't joking.

'When's Nelson kicking you out?' asked Jonathan, getting his diary out of his jacket pocket.

'In about a fortnight's time.'

Jonathan's brow furrowed and he flicked back and forth between pages. They were all covered in his very small, neat American handwriting.

The waiter, who'd been hovering patiently, pounced as soon as I raised my head. I plumped for the haggis, though I didn't feel up to eating anything very demanding now, and without looking up from his diary Jonathan briskly ordered a steak and some fries and some salad and a bottle of mineral water.

'A fortnight?'

'Yes.'

So, was this it?

'Well, you can't stay in my house,' said Jonathan. 'I have some old clients staying there as a favour while they look for property in London. I'm going to be flying out to New York pretty soon, settling some deals, meeting people, seeing how these changes will impact our basic company infrastructure. But there's one very obvious solution.'

'What's that?'

He gave me his tiniest smile, the one that hid genuine excitement. 'You'll have to come with me. Come and live with me in New York for a month.'

I stared at him. 'But I can't!'

'Why not?'

'Well, I can't leave the agency for a *month*!' I stammered. 'I've got appointments, and people booked in. I mean, I'm meant to be organising a stag night for Katie Torrebridge and—'

Jonathan raised his hand to stop me. 'Hold it right

there. Back up. You're organising a stag night for the *bride*?'

'On behalf of the bride,' I explained. 'Old friend from prep school. She wanted to make sure the best man didn't drag Giles off to Amsterdam and get him tattooed or infected with herpes or something, so I'm arranging it all. He thinks I'm a stripper.'

'Tell me you haven't added stripping to your client services,' said Jonathan wearily.

'Good heavens, no!' I hooted. 'I just told him that so he'd think it'd be salacious enough already, and not try to add on any, um, extras. No, the thing is, most British men hate the idea of stag weekends, and having to be all manly and get drunk and spend a fortune on strippers they're secretly too embarrassed to fancy, so I've booked them into a nice hotel in the Lake District where they can go paintballing, and get muddy. Well away from any hooker types, and only four hours out of London on the train. In case they do tie him to a lamp post or something.'

'You think of everything.' Was that a note of terseness or admiration? Given Jonathan's quest for ultimate office efficiency, and his slight antsiness about my more hands-on agency work, it could have been a bit of both.

'So, you see, I can't just up and leave. Much as I'd love to come to New York with you,' I finished.

Our food arrived and I gazed sadly at my plate. My appetite had vanished. One did need a certain amount of appetite to tackle a good haggis.

'Melissa, I'm offering you a month's vacation in New York.' Jonathan sounded confused. 'It's a city you've never visited, something that surprises me actually, and I'd love to show you round *my* town, like you did for me. But, hey, if you'd rather stay here and *work* than be on holiday with me . . . ?' This time, he made his voice jokey, but not quite enough.

'That's not fair!' I protested. 'It's not a question of what I *want*.'

'It is.'

'But, Jonathan . . .'

He attacked his steak methodically, slicing off the fat like a surgeon. 'You reckon I'm a workaholic, but I'm not the one who carries two cell phones, both of which are permanently switched on. And don't deny it,' he added, as my jaw dropped. 'I know you have your work phone on vibrate when we go out. Not even my grandmother needs to go to the bathroom so many times in one evening.' He looked up at me from his steak autopsy. 'I mean, don't get me wrong – I love that you're savvy *and* polite. Most businesswomen I deal with would just take the calls at the dinner table. I just wonder where I fit in to all this. Whether, ah, whether I had higher priority when I was a client?'

'Is this about the wig?' I asked. 'Because—'

'No!' He laughed. 'I don't want to have the wig conversation again, Melissa. All I mean by that is that I'm really proud that you're my girlfriend. And I want you to be my girlfriend when you're at work, as well as at home. Not pretending to be someone else.' He shook his head. 'Besides, I can't risk you running off with someone else, can I?'

Such was Jonathan's innate adultness that he was able to say all this without sounding whiney.

But it really wasn't fair of him to suggest I didn't put him first. If he only knew how much effort I put into looking casual and effortlessly organised in my own time; at least when I was being Honey brisk sauciness seemed to spring forth naturally.

Anyway, my business *depended* on me. It wasn't like I could just get a temp in.

'Jonathan, I can't believe you think that! I mean, you are the first priority in my life.' And that was true. 'And I'd *love* to come with you, you know I would—'

'Then come.' Jonathan held my gaze, and I got the distinct impression that this was something that had been bubbling under the surface for a while. The huffs when I was late because of clients running over. The raised eyebrows about my more, um, *fitted* office wear.

I wriggled in my seat. He couldn't honestly think I'd run off with someone else, could he? *Me?*

'You're asking me to choose between the two things that mean the most to me,' I said in my brave little soldier voice. 'I can't just—'

'It's not a *choice*. You need somewhere to live. You also need a holiday. And I need to have you around.' He smiled, and as he said that, I felt something swell in my chest and my heartbeat quickened.

He took my hand in his again, playing with my signet ring. Was that . . . meaningful fiddling? The blood rushed from my head.

'I guess I could *cope* without you, just. But it wouldn't be living. Will you think about it?' asked Jonathan, as if he already knew what my answer was going to be.

'I'll think about it,' I managed to gasp, as he raised my palm and kissed it, holding my gaze over the top.

'Good,' he whispered.

Honestly, sometimes I felt like the only thing missing from our romance was the Busby Berkeley dance routine.

'Run this by me again,' said Gabi, from beneath a large pair of black sunglasses. 'Mr Perfect wants to take you to New York to live in his flashy condo for a month, while you're homeless, and you don't want to go . . . why?'

'Because I hate letting people down,' I repeated. When she put it like that, it didn't sound so convincing. In fact, it sounded positively wimpish.

'Mel, the only person you're letting down here is me. Do you not understand how much cheaper Kiehl's skincare is in America? I'm economising these days, you know.'

We were sitting on a bench in Hyde Park, eating ice creams and watching people pour out of offices, tearing off their clothes to catch the last of the parching London sun.

'I'll really miss him,' I said mournfully. 'I should have known it was too good to last. And I notice it's not like he's putting *me* in front of his career, is it? Hasn't stopped him taking a job that "requires more travelling".'

Gabi snorted. 'Christ on a bike, Mel, I don't understand you. He's not asking you to move out there! He's just offering you somewhere to live while Nelson does his bloody sailing sainthood!'

I looked at Gabi and could tell she was scowling beneath her huge shades. Evidently she'd discovered the downside of dating someone with innate nobility.

'He told you then?'

'Yes, he told me. And he didn't offer *me* a go in his hammock either. No stowaways allowed, apparently.'

'Well, no. You don't have knotting skills.'

Gabi's well-plucked eyebrow extended above the frames.

'I don't want to know, thanks,' I said hurriedly. 'But it's just impossible. I can't leave, and I can't stay. What on earth am I meant to do?'

She pulled down the shades to give me the full benefit of her sarcastic look. 'Will London really grind to a
halt if you stop telling overgrown schoolboys not to tuck
their shirts into their pants?'

'Well, not *as such*, but I still have regular appointments
with people and—'

'OK, if he's making such a big deal about choosing
between him and work, how about this: tell him you'll
definitely go out there. No question. Jonathan, you are
my lord and master and I can't bear to be separated from
you for ten of your earth minutes. But, really, plan to go
for a *fortnight*,' suggested Gabi. 'I mean, it's not unreasonable for you to take a holiday – people expect it
now and again. If you get ahead of yourself with the
preparation stuff, all you'd have to do would be check
your answering machine and get your emails. And you
can do that from Jonathan's house.'

'That's true,' I said slowly. 'And I don't need to tell
him I'm checking. I could do that while he's at work.'

'Exactly. Then, after a fortnight, if you're still gagging
to come home – though I can't imagine why on *earth*
you would be – you can make up some excuse about
your family having a crisis that requires your immediate
intervention, nip back, deal with anything that needs
dealing with, then nip back again for however long you
want.' She cut me a sideways look. 'I bet you a tenner
you end up coming back to sort them out anyway.'

'You make it sound like going up to Leeds on the
train,' I said, though actually it wasn't such a bad idea.

'Aaron and I used to go to New York for shopping
breaks all the time.' Gabi shrugged. 'It's no big deal.' She
paused. 'Getting through Customs on the way back with
all the stuff I'd bought, now that was more of a problem.'

She sighed nostalgically. 'Aaron used to pay the excess rather than look at all my shopping bags again. Said it gave him flashbacks.'

'Well, you'll be lucky if you get so much as a commemorative parrot from Captain Pugwash,' I said. I'd liked Aaron. For someone who worked in the City, he had a well-developed sense of humour and really good taste in socks.

'Thanks. As long as that's all he brings back from three months at sea,' said Gabi darkly. 'I've heard things about these sailors.'

'I think you're safe with Nelson. He'll have them singing sea-shanties and playing deck quoits, then lights out at nine every night.'

We licked our ice creams companionably.

'You're not scared, are you?' asked Gabi suddenly.

'Scared?' I bluffed. Gabi had a disconcerting ability to see into my head, and then see things even I hadn't spotted. 'What of?'

'Of living with Jonathan. Him seeing you less than perfect without your make-up.' She looked at me significantly. 'Maybe meeting all his ball-breaking friends and relations. And his ex-wife. Things getting serious.'

'Don't mince your words, will you?' I protested. But there was no point fibbing to Gabi. She knew me too well. 'Um, yes, there is a bit of that, I suppose. It's just been going so well, and—'

'Stop worrying,' she said firmly. 'Anyone can see Jonathan's mad about you. And you've already met some of his friends, haven't you?'

I pulled a face. 'Yeah, Bonnie and Kurt Hegel.'

'And they liked you!'

'Um . . . after a fashion.' That had been quite a ghastly

dinner. It was when Jonathan was still dating me in a professional capacity, and the first time he'd seen any of his and Cindy's mutual friends since their separation. Unlike the carefully divided stock portfolios and antique what-nots, they'd maturely agreed not to divide up their friends in the divorce settlement. But between Kurt's relentless interrogation, which I later realised was his idea of light conversation, and Bonnie's searching therapist's eyes, I felt like we were both on trial. Him for his feelings towards Cindy, and me for – well, I felt guilty about things I hadn't thought about in years.

'Pshuh!' said Gabi. 'Just give them the full Honey charm treatment.'

I stared at her, then clapped a hand to my mouth. 'Oh, Gabi! They think I'm blonde! And called Honey!'

She flapped her hand dismissively. 'Tell them you dyed your hair. Main thing is, you've met them, haven't you? And they liked you, and they'll have told everyone else how great you are.' She peered at me. '*Everyone* else. So what's to worry about? So long as that neat-freak Jonathan doesn't catch you hanging the towels up messily, you'll have a great time. Think about it – summer sales in the shops, proper ice cream, Jonathan pulling out all the stops to show you a good time . . .'

American ice cream. Mmm.

Not to mention Jonathan showing me a good time . . .

I wrenched my mind back to practicalities. 'What about the office? What about post? What if people tried to turn up and leave things?'

'Look, if it makes you feel better, I'll call in and look through the post for you,' said Gabi. 'Get your messages.'

'Would you?' A plan was forming in my mind. One that involved Allegra working at my agency without actually shutting it down before my flight landed at JFK.

'I *do have* office experience,' she huffed. 'But I'm making you a list of things to bring back from Bloomingdales, all right?'

So as not to waste any time she got a notebook out of her bag and started on it then and there. I gazed round Hyde Park and was surprised to feel rather excited.

5

Jonathan greeted the news of my decision by taking me out to dinner at Christopher's and plying me with complicated American cocktails. But the next day he had to fly back to start organising his new job, and we had an emotional parting at Heathrow Airport.

Well, fairly emotional. He hated public scenes and I was trying to put on a Stiff Upper Lip about the whole thing.

'Can't wait to see you in New York,' he said, holding me very tightly before heading into the business class check-in. 'I'll come and pick you up at the airport.'

'OK,' I said, and forced a brave smile.

'Don't be late.' He touched the tip of my nose. 'If I do half as good a job showing you New York as you did showing me London, you won't ever want to leave.'

I didn't work out what a lovely compliment that was until I was almost back in Pimlico.

To be honest, I didn't rush back to the house, even though it was Sunday evening, which I usually reserved for armchair detective dramas and the week's ironing. Nelson, being Nelson, had insisted that we start 'going through the flat' in advance of his departure. I'd have preferred to blitz it in one awful go, with gallons of coffee and the promise of a takeaway at the end, but he'd booked space at the Big Yellow Storage Place and was determined to fit everything into the space he'd arranged. And not a box over.

'We need to weed out some of this junk,' he insisted, forcing me off the sofa where I'd slumped, still playing back Jonathan's last, long kiss in my head. 'I've got boxes for storage, boxes for charity shops and boxes for the dump. And when I say dump, Mel, I do mean dump.'

Nelson stood back with his hands on his hips and surveyed the general detritus of several years' domestic bliss with some desperation. 'I mean, we can just ditch all those magazines, can't we?'

He gestured towards the stack of lovely glossy mags, holding the stereo speakers off the floor.

'Well, no . . .' I *needed* those. I looked into my half-drunk gin and tonic and wished I had the energy to mix up another. 'Can't we start in the kitchen instead?'

But there was no stopping Nelson once he got started on 'household tasks'. His father, who was a military enthusiast, had run their family like a sea cadet unit, using a series of whistles to indicate 'task time'. Even now, Nelson and his brother Woolfe got twitchy when the football was on the television.

'You realise how much you could have saved over the years if you'd just read those stupid things in the hairdresser's?' he added for good measure, lifting up the speaker so he could start piling them into a dump box. He brandished a fistful of *Tatler*s in my direction. 'There's over a hundred pounds of idiocy and shampoo ads in this stack alone.'

'I think you'll find half of that pile includes your *Practical Boat Owner*s,' I observed. 'But you're right – go ahead and chuck it all out. They're just taking up space.'

Nelson's packing action abruptly stopped. 'Well, in that case, maybe we should do some *selective* chucking.'

The doorbell prevented me from responding in a way I'd have liked.

'That'll be Roger,' he said, with some relief. 'He said he'd come over to give us a hand.'

My face fell and I gripped my warm G&T harder. 'Roger? Oh, come on, Nelson. It's Sunday night! My boyfriend's just flown back to New York! I've got a hard week coming up. The last thing I need is Roger Trumpet and his Personality Vacuum coming round here to punish me with small talk.'

Nelson gave me a reproachful look. 'Don't be mean. Roger's nowhere near as bad as he used to be. Mainly because of your sterling efforts. You should be proud of him.'

'I am,' I said, pulling a desperate face. 'But not on a Sunday night when we only have one more Sunday night left here!'

'The flat isn't going anywhere! You're just moving out for a few weeks, for heaven's sake!'

'But I was going to iron!' I wailed. 'I thought we were going to make a curry and watch *Inspector Morse*!'

Heavy footsteps were now audible on the stairs leading up to our first-floor flat, and already I could feel Roger's enervating presence begin to drain me of sparkling chit-chat. He did that to a girl. Ten minutes with Roger Trumpet, in a bad mood, was like inhaling chloroform.

'How did he get in?' I demanded. 'Is the front door open?'

Nelson's brow furrowed. 'Now that *is* a good question.'

We didn't need to wonder about Roger's means of entry for long, because there was a brief knock on the front door and then Gabi appeared, with Roger in tow.

'I met him outside,' she explained, wiping the mascara from where it had smudged under her eyes.

Roger nodded at everyone by way of greeting. He wasn't wiping his eyes, but he wasn't exactly looking chuffed either.

'I didn't know Gabi had a key!' I exclaimed, a bit too brightly. 'Nelson?'

'Um . . .' said Nelson. 'Yes. I was going to mention that to you.'

'Were you?' I said, still very brightly.

Gabi sniffed. Her nose was red, and her hair wasn't as perky as usual. In fact, it didn't even look as if she'd bothered to attack the unruly curls with her straighteners. It honestly wasn't like her to be so downcast about a man. Whenever Aaron had gone away on business, she was on the phone to me within minutes, planning where we could go for cocktails. Still, Nelson was different, I supposed grudgingly. He was less a boyfriend, and more a lifestyle. We'd all miss him.

My heart went out to her poor sad face.

'Gabi, would you be a sweetheart and go and put the kettle on?' I suggested. 'I'm gagging for a cup of coffee.' And gratefully she vanished into the kitchen where loud clattering started up.

Roger, Nelson and I stood there in the middle of the floor. Nelson realised he was holding a stack of *Cosmopolitan*s, the top one of which was last year's Ho-ho-holiday sex special, and he quickly put them into a dump box.

'So, how are you, Roger?' I asked, grasping the conversational nettle. 'Looking well!'

Roger pulled a face, which I guessed was meant to

indicate some kind of response. For a young man in his early thirties, who was the heir to a substantial cider and sparkling perry fortune, who lived in Chelsea, and who was in possession of all major mental faculties, Roger cut a very unprepossessing figure. He'd gone through a more urbane phase, when I'd taken him in hand rather rigorously, but since I'd been spending more time at work and with Jonathan, instead of at home on the couch with Nelson and Roger, he'd regressed. Badly. Tonight he was dressed entirely in shades of porridge, and didn't appear to have shaved for about four days. It might have passed as a style statement on a more put-together man, but not on Roger.

Communicating in shrugs and grunts was where I'd picked up, not left off.

'Roger!' I said, more emphatically.

'I'm very well, thanks, Mel,' he said. 'Not much going on, but even less going on for the next three months.' And he shot a wounded glare at Nelson.

'Roger,' said Nelson evenly, 'if you wanted to crew on this tall ship, you should have applied. Stop acting like such a girl.'

'I'm thinking of doing some sailing in the *Maldives*,' he informed me. 'One of my friends has got a *Nicholson 35* that he needs bringing back to England.'

'Roger . . .'

'So I might do that.'

Gabi reappeared with the coffees, one of which she gave to Nelson. 'Milk, three sugars,' she said, and bit her lip.

'Good timing, you two!' I said, before she could ask to keep the mug to remember him by. 'We'd just got started!'

'Yes!' said Nelson in the same 'that's right, Melissa!' tone. 'This box is for the charity shop, this one's for keeping, and this one's for dumping. I'm going to set my stopwatch for one hour, and then we'll go out for dinner, OK?'

'OK!' I said.

Honestly. We sounded like a couple of children's TV presenters. Or parents.

'Fine,' said Gabi, staring morbidly at a bookshelf. 'Are these your books, Mel? *I Do, or Die*? *Why Men Marry Some Women and Not Others*?' She looked inside. 'To Melissa, Merry Christmas, love from Mummy and Daddy.'

I grabbed them off her, and dumped them in the charity shop box. 'No need for those any more! And I never thought I'd be sitting here saying that.' I beamed with delight. 'You know, when I think of the time I wasted on men like Orlando . . .'

Nelson looked up from his stack of CDs. '*I* never thought I'd be happy that you'd taken up with an American estate agent, but after Orlando von Borsch, I'd have given Jack the Ripper a chance.'

'Nelson!' I said. 'He really wasn't as bad as you made out.'

Nelson hated all my ex-boyfriends. Particularly handsome, year-round-tanned, slip-on-shoe-wearing ones like Orlando.

'He was, Melissa,' agreed Roger. 'Definitely. He was a slimy creep. Don't you remember how he made you collect his dry-cleaning?'

'And never gave you the money for it?' added Gabi.

'And twice it included a strapless, backless, split-thigh ball gown?' added Nelson.

I paused. Orlando had had a lot of dry-clean-only clothes. At the time I'd thought it was terribly chic, but now I wondered if he'd deliberately just sent everything there so I'd pick it up for him, free and gratis.

'Well, that was the old me,' I said confidently. 'I was pretty dim in the past, I admit, but not any more. No one takes advantage of Melissa Romney-Jones now.'

'Ding!' muttered Nelson, wrapping one of his model battleships in an old copy of the *Telegraph*, but since we were all feeling rather over-emotional, I didn't pull him up on it.

We packed and stacked in companionable silence for a few minutes.

'Be ruthless with clutter,' intoned Nelson. 'There's going to be no room in the new and improved flat for knick-knacks.' He looked up. 'And I mean that, Melissa.'

'Like this, you mean?' grunted Roger, waving an elaborately wrapped explosion of net and hand-folded paper doves.

'Emery's wedding,' sighed Gabi. She looked at Nelson, who had suddenly become fascinated by a box full of old contact lenses. 'It's so sweet you kept it. Don't you remember, Nelson? That was the night . . .' Her voice trailed off in another uncharacteristic wobble.

I swallowed, as a pang of missing-Jonathan nostalgia hit me. *We'd* got together at Emery's wedding too.

'Oh, for pity's sake,' moaned Roger. 'That's all it ever is round here – snog, snog, snog. It's like being trapped in a fifth-form disco, hanging out with you lot. Don't you ever think what it's like for the rest of us? The ones who aren't completely out of their heads on Love's Young Dream? Eh?'

'If this is about the Hunt Ball, Roger—' I started.

'It's not!' he snapped.

Nelson looked at me. 'Shall we all go out for dinner now? Maybe do some more when we come back?'

'I think that would be a good idea,' I said firmly.

With my flight booked, and all my possessions bar the ones I needed to take to New York checked into Nelson's Big Yellow Storage Crates, I thought it would be prudent to pop home, just to check nothing was about to erupt while I was away. It would be absolutely typical for Daddy to turn up on CNN, accused of embezzling the entire Olympic fund at the exact time that I was trying to impress Jonathan's super-smart friends.

The upside of Daddy's new position of power, according to my mother, was that he was AWOL when I arrived, and, as I found out, she had no idea whether he was engaged on parliamentary or Olympic business, nor did she know when he was going to be back. Not that she seemed unduly concerned.

'Oh, he's got a new secretary, darling,' she said vaguely, keeping her eyes glued to her knitting needles. 'Olympic budget and all that. One, two, three . . . Bugger!' She thrust the knitting at me with an imploring look. 'Have I dropped a stitch?'

We were sitting in the kitchen, which was the coolest room in the house in the summer. Jenkins was sprawled in his basket, near her feet, panting.

'I don't know, Mummy, I don't knit,' I said.

She took it back, and frowned. 'Christ, it's so hard to tell with mohair.'

It wasn't surprising that she was dropping stitches, since her hands were shaking as if she were sitting on a washing machine, but I didn't mention that.

'Daddy's got a new secretary?' I asked suspiciously. Daddy went through secretaries like most men went through shirts. 'Just for his Olympic business?'

'Oh yes, um, Claudia, I think she's called.'

'Right.'

How convenient, I seethed. I could see it now: Daddy probably emailed his secretarial requests along with his office requirements. Blonde, under twenty-three, very good at dictation . . .

Mummy looked up, her face suddenly wreathed in serenity. 'Don't worry, darling. I sent Claudia a little note, in private, just to remind her about Daddy's weak heart.' She smiled. 'Any over-excitement and he could drop down dead.' The needles started clicking again. 'She wrote straight back to reassure me she'd keep an eye on it. So thoughtful.'

I swallowed. 'That's not entirely true, though, is it?'

'No, darling. Well, not as far as we know. But then, who's to say, with your father?'

My mother did a good impression of being ditsy, but sometimes she amazed even me. And when it came to her relationship with my father, frankly there were things it was best not to know.

'You know he's got me researching his international etiquette?' I said. 'I'm rather enjoying it.'

'Is he?' Mummy looked pleased. 'That's nice for you. At least that's one assistant he can't be accused of employing for her looks!'

Charming.

'So, anyway,' I said, changing the subject, 'I'll be away for a fortnight, to begin with. I'm staying with Jonathan in his new apartment!'

Mummy traced a shaky finger along her knitting

pattern and cast a longing look at the big silver box on the Welsh dresser that used to contain her Marlboro Lights, then, with an effort, wrenched her attention back to the pattern, which was for a fluffy hippo.

'And what about work?' she asked tightly.

'Gabi and Allegra are going to answer the phones for me while I'm away,' I said, 'but I am *going* to come back, so don't let Daddy get any ideas about this job for Allegra being permanent.'

Mummy sighed and bashed her needles together. 'Oh, darling, once you see New York, you won't want to come back.'

'I will,' I insisted stoutly. 'My life's here. People depend on me. *Clients* depend on me.'

She peered at me over her knitting. 'If you want your relationship to work out, Melissa, you should think about what's best for Jonathan, instead of *other men*.'

'Mummy!' I protested. 'You make that sound . . . awful.'

'Well,' she said. 'It's true.'

'Anyway,' I went on, blushing, 'Nelson's here, and Gabi and—'

'That's another man,' Mummy observed, clicking away. 'You should think about soft-pedalling that too. I'm sure it must bother Jonathan, knowing another man sees you in your bathrobe every morning.'

'He's my *flatmate*,' I exploded. Honestly, I was so sick of telling everyone there was nothing going on with me and Nelson. 'The fact that he *does* see me in my bathrobe should tell you that there's nothing going on.' I rolled my eyes as my mother raised her perfectly shaped eyebrows with as much sarcasm as someone with maximum Botox could manage. 'Honestly! We're just *friends*.'

'Who's that? Nelson?'

I swivelled round as Allegra swanned in, swishing her long chiffon house-kaftan behind her.

Great. That was all I needed.

'Shut up, Allegra,' I said, on a wave of crossness, then immediately felt scared. Telling Allegra to shut up was second only to telling my father to get lost, and third only to putting one's head into a crocodile's jaws.

'I mean,' I added quickly, as she opened her mouth, and widened her eyes so the whites were visible around the kohl liner. 'I don't think you see it quite the way I do. How's the investigation going?'

She snapped her mouth and her eyes shut, so two thick black lines and one bright red line appeared on her otherwise white face.

'Don't ask,' said my mother quickly. 'We've had Simon here three times this week.'

Simon was my father's barrister. He was the heavy artillery, brought out only for High Court actions and anything that might get into the papers. He was also my godfather, being as how he'd spent more time with my father over the years than my mother had.

'So,' I said brightly, 'shall we talk about my trip to America then?'

'Oh, God, if we must,' sighed Allegra. 'How are you flying? Cattle?'

I bridled. 'Do you mean economy?'

'Allegra,' said Mummy reproachfully. 'Melissa isn't married to a wealthy businessman. She's self-employed.'

Allegra snorted and opened the fridge door to see what was in there. It seemed to be full of bottles of algae and urine samples, which I assumed were her health drinks. Then again, one never knew with Allegra.

'I'm flying economy because there were very few seats

available,' I said. 'It's a popular time of year, and if I'd gone business class it would have cost more than I earn in a month.'

'Poor you,' said Allegra.

I didn't bother to get annoyed. I was proud of earning my own money. Better to travel cattle and pay for it myself than fly first on someone else's credit card, I thought – although obviously I didn't actually say so. That would have been asking for trouble.

'Well, if you must be a martyr about it, you'll need these,' said Allegra, reaching into her bag.

'Allegra . . .' said my mother warningly.

'It's perfectly innocent,' she snapped, throwing me a little brown bottle.

'What is it?' There was a prescription label in Swedish, but oddly enough it wasn't made out to Allegra Svensson.

'Melatonin. Helps you sleep on planes. Knock back a couple of those with a glass of red wine and you'll be out like a light until JFK. Get yourself into first, ideally, drop off, and they'll never be able to shift you.' Allegra helped herself to a handful of Mummy's expensive salted caramels, and swished towards the window. She peered out, opened a window, made an obscene gesture, then slammed it shut, sinking dramatically onto the window seat.

To her credit, Mummy refused to acknowledge any of this performance.

'I wish that police protection man would bugger off. He's making a complete dog's breakfast of the rose garden. I mean, what can they do? Send hitmen in? I can't believe Lars knows anyone more dangerous than Stockholm's worst dentist.'

'I should make tracks,' I said, suddenly longing for

the relative sanity of Nelson's now echoing flat.

'Do you want some jam to take back, darling?' asked Mummy, waving vaguely in the direction of the kitchen cupboards. 'I've got one or two extra jars.'

'Ooh, yes, please,' I said. The local WI made seriously good raspberry jam; it was one of Daddy's perks as regular fete-opener that he got first pick of the preserves stall. 'Is there any raspberry?'

'I think so,' she said, peering at the mass of mohair skewered on her needles. 'Have a look.'

The cupboards in our kitchen were very old, and reached from floor to ceiling, a relic from the days when three parlourmaids, a cook and a scullery maid staffed the place. I swung open the cupboard where the jam and breakfast cereals normally lived, and gasped in surprise.

Five of the six shelves were crammed with a gleaming array of jam jars: strawberry, raspberry, loganberry, apricot, blackcurrant, blackberry, marmalade and various other permutations. There must have been over a hundred cotton-topped jars in there, stretching back into the dusty depths.

'God almighty!' I exclaimed.

'What? Nothing you fancy? I think there might be some lemon curd, if you look, darling,' said Mummy, apparently unperturbed.

'Mummy! I thought you'd got the shopping thing under control,' I said reproachfully. 'You promised. No more binges.'

She put down her knitting and looked a little sheepish. 'Well, it's the WI markets. I have to support them, as the local MP's wife. And there are so many! You can't just patronise one – they find out, these ladies! Anyway, it's such good jam. And it always comes in, you know, for gifts. And when I'm giving people tea.'

I looked at her suspiciously.

'Like the other day,' she said defensively. 'I had a journalist round from *Country Life*. I made her a lovely English cream tea, with four different sorts of preserve. It made a lovely photograph. I knew those silver preserve boats would come in useful eventually.'

She picked up her knitting again.

'You didn't tell them you made it, did you?' I asked carefully.

The needles clicked quicker. 'I didn't say I *didn't*.'

I sighed. Still, how could I get stroppy with her when my whole business was built on pretending to be someone I wasn't?

I helped myself to a jar of raspberry jam and a couple of lemon curds.

'Oh, I nearly forgot,' said Mummy. 'Daddy left a letter for you on the mantelpiece in the drawing room. It must be a business thing – he wouldn't tell me what it was about.'

'Plus ça change,' said Allegra, in a ridiculously outré French accent, just in case we'd forgotten she was still lurking about, 'plus c'est la *même* bloody *chose!*'

How I was looking forward to having that in my office. It would be like having Harold Pinter manning the phones, but without the light relief.

I wandered through to the drawing room. The envelope was tucked behind the marble clock, amongst a crop of formal invitation cards.

I opened it and read the short crested note card inside. In my father's unhelpful handwriting were the words:

*Allegra's blood money to be paid into your account, take
off 20% of same for your etiquette advice, first of month.
Will be in touch. Pls shred.*
    MRJ

Twenty per cent? Of how much? It was typical of my
father not to commit salient details like that to paper; he
was notoriously shred-happy after an unfortunate incident with one of those dreadful bin-stealing tabloid inves-
tigators. It wasn't so much the tax details he was unhappy
about, as the shopping list with twelve bottles of Scotch
and his prescription cortisone cream listed for everyone
to see. What made it much worse, in my eyes, was that
he'd implied that the Loving Care was Mummy's.

Anyway, I thought, tucking the card into the pocket
of my linen trousers, I had other things to worry about.
Knowing Allegra, she'd have negotiated her own wage
direct with my father, and twenty per cent of whatever
she was getting was bound to be decent, if not adequate
compensation for having her around.

Back in the kitchen, Mummy was trying to make her
hippo stand up on the table. I had to swallow a gasp of
horror – its head was the same size as its body, none of
its limbs was equal in length and it appeared to have a
fin. She didn't seem perturbed, and carried on trying to
make it stand with a childlike patience.

Because of its grotesquely misshapen head, it looked
as if it were trying to do some kind of yoga headstand.

'That hippo's got five legs,' observed Allegra from the
window seat. 'Unless you've made it very anatomically
correct? In which case it's positively disturbing.' She
flicked some more V-signs out of the window at the
hydrangea bushes.

'Oh, damn,' sighed Mummy. She tried one more time to coax it into uprightness. It flopped over. She looked crushed.

My heart went out to her. Poor Mummy. 'He's adorable!' I said, wanting to cheer her up. She got so little encouragement from anyone. 'Can I have him?'

'Really?' Her face illuminated with pleasure. 'Of course, darling. Please do. You can give it to Jonathan, if you like?'

'Um, I'll just keep it for myself,' I said quickly. In a box. Under the stairs. 'Right, I'm off. I've got packing to do.' I turned to Allegra and tried to look stern. 'Don't forget you're coming in for a briefing at the office before I go.'

'I hadn't forgotten,' lied Allegra.

'Well, please don't forget. It's important.'

'Yadda yadda yadda,' she replied, gazing out of the window. 'Don't forget your jam.'

I put the jam in my handbag, making a mental note to buy *Country Life* to find out exactly what Mummy had said about her preserving skills.

'See?' said Allegra, turning back to bestow a wolfish smile on us both. 'I'm totally cut out for this lifestyle advice thing. Nagging, that's all it is.'

I gripped my hippo so tightly that he developed a whole new deformity, and left.

6

There were times, living with Nelson, when it was hard to remember that I was living in the twenty-first century and had the vote. Seeing him off on his voyage of educational smugdom was one such occasion, made worse by Gabi's insistence on behaving as if she were starring in her own historical mini-series, minus the costumes and extras cycling gratuitously past on penny-farthings.

Heaving bosoms, though, were very much on the menu. They always were with me.

With military precision, Nelson loaded up my car with his kit, Roger, Gabi and then me, so we could drop him off then wave him away at the docks where his ship was being stocked up with rations, and sails, and crew. I was pretty impressed with the *Bellepheron*: it was a real tall ship, with three masts decked out with beautiful white sails, and a saucy figurehead on the prow. If it hadn't been for the boxes of microwave porridge going aboard, you'd never know you weren't in some BBC2 period drama.

'Will you write, Nelson?' said Gabi, scrunching her handkerchief.

'Gabi, we've been through this before – I won't have time,' said Nelson impatiently. 'But we've got the most modern satellite navigation and communication equipment known to man, and we're docking as often as possible to let people on and off. It's not like I'm going to come back with scurvy and one eye.'

'How about a beard?' she asked hopefully.

'I might manage a beard,' he conceded wearily. 'A small one.'

'And a parrot?' I suggested.

'Don't push it, Melissa.'

Roger slapped his arm. 'Be safe, mate,' he said. 'If you fall overboard, I'm having your new cricket bat, OK?'

'OK,' said Nelson. 'But not the box.' He punched Roger's shoulder.

'Too small, mate,' said Roger, and feigned kneeing Nelson's groin in return.

Honestly, you wouldn't think they'd known each other for over twenty years. Or maybe you would.

'If you two have quite finished,' Gabi piped up meaningfully.

Roger and I turned to her in surprise.

'I'd like to say goodbye to Nelson,' she went on. 'Alone.'

A funny sensation swamped me, and I had to force myself to smile to stop it showing on my face. Roger, who lacked any social graces, didn't bother to disguise his surprise at the new pecking order and dropped his jaw in outright sarcasm.

He drew breath to make his feelings known, but before he could say anything, I said quickly, 'Of course. Come on, Roger,' and hauled him away to an ice-cream stand.

I was quite happy to turn my back on whatever scene was playing out while I got us both mint choc chip cones. When I turned back, however, Roger was staring unashamedly, and I almost felt sorry for him.

Gabi was hanging off Nelson's neck – inevitable, really, since he was well over six feet and she only scraped five feet two if she was wearing heels – and they seemed to be kissing, sort of. Or Gabi could have been giving him a lecture, a few centimetres away from his mouth.

Nelson, I'd noted, didn't lecture Gabi like he lectured me. Maybe because he couldn't get a word in.

'Is this what it's going to be like from now on?' moaned Roger. 'Watching those two carrying on, like . . . like . . . Bollocks.'

I turned my head in time to see him engulf his entire scoop of ice cream in one terrifying downward mouth movement.

'I hope not,' I said, with many-layered sincerity.

He disengaged himself with a slurping sound, leaving a perfect lipstick peak on each side of his ice cream.

'Roger,' I said, 'please don't do that again. It's troubling.'

'All in the tongue action.' He winked at me. 'Chicks dig it.'

'No, they most certainly do not,' I said with a shudder. Things really had slid. 'Where are you *getting* all this stuff ?'

If anyone thought he was getting it from me, my business was ruined.

'Books,' he said vaguely.

'Roger,' I said sternly, 'I think I need to take you in hand again. And with a very firm grip too.'

Roger choked on his cornet, spraying molten ice cream everywhere.

'What?' I demanded. 'What?'

Roger was saved in his spluttering by Nelson yelling, 'Mel! Over here, Mel!' in a voice that could carry through fog.

We looked up, to see Nelson waving me over in his best kindergarten manner. Gabi had disengaged from his neck, and was busying herself checking her mascara.

'At least you're wanted,' said Roger, somewhat sourly.

I went over, and gave Nelson a hug. 'Take care,' I said. 'No showing off to the children.'

'Of course not.' He hugged me back and I buried my head in his broad chest. Nelson was great to hug. He made me feel all tiny and petite. 'And you take care too, in America.' He pushed me away so he could look into my face. 'And if anything happens with Remington Steele . . .'

'I'll let you know,' I promised. 'I'll send a pigeon or something. But, honestly, nothing's going to go wrong. I know it won't.'

'You email me,' he repeated. 'I'll turn the ship round, and come and get you. I mean it.'

'OK,' I said, slightly embarrassed by the intensity of his look. 'And if you sink, let me know too. If the little children stage a mutiny with table forks or something.'

'I'll die first. Now, I've left a list of all the things you have to lock before you leave, all right? And the details for the builders and the electricians. I've made a very specific plan of action, that Gabi's in charge of implementing, and I've asked my brother if he'll pop over and—'

'Nelson,' I said firmly, 'we are all perfectly capable of carrying out your every wish.'

'I know. Well . . . OK, I know.' He looked over my shoulder, then dropped his voice. 'I haven't told Gabi, but this is my emergency number, if you really need to get hold of me.' He hugged me again and slipped a piece of paper into my jacket pocket.

I bit my lip. Even though I was secretly glad he'd given me the number and not Gabi, I still felt a bit awful. It wasn't much fun trying to work out where we all stood these days.

'In case the workmen blow up the house, right?' I said.

'Er, yes,' said Nelson. 'That sort of thing. But, seriously, Mel—'

A loud whistle from the ship interrupted the rest of the conversation.

'I've got to go,' he said. 'I'm meant to be organising the crew.' He straightened his shoulders. 'In fact, they're giving the wrong whistle. I need to get that sorted out before there's a terrible misunderstanding.'

Roger, Gabi and I stood on the quayside as Nelson self-consciously walked up the ramp onto the deck.

'Ship ahoy!' shouted Gabi and waved her hankie. It had clumped where she'd blown her nose into it.

I reached into my capacious handbag and discreetly passed her a fresh one.

'Au revoir!' she bellowed, undeterred by the curious looks we were getting from other crew well-wishers. 'Bon voyage, Nelson!'

'Come on,' said Roger, tugging at my arm. 'Before people start thinking she's got some kind of Lady Hamilton complex.'

'Bye, Nelson!' I yelled and waved.

He waved back, then vanished gratefully below deck.

Gabi stood firm.

'Gabi,' I said patiently. 'It's not like the *Queen Mary*. It's not suddenly going to slide down into the dock while someone crashes a bottle of champagne over it.'

'Won't it?' She looked surprised.

'No. It could be ages yet before they go. They get a little tugboat to . . .' I trailed off, seeing she was still gazing up at the portholes. 'Didn't Nelson make you watch his tall ships videos?'

She nodded and sighed. 'I wasn't really concentrating on the boats, though.'

'Gabi,' I said, sliding my arm through hers, 'let's go home, and have a pot of tea and watch *Upstairs, Downstairs*.'

As we moved away towards where my car was parked, I sensed a dishevelled presence on my other side.

'Can I, er, can I come back as well?' mumbled Roger. 'Only I forgot to go shopping this week and, er . . . you know.'

I put my arm through his too. 'Of course you can, Roger. Nelson left us all a shepherd's pie to remember him by.'

And so the three of us made our way back to the now very empty flat. When no one pointed out the historical inaccuracies in the scullery maids' uniforms, it felt emptier still.

There was only one other task to be got out of the way before I could fly out, and I was looking forward to that even less than waving Nelson goodbye.

I had to hand over the office to Gabi and Allegra.

The one bright spot, though, was that Gabi's moping around the place lasted exactly as long as two episodes of *Upstairs, Downstairs*. By the time she turned up at the Little Lady Agency for her briefing on Monday lunchtime, she was almost back to her normal pre-Nelson self.

By which I mean she was carrying two carrier bags from Topshop and had spent the past hour dunking my chocolate biscuits in her coffee, while divulging the most appalling gossip about the tabloid editor whose house was being sold through the estate agency.

'Right,' I said, checking my watch for the sixth time,

'let's make a start, shall we? No point in waiting any longer for Allegra – she's obviously decided she's got better things to do. So. These *red* files are for wardrobe shopping trips—'

'Just tell me where the wig is,' wheedled Gabi. 'I promise I won't use it.'

'No!' We'd been in the office for an hour and the more I thought about the prospect of leaving Gabi, let alone Allegra, to run free among my confidential files, the more I was beginning to think I shouldn't actually go at all. 'The wig is strictly, and I mean *strictly*, out of bounds!'

Gabi pouted. 'But I only offered to do this because of the wig.'

I looked at her imploringly. 'Please, Gabi. I'm relying on you here. I'm about to put my livelihood into the hands of an egomaniac with the social graces of an underfed tiger, and only you can keep her from decimating my client list. Please. At least wait until I'm out of the country before you start going through the drawers.'

'OK.' Gabi tapped her French manicure on the arms of her chair. 'But if she's not here in the next ten minutes, I'm going to have to go. Selfridges isn't open all night. And,' she added beadily, 'I want you to know that I wouldn't spend two weeks' bonus holiday on anyone else but you.'

'I know. I am grateful beyond words. So is Nelson,' I added in a shameless appeal to Gabi's weak spot. 'More coffee?' I suggested. 'You'll need to know how the coffee machine works. Especially if Allegra's going to be in.'

At that point the door opened with a theatrical flourish and Allegra herself shimmied in, bearing three carrier bags from Peter Jones, a venti iced coffee and a parking ticket.

'I can't believe the traffic wardens in this country,' she spat by way of a greeting. 'They're evil! Evil!' She slammed the ticket on my desk, rattling the Bakelite telephone in its cradle. 'Can we claim this? It's a business expense.'

'You're an hour late,' said Gabi. 'Unless you're here for a different appointment?'

Allegra swivelled in surprise.

Actually, I did too.

'And you are?' she demanded.

'Gabi Shapiro,' said Gabi, extending her hand. 'Pleased to meet you. We'll be working together.'

Allegra turned and looked at me, with an interrogative raise of her Paloma Picasso eyebrows.

'Gabi is my, em, usual assistant,' I fibbed quickly. 'She's very familiar with how the agency operates, so I've asked her to come in while I'm away. To show you the ropes, as it were.'

'Are you saying I can't manage?' demanded Allegra. 'Are you implying I might need . . . supervision?'

'No!' I protested, my resolve melting in the force of her personality. 'But, you know, Allegra, it's very delicate, some of what I do, and it really helps to—'

'Delicate how exactly?' asked Allegra, checking my desk ornaments for price labels. 'Just giving a load of slack-jawed wasters a kick up the arse, isn't it?'

'No, it isn't!' I objected, as my heart plummeted.

'Yes!' said Gabi. 'That's about the size of it.'

I spun round and regarded her with horror. Honestly, I could *feel* the blood draining from my face.

'But . . .' I began.

'She's no worse than Carolyn,' whispered Gabi. 'I can handle her, no problem.'

Carolyn was our old office manager. She was dreadful, but not in the same Wagnerian league of dreadfulness as Allegra.

'Sit down, Mel!' insisted Gabi before I could disabuse her, pushing me cheerily into one of the comfortable leather library chairs I kept for clients. 'Relax! Now, you can tell me and Allegra exactly what you'd like us to do while you're away. *Can't* you?'

I swallowed.

'Yes, do tell us,' drawled Allegra, temporarily looking up from the desk. 'Then you can tell me what you thought you were doing when you bought this revolting desk tidy.'

I looked at the pair of them. I was leaving my business with these two? I must be mad.

'Right,' I said, getting a grip of myself, 'take some notes, please.'

They both stared at me.

'Notes.' I nodded towards the antique roll-top desk I'd bought at Lots Road Auction House and made Nelson drag back for me. 'If you look in there, Gabi, you'll find notebooks and pens.'

'You made your very own stationery cupboard,' she breathed disbelievingly. 'I knew you were psycho about the one at the office but . . .'

'Everyone needs somewhere to keep things neat,' I said. 'Now, have you both got a pen? OK. First of all, daily routine. First thing you do in the morning is check the messages. I tend to get a lot of people phoning during the night. In crisis. Phone them back first, and let them know I'm not here, but I'll be back in—'

'We have to wait until you're back?' said Allegra. 'Where's the fun in that?'

I fixed her with a look. 'Allegra, this isn't a *fun* situation.

This is *work*. And, yes, you *do* have to wait until I'm back. I'm only going to be away for a week or so.'

'Fine,' said Gabi brightly. Too brightly. She looked as if she had a plan, but I couldn't see what on earth it could be, and that was worrying.

'So, yes, check the phone messages, then the post. There might be some bills, in which case they go into the pink bill file. There might be some cheques, in which case they go into the green cheque file. There might be some invoices which go into the blue—'

'Invoice file,' chorused Allegra and Gabi.

'Well, quite,' I said, discomfited.

'This office work business seems pretty straight-forward to me,' said Allegra, stretching out her long legs. 'I should have done it years ago. Piece of cake. The fuss you make, Mel, I thought you'd be *slaving* away.'

'What do you want us to do if anyone phones up wanting an appointment?' asked Gabi quickly.

'Look in my appointments diary, which is right in front of you on the desk.' I didn't mention that I'd already photocopied it three times, just in case of accident. 'I've made a list of how long each standard service takes – wardrobe consultation, general date coaching, that sort of thing – but if it's anything more complicated, then call me.'

'Call you? What if you're in the middle of a romantic moment with Dr No?'

That was a good point. I'd more or less promised Jonathan that I'd be taking a holiday. And I knew he was getting tetchy about my 'work priorities'.

On the other hand . . .

'Text me,' I said. 'Keep it brief and I'll let you know roughly how long it'll take, then book them in for when I get back.'

'Right.' Gabi made a note.

'But remember we don't do any of that pretend girl-friend stuff any more,' I added. 'You have to be really firm about that. I still get about three calls a week from people and some of them can be quite pathetic, but you just have to be firm.' I paused. I had one slightly masochistic client who thought the refusing was all part of the service. He'd bombarded the office with literally hundreds of red roses, until I'd abandoned diplomacy and got Nelson to phone him up, pretending to be the police.

They'd *both* enjoyed that a bit too much, actually.

I shook myself. 'The right *kind* of firm, obviously. It, er, just encourages certain people, but I'll leave it up to you.'

'What else?'

'Don't forget to get some fresh flowers every other day – Nelson lets me budget for that in my accounts. Whisk a duster round this place, because it's really impor-tant to keep it clean for people coming in. Check the diary for birthday and anniversary reminders – clients get three reminders, one a fortnight in advance, one three days in advance and one the day before to leave time to send flowers if they've completely forgotten. If they've completely forgotten,' I added, 'offer to send the flowers for them. And be delicate with the anniversaries. You never know when they might have . . . hit a rough patch.'

'You mean, when they've split up?' growled Allegra, with a toss of her dark hair.

'Well . . . yes.'

'Fine,' said Gabi. 'In which case I'd just get a new set of details for the mistress in the diary, right?'

I blinked. Gabi's relentless practicality might be more of an asset than I'd reckoned. 'Well, yes,' I said again, 'but for God's sake, be nice. You have no idea how much this business depends on being firm but *nice* to people.'

I swung my most beseeching gaze between Allegra and Gabi, two women known for their firmness, but not necessarily for their niceness.

Gabi looked affronted. 'You don't have to tell me that, Mel. I'm the soul of discretion.'

We both knew this was a complete fib. However since Allegra didn't – *yet* – I let it go.

'So, apart from checking your diary, answering your phone and buying flowers, that's it?' said Allegra. 'And for this, you're going to pay me—'

'No!' I said quickly, before she could reveal her astounding Daddy-subsidised wage to Gabi. 'No, er, of course not! That would be awfully dull for you. Um, there are lots of birthdays and September weddings coming up, and with your combined shopping experience, I'm sure you could handle buying some presents, couldn't you?'

Gabi's eyes lit up.

'Check with the client first,' I went on, 'and get them to make you a wishlist, just to get an idea of how much they want to spend. I mean, you can more or less ignore the actual wishlist if the gift's for a woman, because they'll put stuff like socket sets and power drills on it.'

'Unless the woman in question is a rally driver,' Allegra pointed out, with an arch glance towards Gabi. 'My friend Dagmar is a well-known Swedish rally driver and I've always bought her the best spark plugs money can buy. Or art. I wouldn't insult her with perfume.'

'I don't think I've ever been insulted by a present,' mused Gabi. 'But then when you *earn your own salary*, you tend to be more appreciative of the value of money, don't you think, Mel?'

'Well, clearly, between the pair of you, there shouldn't be any problem finding some really wonderful gifts!' I said hurriedly. 'Just make sure you put a note of what you got, who it was for and how you sent it in the purple present file, then I won't accidentally send them something similar next year.'

Allegra smiled patronisingly. 'I doubt it, Melissa. I don't think you and I have very similar tastes.'

I was about to remind her that it wasn't about our tastes so much as the gift-giver's when the phone rang and saved me.

'Now, listen,' I said, putting on my tortoiseshell glasses. 'This is what I want you to do.'

They both rolled their eyes, which wasn't the response I was after at all.

'Hello, the Little Lady Agency,' I said, mentally picturing a cup of hot chocolate. My old Home Ec teacher had taught us that tip for projecting a really enthusiastic phone manner. 'How can I help you?'

'Mel, it's Roger.'

A skin appeared on the hot chocolate and I had to make a real effort to keep my voice alluring, more for Gabi and Allegra's benefit than Roger's.

'Hello, Roger, how are you?'

'Fine. Look, I know what you said before, but I really do need to talk to you about this Hunt Ball. I *cannot* go with Celia. My eczema's come back just thinking about it. I'm begging you, just put on that lovely blonde wig and—'

'I'm sorry, Roger,' I said, pushing the spectacles up my nose. 'As I explained before, I don't offer personal services like that any more.'

Gabi and Allegra sniggered.

I ignored them.

'Not even for a mate?' Roger demanded huffily. 'Nelson's not here. He'd never know.'

'It's not *about* Nelson. Look, Roger, I'd love to help you out, but I can't. I just can't. We'll talk about this later, all right? I'm sure we can come to—'

Roger put the phone down.

'Honestly,' I said. 'He needs a girlfriend, as soon as possible. And a real one at that.'

'What did he want?' asked Gabi. 'Fumigation recommendations? Or a dentist?'

'He wants me to go with him to a Hunt Ball. As Honey,' I said, rearranging the papers that Allegra had riffled through on my desk. 'And did you see how I said no?'

'Tsk. I could have done it,' said Gabi. 'Just give me the wig.'

My head shot up as if it were on a string. 'No, you could not. No!' I said, raising a warning finger. '*No*, Gabi. Before you even *think* it. It's not on.'

'I don't see why not,' said Allegra. 'If it's OK for you to do it, what's the difference? It's just like a franchise.'

I gave both of them a very firm stare, the sort I used on clients who resisted my attempts to chuck out their 'favourite' Thatcher-era boxer shorts. 'It was OK when I *did* it. But now? I no longer do it. So no one does. The subject is closed,' I said. 'Now, let's talk about cleaners.'

7

Naturally, with Nelson's advice about planning ahead ringing in my ears, I'd been rigorous in my to-do lists, up to and including having my big toes waxed, but – of course – I hadn't planned for the jam on the M4 which left me exactly ninety seconds to get from the taxi drop-off to the check-in desk for my flight from Heathrow.

I sprinted through the terminal as best I could in my chic upgrade-me-please mules, and tried not to notice everyone staring at me. I absolutely didn't want to be one of those dreadful arguers you see on *Airline*, who turn up late, then claw wildly at their faces and shriek at the check-in staff that they can still see the plane on the tarmac, but neither did I want to miss my flight.

Panting, I slapped my ticket down on the desk, and smiled as charmingly as I could.

'Hello,' I said. 'I'm on the twelve fifteen plane to New York.'

The check-in girl took my ticket silently and jabbed at her computer.

I waited, breathing slowly to get my heart rate back to normal. 'Oh, what great nails you've got!' I observed. 'How do you keep your manicure from chipping when you're typing all day?'

She looked up, and a faint 'Don't bother' smile crossed

her face. 'I'm very sorry, madam, but the flight's over-booked. We don't have a seat for you on this particular flight, but I can—'

'Sorry?' I stared at her. 'But that's impossible. I booked my ticket ages ago.'

She pointed her chip-free nail up at the clock, and spoke very slowly, as if I were completely stupid. 'Yes, madam, but you're checking in very late. And it's industry policy to overbook flights, but on this occasion everyone has turned up. I'm afraid you'll have to wait and see if anyone takes a voluntary bumping.'

'Oh,' I said, feeling foolish. 'But I really do have to go on this one. My boyfriend will be waiting for me at the other end, and . . .' I stopped, realising how lame this sounded. Behind me was a drained mother with two children and a baby in a pushchair, and two students. The baby was grizzling, and the students were having a frantic argument in a language I didn't know, but it seemed to involve their visas which they were shoving in each other's faces.

I turned back to the check-in girl. 'They're overbooked too, aren't they?'

She nodded.

'And they're ahead of me in the voluntary bumping line?'

She nodded again. 'But if we have to bump you, you'll get compensation, madam.'

I sighed and tried not to think of the romantic welcome Jonathan probably had waiting for me. No compensation would make up for missing that. 'I'll take a seat.'

Now, in my position, I knew Gabi would have pulled every string she could think of – from my business, to my father, to Jonathan's frequent flyer miles – but I hated doing that sort of thing. I never sounded convincing, even when it was true.

I wandered off to get myself a coffee and a newspaper, and when I came back, the check-in girl was negotiating furiously with the students. It sounded as if they had to get back to wherever it was they were going, or else they'd be evicted or their mother would be offered as a living sacrifice to the powers of the dark side, or something.

I hovered, not wanting to butt in, and suddenly felt a large hand smack me on the bottom.

'Melissa!' boomed a voice behind me.

I spun round.

Looming up behind me like a pinstriped drainpipe was Harry Paxton, a business acquaintance of my father's for whom I'd done some Christmas shopping last year. I'd been recommended on account of my extreme discretion apparently (doubtless by my father), which was just as well, since he seemed to have a suspicious number of 'god-daughters' on his list.

Still, he was quite jolly and had tipped me lavishly – even if it was by 'putting a couple of quid behind the counter at Rigby & Peller'.

'Hello, Harry,' I said, extending my hand for him to shake.

He went for a kiss. 'Melissa,' he mumbled into my knuckles. 'And what brings you to Heathrow? Business or pleasure?'

'Oh, I'm flying to New York. Or, rather, I was, until I was bumped off the plane.' I pulled a face. 'It's rather inconvenient, but I suppose I'll just have to get a good book and make the best of it.'

'Can't have that!' exclaimed Harry. 'What nonsense! Come with me.'

He bustled off in the direction of the first-class check-in, and walloped the counter hard until a stewardess appeared.

'Now, see here,' he said. 'I've checked myself into first class, but my assistant has been bumped out of economy by some minion of yours. Should have booked herself in with me, silly girl. False economy, what? Know for next time. Now we need to deal with a fair bit of business before we land at JFK, so I'd be obliged if you could take a look at your screen or what have you, and see if you can't pop her into first with me.'

'Of course, Sir Harry,' mumbled the stewardess, clicking rapidly.

Blimey. I'd forgotten he was a Sir.

'There you go!' said Harry. 'Give the nice lady your passport. That all you're travelling with?'

'Um, yes!'

He beamed. 'Very small clothes, eh? Excellent!'

'Well, no, just clever packing,' I murmured, handing over my passport. I saw her expression flicker when she checked the back. Having an Hon Granny on my contact details as well as Daddy's official MP thing often raised a few eyebrows.

'Jolly good,' boomed Harry jovially. 'Now, how about a quick snorter while we wait for the cattle to load? Rather good lounge here, actually.'

I cast a guilty glance back to the economy desk, where the mother was practically banging her head against the desk, while her children stuffed crayons up each other's noses.

I turned back with a big smile. 'I'll see you there in two shakes! I just have to . . . make a quick call.'

He patted my bottom again. 'Don't be too long. I need

to have a little chat with you about Margery. Her knuckles again. Driving me mad. Need some tips on house-breaking her, what?' And he tapped his nose.

Great. I'd had chapter and verse about Harry's wife's myriad irksome habits before now, but it was a small price to pay for a seat I could fit my whole bottom in. At least I could improve her Christmas present outlook while I was there.

And maybe there was something else I could do to help.

When I was sure Harry was out of sight, I walked quickly back to check-in, and muttered discreetly to the stewardess that I recognised the woman with the baby from a BBC consumer affairs show and that I was sure I'd seen her filming secretly in the loos. Something about an exposé?

I suppose it must have worked, because ten minutes later she was pushing her suddenly angelic kids into the first-class lounge, followed by two very surprised students.

First class was a very new experience for me. The seats were so far apart that Harry had to lean right over to talk to me. And talk to me he did, right through the safety demonstration, right through the explanation of the films on offer, and right up until the stewardesses came round with the first lot of drinks. Then he broke off to order his first Scotch.

From long years of cocktail parties at home, and then office parties at work, I was used to making conversation with men like Harry – not that it involved much actual conversation on my part. Nodding, humming and twitching my eyebrows was about the limit. Still, men were always telling me what a good listener I was.

We'd run through various of his anecdotes about his

time as chairman of the local Neighbourhood Watch committee and his 'zero tolerance' stance on cyclists on pavements, when he leaned over even further, and said, 'Do you fly a lot, then, Melissa?'

'Oh, yes. Holidays and so on.' I nodded.

'Are you a member of the, ah, Mile High Club?'

I racked my brains. Was that something to do with Air Miles? Gabi was obsessed with how many she got on her credit cards, and claimed Tesco's had paid for several upgrades in her flying career.

A light went on in my head. Maybe if I was a member, I wouldn't get kicked out of first when they realised I only had an economy ticket.

'Yes,' I said, nodding harder. 'Yes, I am. Have been for ages.'

'Good!' Sir Harry grinned so hard his eyes almost disappeared. 'Excellent! Well,' he went on, dropping his voice discreetly, 'I'm just off to the little boys' room now . . .' And he winked slowly, on account of the whisky, I supposed. 'I'll see *you* in a moment.'

'Wonderful!' I said, and as soon as he'd gone, I motioned to the stewardess for a glass of champagne and the headphones, and settled down to watch the latest Harry Potter film on my personal video screen.

Half an hour passed very pleasantly, and I'd moisturised twice with the complimentary Jo Malone face cream, when I realised the seat next to me was still empty. Where had Sir Harry got to? I looked round the cabin in case he'd table-hopped to someone more interesting but there was no sign of him.

Oh dear. I hoped something hadn't befallen him in the loo, like a sudden deep vein thrombosis. I'd read they could be nasty.

'More champagne?' The stewardess leaned over with another mini bottle, and I seized my chance.

'Um, I'm rather concerned about my, er, colleague?' I felt myself turning pink with the effort of fibbing and being discreet simultaneously. 'He's been, er, gone from his seat for quite a while now, and . . .'

'Don't mention it.' The stewardess smiled. 'I'll make sure he's OK.'

'Would you? That would be so kind,' I said gratefully, and settled back into my comfy seat.

I watched her walk down the aisle towards the lavatory, knock once – I couldn't hear, since I had my state-of-the-art headphones back on – then recoil backwards from the door in shock. For a horrible moment I wondered if poor Sir Harry had died in there, but he came bustling out almost immediately, adjusting his clothes, nearly pushing past the poor woman as he stumbled back down the aisle.

Turbulence, I assumed. Or constipation. It happened a lot to men his age, if their confided medical histories were to be believed.

He glared at me when he sat down, but I smiled sunnily, and removed one ear of my headphones. 'I ordered you some cold water,' I said. 'You should try to rehydrate if you're drinking at altitude, according to my facialist! It would be such a shame to have a vile headache when you land, wouldn't it?'

He muttered something I missed as I was replacing my headphone, and when I turned back to tell him about the hypnotherapist I'd just remembered about in Parson's Green who could cure his wife's knuckle-cracking, I was startled to see that he'd donned one of those blackout eye-masks that practically covered the whole face. It was like discovering an Elizabethan executioner in the next seat.

Still, it meant that I could enjoy the first-class luxuries undisturbed by conversation, and I spent the remaining five hours toying pleasantly with a number of romantic reunion scenarios, most of which seemed to take place in black and white, and all featured Jonathan and me dancing, gazing into each other's eyes.

I'd often daydreamed about my first trip to New York with Jonathan, pretty much since our first meeting. I was usually bundled up in some adorable fur-lined hood, clutching heaps of beribboned Christmas presents while a fine dusting of snow fell around us and groups of rosy-cheeked youngsters sang carols on street corners. And a yellow taxi came to pick us up and sweep us off to the ice rink for hot chocolate and enormous cupcakes.

As Nelson liked to point out, most of my fantasies have a significant food element.

Jonathan had warned me that New York was 'kind of extreme' when it came to weather, in summer as well as winter, but I'd put that down to his usual 'America is so much bigger/louder/faster' spiel. So I wasn't actually prepared for my clothes, my hair and my luggage to start sticking to me with humidity while waiting in the hour-long immigration queue.

Obviously, I knew it wasn't always Christmas in New York, in much the same way that London wasn't populated with chimney sweeps and cheery flower-sellers, but I did think it was all meant to be air-conditioned. To the point of hypothermia, according to Emery, who'd broken her usual vow of vagueness to ring me from Chicago with packing advice.

'Take nothing at all,' she'd insisted with uncharacteristic certainty. 'Nothing!'

I rolled my eyes at the phone. 'Well, what am I going to wear?'

'Wait till you get there to decide. Go shopping. See what mood you're in. But take something squashy in your hand luggage, in case it's hot.'

Emery, I should point out, was one of those annoyingly waif-like girls who could float around bra-less in Ghost rags and look ethereal, rather than an escapee from *Les Misérables*.

'Mmm. The weird thing is,' she went on, 'I find New York is just like those Scottish castles we used to go to on holiday. It's kind of spooky, actually. It can be really hot outside, like . . . *tropical* . . . and yet inside, everything's freezing. I don't know how they do it. It must be the stone floors, don't you think? Bizarre.'

I stared at my own reflection in the mirror over Nelson's phone table. *How* were we related?

'You don't think it's the air-con, maybe?' I suggested.

'You know me, Melissa, I don't talk about politics,' said Emery firmly.

Now, of course, I wished I hadn't taken Emery's advice because I'd packed the bare minimum of clothes, and then sucked all the air out with Gabi's special vacuum packer. In practical terms, the only outfit I could slip into without exploding my whole carry-on was a slinky silk jersey dress that I'd only packed in my handbag at the last minute because you could screw it into a little ball without fear of creasing.

The fact that such slinky minimalism required several complicated Pants of Steel elements went without saying, but with the humidity rapidly reaching tomato hothouse levels, pretty soon I wouldn't have much choice. I refused to meet Jonathan with sweat stains and a shiny nose. It was hardly Jackie Kennedy Onassis. But then neither was shuffling forwards slowly in a queue while my hair slowly slumped.

Oddly, Sir Harry had vanished off the plane the second it landed, before I could even thank him properly for wangling me such a lovely flight, so I was left to find my own way out as best I could. Once they'd taken my fingerprints and I'd squinted into the security camera, I scuttled into the nearest loo for emergency renovations.

A year of turning myself in and out of Honey Blennerhesket at short notice meant I was pretty good at tarting myself up under pressure: a splash of cold water on my wrists, mouthwash, fresh mascara, and some red lipstick, and I looked almost human. Once I'd wriggled into my slinky dress, I really did look as if I'd travelled over first class. For the final effect, I slipped on my shades, and strode out into the corridor, a whole new woman.

The security guard outside did a double-take.

I flashed him a broad smile as I wheeled my case past. Yes, I did look good. Jonathan was going to be very impressed by my soignée arrival.

He didn't smile back.

I sped up, suddenly overwhelmed by excitement at the thought of being so close to seeing Jonathan again. I wondered what he'd be wearing? His new Savile Row suit? Mmm.

'Miss?'

I ignored it.

'Miss?' repeated the voice.

A new hot flush hit me. Had they found out I'd travelled first class on a discount internet ticket? I walked on. It felt much cooler out here. Presumably they had better air-conditioning once they'd established you weren't an illegal immigrant.

At the arrivals gate, whole families were blocking up the doors, in massive rugby-scrum group hugs, waving raffia donkeys and pushing vast taped-up cardboard boxes full of God knows what.

I scanned the crowd for Jonathan's red hair.

He wasn't there.

My heart sank.

'Miss!' said two new voices.

I looked round. A family of Italians were standing there, giggling at me.

'What?' I asked.

A small boy pointed at my skirt. 'I can see your panties!' He giggled and put his hand over his mouth.

'Nice ass!' added his father.

His mother back-handed him, without even looking.

I slid my hand behind me and touched my own clammy flesh. The improved air-con was in fact courtesy of my dress, which was tucked into my pants. Which were riding up my er . . .

Stammering my thanks, I pulled down the stupid slinky dress, and tried to regain my composure, pretending to look for Jonathan, while my whole body turned hot and cold at the thought of what I'd nearly done.

There must have been hundreds of people out there, waiting for passengers! I felt sick, and not just with the heat.

I hovered at the door, not wanting to walk past him, in case he was hidden behind someone else. Honestly, he could wave or something, I thought. I mean, there's reserved and there's plain unhelpful.

Just as my mood was sinking from disappointment into despair, a small woman with jet-black hair and a neat twinset approached us.

'Ms Romney-Jones?' she said, putting out a tiny little hand to shake. 'I'm Lori? From Mr Riley's office? I've been sent to collect you?'

'Melissa, please!' I said.

'Mr Riley apologises but he's been called out on some urgent business?' said Lori, smiling. 'May I compliment you on your outfit, by the way? You look just like a film star!' Her face dimpled when she smiled. It gave her a very pretty Russian doll look. If I split her between her neat skirt and neat cotton cardigan, there were probably nine other tiny Loris inside, I thought.

I shook myself. Clearly the heat was having a strange effect on my brain.

'That's very kind of you,' I said, trying not to sound too disappointed at the news of Jonathan's absence. Even though I was. Awfully disappointed.

Why couldn't he be here? What was more important than my arriving in New York for the first time?

'He's very sorry not to be here to meet you himself, but he's asked me to take you to his appointment and he'll take you home? We'll get a cab downtown? Are these all your bags?'

'Yes, yes, that's all,' I said, letting her take my wheelie case, while I clutched my handbag to my side. I followed her through the concourse and out into the cab rank, where the hot, airless air hit me like a wall.

'Gosh!' I said, unable to stop myself. 'It's so hot!'

'I *know*!' said Lori, with such passion that it didn't turn into a question. 'This is a cool day, though? It's been much hotter than this?'

'Really?' I said faintly, and sank gratefully into the air-conditioned cab she magicked out of nowhere. For the first time ever, I understood Jonathan's obsession with cars that had powerful air-conditioning as well as seat position memory functions.

We sped through the outskirts of the city, and soon the skyline of tall buildings and bridges started to rise out of the low-level buildings. I couldn't stop staring. Everything was so familiar, from television and films, and yet – there it was! Real!

I'd had a very similar experience when Gabi and I had visited the *Coronation Street* set in Manchester.

'Kind of amazing, isn't it?' said Lori proudly, as the cab driver lurched impatiently from one lane to another. Fortunately, the car was so enormous that I didn't even feel the swerve.

'Absolutely.'

'You'll find it very big at first? But you'll soon get used to it?' Her mobile phone rang. 'Would you excuse me?' she said politely.

We carried on into Manhattan, with me getting progressively more excited and fluttery at the thought of seeing Jonathan, and Lori getting more and more calls on her mobile, which she dealt with in a courteous undertone. I kept hearing the words 'Mr Riley' and 'schedule' and 'impossible'.

At last, we pulled up outside an impressive mansion block, with a long green canopy and a doorman who held the door for us as we went in.

'If you'd like to wait here, Mr Riley will be finished in a few minutes?' murmured Lori in suitably hushed tones as we entered the lobby. 'I'll go and get you a coffee, and something to eat, if you'd like?'

I was quite happy to sit and refresh myself in the discreet splendour. The lobby of these apartments was more lavishly appointed than most London hotel bars: oak panelling, brass light fittings, vast green plants. It also had bone-chilling air-conditioning which was raising all the hairs on the back of my arms in a most gratifying manner.

'I'd love a cup of coffee,' I murmured back. 'And a muffin or something, if you think I've got time. And if you think they wouldn't mind me eating in here,' I added, partly as a joke. Just partly, though.

'Whatever you want?' murmured Lori deferentially, and it dawned on me that the reason she was treating me like some kind of visiting royalty was because I was Jonathan's guest.

It was easy to forget just how important Jonathan was in this company. I blinked. So it rather behoved me to behave accordingly. Which meant less like a dumbstruck tourist, and more like a friendly but equally successful businesswoman.

'That would be kind,' I said with a smile. 'Thank you.'

Lori backed out of my presence, went up to the concierge to murmur a few more words to him, and I was left sitting on the huge velvet sofa, appreciating the fine art and the immense explosion of fresh flowers in the fireplace.

The fireplace was roughly the size and depth of a small car, and carved out of big chunks of marble. It looked as if it could have been shipped wholesale from Windsor Castle, complete with secret priest-hole in the back.

While I was pondering how much an apartment in this block must cost, I heard footsteps on the parquet hall behind me, and a few low-spoken words of conversation. I knew it was Jonathan, winding up his business with some clients, and a shiver of anticipation ran over my skin. Not wanting to turn round and gawp, my ears twitched all the same, and I picked up the words, 'board meeting . . . personal references . . . pets . . .'.

Then there was some manly well-wishing and arm-slapping, the doorman was thanked in an undertone, and after a few tantalising seconds, the smell of Creed came closer, bent over, and placed a soft kiss on the nape of my neck.

'Hello,' Jonathan whispered in my ear, his breath warm on my skin. 'How very nice to see you.'

Every hair on my body pricked up and tingled, but I made myself turn round very slowly in the manner of Rene Russo in *The Thomas Crown Affair*.

When I did, it was worth it. Jonathan was looking heart-stoppingly businesslike in a sharp navy-blue linen suit, with a creamy shirt and a liquid-gold tie. His hair was perfectly groomed, and he showed no signs at all of the raging heat outside.

He looked a little tense, but then he was at work, after all.

'Let me see you,' he said, taking my hand and making me stand up. 'You're telling me you've just got off a seven-hour flight? I don't believe you. You look wonderful!'

'Thank you.' I glowed. 'Just something I found in my handbag.'

He leaned forward and kissed my cheek, lingering long enough to smell my scent and for me to smell his cologne. I knew he wasn't going to pull me into a dramatic embrace in front of the concierge, and for some reason that sort of discreet kiss was even more exciting.

Jonathan could be really very Rhett Butler when he wanted to. It was positively knee-buckling.

'In fact you look even more beautiful than I remember,' he said, right into my ear, close enough for me to feel his breath. 'And,' he added, in a husky undertone, 'I've been remembering . . . quite often.'

I wanted to be equally mature and restrained, but I couldn't. 'I've missed you,' I said impulsively, unable to hold it in any longer. 'It's felt like ages.'

'And I've missed you,' he said, and put his hands on either side of my face, pulling me close and kissing me passionately.

Lori coughed behind us and we jumped.

Well, I jumped. Jonathan just turned round and took the coffee from her with a quick thanks, then handed it to me. She smiled, nodded slightly to him, then opened her mouth uncertainly, only speaking when he raised his eyebrows in encouragement.

'Will you be going back to the office this afternoon, Mr Riley?' she enquired. 'Because I can have those papers sent over to you this evening if you want to look at them before tomorrow's board meeting? And I have the references for the Grosvenor apartment?'

'Right,' said Jonathan, shooting out his cuffs to adjust them as he thought aloud. 'OK, cancel everything for the rest of the day, and have whatever you think most urgent sent over to me tonight. I'll take a look at it. And, Lori, thank you for collecting Miss Romney-Jones from Kennedy. I appreciate your time.'

'Yes, thanks very much,' I added. 'I'd never have found my way here by myself!'

Lori smiled until she dimpled up, nodded shyly, and then excused herself.

'You want a cup for that?' asked Jonathan, when she'd gone, nodding at my Starbucks cup.

'No, no, it's fine,' I said.

'Go on, I know you like a proper cup for your coffee.'

'No, honestly, don't worry about it,' I said, confused. Where was he going to get me a cup from?

'Listen,' he said, his face perfectly serious, 'why don't we nip upstairs and borrow a cup and saucer from the apartment I've just viewed?'

I stared at him, then laughed. 'Oh, don't be silly! You can't do that!'

'Would that be very unprofessional of me?' Jonathan gazed at me, all innocence.

Was he winding me up? 'Well, yes,' I spluttered. 'Of course it would!'

'Melissa,' he said solemnly, 'I don't like to follow the rules all the time. Come on, I've still got the keys.'

And he set off for the lift.

I trotted after him in a state of some confusion, my heels clicking loudly on the black and white floor. I was surprised that the concierge didn't try to stop him as he called the lift.

'Listen, Jonathan, I really don't want to—'

'Shh!' he said, putting a finger on his lips.

'But I don't want you to—'

'Shh!'

He waited until the wrought-iron gates shut behind us, then leaned forward and gave me a long kiss. It was such a long kiss, and his hands moved with such delicious confidence over my tingling body, that I barely noticed when we reached the tenth floor.

Jonathan, though, had better timing, and stepped briskly out of the lift the minute it stopped moving.

'Now, which one was it?' he mused to himself, looking at the keys.

I had to admit that I was getting an idea of what he might have in mind, and although I was shocked to the core at the out-of-character naughtiness of it – well, perhaps that was what was so exciting.

He pretended to try various keys in the forbidding oak door until one fitted. 'Ah, here we go,' he said, and lifted a foxy eyebrow in invitation. 'Can I invite you in for a . . . cup of coffee?'

'OK,' I said, lifting an eyebrow flirtatiously. 'But you'd better find me a saucer too.'

'Something saucy?' he enquired.

'No, a saucer.'

'I'm sure I can rustle up something,' he said, and pushed the door open for me to go on in. I slithered past him, so he could see just how slinky my silk dress was, then I stopped in my tracks.

When I say this was an apartment, I mean it was an apartment in the sense of a *state* apartment. Everywhere I looked was either oak-panelled, gold-plated or draped with fabrics.

'Crikey,' I breathed. 'Is the owner still here?' I stepped into the hallway, which had ornate brass light fittings, converted, I guessed, from the originals. The smell of myrrh and cloves and beeswax polish floated through the whole apartment.

'No,' said Jonathan, suddenly sounding quite brisk.

I wandered slowly through to the sitting room, which was massive – bigger than Nelson's whole flat, I reckoned. Long windows, hung with deep red velvet curtains, looked out onto parkland, and an old glass chandelier hung from the high ceiling, sending slanting diamonds of refracted light all over the crimson walls. The room was dominated by three huge leather sofas, and some striking modern paintings, with a long oak table running the length of one wall, on which sat a wide glass bowl, containing about three hundred pounds' worth of expensive dried rose petals, flanked by a couple of massive fig-scented candles. I could smell them from the door.

The overall effect was stylish, modern, but at the same time curiously empty. There were no bookshelves, or photographs, or anything personal at all. The sofas were grand, but didn't invite you to get comfy on them. They didn't even invite you to take your socks off. And the view was there to be seen, just as much as you were meant to admire the paintings – I knew I should know who they were by, but I didn't.

Suddenly, I didn't want to wander any further. I wasn't sure I still felt slithery or flirty either. But I swallowed and tried to summon my best seductive smoulder.

'So,' I said, leaning up against the wall saucily. 'That's the sitting room. Are you going to show me the bedroom now?'

He was staring into space, and seemed to shake himself back to life when I spoke. 'Yeah, yeah. A cup, right?'

And he walked through a doorway into the kitchen.

Red-hot humiliation swept over my face. Argh.

After a moment's frozen embarrassment, I followed him, hastily rearranging my dress. Whatever sauciness he'd had in mind seemed to have evaporated too. Maybe he was reminded of problems on the deal – maybe it had been a tougher meeting than he was making out.

The kitchen, by contrast, was like the interior of the *Starship Enterprise*: everything was stainless steel and looked professional quality. There were no visible handles on anything and I could see our reflections in everything from the walk-in fridge to the matching dishwashers.

'Wow!' I said, trying to sound normal. 'Nelson would love this! Is the vendor a chef?'

'No,' said Jonathan, opening a cupboard. 'The vendor is a woman whose idea of home cooking was to put Thai fusion take-out on her own plate instead of getting a maid to do it.'

Oh. I frowned.

He handed me a bone china cup and saucer with a fine band of silver around the edges.

'Thank you,' I said, carefully decanting the contents of my takeaway cup. It wasn't like Jonathan to be so dismissive of his clients.

'Want a side plate for the muffin?' he enquired, offering me a matching tiny cake plate. 'Never been used. Part of an eighteen-place dinner service too. Look.' And he swung open the cupboard door to reveal more china than I'd seen in one place outside Peter Jones's homeware department. 'Never been through the dishwasher.'

I took the plate, trying not to let my surprise show. 'How do you know all this?'

Jonathan's mouth made a flat line. 'It's my old apartment.'

I blinked in shock. 'Sorry?'

'It's where Cindy and I used to live. She's been living here while I've been in London. I know, I know,' he added, raising his hands, 'she was meant to sell it as soon as the divorce went through but the market's been slow. And now the . . .' Jonathan didn't often swear. He swallowed. 'Cindy's put it on the market with Kyrle & Pope and wants *me* to broker the sale.'

A heavy weight plunged in my stomach, like a duck being shot and falling vertically to earth. I put the cup and saucer down as if they were red-hot.

Cindy.

The mere mention of Cindy made me feel nervous. And underdressed. And under-achieving, and, for some reason, cross. She'd behaved appallingly to Jonathan, and yet he'd put up with her shenanigans for years – so he must have really, really loved her. I'd never met Cindy, and he virtually never talked about her, but the few fragments I'd picked up were enough to paint a pretty disturbing picture: how she set fire to things at parties 'to get the atmosphere going', how she put her own secretary on the Atkins Diet, that sort of thing.

I'd only ever seen one photograph of Cindy, which I'd found hidden in a drawer at Jonathan's house – by accident while I was looking for a bottle-opener, I might add. It was taken at some very smart function; he was in a dinner jacket, looking tense, and she was wearing a long, straight, severe dress in crimson silk that emphasised her long, straight, severe figure. Also her long, straight, severe face, which could, as Gabi would have said, have done with a few pies. Her hair, fortunately, was neither long, nor straight, but wisped around her head like a candy-floss crash helmet. It wasn't fooling me, though – I knew, left to its own devices, it too would be long and straight.

My inner TV detective told me at once that she was the sort of cow who smiled sympathetically while she was sacking you, and boasted about 'playing hardball with the guys' while claiming her haircuts as business expenses.

Well, I didn't *know* that, to be fair. But who's fair about their boyfriend's ex?

Actually, the one major definite fact I knew about Cindy summed her up for me: she and Jonathan split up when she found out she was pregnant with his brother Brendan's baby. With whom she was now living.

You see? *Not* a nice woman.

Jonathan and I had had one shortish heart-to-heart about her, after we started dating properly. It was triggered by the arrival of a birth card, announcing the Gift of a Son to Brendan Riley and Cindy Riley. Kind of lucky that etiquette spared her blushes there, I'd say.

'She wasn't always a ball-breaker,' he'd insisted, after I'd expressed some surprise over the protocol of announcing the birth of your ex-husband's new nephew. 'Until she went into advertising, she used to read her horoscope every morning.'

'And what sign was she?'

'Aries,' he'd replied glumly. 'The ram.'

'Oh, a fire sign!' I'd said inappropriately.

Jonathan had just looked at me, with weariness written all over his face, and said nothing.

I hadn't liked to ask, but at that point he'd volunteered a quick rundown of their married life: they'd met at a formal dance when his New England boys' school had hosted her New England girls' school – that much I could sympathise with – and she'd won his heart by arguing with him all the way through a foxtrot. They'd then dated through university (Princeton for him, Brown for her), and married on graduation while she was still Lucinda, with the reception at the New York Yacht Club, and the honeymoon in Antigua.

What with Jonathan being a career realtor, and Cindy working her way swiftly up the ladder at her advertising agency, they'd had a series of nice apartments, and I knew their final marital home had been pretty smart, but it was only now I was standing in front of a twenty-thousand-pound kitchen range that I was starting to see the extent of what they'd had between them.

I gulped.

And the fact that she wanted *him* to sell it demon-strated, to me, anyway, just what a cow she was.

'I guess she wants to make sure I get the best price,' he added. 'She knows I don't broker sales any more. But she told the company that only I could deal with it, or else she'd take it elsewhere. And' – he waved a hand around – 'as you can guess, there's a pretty big commission on this.'

'I can imagine,' I said weakly.

Jonathan's mouth set into a lipless line again. 'Obviously it's in my interests to get as much as I can for it. But, mostly, I don't want to give her the satisfac-tion of showing her that I care. If she's trying to make me feel bad about the divorce, it's not working. It's just an apartment to me. It's not like it has sentimental value.'

The toughness in his words broke my heart, because I knew he couldn't possibly mean it.

'Oh, don't say that!' I exclaimed. 'That's not true! You *must* have had some happy times here.'

He sighed and wiped a hand across his face, then held out his arms. I slid into them gratefully, and squeezed him tight. I could feel his lean muscles beneath his thin shirt. We fitted together neatly.

'Melissa,' he murmured into my hair. 'I have more happy memories of the six months I rented that house in Barnes, when I first met you, than I do of six years of owning this place.'

'Really?' My heart skipped.

'Yes, really.' Jonathan traced his lips along my fore-head. 'That's when I knew how unhappy I'd been, because being with you made me feel like a different person.' He held me at arm's length, so I could look into his eyes and see how serious he was. 'You woke me up.

Those trips round town with you. You know I used to scour guidebooks, trying to find new farmers' markets and stately home Masonic halls and umbrella shops I could ask you to take me to?'

'You did?' I pretended to pout. 'And I thought you were interested in the history of London!'

'Well, yeah. That too. But I was more interested in being with you.'

I sank back into his arms. 'It was a pleasure. Even the Masonic halls.'

'So the least I can do is return the favour,' he went on, stroking my hair. 'And you know what? I think you'll like New York.'

'I'm sure I will.' I pulled away from him. There was something echoing and chilly about the apartment, and it wasn't the air-conditioning. 'But, um, can we go back to your new place? It's not that I don't like this flat, but . . .'

I looked at him, trying to not say, 'But I don't want Cindy hanging over us.'

Jonathan shrugged. 'Listen, Melissa, I wanted to show you this partly because I wanted you to know what I'm leaving behind. Cindy and I are selling this apartment because neither of us wants to live here. And believe me, there are hundreds of clients on our list who would kill to get in this building. It's easier to get into Congress than it is to get in here. But I want to move on.'

He fixed me with his special extra-determined look. 'I want to move on with *you*.'

My skin tingled with excitement as blood pounded to my extremities. 'Good,' I said, trying to appear cooler than I felt. 'That's . . . that's . . . good.'

Jonathan looked at me, his head tilting to one side. '*Good?*'

I opened my mouth again, but I wasn't sure what I was supposed to say. I was, after all, standing in famous Cindy's spectacularly appointed kitchen, with bits of American Airline pretzels still lodged in my back molars, and here was Jonathan offering to chuck away this lavish apartment so he could start a whole new life with me. The clammy, jet-lagged woman whose dress was sticking to the back of her thighs.

It was rather overwhelming – in a good way, obviously.

'British understatement,' I said. 'We like to fall back on it in times of . . . astonishment. I mean . . .' I spread my hands in apology. 'I'm hardly going to say, "Hurray! You've divorced your wife and got shot of your flat!" am I? But, yes, I think it's for the best that you want to move on. Much healthier.'

Jonathan's face relaxed. 'For a moment there I thought you were pissed that I was selling this place.'

'God, no!' I spluttered. Then a thought occurred to me. 'You're not *still* living here, are you? I mean, this isn't your . . .'

His smile increased. 'No, I'm not. In fact, I've already bought somewhere else. Much more your style, I think.'

He picked up my plate and poured the cold cup of coffee down the sink, rinsed them both, and replaced them in the cupboard. 'I think we've spent enough time in this place, don't you? Let's get a cab home.' And he put an arm around my waist and escorted me out of the kitchen, back into the plush reception room, where my small wheelie bag sat, dwarfed by a couple of shoulder-height modern vases.

Home. I liked the sound of that.

8

Jonathan summoned a cab out of the surging traffic with the merest twitch of his hand, and we set off downtown. It was as much as I could do to stop my eyes flicking from side to side at the array of familiar shop names and/or commenting on the powerful air-conditioning now reviving me nicely.

Jonathan, meanwhile, had got straight onto his favourite topic: houses, the acquisition and improvement thereof.

'It was the quickest deal ever, *ever*. I just fell in love with this property the moment I walked in the door,' he was saying, his eyes shining. 'It never even went on the market – I was meant to be checking it over for an old family friend, but as soon as I saw it, I just thought, I've got to have that! So I did!'

'Really?' This opportunism sounded somewhat out of character for Jonathan – in fact, it rather smacked of my father's behaviour – but my attention was temporarily distracted by yet another amazing-looking deli. There were Gaps everywhere. Really *big* Gaps. I wriggled in my seat with excitement.

'I wanted something very different from that Upper East Side apartment I had with Cindy,' he went on. 'Somewhere I could have a library, and a study, if I wanted, and not have to kowtow to the co-op board whenever I needed to have the plumbing fixed.'

I'm not saying I wasn't listening, but there was an awful lot to take in, all at once, so I just nodded and carried on trying to fit everything together in my reeling head.

'It's quite a different neighbourhood too,' he said. 'You know how you used to tell me that London was like a bunch of villages, all joined up? Well, this really is a village. Greenwich Village. It's kind of like London in some ways.'

I turned to him, and squeezed his hand tighter. We were holding hands in the cab – Jonathan and I shared the same strict rules about what was and wasn't acceptable on public transport. Anticipation is underrated, in my book. 'I'm sure I'll love it.'

'I hope so,' he said solemnly, and for a moment he sounded almost nervous.

The neighbourhood was definitely getting less city-like as the streets narrowed and became more residential, with trees shading the pavement between tall Victorian town houses. Passers-by were walking dogs, and sitting outside at table cafés, and generally looking more boho than they had been a moment ago. Boho in an expensive, Notting Hill way, though.

Jonathan indicated for the cab to stop outside a brownstone house, with steps up to a dark green front door. It was second to the end of the street, near a cobbled crossroads, and had a tall tree shading its porch, with ivy curling around the iron handrails, winding down to the basement windows. And, rather prettily, instead of just being a number, the street had a name: Jane Street. I liked that.

'Here you are,' he said. 'Home sweet home. Whaddya reckon?'

To be honest, it wasn't quite what I was expecting of Jonathan's New York residence. It was really rather old-fashioned and understated. Homely. It reminded me, in fact, of Sesame Street, although I didn't say this to Jonathan.

'It's beautiful,' I replied and smiled broadly. The hint of nervousness vanished from his eyes and he smiled back, showing his perfect teeth.

'Good,' he said. 'I'm so glad you approve.'

While Jonathan was paying the driver, I peered out of the window at the house, preparing myself to step back into the muggy air. Actually, on closer inspection, there was something slightly, well, less tended about this house compared to its neighbours. The paint on the door, for a start, seemed to be bubbling, and the lion's head knocker was dull.

Jonathan got out and opened my door for me. 'Quick,' he said, making flapping gestures with his hands. 'Let's get in before the humidity kills you.'

I followed him as he hoisted my bag effortlessly up the steps and turned his key in the lock. The door, I could now confirm, was definitely flaking in places.

'So,' he said, stepping back to let me into the cool, tiled hallway. 'First impressions?'

'It's . . . it's full of character,' I said.

It was full of packing cases. And beyond the packing cases, I could see some delightful details: a big fireplace with lovely original tiles in the sitting room, between two long sash windows, and flower-petal mouldings on the ceiling. But the packing cases were pretty much the dominant feature, in the hall at least.

Above that, though, was a light, airy smell of shaded rooms and old wood. It smelled of grandmothers and faded wallpaper and books and dusty lamps. Not an unpleasant smell at all, to my nose, but one that I knew was a sign that the whole place needed doing up. I hoped he wouldn't do it up too much. And there was another smell too, that I couldn't quite put my finger on, but there was something familiar about it.

'Excuse the mess,' Jonathan explained, his footsteps echoing on the tiles as he led the way through into the long sitting room. 'Not everything's unpacked, because the designers and the builders wanted to see it as it was. And I've been really busy, setting things up in the office. But don't worry – I've got people coming to take care of everything on Monday.'

I stared at his retreating back. 'Builders?'

'Ah.' He stopped, and turned round. He had the grace to look a little sheepish. 'Well, yes. As you can see there's a fair amount of work to be done to bring this up to its full potential, and—'

'You didn't mention you had *builders in*,' I said. 'When you offered this as a refuge from the building work going on in my own house.'

'Well . . . it wasn't my plan,' said Jonathan, putting his hands on my arms. 'You'll hardly notice a thing. They're going to start at the top and work down, and it'll be mainly designers for the next few weeks, anyway. The builders won't be starting for a while. There are several teams of construction guys and architects and lighting people and so on to co-ordinate, so I don't anticipate any actual hammering for a little while.'

'I see.' I looked around. How much had he unpacked? 'It's a huge place.'

'Well, exactly. You'll never notice they're here. Want to know what the plan is?' he said, eyes twinkling with excitement. 'My architect's working on converting it into two apartments – one to rent out on the top floor, and the other for us to live in. What do you reckon?'

In a way, it was flattering that he'd even wanted me to interrupt his new house plans. Nothing usually came between Jonathan and an important property. 'That sounds very clever. How long do you think it'll take?' I asked. 'To get it the way you want?' I smiled. 'Now, admit it – was that why you invited me over? So I could manage the project for you? You just wanted the Little Lady Agency services at mates' rates, didn't you?'

'No,' said Jonathan, not getting the joke. 'No, not at all. You won't have to lift a finger. I've got the best designers in New York on board, and some great architects. They're coming up with the plans.'

That, I supposed, was the difference between Nelson and Jonathan: Nelson had agonised over authentic paint colours and appropriate carpets for days, whereas Jonathan was too busy for messing about. He just called in the experts and set them to work.

Still, it would be nice to offer some advice. Somewhere.

'I'm working on the actual schedule, but I've got some really great ideas and it's just a case of dovetailing the contractors so everything . . .' He suddenly stopped, and cupped my cheek with his palm. 'Are you mad? I guess I should have said. But I really wanted you to come over, and I thought I'd have got more done by this stage, and . . . You *are* mad, aren't you?' He stuck his hands in his hair and the smooth effect was instantly ruined as the waves sprang back rebelliously. 'I should have been more upfront. I apologise,' he sighed. 'But I thought you wouldn't come and I've missed you. You wouldn't believe how I've missed you, Melissa.'

Really, he could look so vulnerable. Especially when he apologised in his suit.

'Oh, Jonathan,' I said, sliding my arms around his waist. 'It would take more than a few electricians to stop me coming to see you. Now, please tell me you've at least unpacked somewhere for me to sleep?'

His tense face broke into a smile, then went serious again. 'But of course. You don't think I'd have been so ill-mannered as to have invited a guest without clearing out a guest room?'

I squeezed him, even though by now I was tingling all over with excitement. It had been quite a while since I'd seen him, if you know what I mean.

'Guest room?' I said.

'That's right. I even checked with one of your British etiquette books about getting the right flowers, the water vase, the selection of amusing bedside reading.'

For a moment, I wondered if he meant it. He did take my tips about etiquette extraordinarily seriously. I squirmed, not sure if I'd made the right assumptions. We weren't, after all, living together and he was, in many ways, terribly old-fashioned.

'But in fact,' he said, leaning closer, so his lips were right over mine, 'the master bedroom was the first room I got ready. And I think you'll prefer it.'

'I'm sure I will,' I murmured, my eyes closed, totally forgetting how sticky I still was after the flight, as his familiar smell came closer and closer, and I felt his breath on my skin.

Just as he was about to kiss me, a frenzied howling and scrabbling tore through the air, making me jump so hard I accidentally head-butted Jonathan's nose.

'What the hell is that?' I yelped as the howling increased to a deafening pitch, accompanied by the sound of wood being attacked.

Jonathan clutched his face. 'That's my new flatmate,' he said, with enough venom to be heard through his cupped hands.

'Your what?'

'Blame Cindy,' he said heavily, and, taking my hand, he led me through the sitting room, which I now saw held a couple of distressed leather sofas and some stacks of books, through to the kitchen.

The howling got louder as we approached the back door.

'Jonathan, what on earth is it?' I demanded, mentally picturing a Labrador or a boxer, at least. So that's what I'd smelled: eau de hound.

'Stand back,' he warned, and undid his cufflinks, folding back his pristine cuffs to his elbows. Then he rotated his shoulders, braced one foot against the door, and turned back to me. 'I mean it, honey. Get back behind the table.'

'Oh, Jonathan, don't be . . . OK.' Seeing the look on his face, I moved aside one of the dining chairs and stood behind the table.

'Right,' he said, more to himself than me, then yanked open the door.

A flash of white shot out like a furry bullet and, with superb timing, Jonathan managed to snatch it by the collar with one hand, and the rear end with the other, scooping it up into the air like a rugby ball.

I don't know who was more surprised: me or the dog.

On balance, probably the dog, since it stopped barking for three seconds, long enough for me to see that rather than being the Hound of the Baskervilles, it was actually a West Highland terrier, roughly the size of my overnight bag. And when it stopped barking, it forgot to put its tongue back in, which made it look exactly like the loo-roll cover the matron had in the sick-bay lavatory at school. Pom-poms for its head and ears and everything.

'Good Lord,' I said, trying not to laugh.

Obviously, it was one of those dogs who responded poorly to owner amusement, and it threw its head back and went into a deafening yapping of complaint.

'Shut up! Shut up!' yelled Jonathan helplessly.

'What's it called?' I shouted.

'Braveheart!' shouted Jonathan, as if it pained him to say it aloud. 'I didn't choose the name. Get the dog food out of the fridge!'

I opened and closed appliances until I came to the fridge. There wasn't much in there, apart from some milk, some bottles of champagne and a plastic takeaway box.

'I can't see anything!' I shouted back over the sound of indignant barking.

'The box,' yelled Jonathan. 'It's the box of stuff.'

I pulled out the plastic container, confused. 'But this is takeaway, isn't it? There's pasta in here and everything. Are you sure it's not—'

'Braveheart has a dietician,' he roared. 'Now if you look in the cupboard next to you, there's a dog bowl.'

I opened the cupboard. It was empty, apart from what looked suspiciously like a porcelain soup plate.

Now, I know my mother was a bit daft about her ghastly animals, but this was really ridiculous. It had a crest on it. In gold leaf.

'Jonathan, you can't be . . .' I stared at him, as he and Braveheart tussled with each other. 'Darling, stop shaking the dog,' I added, before I could stop myself. 'It won't help.'

'I'm not shaking him,' said Jonathan through gritted teeth. 'He's shaking me.'

Braveheart turned his pompom head and snarled in my direction, as if to say, 'Make it snappy with the food, woman.'

Hastily, I tipped the contents of the plastic box into the bowl and set it down on the floor, by the huge stainless-steel swing-top bin.

Jonathan let go of the dog, which catapulted himself across the kitchen floor, skidding only momentarily on the tiles, before sinking his nose into the dish of aromatic pasta verdi.

'It's Cindy's dog, she got him while we were still going to counselling, she thought it might bring us together,' Jonathan explained rapidly, taking advantage of the temporary silence, broken only by the sound of slurping, and a china bowl being scraped round the floor. 'Other people have babies to patch up their relationship, but Cindy couldn't timetable a hospital stay into her development programme at work, plus she, quote, "resented the penalty of stretch marks", unquote, so we got a West Highland terrier. He's got a longer pedigree than I have and his ancestors belonged to Queen Victoria's mother's companion.'

I felt my eyes widen in horror. I've never subscribed to the insanity of warring couples having a baby to 'bring them together' but I didn't think getting a puppy was much better. Both required constant attention, peed everywhere and howled during the night, guilt-tripping their way to getting what they wanted until both parental parties were simply too exhausted to argue any more.

And, more selfishly, I wasn't sure I was ready to hear the entire history of why Jonathan and Cindy had or hadn't managed to start a family, condensed into the time it would take this evil little mutt to scarf up a gourmet meal.

'He's certainly a handsome thing,' I said instead, trying to be positive. Because, to be fair, Braveheart was handsome. As small dogs went, he looked every inch the pedigree specimen, all perfect snowy coat and shiny black button eyes. And sharp little teeth.

'Typical Cindy to get a white dog in New York,' said Jonathan, unrolling his sleeves with more of his usual wry humour. 'He's ridiculously high-maintenance. Braveheart has more staff than I do, and he costs about as much to run as Cindy's car. You know he has his own passport? And microchip? And matching travel bag?'

'Do you like him?' I asked.

'No,' said Jonathan.

'So why is he here? Did you get joint custody when the divorce happened?'

'Ah.' Jonathan paused in putting his cufflinks back in. 'Well, no. Cindy wanted Braveheart as one of the disposable assets from the house, and I was happy to let her take him because I was in England.' He pulled a face, as if to say 'Which I miss already', then went on, 'But then when Parker arrived—'

'Parker?'

'My nephew,' deadpanned Jonathan. 'Cindy and Brendan's baby.'

Oops. I should have remembered that.

But, really, Parker Riley. Honestly. What sort of name was that? He was a baby, not a fountain pen.

'How, um, charming,' I said, embarrassed.

'Yes, well, when Parker arrived, Cindy decided that Braveheart's hilarious table manners weren't so much hilarious as lethal, so she dumped him here. Actually, no,' he corrected himself. 'First of all she dumped him in a very expensive doggy rehab centre, for him to await my return to Manhattan, and then when she heard I got back, she told me where he was, and gave me the option of picking him and his scandalous room service tab up, or of getting rid of him altogether. Although that option, she told me, would make her very sad indeed.'

I'm sorry to say that I couldn't stop myself snorting. 'That's big of her,' I said disapprovingly. 'I hope she doesn't do the same thing to Parker when she gets sick of him.'

'Now, don't you go getting the idea that Cindy doesn't care about her Scotch baby,' he said, wagging a finger at me. 'You'll find, if you open that drawer there, that she's made a list of all his needs, so I can look after him properly.'

I pulled open the drawer, which should have held a cutlery tray and a jumble of whisks and broken nut-crackers. Instead it held a single laminated A4 sheet and a state-of-the-art presentation bound folder.

'Important numbers,' I read. 'Braveheart's walker. Braveheart's veterinarian. Braveheart's canine dietician. Braveheart's groomer.' I looked up. 'Does Braveheart have an astrologer?'

'Not yet.' Before he could carry on with whatever he looked about to say, the phone rang in the sitting room. 'Ah, damn. I told them not to call me at home. Look, I'll just get that. If he starts playing up, get him into the vestibule and shut the door, OK?'

'OK?' I eyed Braveheart nervously.

My father, who was wrong about most things, was right when it came to dogs. He reckoned that a strict ratio of owner height/dog size should apply. Anyone over five feet seven, according to him, should have Labradors or bigger; anything smaller than that looked camp. He would permit Jack Russells – a breed he secretly admired

for their tenacious refusal to let go of trouser legs – as
a supplement to a larger dog, like an Irish wolfhound or
something. Dogs small enough to fit into a handbag, as
far as he was concerned, might as well be cats.

Braveheart finished chasing the bowl around the floor
in his efforts to remove the last forensic traces of supper
– as I would, had I been served that – and stared at me.
I could tell he was spoiling for a fight. He reminded me
of a diminutive Welsh estate agent at Dean & Daniels:
two gin and tonics on top of his residual Napoleon complex, and he'd start getting pushy with men twice his
size. I'd had to administer first aid more than once at
leaving parties.

'Hello,' I said, trying to be nice. Generally, I took quite
a firm line with dogs, but this was Jonathan's dog. Actually,
it was Cindy's dog and I wouldn't have put it past her,
by now, to have fitted him with a microchip voice recorder
to find out what was really going on in Jonathan's life.

Braveheart growled, his teeth jutting over his drawn-
back lips in a show of small-dog belligerence.

'Now, come on. I'm sure you're a lovely chap,' I said,
leaning over to stroke him. 'No need for all this grumpiness! We're from the same country, practically.'

Big mistake. He waited until my hand was millimetres
from his wiry coat, and just as I was congratulating myself
on charming him into submission, he turned with lightning speed and sank his teeth into the fleshy part of my
hand.

'Bugger!' I hissed, not wanting to draw Jonathan's attention, and lifting my hand up to suck it better. To my horror,
Braveheart clung on, until we were both eye to eye.

I swear he narrowed his eyes at me.

With a superhuman effort I managed to disengage his

jaws – I knew there was some clever trick that Mummy had once employed to remove a Jack Russell from Emery's leg when its jaws had locked, but funnily enough it escaped me for the moment – and sent him skittering across the kitchen floor.

My skin was unbroken, fortunately, but a series of cross little marks were now stamped into my hand.

'You little Scottish . . . bugger!' I hissed at him.

Braveheart panted back, unbowed.

In the sitting room, Jonathan was conducting a yes/no conversation with someone, and I heard his voice getting nearer.

He reappeared in the doorway and I hastily rearranged myself into a semblance of normality.

'Sorry,' he mouthed, then nodded to Braveheart who was sitting, stunned, in the corner, preparing himself for his next attack. 'Well done! Never heard him so quiet!'

I nodded back, hiding my hand behind my back.

'Won't be long,' Jonathan finished and walked back into the sitting room. 'We'll be there . . . Of course, I'll mention it. No, it won't be a problem . . .'

I sat down at the kitchen table and rubbed my eyes. All I really wanted now was a bath. A bath and a cup of tea, and a change of clothes, and maybe something to eat, actually, then I'd feel more like . . .

What was that faint growling, ripping noise?

I opened my eyes very slowly to see Braveheart with his nose deep in my handbag. It was, as I may have mentioned, a large handbag. It looked as if it was consuming him, slowly, like a Venus fly trap.

'Oh no, you don't,' I said, in what I hoped were jolly, unthreatening tones, and reached over to pull it away from him.

The growling intensified and Braveheart increased his purchase on the bag.

'Now, don't be silly!' I said, pulling harder.

He tugged the other way, getting his head looped under one of the handles.

I glanced over towards the sitting room. Jonathan was still talking, albeit in 'winding up' mode.

'Give!' I hissed, pulling at the bag.

Braveheart's lips lifted again, almost in a smile, and he started to walk backwards, so we were engaged in a very undignified tug-of-war.

'This is ridiculous!' I hissed, and made a lunge for the bag.

Of course, this just tipped the whole thing up altogether, scattering the entire contents over the kitchen floor: lipsticks, tape measure, white handkerchief, my travel socks, mobile phone, purse, spare purse, change purse for tips, sunglasses, whistle, breath fresheners, mini manicure kit, keys, useful addresses written on business cards, compact, Nurofen, Allegra's bloody melatonin, the dress and underwear I'd changed out of at the airport, diary, notebook – all sent bouncing and rolling across the tiled floor.

Immediately I fell to my knees, trying to jumble everything back into the bag before Jonathan came back in and saw what a bizarre collection of nonsense I'd carted across the Atlantic with me.

I was searching in vain for the missing right-eye contact lens case when I realised that once again Braveheart's hysterical barks of triumph had gone quiet.

When I looked up, I saw, to my horror, that he was silent because he was licking something off the floor. I crawled nearer, on my hands and knees so as not to frighten him, and saw that the top had come off Allegra's melatonin bottle, and Braveheart had one white tablet balanced on his tongue.

He also had my knickers on his head, an ear poking jauntily through one leg hole with a frill of lace drooping over one eye. But I wasn't so worried about that for the time being.

I grabbed the bottle and slammed my hand over the remaining pills. How many had he taken? I looked so ridiculous that Braveheart forgot to put his tongue back in and for a second I nearly managed to grab the tablet off him. But then he swallowed it, and snapped at my fingers instead.

'Oh, God almighty!' I breathed. This was all I needed. Dog poisoning. There was no way I could turn him upside down and shake it out of him, and I wasn't going near those jaws again.

I grabbed my mobile phone and dialled my home number, praying that Allegra wasn't tying up the line quarrelling with Lars.

It rang and rang. I kept my eye on Braveheart who was now truffling round the kitchen for more food, howling to himself for amusement. When he passed the door out to the vestibule, I took the opportunity to shove him in and shut it. Immediately he set up a loud protest but for the moment, as far as I was concerned, that was a good thing.

'Come on, come on,' I muttered, turning nervously to see where Jonathan had got to in his phone conversation.

'I've got nothing to add to my previous statement. I really can't comment further,' said my mother's voice, very insistently. 'I have *nothing more* to say on the matter. And neither has my husband.'

'Mummy?' I said, moving out of the kitchen into what looked like a scullery of some kind.

'Hello, darling!' she said enthusiastically. 'Where are you calling from?'

This was her discreet finishing-school method of working out which of her daughters was ringing, since she could never tell us apart on the phone.

'New York,' I said heavily. 'It's Melissa. Look, Mummy, that melatonin Allegra gave me – what would happen if, um, if a dog ate some? A smallish dog.'

'How small?'

'About the size of a West Highland terrier,' I said with a nervous glance towards the now silent vestibule.

'Oh, nothing, I shouldn't think,' said my mother. 'Might get a bit sleepy. I sometimes give the dogs Nytol if I have to take them up to Scotland in the car. They don't mind. I expect they feel as if they've been smoking dope. Probably gives them lovely dreams!'

'Mummy!' I said, scandalised. 'You drug the dogs?'

There was a movement in the hall, and I heard Jonathan's voice coming nearer. '. . . I'll tell her. No, I don't think . . . Yes, it's marvellous, I've got Cooper's designer coming over . . .'

'It's all homeopathic,' insisted Mummy. 'No worse than feeding them tea and biscuits, like Mrs Bleasdale does.'

'So it should be fine?' I repeated. 'To be absolutely sure?'

'Don't see why not,' she said. 'Just don't get him addicted. Valley of the Dogs and all that.'

Relief flooded through my system, followed by awful guilt.

'Thanks,' I said, then heard Jonathan wind up his conversation. 'Look, I'll speak to you later, Mummy. But thank you.'

I hung up, and scuttled back through into the kitchen. I opened the door to the vestibule and found Braveheart there, still chuntering to himself but in a more docile fashion. To test Mummy's theory out, I took my life into my hands and scooped him up.

He looked at me crossly, then seemed to settle himself in my arms like a baby and then broke wind gently.

At this point Jonathan walked back in and practically did a double-take.

'You're kidding me!' he said. 'How in the name of God did you do that?'

'Oh, er, dog training tips from my mother,' I mumbled.

'Really? Wow. You never cease to amaze me, Melissa,' he marvelled. 'Is there anything you can't do?'

Braveheart managed to pull back one lip, exposing his teeth, and I knew I'd just stored up a whole lot of trouble for myself.

'Oh, um, I have many hidden talents,' I said.

'Speaking of which,' said Jonathan, taking Braveheart out of my arms. 'Why don't we put him in his basket, and let him get a nap before the walker comes, and we can . . .'

He let his voice trail off seductively, as he nuzzled his nose into the crook of my neck, and murmured some rather outrageous things into my ear.

I dragged my guilty conscience away from the image of the dogwalker hauling a semi-conscious Braveheart round the park and instead let myself be led up to Jonathan's newly refurbished master bedroom.

Well, to be honest, I didn't need much leading.

9

To say I wanted to make a good impression at Bonnie and Kurt Hegel's Welcome Home party was the understatement of the year. I'd never been to a 'casual get-together' that came with its own engraved invitation, now propped up on the mantelpiece.

As I'd told Gabi, our meeting at the Oxo Tower had been rather fraught; Bonnie had more or less admitted Cindy had despatched them to size me up, and even though she assured me over coffee that I wasn't nearly as bad as she'd expected, I was rather dreading a second inspection, this time on Cindy's home turf.

'I've booked in for a blow-dry,' I informed Jonathan over breakfast coffee. I felt too hot to eat much, but he'd already put away a bowl of power granola and yoghurt. I'd never had him down as a muesli man. It also turned out he had a very messy bathroom and five multi-vitamins with his coffee. The things you learned when you lived with people.

'Blow-out,' he said without looking up from his papers.

'Blow-out,' I corrected myself, 'and a mani-pedi and what have you, and . . .' I paused. 'What time are you going to be back tonight? Because I don't really know what to wear. I could do with your expert opinion.'

Jonathan jotted a final note on his sheaf of notes, clicked the pen with a flourish and shoved it into his top pocket. Despite the heatwave predicted for the day, he was already in his suit, with a spare shirt, freshly laundered, in his briefcase for later.

'Don't know. I've got a mad day. But, sweetie, whatever you wear, you'll look a million dollars.' He smiled. 'You always do.'

'But everything I've brought with me is . . .' I trailed off. I didn't want to tell Jonathan that all my Honey clothes, the ones that made me look curvaceous and bombshell-y, required the sort of underpinnings that could stop bullets. I'd die of heat exhaustion within half an hour, and swooning into the canapés was a pretty drastic way of breaking the ice.

A deranged yapping at the door prevented me from explaining this to Jonathan. The yapping soon turned into dull thuds, suggesting that Braveheart was hurling himself against the glass like a football hooligan.

'Can you deal with Braveheart?' sighed Jonathan, finishing up his coffee, and sliding his briefcase off the table. 'I can't. You seem to have a knack with him.'

I swallowed guiltily. Braveheart needed a dog psychiatrist, not a trainer, and I didn't have enough melatonin tablets to drug him for my entire stay, even if I wanted to. But Jonathan was beaming at me like there was nothing I couldn't do. 'I'll try,' I said weakly.

'That's my girl.' Jonathan beamed. 'I love that about you, Melissa. You're a can-do sort of woman. None of this "We'll have to get a specialist dog behaviourist in" nonsense.'

I smiled bravely and made a mental note to call my mother for dog tips. Ones that didn't involve turning them into junkies.

'Anyway,' he went on, making his way to the front

door, 'I appreciate that you're a little daunted by tonight, but, honestly, there's no need. It's just a very small, very informal party. You'll be among friends – Kurt and Bonnie already love you to death.' He paused, then had an idea. 'Hey, do what I do – go to Bloomingdales and get one of their shoppers to pick something out for you.'

'I could do,' I said slowly, thinking of the air-conditioning. And the sales. Maybe they'd have some magic American underwear that could suck in my stomach without giving me internal haemorrhaging.

'Look, whatever you wear, you'll still be the most beautiful girl there,' said Jonathan seriously. 'Don't forget that.'

I blushed. 'Oh, stop it.'

'I mean it.' Jonathan reached into his pocket for his wallet, picked out a card and chucked it across the table. 'But treat yourself – go to Bloomies and charge it. Call it my welcome to New York treat. OK?'

'You don't have to,' I began, not wanting to seem like I was angling for presents.

'I want to,' he said firmly.

Did Cindy need buying off with clothes? 'Thanks,' I said, as graciously as I could. 'I'll get something special.'

'Jesus, what is he on?' Jonathan shot a weary look at the source of the thudding and howling, then turned back to me with a relieved smile. 'I'll see you later.'

As soon as I'd kissed him goodbye on the front step, however, the howling and thudding stepped up a level.

Steeling myself, I went over to the utility room door.

'Braveheart!' I cooed in my best cajoling tone. I didn't want him running riot while he was in this frenzy. 'Calm down. Calm down, and we'll have some lovely breakfast!'

In response, the yapping turned more outraged.

'Please?' I tried opening the door a notch, in case the

fury was being caused by his imprisonment. I'd only edged the door open a tiny crack when the powerful force of a small dog shoved it, and me, out of the way.

His centre of gravity was lower than mine, and my high heels slipped out from under me as he shot past. I landed squarely on my backside, so hard that the glasses rattled in the dishwasher. After years of hockey I was used to falling over, but, even so, I felt strangely embarrassed. As if Cindy herself had trained her dog to humiliate new girlfriends.

When I turned round, Braveheart was sitting on the kitchen table, his tongue out, quite obviously laughing at me.

'Fine,' I said, in a cheerful, but firm tone. My mother used to say it was all about tone with dogs, not words. 'If that's the way you want to play it. I'm going to take you for a walk so long that you'll be too exhausted to mess me around, you snotty little yap-dog. Let's see whose got longer legs then, eh?'

Braveheart panted, his pink tongue sticking out in a broader smirk.

Walking him in this heat might finish me off, but I wasn't going to let a dog that size get the better of me. I might be perspiring from places I didn't even know had perspiration glands, but I still had my pride.

A quick call to Mummy revealed the magic secret of food bribes and firm looks, a tactic she assured me could be used on small dogs, medium dogs, large dogs and all husbands.

To my surprise, it worked. Once I'd lured Braveheart onto his lead, by shameless use of cold roast chicken breast, combined with a surprise attack-lunge learned from years of self-waxing, we set off down Jane Street.

Even though it wasn't yet nine, the air was already thick with heat and I was grateful for the shade offered by the trees that lined the street. Really, I thought, admiring all the pretty shutters and brownstone stoops, you'd hardly imagine you were in New York at all, walking around here. It felt more like Bloomsbury. There were even a couple of blue plaques.

Braveheart, despite his twice-daily dogwalker sessions, wasn't as submissive as I'd have liked on the lead, and it quickly turned into a battle of wills. Embarrassingly so, given how small he was. Every time we passed another dog and owner, he'd snarl and carry on as if he were some kind of Irish wolfhound.

It quickly fell into a routine: we'd spot another dog in the distance, Braveheart would start growling, I'd wave gaily and carol, 'What a splendid day!' in a distractingly English accent, then haul him across to the other side of the road before any damage could be done. The owner, throughout this performance, would keep their shades on, and step up their walking. The other dog would remain baffled.

We'd crossed the street about ten times before we reached Washington Square Park. Braveheart made it very clear to me that Washington Square Park was not the sort of park in which he was used to defecating. I'd never seen a dog relieve himself against a tree so disparagingly. Even the old men playing chess at the community boards around the square seemed to notice.

I sat down on a bench in the shade of a tree, wrapping Braveheart's lead firmly round my wrist and took my mobile phone out of my big handbag.

It was two in the afternoon in London. If I called the

office now, I could have a quick word with Gabi, put her mind at rest about any problems and settle my own worries at the same time.

Jonathan need never know. I wouldn't mention it.

Guilt spread through me. I'd said I wouldn't, and I didn't want him to think I was putting work before him. I wasn't! But I needed a business to go back to, and with Gabi and Allegra in charge . . .

My fingers were dialling the office number before I could stop myself.

As the phone rang at the other end, I got out my lovely leather-bound notebook, and let my eyes wander round the square. One professional dogwalker was exercising ten dogs at a time, on those leads with multiple dog attachments. As she sailed past, propelled by ten dog-power, she looked like a huskie driver who'd lost her sledge a few blocks back. I couldn't tell if this was a problem for her or not, as her eyes were hidden behind Oakley shades.

To my surprise, the answering machine cut in and I heard my own voice.

'Hello.' How posh did I sound? 'You've reached the Little Lady Agency. I'm afraid we can't take your call right now, but if you leave your number and a short message, we'll call you straight back.'

At least Allegra hadn't taken it upon herself to change the message, I told myself. But where were they? I'd told them they could do shopping appointments, as long as one of them stayed in to answer the phone.

There were a couple of bleeps, then a worried-sounding man's voice said, 'Marks and Spencers have stopped making their Breathe-Easy socks. I can't wear any other kind. This is Julian Hervey. Please call me back. Um, cheers.'

I made a note.

'Hello, Honey. It's Arlo Donaldson here. Look, I'll get to the point: I've been invited to a shoot up in Scotland, and the host's new girlfriend is the woman I, er, had to jilt last year. You might remember – you phoned up as my mother and told her I'd taken religious orders? Daisy? With the nose? Um, well, thing is, it's frightfully good shooting, and there's a decent still up there too, so I rather want to go, so could you, er, advise? Thanks very much.'

I shook my head in disbelief.

'Hello. Melissa? It's Roger. Listen, have you thought any more about this Hunt Ball? I won't tell Remington. I'm . . . I'm . . . Look, I don't mind paying you double.' His voice sounded quite desperate, and I could hear music in the background. It sounded like Jeff Buckley. He must really be missing Nelson, I thought. 'I've been getting calls from Celia and . . . Oh, just ring me, woman.'

I sighed, and scribbled 'Call Roger' on my notebook. I'd have to get tough.

The answering machine gave me the option to delete my messages and I paused, before leaving them on. Hadn't the girls listened to the machine? What were they playing at? What if someone had had a frightful emergency and needed immediate advice?

Before I could dwell too much on that, a sharp pain in my left calf dragged my attention back to the immediate set of problems. Braveheart had circled my leg with his lead, effectively tying me to the bench, and was hauling himself round and round until the blood supply to my foot was more or less cut off.

He looked up at me with an expression of supreme devilment as pins and needles shot up my leg.

I glared down at him.

Braveheart started his laughing/panting thing and his boot-button eyes twinkled malevolently.

While we were staring each other out, a passing dog-lover screeched to a halt on her rollerblades, bringing her spaniel to a neat emergency stop next to her. 'Oh, my God! Your poor little baby!' she wailed. 'Is Mommy not looking after you?' she added, with an accusing glance at me.

Braveheart whimpered pathetically and choked himself a little more.

'Oh, it's just a game he plays,' I said briskly. 'I think his previous owner was . . . a little funny.'

'He's a rescue pup?' said the lady, putting a hand to her chest in sympathy.

'You could say that.'

'Well, then, the very best of luck to you.' And she skated off.

I glared at Braveheart. This really wasn't on. I was as sorry as the next animal-lover for pets who hadn't been trained, but frankly he was milking it.

'Right, you little bugger, if that's the way you want to play it,' I said, in my best nannying tone, and unclipped his lead, keeping a tight grip on his collar. He started to growl warningly, but I ignored him, as I unwound the rest of the lead with one hand, then unzipped my bag.

The growling intensified as I lifted him with two hands into the bag, and then swiftly zipped it up, leaving his big fluffy head sticking out at one end.

A lady's handbag can never be too big, that's what I say.

I wrapped the lead around my wrist, and got up, hitching my bag over my shoulder, so Braveheart was left snarling impotently under my arm. Good job I knew for a fact that his bladder was empty.

'You and I are going to be great friends, but we're going to have to work at it,' I muttered to him, under my breath so none of the chess players would think I was one of those ridiculous women who carried their dogs around in bags and talked to them as if they were children.

Braveheart growled, but didn't struggle any more. And when I let him back on the lead, a few blocks further on, he almost walked to heel.

At home, as per Cindy's laminated instructions, I put Braveheart back in his vestibule with some food and MooMoo, a disgustingly slobbered toy cow, and walked up to Bloomingdales with Jonathan's card burning a hole in my purse. It was a bit of a trek, but the ever-changing display of shops took my mind off the distance I was covering. Plus, every calorie counted when it came to the sort of clothes I knew I'd have to squeeze into.

I explained to the charming personal shopper, through the door of the enormous changing room, that I needed some underwear that would reshape my body in the manner of plastic surgery and yet remain invisible beneath sheer clothing. Instead of laughing in my face and suggesting Pilates, Hanna (we were on very friendly terms immediately) nodded seriously, went off, and came back with an armful of what looked like skin graft. Then another armful of slinky cocktail dresses, and, every five minutes, another three pairs of shoes.

Amazingly, within an hour, I had not only a whole new outfit, but a whole new body underneath.

I looked at myself in the flattering mirror. Even if I was jittery on the inside, on the outside I looked like I'd bought a confident new personality along with the sky-scraper sandals.

Plus, I wasn't going to argue with a shop assistant like Hanna. She definitely knew best.

'I'll take it all,' I said, and handed over Jonathan's charge card.

Kurt and Bonnie lived in an apartment on the Upper East Side. It wasn't like London, where the street names gave you a clue to an area's flavour; the more upmarket the Manhattan address, I was discovering, the more dis-creetly numerical it was.

Technically, in London terms, I suppose it was within walking distance, but Jonathan took one look at my heels and hailed a cab. Not that I was complaining. I'd spent longer getting ready for this party than I'd done for any event since Allegra's twenty-first birthday party, where we all had to dress up as eighteenth-century aristocrats with powdered wigs.

Jonathan, of course, was looking effortlessly chic in a fresh shirt and linen summer suit. He had the kind of expensive style that transcended meteorological interven-tion, and a wardrobe filled with proper suit bags.

'You really didn't need to go to this much effort, sweetie,' he said, for about the billionth time.

'Oh, I didn't!' I insisted, shifting nervously in my seat so as not to wrinkle my dress. According to my new best friend Hanna, it was a 'never fail Lilly Pulitzer', what-ever that meant. 'Tell me again who'll be there.'

'Bonnie and Kurt, whom you know already,' he replied patiently, 'Paige, who was at college with Cindy, David and Peter, who are realtors, Bradley, who's a friend from Princeton—'

'*House!*' I said excitedly.

'I'm sorry?'

'*House!* Isn't that where *House* is set? Princeton?'

'Are all your cultural references TV-based?' Jonathan's mouth screwed up wryly. 'Well, yes. It's also one of the finest universities in the United States.'

'Oh, yes, yes, absolutely,' I said, but, to be honest, since I saw the Princeton-Plainsboro Teaching Hospital on a more regular basis than my own NHS clinic, this fact was more significant.

'I went to Princeton,' Jonathan reminded me, since I'd forgotten to comment. 'And so did Bradley and Kurt, and a few others whom I think Bonnie will have asked. But don't mention any of that to anyone else there, because I think Bonnie went to Harvard, and it's rude to rub her nose in it.'

I made yet another mental note.

When we arrived, a liveried doorman opened the door of our cab for us, and directed us under the long canopy into the apartments. Jonathan announced us at the desk to another doorman, then we were allowed up in the stately elevator to the Hegels' apartment, where, finally, the door was opened by a butler.

I was seriously impressed by that. The smallest house I'd encountered a butler in had seven bedrooms and a paddock.

Bonnie and Kurt were standing just inside the door, chatting animatedly while jazz music burbled in the background. Since they both waved their hands around to illustrate their points it looked as if they were simultaneously signing the conversation for the deaf.

'Bonnie, Kurt,' said Jonathan, shaking Kurt's hand, and leaning forward to deposit a kiss on Bonnie's cheek.

'Hello!' shrieked Bonnie, throwing her hands in the air, then clasping me to her bony bosom. My upper chest was pressed up hard against a splendid blown glass necklace. 'So good to see you! But look at *you*! You dyed your beautiful hair!'

Kurt peered at me, his bald spot glinting in the soft lights. 'You dyed your hair. Why did you do that, Honey? It was exquisite. Wasn't it exquisite, Bonnie? Didn't we say that you really did look exactly like a young Brigitte Bardot with that beautiful hair?'

I looked anxiously at Jonathan, who simply smiled and put his hand round my waist.

'I think she looks exquisite however she wears her hair. And, ah, guys, I'd prefer it if you introduced Melissa as Melissa this evening, not Honey?'

Bonnie tipped her head. 'Don't tell me. Honey is your *special* name, right?'

'Exactly,' I said, not wanting Jonathan to do all the talking for me. 'I won't tell you what I call Jonathan.'

Bonnie let out a cascade of tinkly laughter. 'Oh, you are so funny! Let me get you a drink.'

She waved at a waitress who was circulating with a loaded tray and handed Jonathan a glass of white wine. 'Sancerre for Jonathan, as always, but what about you, *Melissa*?'

I looked sideways at Jonathan, who was already being dragged off in conversation with two other men, both clapping him enthusiastically on the back. 'Welcome *back*!' one roared. 'How're your *teeth* after a year in London, fella? Still there?'

'I'll have a sparkling water, please,' I said firmly. I needed to concentrate hard if I was going to make the right impression.

'Ah, now, can't I get you some champagne? Go on.

Just to celebrate Jonathan coming home – and you coming back with him, of course,' she added quickly.

I took a flute from the tray. Demurring too much always looks bad, and I didn't have to drink it all, did I?

'Now, let me find you some people to chat to.' Bonnie scanned the room. There must have been about thirty or forty people, a number which barely touched the walls of the huge reception room. Like Jonathan's old apartment, it was all wood panelling and chandeliers, although in a more minimalist style. 'We're all old friends here,' she went on. 'With some new faces, just to mix things up. But don't let that put you off!'

Yet another small waitress appeared at her elbow and murmured something in her ear.

'What do you mean they've *flopped*?' she demanded. 'They're canapés!' She turned back to me, flashing a brilliantly white smile that didn't disguise the sudden strings of tension in her neck. 'Tiny problem with the themed canapés. A surprise for you and Jonathan. Would you excuse me a moment?'

And she shimmered off in a gust of Chanel.

Fortunately, I'm not the sort of person who lurks in corners at parties, so I looked round for someone to talk to. I find if you smile in at least one direction, someone will come over without you having to crash a conversation.

Before I could engage anyone in seasonal weather pleasantries, though, my attention was drawn to a conversation happening just behind me, in the corner.

I say conversation. It was more a desperate attempt by one woman to extract more than two words from a remarkably sullen man.

He was wearing head-to-toe black, accessorised with

dark shades, despite the fact that we were indoors, and an absolutely foul scowl. While the poor woman was trying to chat, he was shoving mini Cumberland sausage rings into his mouth as if he were in a timed eating competition, then using the cocktail sticks to pick gristle from between his teeth. From where I was standing, it was like watching a human cement mixer.

'So you're British!' she was saying.

The man grunted.

'Wow!' she said desperately. 'I'd love to spend time there. Such a great country!'

'You reckon?'

'Oh, yeah . . . I mean, Tony Blair! I'm a big supporter of . . . his fair trade commitments!'

Crikey, I thought. She must really be scraping the bottom of the conversational barrel if she's on to Tony Blair already.

The man paused in his systematic consumption of the eats table. 'He's an effing idiot.'

The lady took a step back. 'Oh really? You think so?'

I narrowed my eyes. I might be very, very wrong, but this beast seemed oddly familiar. Something about the 'effing' – it bespoke a certain type of Englishness: one I came into contact with pretty much every day.

And there was something else. Something I recognised from somewhere . . . My mental Rolodex flipped wildly. Was he an old client? Someone I was at school with?

'And that gobby hag of a wife!' Even with his shades on, I could tell he was rolling his eyes.

'Cherie? Oh, but she's a great role model for professional women! Don't you—?'

'Are you *insane*? Do you not have *eyes*?' he interrupted her. 'What is *wrong* with this country?'

Now, I was no big fan of Cherie Blair, but if this was meant to be a Welcome to New York party for me as well as Jonathan, I simply couldn't stand by and let this buffoon do such an appalling ambassadorial job for the motherland.

As I took a step forward and prepared to launch myself into the conversation, to my horror I heard him say, with a distinct nod towards her chest, 'So, are those real then?'

'Pardon me?' she enquired.

'The girls there.' He nodded, as if he were genuinely interested, rather than trying to come on to her. 'Are they real?'

Silently, she clapped her hand to her cleavage. 'I don't . . .'

That was the final straw. I couldn't stop myself.

'Pearls!' I said, intervening briskly. 'Ah ha ha! He means your necklace! It's, er, cockney rhyming slang! The girls . . . pearls!'

'But I'm not wearing any,' she said coldly. 'This is a sapphire necklace.'

I took a closer look. Indeed it was. About three apartments' worth too. 'Gosh, so you are! Isn't it gorgeous? No, it's, um, just one of those generic terms! Means all jewellery. The girls, you know – what you keep in your jewellery box.'

There was a brief moment while we all digested this nugget of information, broken suddenly by a dirty snigger.

'As in . . . pearl necklace!'

I glared ferociously, and he quickly shut up.

'How interesting language is.' She shot the rude man a haughty glare. 'For a moment, I thought you were being offensive. Would you excuse me while I . . . freshen my drink?'

She said it in a tone that clearly meant 'go somewhere far, far away from you, you charmless oaf'.

'You've still got half a glass of wine there,' he pointed out.

She paused, looked at her glass, then looked back at him. 'I think I need something stronger.' She flashed me a cold smile. 'Excuse me.'

I stepped aside to let her past, and realised that I'd managed to leave myself trapped with him. And now he was peering at me, as if *he* recognised *me* from somewhere.

My mind whirred, trying to work out why this particular brute seemed so familiar – not easy when he was wearing sunglasses indoors. But that thick black hair, the consumptive complexion, the voice . . .

'Do I know you from somewhere?' he demanded, removing the sunglasses, and I knew at once who it was.

Godric Ponsonby.

Or, as he'd been universally called, when I knew him for a few brief months in 1994, Oh-Godric.

A hot flush started in my forehead and spread rapidly down throughout my body.

Oh-Godric and I had had a fleeting flirtation, and even more fleeting backstage tussle during the final-night party of a school production of *A Midsummer Night's Dream*. My girls' school had had to borrow some men from the nearby boys' school, and Godric had been one of the few artistically inclined volunteers. I wasn't acting, though – I was in charge of wardrobe, and pretty busy with it, too: the boys seemed to be constantly damaging their doublets, and insisted on personal repair attention, usually while they were still wearing them. Godric was the worst offender. He had a long list of fabric allergies too, and consequently, by the final night, we were on such intimate medical terms that snogging was more or less inevitable.

I cringed at the memory. Even then, I wasn't naïve enough to believe I was Godric's first choice for drunken grappling. Emery, in the throes of her Goth Actress phase – she was growing her eyebrows out like Imogen Stubbs – was the star of the show, and had the male fairies following her around like geese. I suspected she'd given Godric the flick, and so on the last night he'd consoled himself with literally pints of punch and a quick roll around the props cupboard with me.

Actually, it would have been quite romantic if he hadn't had a 'bad reaction' to whatever everyone had been doctoring the punch with, vomited all over Bottom's head, and broken out in hives. Matron had taken the night off so I had to drive him to the local A&E, still in his M&S opaque tights, still vomiting, and I never saw him again after that. Just as well, really, given what I knew about his, er, inside leg measurements.

Obviously he recognised me too, at exactly the same moment, and presumably suffered the same excruciating mental slideshow.

I wondered if he'd be discreet enough to pretend we hadn't even met, and start again. After all, one doesn't like to start reminiscing about love bites and curaçao vomit at a smart Manhattan cocktail party.

'Melissa?' he said, peering at me, then dropping his line of sight a bit lower. 'Melons?'

I ignored the Melons bit. Fine. There was no getting out of it. 'It is!' I said. 'Hello!'

'You don't remember me, do you?' The mixture of grumpiness and chronic shyness hadn't changed much in ten years. At least I knew he wasn't deliberately being rude to that woman. Godric never did have much in the way of social confidence. From my sewing chair in the wings, I'd noted the other thesps had affected gloomy self-doubt, but with him it seemed painfully real.

Still, that didn't excuse much *now*. Good heavens above, no.

'Of course I do!' I protested. 'It's Godric. Godric Ponsonby!' For a second, I moved forward to kiss him on the cheek, then thought better of it and put my hand-out to shake instead. 'What are you doing in New York? Do you know Bonnie and Kurt?'

'Who?'

'The hosts?' I raised my eyebrows in Bonnie's direction but she'd vanished into the throng again. 'Um, well, do you know Jonathan then? Jonathan Riley? The party's in his honour.'

'Who?' he grunted. 'No. I don't know any of these tossers. Didn't even want to come. It's a crap party.'

'Yes, you do! You know Jonathan,' interrupted a small, dark woman, who'd appeared from nowhere. '*Jonathan* found you that awesome apartment in Tribeca! Hi!' she said, grabbing his arm and looking up at me intently. 'Paige Drogan.'

'Hello,' I said. 'I'm—'

'No, *I* should do the introduction,' grumped Godric. 'Manners! Paige, this is Melissa Romney-Jones, Melissa, this is Paige Drogan, my agent. Don't suppose you've got a job, have you, Mel?'

But I was still gawping from the previous revelation to rise to that. 'Your *agent*?'

'Yeah, 'm an actor,' he muttered.

'No!' I gasped. 'What? A proper one?'

Paige laughed prettily, and smoothed back her short coffee-coloured hair. She was wearing a tortoiseshell wrap dress that emphasised her pepperpot curves, finished off with bright yellow shoes. She reminded me of a wren.

'He's being very modest,' she chuckled. 'Ric's about to be huge over here. He's starring in a very significant film, which opens in a few months, and that's going to really launch him onto the next level, but he already has a market presence with some very well-received television work. You may have seen him in *ER*?'

I shook my head. 'Um, we're rather behind you, I think.'

'And he's working on some stage projects, aren't you, Ric?' She nudged him. 'Ric?'

He nodded sullenly.

Paige put a little cupped hand to her ear and tilted her head to one side. 'I can't hear you, Ric, this party's awful loud. What was that?'

'I'm in *The Real Inspector Hound*,' he managed. 'It's not a very good production, and the director doesn't know what he's talking about, but, you know . . . At least it's proper theatre. Not like wasting time with those film wankers who—'

'Ha ha ha!' laughed Paige in a transparent attempt to drown him out. 'Ha ha ha! Ric, honey, can you go and get me and Melissa some drinks, please?'

'She's got a drink,' he pointed out.

'Well, I'm sure she'd like another,' said Paige firmly.

'Ungh,' grunted Ric. It was a sound I heard about nine times a day on average – a combination of resentment and resignation – and sloped off in the direction of the waiters.

'I saw what you did there,' said Paige at once. 'With Lucy Powell? Thank you for that. Ric's a sweetheart, but he's kind of . . . unpolished!'

'Yeeeees,' I said, wondering if unpolished was an American euphemism for barely socialised.

'So, anyway, let's talk about you – you're the famous Melissa!' She beamed at me with a scary intensity.

I suddenly felt lanky and un-put-together, my new outfit, perfect hair and manicure notwithstanding.

'Yes, I am,' I said.

'I'm Paige,' she said. 'Paige with an i. I was at Brown with Cindy, but Jonathan and I go *way* back too. Like Ric said, I'm an agent. For actors.'

'How interesting,' I said, ignoring the flicker of panic that ran through me at the mention of Cindy's name. I really had to knock that on the head. It wasn't like she was *here*. 'Anyone I know?'

Paige reeled off a list of clients, some of whom sounded vaguely familiar, then shook my hand very hard, twice, then dropped it. 'So. You and Jonathan, huh?'

What did that *mean*? I didn't know what to say, so I just smiled and nodded.

'I bet Jonathan's glad to get his home insurance premiums down again!' she cackled, then switched her face back to serious. 'So you're English?'

'Absolutely,' I agreed, relieved to be on safe ground. 'Many generations.'

'Yeah, yeah, yeah, yeah, yeah. Married before?'

'Um, no.'

'Kids?'

'No!'

'Cool. OK, I'm building up a picture here. What is it you do?'

I was starting to feel slightly interviewed. 'I run a . . . a life management consultancy,' I said defensively.

The upside of New York was that no one lifted their eyebrows and snorted at this, as they would have done in London. Paige, on the contrary, actually looked impressed. Though that may have just been a holding expression until she worked out what it was that I did.

'Yeah? Whereabouts?'

'In London? Victoria?'

She gave me a 'more information?' look.

'Near Buckingham Palace?' I hazarded, with some truth economy, I must admit. Well, my office *was* near Buckingham Palace. Compared to, say, Brent Cross Shopping Centre.

'Right,' she said, arching her perfect brows above the frames of her square-framed glasses. 'And what type of client relationship is your specialty? I mean,' she added before I could reply, 'please God tell me you're not one of those terrible women who play with colour swatches and tell men to floss!'

And she laughed one of those blood-chilling power-laughs. The sort with no humour involved whatsoever, the sort that give you a sort of conversational deadline: prove me wrong by the time this laugh dies away.

The temperature seemed to ramp up a couple of degrees at this point, despite the air-conditioning, and beads of sweat began to pool in the cups of my Lycra skin-graft bra. Was it going to be this hard-going all evening? It wasn't like mingling at London parties, where I could get by on gossip and connections. Here, I felt as if I were at some kind of large-scale interview, where the whole panel were Jonathan's friends.

To my horror, even as I was wishing I could click my

heels and be back in Nelson's comfy sitting room, I felt a familiar tingle up my backbone, as my whole posture started to shift. My hips went slightly forward, pushing out my ample bosom, shrinking my waist and lengthening my back.

Honey. I dragged Honey's personality in front of mine like a riot shield. Even though there was already a little voice in my head telling me it probably wasn't a good idea.

'Actually, I run a life coaching agency,' I said breezily. 'I work with a variety of clients, mostly male, from a broad social spectrum.'

Paige nodded more slowly, but didn't look totally convinced, so I found myself ploughing ever onward.

'It's terribly old-fashioned, in some senses, but I find simply harnessing some of the more traditional aspects of etiquette is really rather empowering for many men.' I smiled. 'Providing them with social parameters from which they can build their own relationship bridges, on a professional as well as social level. And through positive role reinforcement, from a feminine perspective, I'm able to encourage them to project and visualise an idealised version of their own persona, and guide them towards attainable targets.'

Paige was nodding hard now. 'Uh-huh. I can see that, the way you handled that moment there with Ric. It was pretty slick. And you're doing that over here?'

'Um, I'm on holiday right now,' I hedged. Honestly, my heart was beating so fast. Where did all this stuff come from?

'But you could be, yes?'

Jonathan was on the other side of the room, deep in conversation with a man who kept jabbing at his shoulder.

'Well, I don't see why not,' I said, more to sound professional than anything else. 'I'm sure American men have their own sets of hang-ups.'

'Oh, my God, yes.' She nodded frantically. 'And therapy isn't always the answer.'

'Well, quite,' I said, as if I didn't think therapy was a licence to whinge. 'One can't blame one's mother for everything.'

Paige threw her head back and cackled. Then she snapped it back to fix me with a fierce look. 'Listen, Melissa, I could use your help.'

My heart sank. The last thing I needed was to get involved in someone else's relationship. Especially someone who knew Jonathan. 'Oh, honestly, Paige, I don't really know much about American men and—'

'It's not an American man,' she said. 'Can we meet for a coffee this week? I'd really love to talk with you.'

I made demurring noises, casting my gaze around to see if Jonathan had moved into hearing distance. 'Well, I am meant to be on holiday, and Jonathan isn't . . .'

She intensified her gaze until I could almost feel it on my face. At the same time I felt my will to resist evaporate.

How did she do that? I wondered. What an amazing trick. If she could teach me how to do that, I could have Braveheart eating out of my hand in seconds.

'Well, OK,' I conceded.

Paige smiled.

That Sphinx-like smile was worth learning too, I thought, dazed. It just made you wonder what you hadn't noticed.

Fortunately Godric chose this moment to reappear, with four glasses of wine squashed in his hands, as if he was schlepping drinks from the bar at the White Horse.

Paige rolled her eyes. 'Ric! I keep telling you. Just ask the waiter to bring you what you want! You don't have to carry them across the room like that! You're not a server!'

'Shut up,' said Godric.

I started to move backwards in my patented party extrication method: inch away until you make sufficient corridor for other people to pass between you, wave hopelessly as if being swept out to sea, then leg it.

'Call me!' mouthed Paige.

I smiled vaguely at both her and Godric, then slid off to find the loo.

No sooner had I extricated myself from that particular minefield than a tall woman with magically unsupported breasts appeared in front of me.

'Hi!' she said, extending a hand. 'Jennifer Reardon. I'm a colleague of Bonnie's. And a friend too, of course!'

'Hello,' I replied, fixing her name in my head. 'I'm Melissa. Melissa—'

But she interrupted me before I could finish my introduction. 'Are you *British*?'

'Yes,' I said. 'I am. I'm—'

'Oh, my God, I was *right*!' she said, clapping her hand to her chest. 'My instincts are so good for these things? I saw you talking to Ric Spencer over there, so I figured you must be the writer Bonnie was telling me about. The column in the London *Times*, right? Hi, I am so pleased to meet you! Now, call me nosey, but have you got any inside stuff on this new girlfriend of Jonathan's?' she went on, with a giggle. 'I've been out of the country for a while so I'm a little behind on the gossip. He's been really tight-lipped about her – which makes you wonder, huh?'

I opened my mouth to put her straight but she didn't give me a chance to speak.

'She's British too, right?' she demanded gleefully. 'I was at Cindy's for dinner earlier this week – she's his ex-wife? She might come along later, actually, if she has time – and she was telling me she heard he was dating this blonde girl called Honey or Happy or something like that. Totally too young for him, and soooo rebound! I mean, it's an understandable reaction, breaking up with your wife of all those years, but, eek!'

Jennifer pulled a face, then touched my forearm in an 'oh, we're so awful, aren't we?' gesture. My stomach shrank. I knew I should say something before she dug herself in any further, but my throat had suddenly gone tight with horror.

'And Cindy totally thinks it's because he's cut up about her and Brendan, but, listen, who wouldn't be? It's a terrible, terrible situation, but sometimes you've got to go with fate, know what I mean? What's meant for you won't pass you by? Their baby is the cutest, cutest thing. Parker? Isn't that an adorable name? I could eat him up! Not literally! Ah ha ha ha! He so has Cindy's eyes. Anyway, I must catch up with Jon in a minute because I need to give him a message from Cindy. Do you know if he's brought rebound girl along tonight?' She craned her neck around to see past my stunned face. 'I don't see any blondes in here. I guess she'd stand out, right?'

Jennifer was rattling on at about ninety miles an hour, and so probably didn't notice the silence falling around us. I've been there myself – you're so busy dishing out the gossip that you can't hear anything but your own voice. But since I hadn't spoken for what felt like an hour, to me the shocked hush was all too apparent.

So much for people claiming never to eavesdrop at parties.

'You know her, huh?' she said, seeing my crestfallen expression. 'Oh, nuts. Have I put my foot in it?'

'Melissa,' said Bonnie unwittingly, bowling up behind me with a tray full of food. 'I had to show you these myself – aren't they darling? Jonathan's had three already.' And she shoved a plate of miniature Yorkshire puddings filled with shavings of roast beef and wisps of horseradish under my nose.

She looked up when I didn't speak, and neither did the seven people immediately around us. I felt sick.

'Oh, now don't tell me you're low-carbing!' said Bonnie, taking my silence the wrong way. 'Jonathan loves you just the way you are! He told me so! He says one of the things he loves best about dating you is that he can always order a starter and a dessert without feeling bad!'

I could almost hear the penny drop in Jennifer's head. It probably didn't hit much on the way down. A ghastly recognition slid over her face, and her eyes went glassy with embarrassment.

If I'd been Honey, or even Gabi, I might have made a scene and stalked out, but this wasn't my party or Jennifer's. It was Bonnie's, and she'd gone to a lot of effort. I wasn't going to let someone else spoil it, and make a show of myself into the bargain. I'd show them how we British could rise above sticky moments. Even if we did want to sprint, sobbing, from the room.

'Oh, I can't stand girls who go out for dinner and never eat! What on earth's the point?' I said, taking a Yorkshire pudding and racking my brains for the most outrageously untrue thing I could think of to break the tumbleweed. 'Now, tell me, is it true that all shopping is free for tourists on Sundays? I'm sure I read it somewhere.'

At once, about seven different voices joined in with outraged denials, and then suggestions for outlets that had such amazing values that it might as well be free.

Jennifer melted into the background, mumbling something about having a top-secret sample sale leaflet in her bag somewhere.

I managed to keep the shocked tears pricking my eyelids at bay by frantically nodding my head and raising my eyebrows, hoping fervently that Jonathan hadn't overheard. I couldn't see him anywhere and, for a moment, I really wished he didn't think I was so good at parties that I could be left alone with a crowd of complete strangers.

And then I felt a familiar hand on the small of my back, and a sudden warm breath on my neck.

'Sorry, but I couldn't leave you alone a minute longer,' Jonathan murmured. 'I've been studying your rear view for ten minutes now, and I don't see why these people should have the monopoly on the front.'

He smiled at the guests around us. 'So you've all met the reason I couldn't leave London?'

Relief flooded through me as conversation started up again, and I noticed how everyone now met my eye. But even with Jonathan's hand resting lightly on my hip, I still needed a moment to pull myself together, and, after a brief comparision of public transport systems, I excused myself. On my way out, I had a quick glass of champagne to revive myself, then, since there was no one looking, another.

My heart was still hammering as I splashed water on my wrists in the marble-lined bathroom. I gazed at my face in the vast, subtly lit mirror as I reapplied my lipstick, and wondered forlornly if Honey would have handled the situation better. I always seemed to come out with better repartee when I was wearing that wig.

No. I didn't need the wig to be polite. Manners, that was all one needed. Besides, I reminded myself, smoothing down my Jackie O flick, all glossy and chocolate brown where the stylist had serumed me to death, Jonathan chose Melissa, not Honey. Of course his friends would be suspicious of any new girlfriend. It was only natural. I just had to persuade them that I was worthy of him.

But in this magnificent apartment, surrounded by all these people who knew Jonathan so much better than I did, it was easier said than done. Jennifer's words seared across my brain. Was that what they were thinking – that I was just some rebound bimbo Jonathan was dating while he was still grieving over Cindy?

God. How I wished Nelson were here to give me a boot, or Gabi. I opened my bag, and took out my mobile phone, then resolutely put it back. Gabi would be in bed right now, and Nelson would be . . . well, I wasn't going to phone Nelson at the very first inkling of trouble.

I took a deep breath. You'll just have to show them how suitable you really are, I told myself. Then, I turned on my heel and strode back down the parqueted corridor.

Jonathan was in an excellent mood on the way back.

'You were a big hit,' he said, squeezing my knee in the cab. 'Everyone was raving about how great you are. I love how you just talk to everyone.' He gave me a look. 'I was watching you all evening.'

'Isn't that what you're meant to do at parties?' I asked. 'Talk to people?'

Jonathan pulled a face. 'Well, no. *Some* people like to get conversation buzzing by telling the hostess she needs to lose ten pounds, then pulling her outfit to pieces.'

It had been bad enough having Cindy's presence hanging over me at the party, but I wasn't having her in the cab with us afterwards. 'They were terribly nice people,' I said firmly. 'Especially Bonnie and Kurt. Remind me to have some of that Cheddar cheese they liked so much sent over when I get home.'

Jonathan turned to me, his face very serious. 'Bonnie told me about Jennifer putting her foot in it tonight. I'm so sorry. You were very dignified, and she's grateful to you for not taking offence. It's my fault. If I'd been there two minutes sooner . . .'

'Oh, that.' I shrugged it off. 'I just did what any well-brought-up person would do.'

'Well, Bonnie was mortified. She's going to speak with Jennifer. Set her straight. Jen's always had a big mouth.'

'Well, at least she knows I'm not a blonde bimbo now,' I joked.

'No.' Jonathan looked me in the eye. 'She's going to tell her that I'm very serious about you, and think you're the best thing that's ever happened to me. Blonde, brunette or redhead.'

'Oh,' I said, looking down at my lap. My insides glowed with delight to hear him say that, but – well, the whole evening had been somewhat overwhelming. I couldn't quite push that 'rebound' word out of my head. 'I'll bear that in mind.'

'But, Melissa . . .' He bit his lip. 'That's why I want you to be really careful about what you say to people about your job. It's not that I don't feel proud of what you do, but I—'

'Don't want people to think that you're shacked up with a hooker,' I interrupted. 'I know. I'm not stupid! It isn't the sort of thing I'm likely to bring up in conversation, is it?'

He gave my hand a little shake. 'Don't take it the wrong way. It's complicated, and I don't expect them to understand. I mean, I sort of explained to Kurt and Bonnie, but . . .'

'I know,' I replied quickly. 'I'd hate to do anything that made you feel embarrassed. But I don't want them to think I'm some idle It-girl who doesn't *do* anything. I have a business!'

'I'm never embarrassed by you,' he said. 'But I know how helpful you are, and I don't want you to get into a situation where *you'd* be embarrassed. It's not like London. People are . . . different over here. You give people like Paige Drogan an inch, they'll take a mile. Not that I don't think you can handle it, but, you know. Just don't let anyone talk you into dishing out advice. You're on holiday. Having a break. OK?'

'Jonathan, I *know*. I won't.'

'Good,' he said, sounding relieved. 'I knew you'd get it. I saw you talking to that idiot Ric Spencer – Paige didn't try to palm him off on you, did she?'

'Um, not exactly.' I didn't think it was the best time to mention that Paige had asked me to see her. I'd just have to invent some prior appointment to get out of it. 'She mentioned something about you finding an apartment for him – you remember him?'

Jonathan groaned. 'Do I? Yeah, slightly. Paige sometimes gets us to find short lets for her *more high profile* clients while they're in New York, and she made me spend an interminable day with that . . . that . . .'

'Oik?'

He clicked his fingers and pointed at me. 'Good word. Oik. Jesus. I mean, sure, the guy can act but . . . euch. I don't know if he means to be rude, but I've never come so close to punching someone in the head.' His expression softened. 'I only put up with it because he was from London and he kind of reminded me of you.'

'Well, I'm touched. Actually, I do know him, vaguely,' I admitted.

'Not a client? Please God.'

'Do you *mind*?' I said. 'You think I'd release something like that back into the community? He'd hardly be an advert for the agency. No, I had a brief . . . moment with him when we were at school. Let's not talk about Godric now.'

'Godric?' Jonathan looked amused. 'Ric's short for Godric? Now if I'd known that while I was putting up with his belly-aching . . .'

'Family name. Some kind of inheritance issues, I think. Anyway,' I said, more emphatically, 'forget all that. Here we are, in a taxi, in New York, our first proper date . . .'

Jonathan gave me a stern look. 'What are you suggesting?'

So I showed him, and such was his good mood that he went along with it for at least three blocks.

10

As it turned out, Paige didn't allow me time to think of a reason not to see her, as she called me so early the next day I assumed it was an emergency from home.

Fortunately Jonathan had already left for his 6 a.m. squash date and breakfast meeting.

'Hello?' I mumbled into my mobile. 'What's happened?'

'Hi, it's Paige Drogan here!' She sounded unnaturally cheery. 'Can we meet this morning?'

I fumbled around for a reason to say no, but my brain was still fuzzy. 'Um, well, I have . . .'

'It'll only be for half an hour. Can we say . . . eleven o'clock?'

With a massive effort, I rallied myself into social fib mode. 'Oh dear, I have some appointments scheduled for today.'

There was an ominous pause. 'I thought you said you were on vacation?'

Paige's voice made me feel uncomfortably as if she were in the room. 'Yes, well, I am, but I'm meeting some people while I'm—'

'Then you're going to be around? Great! I'll text you my office address, and I'll see you at eleven. Thank you so much, Melissa. I look forward to speaking with you later!'

And the line went dead.

I stared at the phone in my hand. My eyes were still barely focusing in the half light coming through the slatted shutters. I sniffed, suddenly conscious of the really quite awful stench of sleepiness hanging over the room. Despite the fresh white roses Jonathan had thoughtfully had delivered to put by the bed, it smelled like a rugby team had kipped on the floor overnight, in their dirty kit and with the post-match curry boxes.

Damn. I'd already failed in my intention to get up first every morning to make sure Jonathan saw me only in a fragrant, cosmetically enhanced state. But even Roger's flat didn't smell like this. It couldn't be *me*, could it?

I rubbed my eyes and sat up, at which point I realised that Braveheart was sleeping on the bed next to me. When I nudged him with my foot, he growled in his sleep, bared his sharp little teeth, and broke wind.

No wonder Cindy and Jonathan's relationship had taken a turn for the worse. I knew a friend of my mother's who'd encouraged her Great Dane to sleep on her bed for the express purpose of keeping her randy husband at bay.

'This won't do, Braveheart,' I sighed, and scooped him up, protesting loudly, to return him to the kitchen. His crate in the vestibule showed all the signs of a break-out from the inside.

He sat in his basket and chuntered as I made some breakfast. It was rather sad, I thought, that as long as Braveheart had some attention, he more or less behaved himself. He wasn't an evil dog. Just a histrionic one. The more I scratched his ears and praised him for his attempts at walking to heel, the harder he tried. I'd had slower results from some clients in the sit and stay department.

If Jonathan wasn't going to allow me to train men in New York, I thought, toasting myself a bagel, I was definitely going to sort out Braveheart.

After a challenging walk from Jane Street to Yolanda the dogsitter's place, where I dropped Braveheart off amidst much toddler-esque howling and yapping, I got out my map and headed for Paige's SoHo office, rehearsing my array of polite refusals as I went. I'd come up with about three by the time I got there. It wasn't as easy as you'd think, not if I didn't want to come across as under Jonathan's thumb, or scared of a challenge, or a million other impressions I didn't want to give.

It took me a little while to find Paige's office, since once I got into SoHo I found myself awfully distracted by the numerous pavement stalls selling cheap necklaces and hand-made bags and things that would make perfect Christmas presents. Ten years in London had prepared me for the sharp elbows and huffy tuts of fierce pavement traffic, but the wafting smells of hot coffee, and cakes, and doughnuts kept throwing my attention disastrously.

Eventually, I found Paige's office: on the eleventh storey of an impossibly elegant block, where tall columns stacked on top of columns, each with carved swags at the base, grimy with city dirt. I straightened my skirt, smoothed my hair, and was directed into the lift by the security men at the desk.

There were two other people in the lift with me, both too cool to acknowledge any other presence, and when I stepped out at the eleventh floor I was surprised to find that the inside of the office was as modern and stripped back as the outside was old-fashioned. I swallowed as I pushed open the glass door and went in. It wasn't the 'put you at ease' style I'd tried to achieve in my own office. It was the sort of place where you automatically wanted to walk straight out and buy entirely different clothes to the ones you foolishly thought were pretty snazzy when you got dressed that morning.

'Ms Drogan is very busy this morning,' the receptionist informed me, as if it was par for the course. But before I had time to settle myself with American *Vogue*, Paige herself appeared, in a black outfit, complete with phone headset.

'Put all my calls on divert. I'll take it from here, Tiffany,' she said, ushering me into her office with some urgency. She gestured for me to sit down, then poured me a large decaff coffee from her own personal machine, and got straight down it.

'Melissa, I'm so pleased you could make time for me? I do appreciate that. But you're busy so I won't waste time – here's the thing,' she said, tapping the empty desk with her pen. 'As you know, I'm working with your friend, Ric Spencer.'

She paused, and smiled before I could point out that 'friend' was rather overstating things. Paige had a lovely smile. I smiled back without even thinking.

'I love your dress,' she added. 'So cute! Anyway, I was really impressed with how you handled Ric's . . . communication malfunction at the party. I don't know if you realised, but Lucy Powell is quite an influential arts writer, and—'

'Oh, it was nothing, really. But, before we start, Paige, I have to—'

She tipped her head to one side. 'To be honest? I'm surprised you didn't know about Ric's success over here

– he's hot. He's spent the last year working on this film, and let me tell you, Melissa, when it opens, Ric is going to be seriously big. I mean, front of *Vanity Fair* big. You know?' she added, peering at me. 'You read that? The fold-out over edition, with all the hottest young actors on it? I'm speaking with some people about having him on there. We're just talking positioning right now. I need to have him third in from the left. No further. I don't want him on the fold.'

'Wow,' I said, struggling to equate this with the puking Goth with the low nylon tolerance I'd known. '*That* big, eh?'

'*Oh*, yes. So, listen to me here, Ric's got the looks, he's got the talent, he's got the best management in New York, but . . .' She let her voice trail away and raised her palms to heaven.

'But . . . ?' I repeated.

'But he hasn't got the . . . *tseychel*. You know?' Paige blinked rapidly.

'Oh,' I said. The *what*?

'Yip. And you need that. You need to be able to *charm* people into loving you, and there's just . . . he can't do it,' she finished briskly. 'I mean, you never have to tell Colin Firth to stop staring at interviewers' tits, do you?'

'Well . . .'

'And I'll level with you here, Melissa, I'm thinking that's how I want to pitch Ric. Mr Darcy. You know, he's got this great public school background, he's got these classically brooding features, like he's got this crumbling stately pile that's falling into the sea because his family spent the inheritance on gambling, then duelled each other to death with blunderbusses – that sort of feel. You know? I'm talking lakes. I'm talking

vintage cars in the drive, I'm talking *class*. Mysterious.
But definitely upmarket.'

It sounded to me rather as if Paige was describing my
own hellish family, but I didn't want to sound like I was
getting involved.

'I see,' I said.

'I mean, is that right?' Paige looked over the top of
her scary picture-editor glasses. 'I'll level with you. I don't
know what sort of background he has.' She threw her
hands in the air again. 'Ric won't tell me. I have to drag
details out of him' – she made scarily convincing clawing
gestures as she said this – 'all it says on his résumé is
that he was expelled from three schools and loves Wilkie
Collins.' She coughed. 'His *old* résumé. Obviously I've
worked on that with him since.'

'Mmm.' I could understand that omission. A certain
proportion of the public schoolboys I knew, mostly the
ones who didn't work in the City or the armed forces,
vehemently denied they'd ever been near a blazer, let
alone a prep school. Being posh was arty career death
in London if you wanted to be taken seriously. Bobsy
Parkin's brother Clement ran a T-shirt company in
Clerkenwell and you'd think he'd grown up in a squat in
Hackney. Especially now he insisted on being called DJ
CP.

'Ric's a man of few words,' Paige went on, 'and when
he does speak, it's . . . kind of hard to make out what
he's saying. He *sounds* quite posh. But of course, when
he's *acting*, he's fine! Beautiful articulation. He was in
two episodes of *ER* and oh, my God! The way he
described symptoms? I'd love to have a doctor like that.
The only episodes I've ever understood. Ever. Period!'

Her hands now made chop-chop gestures. I was getting

terrible manicure envy. New York grooming was on a whole new level, even for me. I folded my hands into one another.

'It sounds like you've got everything under control,' I said nervously. 'I can't think what you'd need—'

'I need *you*, Melissa,' barked Paige passionately. 'I want you to come on board and help Ric make it here in the US. I'm thinking in terms of a . . . personality makeover.' She broke out a wide and very white smile. 'Nothing too radical. Just, ah, encourage him to speak up, and be polite.'

I scrutinised Paige, trying to work out what she wasn't telling me. I might be naïve on occasion, but I'm not daft, and there seemed to be a few gaps here.

For one thing, he was an actor! On television! I didn't know any actors, but even I knew that they generally did what they wanted, and got away with murder. Wasn't it one of the perks of the job?

Second, I was beginning to wonder, queasily, if I hadn't rather overstated my own agency in an effort to keep my end up at the party. What exactly did Paige think I did? Did she imagine I was one of those *executive* makeover people?

I gulped.

Then there was Godric himself. If he'd turned up at my office, wanting advice on smartening himself up for the Fulham dating market, I'd have considered it a tough assignment. But Paige wasn't talking about improving his chances with a few Fionas, she wanted me to sort him out to international publicity standards!

No, I couldn't do it. It was asking for total humiliation. Not to mention the fact that Jonathan had specifically told me not to start getting involved in any work. And especially not with Paige.

I took a deep breath. Saying no wasn't one of my strong points.

'Paige, you know I'm terribly flattered that you think I could help out here, but don't you have all sorts of specialists you could be employing?' I protested. 'Voice coaches, and, um, movement people, and . . .' I tried to remember the lists of people they had on film credits, after best boys and make-up artists to the assistants and that sort of thing.

Paige pushed her glasses back up on her nose and looked at me. 'But I want *you*.'

'Well, that's awfully kind of you to—'

'Melissa, let me level with you.'

This was the third levelling we'd had. Things were pretty flat between us by now.

'I need someone *discreet*. Ric's at a delicate stage in his career, and I'm loving his naturalness. Everyone's loving his naturalness. I don't want any gossip about *coaching* to impact that? And what could be more natural than to have someone like you, someone well-spoken, from his own jolly homeland, just reminding him, by being there, how he should be behaving? You'll look like his PA, or an old friend, not some kind of crutch.'

I could see where she was coming from but I still wasn't convinced.

'Paige, this may sound very odd, but being posh . . . it's not the advantage you think it is at home. I mean, he might be trying very hard *not* to be, er, Hugh Grant, and if he's decided that's not him, I don't think anything I say can—'

But that just sent Paige off into a litany of how much everyone loved Ric and how his film was going to reach an unprecedented market share and end up with Mattel action figures of him in Wal-Mart, and her hypnotically soothing monologue gave me a moment or two to think.

Despite myself, I was starting to be intrigued, and not a little tempted by the idea of working with someone who was about to be famous. Properly famous. I mean, how good would it be for the agency's reputation back in London when I got back, not to mention the gossip I could dangle in front of Gabi?

I wrestled with my conscience as Paige's mellifluous tones and sing-song accent lapped gently at my ear. Maybe this could even be the start of a legitimate business in New York; OK, so Godric was a bloke, but really this *was* life coaching, not pretending to be anyone's girl-friend, and that was what Jonathan – understandably – had had such a problem with, wasn't it?

I began to soften to the idea, despite the alarm bells going off in some distant part of my brain. How badly could it go if I just saw Godric for coffee and put him straight about a few things? Not saying 'what' and making sure he smiled now and again. He looked like he needed a bit of help on that score. And we did have, um, some history. It would look frightfully rude if I refused to see him . . .

'. . . favour for a friend?' Paige gave me a meaningful look and I realised I should have been listening harder. As usual.

'Um, well, yes, I suppose so,' I said, caught off-guard.

'Melissa, I am so thrilled!' she exclaimed, delighted.

I panicked. What had I just agreed to? She was acting like I'd offered to marry him.

'But . . .'

'I just know you'll be able to help him in ways I never could.' She smiled conspiratorially. 'I could tell you had a special talent right there at the party. Have you ever thought of working in PR?'

I bit my lip and gathered up what remained of my concentration in this heat.

OK, so maybe this was a little nearer to the whole man management thing than Jonathan would necessarily like, but it wasn't like I'd be pretended to be Godric's girlfriend. I'd be acting as his chaperone. His . . . manners coach. The fact that he was a rude *man* was neither here nor there; if Paige had a rude actress she'd be asking me to do just the same job. And if it went well, it might give me a footing to work here, as well as in London, and if Jonathan and I were going to make a go of things, that might be important.

And, I conceded, it would be nice to have some spare cash. I wasn't earning anything while I was on holiday, after all. And the rent still had to be paid on the office. Besides, every time I left Jonathan's house I stumbled upon another shop selling fabulous little skirts or shoes that you just couldn't get in London.

As long as you don't promise anything just yet, I told myself.

'Well, maybe if Ric and I meet for a coffee and see how it goes from there?' I heard myself say, in polished Joanna Lumley tones.

'Fabulous. Fabulous. I can't tell you how glad I am that you believe in this as much as I do,' gushed Paige, and jabbed a button on her phone, adjusting her headset so she could talk into it. 'Would you excuse me one second?'

I nodded.

'Hello, Tiffany, is he here yet?'

Paige had invited Ric here already? Before she knew I was going to say yes?

Confident, huh.

Paige's brow furrowed. 'Tiffany, sweetie, you're mumbling. You can't mumble. It wastes my time and it makes you sound dumb,' she said, in a gentle but steely voice. 'Well, where is he? Have you called him?'

I tried not to meet Paige's beady eye, and fixed my attention instead out of her huge window. All I could see was a lot of other windows, in the looped arches of the block opposite.

'He's *what*? *What*? Tiffany, sweetie, I don't want to be hearing that!' Paige's face darkened and she pressed one perfectly manicured nail against her cheekbone until the skin went white around it under her blusher. 'No call? Nothing?'

There were other people in the windows opposite. They were also staring out. I thought about waving, then thought again.

'And you've paged him? Just twice? Keep paging!'

Paige had a way of delivering all this that bespoke of a titanium fist in a velvet glove.

That was agents, though, I guessed, and shivered as she stabbed at the button on the phone to cut Tiffany off, mid-protest.

'Well, I had hoped to have him here,' she said with a little 'what can you do?' shrug, and I guessed she'd wanted to open the door and wave Ric in as soon as I'd agreed, in the manner of a dating game show.

Presumably, if I hadn't agreed, she'd just have wheeled him in anyway, and showed me how dreadful he was until my professional pride was sufficiently roused to sort him out.

'Never mind,' I said brightly. 'I'm sure we can arrange a meeting soon. I have quite a few windows in my—'

'No, I need you to meet with him ASAP,' interrupted Paige, with an apologetic moue. 'Can I call you just as soon as I've tracked him down? The publicists are on my case, wanting to set up long lead-time interviews, and I need to have him good and prepped.'

'Right,' I said. 'Well, I'll just—'

Paige held up a hand. 'Would you hang around here for a half-hour? He can't be far away. I told him ten thirty.'

I smiled politely. 'Paige, I'm meeting Jonathan for lunch at one, and to be honest with you, I don't know New York that well, so I was planning to leave a little longer to find—'

'A half-hour.' And now she wasn't beaming so fully. In fact, her eyes had gone a little glinty. 'Thirty minutes, Melissa. That's all I'm asking of you.'

I forced my lips into a smile. 'But even if he arrives in the next thirty minutes, I still don't have very long . . .'

'Oh,' said Paige, with a touch of sadness in her voice. 'I thought you'd understand how time-sensitive these things are.' She paused, then added, 'Did you say you ran your own business?' as if she'd heard wrong.

Something in me cavilled at that.

'Well, half an hour. I really must go after that. But if it's all the same to you, I'll wait in the café over the road,' I added. 'I have some calls to make.' I paused too. 'I need to check in with my assistants at the office.'

I smiled to underline that this was my final offer, and Paige was smart enough to nod curtly. 'You have your cell phone switched on?'

'Not during a meeting,' I replied. 'That would be terribly bad manners.'

Paige beamed. 'Oh, you! Well, if you could turn it back on now?'

'Naturally.'

Not that I was going to answer it on the first ring, though.

When I'd settled myself into a corner seat in the Starbucks over the road, with a bucket of cappuccino and a slab of blueberry coffee cake that couldn't possibly be as low-fat as it claimed, I turned my phone back on and immediately it ding-donged with new messages.

'Mel, it's Gabi. I can't find Allegra. She's not been in all day, she won't answer her phone, and she's left me a note to pick up her bloody car from the garage. Can you have a word with her? She's . . . [sound of a door banging] Oh, hello. What time do you call this? [muffled response] I don't *care* what your barrister says! I'm on the phone to Melissa right now, actually. Do you want to talk to her? No? And you can put that down. You can . . . [not-so-muffled crash]'

I closed my eyes and massaged my forehead.

'Hello, Melissa.' My eyes opened. It was an American voice. 'My name's Agnetha Cooke, we spoke briefly at Kurt and Bonnie Hegel's cocktail party? You might recall we had a discussion about *tea*, and I was wondering if you could give me the name of the place in London you mentioned that did that special *tea* you were talking about?'

God, what had I told her? By that stage in the evening I was barely registering names, let alone recalling advice, such was the high-pitched note of stress in my brain. I made a note to call her back.

As I was jotting down Agnetha's many phone numbers, I let my eyes wander around the room. New Yorkers were, on the whole, not so different from Londoners, really. SoHo, NY, had much in common with Soho, W1:

trendy black-framed glasses, strange clothes, laptop bags, people wearing sunglasses indoors . . .

My eyes stopped wandering as they fell on a familiar figure in shades.

Godric.

He was reading a thin book, very intently, and drinking espresso. I assumed, from his black clothing and existentialist demeanour, that it was something in the original French – Voltaire, or Sartre, or something. Emery had gone through a phase like that. Although in her case the books were chosen because, being short, they took up less space in her handbag.

As I watched, his phone rang, two people turned to glare at him, and he sent it to 'busy'.

Honestly. Lateness I could forgive if one had had to save the life of a passing lollipop lady, or rescue a cat from a burning house, but not just because one had reached a gripping argument for free will.

I got up and moved purposefully across the café, slipping onto the easy chair opposite his. 'Hello, Godric,' I chirruped. 'Aren't you meant to be in a meeting right now?'

He looked up bewildered, realised it was me, and let his shoulders slump down into ennui mode again.

'Maybe, maybe not,' he said defensively. Then he looked up, and added, 'How do you know that, anyway?'

The phone rang again, and we both stared at it. Godric sent it to 'busy' once again.

'Because you're having the meeting with me,' I said firmly.

'Why?'

'Godric, would you take off your sunglasses? I know it's sunny outside, but it's rather rude to the person you're talking to.'

'I need them for privacy reasons,' he sulked. 'Don't want to be recognised.'

'Please? It makes an enormous difference.'

He huffed, but removed them, rubbing his eyes in the unexpected sunlight.

'Thank you!' I said. 'Gosh, now I see you properly, you've hardly changed!'

He hadn't, actually. The ludicrously long, dark eye-lashes, and purplish shadows beneath his round brown eyes were just the same as I remembered from when he was advancing on me in the props cupboard, hands already splayed for groping. Godric was one of those boys who always looked hung over, regardless.

I could see why Paige was so sure teenage girls every-where would be squealing in excitement over him. If he were my boyfriend, though, I'd be forever itching to take him on a brisk walk and get some colour into his cheeks.

Still, mine was not to reason why.

'Right, can we go over to Paige's office, please? I have a lunch appointment today and I don't want to be late.'

'Do we have to?' Godric managed to sound both bored and annoyed at the same time. 'I'm busy too.'

'Doing what?' I enquired sweetly.

'Researching.'

I looked at his book. He was reading *James and the Giant Peach*.

'I'm an actor,' he snotted, in response to my raised eyebrow. 'You wouldn't understand.'

If I hadn't been so hot and on edge from my own meeting with Paige, perhaps I'd have been more intimidated by his attitude, but there were limits to how long I was prepared to hang around waiting for anyone.

'Well?' I said, gathering my notebooks together and

pushing my chair back. 'Shall we go across there now? Sooner we do it, the sooner we get out, and we can both carry on with our busy days.'

Godric regarded me sullenly. 'What if I don't want to go?'

I stopped. 'Godric, it's a business meeting. About your business.'

'Then it's my *business* whether I go or not, surely? Not any of yours?'

I wasn't sure how to respond to this without being actively rude, but by now all I wanted was to get back to Jonathan's house, get out of my smart clothes and get in the shower before meeting him for lunch.

'In that case, I'll just have to invoice Paige for three wasted hours of my time, which I'm sure she'll dock from whatever you're earning.'

That seemed to galvanise him into action, and in ten minutes all three of us were back in Paige's office, setting up an appointment for Godric's – or Ric's, as I now supposed I had to call him – new set of publicity photographs. And somehow, I found myself agreeing to 'pop along' with him, just to hold his hand and keep him calm.

'But I don't need anyone to look after me,' protested Godric, in appalled tones. 'What do you think I am? A baby or something?'

'Work with me here,' said Paige lightly. 'OK? We don't want a repeat of the Balthazar incident, do we?'

And they shared a look of such mutual distaste that even I shrank back in my chair.

'I need a slash,' announced Godric, shoving back his chair, and shuffling out of the room in high dudgeon.

'I can't believe you got him over here,' whispered Paige. 'How did you do it?'

'I just told him we had to go,' I said. 'And he came.'

Paige clasped her hands together. 'You are so good! I told you, I can't get him to do anything, but he's responding to you!'

'It's all in the tone,' I said, vaguely aware that Mummy had said exactly the same thing to me when she was detailing how to bring Braveheart to heel.

I had a grim feeling Godric was going to need more than chicken scraps and ear tickling, however.

11

'So what are you up to today?' Jonathan said, raising his voice to make himself heard over the plaintive sound of a histrionic dog being ignored in a box.

It felt awfully cruel, but we were, on my (OK, my mother's) strict instructions, disregarding Braveheart's outrage at being placed in the crate of doom while we ate our breakfast, to teach him first that his crate was a fun place to be, and, second, that only human beings had breakfast actually on the breakfast table.

Easier said than done, when Braveheart was emoting like Barbra Streisand.

In desperation, I spun round in my chair and tried the Look. The one I gave idiot boys like Jem Wilde when they messed around with depilators in Liberty.

To my surprise, and his, Braveheart shut up.

'Hey! Melissa, you haven't lost your touch!' Jonathan pointed at me and clicked his fingers in delight – an annoying gameshow-host tic I thought I'd cured him of when he first moved to London.

I gave him the Look and he stopped too, and stared at his fingers.

'Sorry,' I said. 'Force of habit.'

'So, what are you up to today?' Jonathan bit into his wholegrain bagel. 'I'm really sorry about missing lunch yesterday,' he added for the ninth time.

'Jonathan! Honestly! I don't mind,' I replied, also for the ninth time.

He looked apologetically over the table. 'I thought Lori had cancelled, but apparently the Schultzes had flown back to New York specially to make the viewing, so I just had—'

'Forget it,' I insisted. 'It's not your fault you're in demand.' I'd caught a glimpse of his printed schedule and it seemed logically impossible, with more meetings than spaces to put them in. He had, however, pencilled several 'Melissa?' entries, which made my heart flutter. 'Anyway, I had a lovely time, drinking coffee, people-spotting.'

'It's not what I had in mind,' he said, sticking his fingers into his hair. Jonathan looked stressed already and it was barely eight. It was a new kind of stress too. Not the old London stress I knew so well. 'And, believe me, I'll make it up to you.' His face brightened. 'I've asked Lori to help you out with any arrangements you'd like to make – you know, if you want to make a boat trip, or go up in a helicopter, or something of that sort.'

'Oooh, lovely!' It wasn't the same as him taking me though. But, looking on the bright side, Lori seemed to know quite a lot about sample sales. She'd already emailed me links to about ten.

As if he could read my mind, Jonathan added, 'You know, I so wish I could be showing you round myself, but work is just *insane*.' He shrugged again. 'I'm so sorry. But how about we go out for dinner tonight? As you can see, my kitchen isn't yet at the cordon bleu standard I need to create culinary magic myself.'

I beamed. 'I'd love that.'

'Where do you want to eat?'

'I don't know. Somewhere that's special to you.' I hesitated, not wanting to say 'but not somewhere you used to go with your ex-wife'. 'Somewhere with a great view,' I added quickly, before he could say something about getting Lori to check out Zagat's newest guide.

'Well, I know just the place.' Jonathan shot me a wicked smile, then checked his watch. 'The walker should be here to get Braveheart at half past eight. I've asked that he stay there all day, until we get home. Better than being cooped up here in his box, right?' He raised his eyebrows, hopeful that he'd done the right thing.

I looked over at Braveheart who had set up a low-level whimpering, with his head on his paws. I'd misjudged him: he had more emotional range than Barbra Streisand. 'And what'll happen to him with the walker?'

'Guess he'll be in a bigger box there, with some other dogs.' Jonathan started to pack up his papers. 'Be good for him. He can make some buddies.' He kissed me on the top of my head. 'You can invite them for tea and English crumpets. Mmm, Melissa. Do you smell this delicious all the way down?' Jonathan murmured.

He swept my hair over one shoulder, and kissed the nape of my neck. Little tingles ran up and down my spine.

Braveheart started yapping crossly, and Jonathan broke off with a vexed sigh.

'I'll take him with me today,' I said impulsively. 'He obviously needs more attention, and he really needs to learn who's boss.'

'Shouldn't that be *me*?' asked Jonathan, with a wry grin. 'Anyway, I'll leave it up to you – after all, you're the one with the magic touch when it comes to that mutt.'

'Well, it's not so hard, really.'

'Hey! Don't sell yourself short! He wouldn't let Cindy

pick him up, not even when he was a puppy. I was telling Kurt about your magic touch and he wants to talk to you about this dachshund of his sister's.' He winked. 'Now if you need a job in New York, that might be something to think about?'

Emboldened by this, I decided to come clean about my meeting with Paige and Godric. I was a rotten liar, and I hated the idea of not being upfront with Jonathan. Besides, if I told him from the start, he could hardly be mad.

'Well, actually, I'm sort of trying to explore that avenue myself,' I said. 'With people, obviously, not dogs. Training, sort of.'

Jonathan looked surprised. 'I thought we agreed you were on vacation?'

'Yes, I know, but I, er, I've sort of got a freelance job.'

Jonathan's surprise turned to suspicion. 'Which is?'

I took a deep breath. 'You remember the actor we met at Bonnie's party?'

He nodded warily. 'Not Ric Spencer.'

'Yes, well, Paige has asked me to pop along to a photoshoot he's doing today, to keep an eye on him, as it were.'

'In what way, "keeping an eye on him"?'

'Just . . . keeping an eye on him. Making sure he looks OK in the pictures. Trying to get a smile out of him. Stopping him insulting the photographer so badly he walks out.' I laughed merrily.

'Melissa, that sounds like a hell of a lot of work,' said Jonathan, less merrily. 'The guy is a moron. I mean, I know he's British and a—' his face twisted up very slightly 'a *friend*, and you feel some kind of obligation, but c'mon . . . This is Paige's job.'

'No, it's not!' I said. 'It'll be fun. It's just for an hour or so this morning, and I'll get to see Central Park, and maybe get some top gossip for Gabi, and—'

'It's just a one-off?' he demanded, fixing me with a firm look.

'I haven't agreed to anything,' I hedged. 'Exactly.'

'Ding!' went Nelson in my head.

'Well, OK, just do this, then tell Paige to hire him some kind of therapist,' said Jonathan. 'I mean it. I don't want you spending your vacation stressing yourself out with idiots. Is Paige paying you for—'

Before he could go on, his mobile bleeped with a message and his brow furrowed as he read it. 'Oh, Christ,' he muttered, under his breath. 'Not again.'

'Trouble?'

It was his turn to look a little evasive. 'Nothing I can't handle. Listen, honey, I've got to make tracks. Call Lori if there's anything you need,' he said. 'She's more than happy to help you out. I'm going to be pretty tied up all day, but I'll let you know about dinner. We'll work out the logistics later, OK?'

I smiled and gave him a kiss goodbye. Then another one, in the hallway by his antique hat-stand, then another, on the tree-shaded doorstep. Jonathan was the best kisser I'd ever kissed, bar none. It was all in the way he held me, carefully but firmly, as if I were a fragile ornament, then kissed me like I was anything but.

Maybe it was a good job he was so busy, or else we'd never leave the house.

Braveheart and I set off in the direction of Central Park, with me feeding him snippets of organic chicken breast and heaping him with praise every block or so, as per instructions. I had to admit that when Braveheart was behaving he looked pretty cute. While I was wearing a simple cotton dress and a large hat to keep the sun off my face, he was sporting an outrageously expensive tartan dog collar and Tiffany dog tag, with his fur gleaming in the sun like fresh ice cream after his wash and brush-up at the dogwalker's yesterday. Frankly, Braveheart looked more Park Avenue than I did, and he was walking along like he knew it.

I found Godric lurking by the entrance nearest the John Lennon Strawberry Fields garden, as prearranged by Paige so we'd 'feel at home'. He was smoking a cigarette furtively, and wearing dark glasses, a dark cotton polo-neck, and a dark pair of trousers, despite the heat. He looked like a cartoon Frenchman.

Even as I was waving at him and he was shuffling in response, my mobile rang, and a wave of advance guilt hit me in case it was Jonathan. But it wasn't. It was Paige.

'Are you there? You're with him, right?' she demanded, without preamble.

'Yes, I'm here,' I said.

'Good, because he *cannot* be on his own.'

'Why?' I asked, regarding Godric curiously. 'Is he liable to run off?'

Paige laughed as if I were being deliberately obtuse. 'Oh, you're funny! No, he's liable to be mobbed by fans, Melissa. He needs someone with him to make sure there are no *incidents*.'

Absolutely no one was clamouring to mob Godric, as far as I could see. Apart from a pregnant woman on rollerblades who wasn't bothering to hide her disapproval of his smoking.

'Well, I'm here now,' I said. 'There's no sign of the photographer though.'

A mobile phone rang in the background of her office, and I heard Paige pick it up, coo, 'Be right with ya!' then clunk it down. 'Tiffany!' she snapped, off phone. 'It's Brad again! Do you ever listen to a goddamn word I say?'

Godric looked as if he were about to slope off into the park, so I raised a warning finger at him, and to my surprise he stayed put. While it was working, I raised another finger at Braveheart, who obediently sat down and eyed my handbag.

'Melissa? Yeah, great, you with me?' demanded Paige. 'As we discussed in our meeting, Ric's had lots of pictures done before, and we just can't get them right. I told him to bring them with him so you can get an idea.' She clicked something in the background – her pen? Her knuckles? I couldn't tell. 'I keep telling him, I'm OK with a bit of smouldering, I'm cool with *one* moody shot, but I need some smiles! I need charm! He just does this . . . face. I don't know how to describe it. You'll see. He never does it when he's working, for some reason. Just when he's in an expensive photo session. So, yeah, this is like the seventh photographer he's worked with, and he's costing us, so I'd appreciate it if you could control things a little?'

'Um, but what do you mean by that? Roughly?'

Paige clicked again. I guessed telepathy probably featured prominently in Tiffany's job description.

'Just talk to him. So he knows what to project? These pictures, they're going to go out to casting agents, for all sorts of different jobs, yup? So I wanna see Hugh Grant, but I need Hugh Jackman as well. Know what I'm saying? I need Colin Firth, but also Colin Farrell. I need some *range.*'

I looked at Godric, who was indeed toting a leather portfolio under one scrawny arm. So far all I was seeing was a fifth-form would-be poet with low alcohol tolerance who'd inadvisedly taken up smoking to impress my sister – but that probably wasn't one of the looks Paige wanted. 'OK,' I said. 'I'll do my best.'

'Great,' said Paige, over the sound of the phone ringing again. 'Should only take an hour or two! Tiffany! Tiffany! Don't mumble at me!' Now there were two mobile phones ringing.

I rang off to save her the bother of hanging up on me.

'Morning, Godric!' I said, walking over to him. 'How are you today?'

'Is that your dog?' he demanded. 'I can't *stand* yappy little dogs.' He bent down to Braveheart's level. 'They should be put on spits and *eaten*!'

Braveheart paused then snapped at his nose with precision timing, and Godric leaped back with a yelp.

'Godric, this is Braveheart. Braveheart, this is Ric Spencer. Right, well, now you two have got to know each other,' I said, tugging at the lead. 'Is that your portfolio?'

'Yes. It's shit.' Godric handed it over.

'Can you take him for a moment?' I asked and handed control of Braveheart over while I flipped through the photographs inside.

Paige was right: they all bore the hallmarks of very expensive lighting and artistry, but Godric was projecting variations on the same emotion in every single one of them. Acute awkwardness.

Admittedly he'd really got 'awkward' nailed – even in black Armani, leaning against a glass wall, he looked like a teenager waiting outside an STD clinic – but you could hardly cast him as James Bond on the basis of these. Not unless you were setting it in a prep school.

I carried on flipping through the glossy photographs. Godric in black tie (strangulated), Godric in riding outfit (mortified), Godric on top of a skyscraper (embarrassed). Then, right at the end, were some photos of him on stage, in the sort of frilly white shirt that even Allegra would have rejected as too attention-seeking, and it could have been a different person.

'Wow!' I exclaimed, pulling them out. 'What's this?'

Godric leaned over. 'Oh, that. I was in a production of *Dracula*. Just a little thing, up in Edinburgh, couple of years ago. I was Jonathan Harker. Got some good reviews, actually.'

'I bet.' In these photos, Godric looked really rather foxy, with his dark fringe flopping into his eyes, and his face animated with terror. I think it was terror, anyway. There was a seven-foot bat behind him.

'So how come you can't do *that* in *these*?' I asked, shaking the other photos. 'Eh?'

He shrugged and surliness returned to his face like a cloud. 'Not an effing model, am I? Can't stand all that stuff. It's a waste of time.'

Before I could give him a brisk lecture about how making an effort for an hour could help his career no end, a large man with two shoulders-full of bags hoved into view.

'Ric Spencer?' he asked.

'Yeah,' said Godric, without removing his shades.

'Dwight Kramer. First up, let me tell you – I loved you in *ER*,' said the photographer, unpacking his first bag with military precision. 'When you gave up your kidney? My wife cried so much I thought she was ill.

No, I gotta be honest' – and he clapped a hand over his chest to demonstrate manly emotion – 'we *both* cried, man.'

'Oh, er, thanks,' muttered Godric, staring at his feet. 'I hated it.'

Dwight boggled.

I nudged Godric hard and spoke quickly to cover the man's confusion. 'Hello, Dwight, I'm Melissa. I'm, er, a friend of Ric's. From home. In London.'

'Pleased to meet you, Melissa!' We shook hands warmly. 'Do you have any particular ideas for this shoot?' asked Dwight. 'Any special angles? I'm very open to direction.'

'Don't make me look a prick,' Godric mumbled. 'If you can manage that. It's about me, right, not about what a great artist you are.'

I swallowed. I'd only been in New York a few days, but it had really struck me how much more accommodating people were, even when they didn't really mean it. I kept reading how New Yorkers were meant to be fearsomely rude, but compared to London, where you could literally go into labour on the Tube only to have people tut about you for not moving down the carriage, the general air of friendliness was noticeable. It might have been something to do with the tipping culture, but even so . . .

Although I knew, by London standards, Godric was just being a bit self-deprecating, maybe grumpy, by American standards he was edging towards sectionable rudeness.

'Why don't we have a walk further into the park?' I suggested, hoping that moving out of the sun might sweeten Godric up a bit.

'I'm cool with that,' said Dwight agreeably, and we set off.

I hung back a bit to let Godric slope on ahead. He'd handed Braveheart back to me, all the better to shuffle along with his hands in his pockets.

Braveheart was trotting at my heels now, nosing my bag and looking positively charming. I felt a surge of warmth towards him. If Jonathan couldn't be with me during the day, then Braveheart was the next best thing. We were *sharing* him.

'Ric always like that?' asked Dwight.

'Oh, God, no. Sorry about that. He's rather tired,' I confided. 'You know what these actors are like. Up all night rehearsing, learning lines . . .'

'Drinking,' added Dwight, with a wink.

'Goodness, certainly not!' I protested, Paige's words about polishing Godric up into a Ye Olde English Gentleman Actor ringing in my head. 'He's really not like that at all. Ric's terribly serious about his acting. He reads and reads and . . . you know.' I made a 'oh, *Ric*' face. 'He's just rather wrapped up in his new role right now. Normally he's the life and soul – the most *beautiful* manners.'

As I said this, two lady joggers swerved to avoid Ric who was shuffling like a Dementor down the middle of the path.

'Jet-lagged,' I explained quickly.

But Dwight was looking at the joggers. 'Did you see that? Did you see who that was?'

I craned my neck round, but they'd gone.

'No?'

'That was Reese Witherspoon. With a trainer, I guess. You never know who you'll run into, walking their dogs or what have you.'

'Really?'

'Oh, yeah. Well, you got all the stars in those apartments over there.' And Dwight proceeded to reel off a list of famous people who lived nearby, and then another list of what his photographer friends had caught them doing on camera. And I thought London was bad for that kind of thing. How wrong can you be?

After a while, Dwight found a nice quiet corner of the park where the light was falling beautifully through the trees. I sat down on a bench and watched while he set up the shot, moving Godric backwards and forwards, trying to coax him into showing some of his famous dramatic sensitivity.

But as soon as Dwight raised his camera to his eye, Godric's face instinctively rearranged itself into the awkward photograph face much beloved of self-conscious men all over Britain: eyebrows aloft, strange, apologetic smile that suggested some gastric indiscretion, coupled with a gentle hunching of the shoulders. He did it every time: Dwight would talk, Godric would listen, stare into the distance, then look back with exactly the same expression. It was like trying to make a teddy bear sit up: things looked hopeful until you moved your hands, then it slumped down again into the same lifeless hunch.

'Um, Ric, why don't you look away for three seconds, then look back and think of your favourite thing in the whole world?' I suggested helpfully, passing on a particularly useful Home Ec tip that had seen me illuminated with joy in numerous party photos as I thought about Nelson's carrot cake while hugging spotty youths. 'Try that!'

Godric flashed a pitying glare in my direction. 'You want me to think about *Hamlet*? Or the wreck of the

Titanic? It doesn't quite work, does it? We're not all finishing school *bimbos*.'

'OK, then, how about getting a curtain call for *playing* Hamlet at the National with, er, Kate Winslet?' I suggested.

He cast his eyes up to heaven, then glowered at me. 'Why should I take advice from someone who clearly knows nothing about the legitimate theatre?'

'Well, you're the expert, *Ric*,' I said sweetly, 'having done so many of these photo sessions before.' And I went back to training Braveheart to sit and stay with my final scraps of chicken.

The charade went on for another twenty minutes, with similar results. Or, rather, lack of results. It was interesting for me though: sitting comfortably in the shade, I could watch the stream of New Yorkers walking their dogs, rollerblading, jogging, arguing, eating their lunch, sunbathing, with the Manhattan skyline rising above the trees behind like a film set. Some of the passers-by, I noticed, even glanced at Ric as if they recognised him. But then again, they might just have been wondering who the grumpy bloke having his photograph taken was.

Eventually, I could see Dwight was struggling, as Ric's face reddened in the sun. 'Shall we go and get a drink?' I called over. 'Maybe look at a different location?'

Gratefully, they followed me back onto the main path, and we wandered further into the park, where I insisted we stop at an ice-cream stall. Godric initially refused, and then succumbed to a chocolate-pistachio cornet, which he ate with incongruous enthusiasm for a man dressed head to toe in black.

'You take the little fella to one of the Central Park dog

runs?' asked Dwight, nodding at Braveheart, who had now tired of being obedient and cute, and was charging at passers-by.

'I don't, no,' I said. According to Cindy's notes, Braveheart was a member of no fewer than three private dog runs, one of which even offered single-sex walking hours.

He laughed. 'Gotta get on the right dog run, hey? I know what you ladies are like with your dogs.'

I started to say that he wasn't mine, but as I looked down, I realised that his extending leash had extended so far that I couldn't actually see him. There were bushes and such like in the way, and only his red lead vanishing into them.

My heart sank. 'Braveheart!' I called, quietly at first, trying to ravel the lead back in. 'Come! Come here!'

I turned to Dwight. 'Sorry about this. I'm training him. He's rather stubborn.'

'Can't you control that thing?' demanded Godric loftily. 'I mean, how hard is it to control an animal you could easily stick on a barbecue? Surely he weighs less than your ludicrous handbag?'

Godric was really starting to get on my nerves. He had absolutely no reason to be so rude, especially to people who were trying to help him.

I got up to wind in the lead before I told Godric where to get off. It went round a wastebin, through a bush, and at last I spotted him.

'Braveheart!' I yelled furiously. He was over by a tree, enthusiastically mounting a spaniel who didn't seem to know quite what was going on.

Her owner, however, did, and he seemed pretty livid.

'What the hell you doing?' he screamed, flapping his

hands at the dogs. 'What the hell? Get off! Get off! Oh, my God! Call the police!'

Braveheart flashed him an 'oh, do just leave us to it' look that my father would have been proud of and carried on thrashing away.

Well, that was it. It was one thing being shown up by the rudeness of a recalcitrant semi-client, but to be shown up by my own dog? In normal circumstances, basic manners would have dictated that one ignored the thrashing and let nature take its course, but this was something else entirely.

'Braveheart!' I thundered, bright red with nine different types of embarrassment. 'Braveheart! I can't *believe* this behaviour! Come here *right now*! *Right now!*'

Dwight and Godric flinched at the steel in my voice.

'Christ,' I heard Godric mumble, 'Maggie effing Thatcher or what?'

With one final thrust, Braveheart dismounted and trotted over to me, leaving the spaniel swaying slightly. I bent down to his level and gave him my Grade One Look of Severe Displeasure, complete with the Strict Finger of Disappointment. 'Never, *never* do that again,' I hissed, 'or I will tan your sorry Scottish hide from here to Aberdeen, pedigree or no pedigree!'

I was pleased to see him quail and lie down in grovelling supplication.

I stood up and prepared to grovel myself to the owner. Never actually having owned a dog myself, I wasn't sure what the correct procedure was. Did I offer to pay for the morning-after pill, or something? Should I insist that Braveheart marry her?

'Hello. Melissa Romney-Jones. Hello. Gosh, I'm terribly, terribly sorry. If it's any consolation,' I said, trying to be wry, 'he does have an excellent pedigree. And wonderful taste in bitches too! What a lovely dog you have: What's she called?'

The man looked outraged. 'His name is King Charles.'

I blanched. 'Oh, heavens, I do apologise. Um . . .'

'Your freakin' dog has just assaulted my show champion, in broad daylight, and you're sayin' sorry?' His voice was getting higher and higher, and I wondered if he was maybe taking this a little too personally. 'And God knows what disgusting British diseases he's spreadin'!'

So much for New Yorkers being friendly.

'Now, hang on a mo,' I said, 'he's actually an *American* dog, with Kennel Club papers and . . .'

But the man was pointing and stepping nearer. Invading my space, as Gabi would have said.

I kind of wished Gabi was here now. She had no problems about settling disputes in public.

'Women like you are what spoil these parks for proper dog-lovers,' he spat. 'Coming here with your stupid little dogs, and your attitude – oh, I'm too busy to train him! That's for someone else to do.' He stopped flapping his hands around in imitation of some Park Avenue dog-owner, and stepped even nearer, the better to jab his finger at me. 'Maybe if you spent less time sitting on your fat ass, which, may I add, is about to bust out of that dress – don't you *have* StairMasters in Britain? – maybe if you spent more time running in the park with your dog instead of sitting there eating ice cream . . .'

I flinched at that. I mean, criticise the dog, by all means, but . . .

'What did you say?'

I turned round. Out of nowhere, Godric was now

standing right up underneath the angry man's nose. I suddenly realised how tall he was – he stood a good head over Angry Dog Man and, as if to emphasise his outrage, he'd even removed his shades.

Not that Angry Dog Man seemed that worried. 'Who're you?'

'What did you say to her?' demanded Godric.

'That your little doggie?' the man sneered. 'Well, now it all makes sense.'

'Godric, just leave it,' I said, aware of a crowd gathering a safe distance away. 'I'm sure once we've all calmed down, we can—'

'I *am* freakin' calm, lady!' shrieked Angry Dog Man. 'You're the one with the problem!'

I quailed, despite myself. I really hate being shouted at. 'Look, please . . .' I stammered.

'Don't speak to her like that,' said Godric ominously.

'What?'

'I said, don't speak to her like that. Are you stupid, or just ill-mannered? Don't you *know* how to behave towards a lady?'

'Godric, listen, please don't—'

'Will you *can* it, you fat bitch?' Angry Dog Man snapped, and then seemed to hurtle sideways as Godric's fist connected with his jaw and sent him reeling.

The crowd gasped. To my horror, I heard the rattle of camera shutters, and spinning round to tell Dwight that this wasn't really the time, I realised that it wasn't just him taking pictures – there was another photographer there too, and they were jostling one another for position, as Godric and Angry Dog Man rolled around punching each other.

Oh, God, this was dreadful! A whole range of horrors

ran through my head: Godric's famous face maimed, Godric up in court, Paige suing me . . .

I racked my brains for what celebrities were meant to do in this situation but all I could think of were pictures of Sean Penn brawling with the paparazzi while Madonna put a bag over her head. Clearly that wasn't going to cut it here, so I grabbed the nearest bowl of dog drinking water, hurled it over the pair of them to shock them into breaking it up, then turned to put my hands over the camera lenses.

'Quick, quick!' I shouted, in a desperate distraction attempt. 'The dogs are getting away!'

That at least was true: the spaniel was making a break for it, with Braveheart in hot pursuit. Angry Dog Man struggled to his feet, glaring furiously between Godric – who had the classic public school slap-and-roll fight technique down pat – and his vanishing show champion. With a fearsome growl, he set off after the dog, jabbing his fist.

'I'm coming back!' he yelled, pointing at us. 'Don't think this is over! I know who you are! I'm coming back!'

I dragged Godric to his feet and brushed the grass off his polo-neck. My heart was still hammering with shock, and I was glad to have some briskness to hide behind. Manners are the corset of the soul, I find.

'That was terribly chivalrous of you, Godric, but next time you want to defend a lady's honour,' I said, brushing hard, 'can you please check for paparazzi?'

'I don't care how fat your arse is,' muttered Godric, 'he had no right to talk to you like that. It was out of line. Can't stand it when people are rude. Makes me mad. Effing American yob.'

But he looked quietly pleased with himself, and I

couldn't help feeling flattered, in an uncommonly medieval way. Even though I was really very angry with him about behaving like that.

Still, no one had ever defended my honour before. I mean, apart from Nelson. And never with *fists*.

'Oh, my God,' said Dwight. 'You want to see *these*.'

We spun round. He proffered his camera, showing us the images on the digital screen: close-ups of Godric's face, doing enraged, surprised, defensive and, finally, quite chuffed.

'Aren't they great?' he enthused. 'I mean, yeah, extreme way to get them, but hey! It worked. There's got to be five, six great shots there.'

But it wasn't those photographs I was worried about. I was more concerned about the ones in the camera now heading off at high speed towards the nearest exit.

12

They say that nothing spoils your appetite like a guilty conscience, and I can confirm this is true. In my experience – and believe me, I generally make Augustus Gloop look picky – extreme desire also renders me less than peckish, so a combination of the two meant that Jonathan's promised romantic dinner was off to a bad start before the food even arrived.

He'd gone to some effort too, to make up for missing our lunch: he picked me up in a cab at six, postponing appointments on his phone as we went, then refused to tell me where we were going. I think he might have made the cab drive round the city for a bit to confuse me – which he needn't have bothered doing because I had no idea where we were anyway – until we ended up at a rickety-looking jetty, down by the river, next to a five-lane intersection and bridge combo.

It wasn't Jonathan's usual style, I had to admit.

'Um, is it some kind of special seafood place?' I hazarded, not wanting to sound disappointed.

'Not really.' He was scanning the quayside, then suddenly strode off, pulling me by the hand after him. 'Here we are!'

We were standing in front of a little landing deck, with the gangplank ready extended into the launch. I looked uncertainly at the small tugboat bobbing in the choppy waters. It was a two-level tourist contraption, with rails around the top, and it didn't look all that sea-worthy to me. Underneath it, the river was churning away ominously.

'Get in!' Jonathan handed me up and over the gang-plank, gesturing for me to go up the stairs to the front of the top deck. We were the only people on the boat, and when he'd fastened the chain behind him, the cap-tain hurled the mooring rope and plank onto the deck behind us with carefree abandon, and, with a lurch, the little boat set off.

The view, though, took my mind off any impending seasickness at once. I leaned against the front rails and watched the skyscrapers and riverside office blocks pass by in a glittering collage of glass and steel, brick and marble. The sun was setting behind them, sending fin-gers of orange light through the spaces, picking out flat panes of glass and frosted curlicues like multicoloured jewels, shifting with every new wave that lifted and dropped us.

Jonathan appeared behind me, holding onto the rails to keep me steady, and I leaned back happily into his chest, feeling his chin tuck protectively over my head.

'I keep forgetting the city's so close to the water's edge,' I said, the stress of the morning vanishing as the wind blew strands of hair around my face. 'It's so beautiful.'

'Isn't it? I love this. You remember when you took me on the London Eye, and told me how proud you felt of London when you saw it all spread out underneath? Well, this is my favourite view of Manhattan. From the river, with no people in the way. In the evening, preferably.' He lifted his hand and sketched a line along the jagged row of offices and apartments in front of us. 'All those windows, all those apartments . . . I love looking at them, and imagining what they've seen going down this river, you know? The ships, the people, the seasons. We can come and go, but this all stays pretty much the same. I like that. Buildings. They're kind of . . . comforting.'

I didn't say anything, but I smiled and relaxed back against him.

Jonathan tucked his head tenderly into my neck. 'I want to share all of *my* New York with you, Melissa. My house, my friends, my life.' He paused. 'It's not just about where you live, what you have. It's about who you're with. I know you get that, and it means a lot to me.'

'I know,' I said, quavering just a little at the responsibility involved there. Could you ever really share friends who'd known one party so much longer? And how was I meant to share them with Cindy? 'But . . .'

He leaned back, so his arms were round me once again, and we were both looking out at the skyline scrolling along in front of us. 'Don't say anything,' he said, putting one finger over my lips. 'Let's just enjoy this view.'

And we sailed on in silence, alone on the little boat, surrounded by our thoughts. I felt so happy, wrapped up in Jonathan's arms, that I barely even noticed how we were pitching up and down on the wash, until we reached the restaurant at the other end and I nearly slipped off the gangplank in my high heels.

It wasn't just some seafood place. The menu was about a metre square, there were three waiters to our table alone, and the piano player switched to playing selections from *West Side Story* when we walked in, almost as if Jonathan had arranged it.

'This OK?' he asked.

'Absolutely!' I said.

We held hands until the starters came, then talked about New York, about London, about his new colleagues, about my sightseeing, about Braveheart. We even touched again on Cindy, obliquely.

'I haven't talked like this for the longest time,' said Jonathan suddenly.

I put my fork down in readiness. I have a terrible habit of having my mouth full at inopportune moments.

'You know why?' he went on. 'Trust. It's so great to have trust.'

I smiled nervously. 'Good.'

'I know I sometimes take the rise out of you for being a little bit . . . innocent,' he said, stroking the inside of my wrist, 'but I love that you're so open with me. I can trust you absolutely.'

'Well, of course,' I said. 'What's the point otherwise?'

'And I hope you trust me?' he added. 'You'd tell me if there was anything on your mind, wouldn't you? Anything you weren't happy about?'

I bit my lip and nodded hard.

'Ding!' went Nelson's voice in my head.

In the candlelight, I could see Jonathan's face was wreathed in smiles. He looked so happy. Relaxed even.

Over the water, the lights of Manhattan had come on, and were glowing through the gathering evening dusk. The Empire State Building was lit up in red and green, and I could see the Chrysler Building rising elegantly over the peaks and spires of the dark city.

It was perfect.

Now wasn't the time to admit my stupid, immature Cindy fears, or tell him about today's Godric fiasco.

'Melissa,' said Jonathan quietly, pushing his fingers through mine. 'You know I love you, don't you?'

My head snapped up to look at him. It was the first time he'd said it. In my chest, my heart swooped and dived like a swallow.

'I do!' I said. 'I mean, I love you too.'

And undemonstrative Jonathan leaned over the table and kissed me on the lips. He tasted delicious.

I wasn't telling him anything after that, believe me.

The next morning, I didn't exactly spring out of bed, due to the crashing champagne headache pinning me to the Egyptian cotton pillows. But Jonathan was already in his shower when I prised my eyes open, and he was singing selections from *High Society*. He had, I noted distantly, rather a good voice.

Not wanting him to see me looking like a toad, I stumbled out of bed and into the other bathroom, where I splashed water on my face to wake up, then lavished moisturiser penitently over the resulting pinkness. When I looked nearly human, with Jonathan still bellowing away next door, I pulled on my linen trousers, a vest and shades, and took Braveheart out for his morning constitutional. OK, so I also took the sneaky opportunity to check my mobile for business arising at home.

There were three texts and a couple of messages. One from Nelson ('Do not get in unlicensed minicabs!'), one from Gabi ('Best place for men's shirts with extra long arms?') and one from Allegra ('Gabi nightmare. Please sack'). As I was reading that one, another arrived, this time from Gabi ('Tell yr sis office opens at 10!! Not 3!! Fed up of slacking! Can I fire her?').

Oh, God. Were they doing this in front of clients? I shook myself. Why was I surprised? The main thing was that they were actually in the office at all. Because, if they weren't, who was answering the phone? Or checking the diary?

I took a deep breath. I was meant to be on holiday. On *holiday*. I needed to prove to Jonathan that I could leave the office alone.

And, anyway, wasn't I going to fly back and do an emergency patch-up job fairly soon? I knew Gabi and Allegra were never going to be best mates, but they might settle down, if I left them to work things out. Stranger things had happened.

One, I told myself, it's not for long.

Two, Gabi won't do anything Nelson wouldn't approve of.

Three . . .

Visions of Allegra remodelling Chelsea bachelors' pads in the style of Hogwarts filled my head.

I shook myself.

Three, it might teach some clients what good value I really was.

I fired off quick responses to each message, picked up the gossipy papers that weren't filled with dry financial news (i.e., the ones that Jonathan didn't already get) and bought some extra chicken breast from the deli on the corner. I also grabbed a coffee, to jumpstart my morning personality before I had to talk to Jonathan, and, after a brief power struggle near some pigeons, Braveheart and I returned home, feeling really rather New York-y.

Jonathan was already sorting through his mail at the table and beamed approvingly at me when we walked in.

'You know what I *love* about you?' he asked.

'My winning way with small dogs?' I suggested, stuffing Braveheart in his crate with some chicken and MooMoo.

'Well, that too. But mainly I love the way you look so gorgeous first thing in the morning!'

I peered at him. 'Do you have your contact lenses in, darling?'

He nodded. 'Of course I do! You just look . . . *natural*. Like a peach. That's nice. Not like these women who have to spend hours and hours plastering themselves with make-up and mascara and what have you before they'll even step outside.'

My initial beam of pleasure faded slightly into wanness. Was that a compliment or a ghost dig at Cindy? The two weren't mutually exclusive, I was beginning to realise. Cindy wasn't a yardstick I really wanted to be measured against. I mean, if Jonathan had seen me before I'd had my magic coffee remedy, he'd know that my real natural morning state could frighten unsuspecting pensioners into thinking the Grim Reaper was near.

But Jonathan had spotted my shopping. 'Hey! You picked up the scandal rags? Homesick for celebrities falling out of nightclubs and showing their panties? C'mon, let's see. You want more coffee? Here, let me get you some.'

I gave him the *New York Post*, while I flicked through *Star* magazine, and we shovelled up our granola contentedly.

I paused, as the comforting warmth of solid food spread over me. This was what I'd come over for, I thought happily. Little moments like this, sharing breakfast with the Man I Loved. I wasn't saying that the expensive dinners and armfuls of roses weren't amazing, but it was the small intimacies, seeing how clinically Jonathan spread butter on his bagel, how he dissolved exactly half a lump of sugar in his espresso, that—

'Oh ho, Melissa!' said Jonathan suddenly, peering up over the paper with a mock-disapproving look on his face. Or was it real disapproval? It was so hard to tell. 'Oh dear, oh dear, oh dear.'

'What?' I put my coffee cup down. 'Oh, God, it's not Allegra, is it? Tell me it's nothing to do with her court case.'

Jonathan looked puzzled. 'Why would anyone care about Allegra? No, it's that *friend* of yours.'

'Which friend? Not Nelson?'

Jonathan pretended to look disapproving. 'No. Your ex.'

'*Orlando?*' I spluttered.

He frowned. 'Who?'

'Let me see,' I said, pulling the paper off him.

To my horror, on page six, there was a blurry shot of Ric pounding Angry Dog Man, with a large black Letterbox of Privacy over his eyes.

My flowered cotton dress, meanwhile, was clearly visible in the background, accessorised with a retractable dog lead and no dog. I looked shocked, and rather stupid. Well, the portion of my face that my hat wasn't concealing looked shocked. Thank heavens for small mercies.

Gosh. There really was quite a lot of that skirt. Angry Dog Man might have had a point about the size of my rear end.

'Oh, it's *Godric*,' I exclaimed. 'I thought . . .' I trailed off as the full implications rolled over my brain like molten tarmac.

Godric. Oh, hell.

'"Which rising Hollywood star-to-be was seeing stars in Central Park yesterday morning?"' Jonathan read aloud. '"His agent, noted industry tigress, Paige Drogan, was quick to leap to the hot-headed hot-shot's defence.

'As I understand it, there was a lady's honour at stake and my client isn't ashamed of his good old-fashioned English manners.'"' He looked up. 'That is Ric Spencer, right?'

'Um, yes,' I said uncomfortably.

'Wow. We're Page Six celebrities once removed! "The British bruiser refused to identify the lady in question,"' Jonathan read on, '"but we'd love to know what the unfortunate dog-lover said to offend him quite so much."' His voice slowed down and he raised his eyes from the paper. 'Melissa, that's *you* in the background, isn't it? That's the dress you were wearing yesterday.'

I drew in a deep breath. There really wasn't any point in lying; after all, hadn't I told Jonathan where I'd been?

'It is, yes,' I admitted. 'It happened while we were doing that photoshoot I was telling you about.'

'So why didn't you mention the punch-up last night? And the cameras? And the noted industry tigress?'

My stomach tightened with tension, and, even though I had absolutely no reason to, I felt terribly guilty all of a sudden.

'Oh, God, because it was all so embarrassing, and we were having such a lovely dinner! I didn't want you to worry about it, and I thought I'd managed to convince the photographer that it was a silly misunderstanding, and . . .' I spread my hands. 'What can I say? I felt ridiculous. I hoped it would blow over.'

Jonathan opened his mouth to speak, then closed it again. 'Don't keep secrets from me,' he said.

'It's not a secret!' I protested. 'I told you I was meeting Godric yesterday.'

'You didn't say you were going to end up in the *Post*.'

'How could I?' I objected. 'I had no idea! You think I wanted that to happen? I . . . I'm *mortified*.'

And I *was* mortified too. That was truly appalling publicity to get a rising Hollywood star, especially one who was meant to have impeccable manners. Paige would be incandescent, and quite rightly so.

'Mortified, why?' said Jonathan coolly.

'Because I was meant to be keeping an eye on him, and he ends up in the papers!' I said without thinking.

He gave me a level stare. 'Not because my friends might see this and wonder what you're doing being defended by another man? A good-looking Hollywood actor man?'

'No!'

'Oh, yeah, I forgot. Who just happens to be an ex-boyfriend of yours?'

Jonathan said all this in a very light adult way, but I could tell from his face that he wasn't entirely joking.

'Oh, don't be so silly!' I burst out. 'He's not an *ex*! We had a brief snog, in a *cupboard*, when we were both at school! That's years ago! Anyway, I made sure no one knew who I was and everyone knows I'm with you. Why on earth would I be . . .' I trailed off. It was just too obvious for words, surely?

Jonathan sighed. 'Melissa, tell me the truth. Has Paige hired you to pretend to be this jerk's girlfriend? Because I can kind of understand why he might have trouble getting a real one.'

'No!' I insisted. 'Jonathan, I gave you my word that I'd never do that again. All that is absolutely, definitively in the past. Paige just wants someone to act as a sort of . . . manners coach for Godric.'

A thick silence fell over the kitchen table.

'And that is all,' I added aloud.

'I don't mean to get heavy with you here.' Jonathan looked wounded, but patient. 'But I've been meaning to say this to you for a while. You might not think you're putting on a wig and pretending to be *Ric's girlfriend*, but, as far as I'm concerned, there's not much difference. I know you. You get *involved* with these guys. You *care* about them. And . . . I don't know. I worry about people taking advantage.' He hesitated, seeing me bridle.

'And call me a jealous, mean, possessive boyfriend,' Jonathan went on quickly, 'but I only want you caring and getting involved with *me*. You want to advise Agnetha on her tea parties, or run seminars for ladies about how to organise wedding showers, that's fine. Go ahead. But do me a favour and leave the guys out of it?'

'But it's not *like* that!' I said. 'If Godric was a useless, rude woman who needed some help presenting herself, would you still have a problem with my helping out?'

Jonathan thought. 'I don't know. I think women are just as capable of forming crushes on you as men are, to be frank.' He cut me a teasing look.

'I don't think so,' I said haughtily. 'You're moving the goalposts.'

'Is that a fact? How far do you think your goalposts could move?' He lifted an eyebrow and I had to look down into my granola to retain my haughtiness.

OK. So, it was his house. I was in his country. They were his friends, and he did have a position to keep up. It wouldn't do the whole Cindy situation any good if I kept being photographed with Godric.

What I did in London though was definitely my own business.

'Fine,' I said. 'I'll talk to Paige and tell her I can't see Godric again. But honestly, Jonathan, you're so wrong about Godric. He's not a sex symbol at all. He's just this hopelessly shy idiot, with a monobrow, who read too much Arthurian legend when he was young and thinks that women should—'

'Nu-uh!' said Jonathan, raising his finger to stop me. 'Don't tell me that. I want to go into the office today and tell everyone that my girlfriend is hanging with Ric Spencer!'

'Jonathan, I'd be surprised if they even know who he is.'

'They will now,' he said, tucking the paper into his briefcase. 'He's a hot-headed hot-shot from Hollywood.'

'He's a fat-headed fuck-wit from Fulham, more like.'

'Well, you are the hotline to the gossip, honey.'

I thought Jonathan had let it go, and I was pouring myself another coffee, when he added, as an afterthought, 'So what did this guy say about you? To get such a beating from a geek you kissed ten years ago?'

I looked up, startled. My hands were a little shaky from my hangover, and the coffee slopped into the china saucer.

Jonathan tipped his head to one side. 'I mean, the girls at work will need to know that.'

'The man made some personal remarks about my weight,' I said stiffly. 'And implied that Braveheart was out of control.'

'Well, he deserved all he got then,' said Jonathan. 'Right, I need to scoot. Give me a ring if you have coffee with any more Hollywood actors, yeah? Got to get my story straight for the reporters.' He paused. 'I intend to be a red-blooded realtor from . . .' His brow creased.

'We'll work on it,' I said.

When Jonathan had left, with me promising faithfully that I'd definitely get round to going to the Metropolitan

Museum of Art today, I readied myself for some quality grovelling.

In addition to rehearsing my apology to Paige for propelling her client into murky publicity waters, that involved ironing a proper dress, putting my hair in proper rollers, and finding some proper hosiery. I needed as much reinforcement as I could manage, and in times of crisis I'd always derived enormous support from knowing that I had the right shoes and underwear.

Jonathan's master bedroom was large and airy, and even though he was planning to have the whole thing redesigned to make maximum use of space, blah, blah, blah, walk-in closets, blah, blah, blah, I rather liked it as it was: bare floorboards with a huge brass bed in the middle, with a view of the leafy green tops of the trees outside, and the rich brown façades of the houses opposite.

I wasn't surprised to find he had a cleaner four days a week, even with the house in pre-decoration state, and I'd already invested an hour in 'making nice' with her and a box of fresh cinnamon doughnuts. Concetta told me some very shocking things about Jonathan's bathroom habits. Then again, a man as tidy and controlled as he was had to have some area of mess, I supposed.

Braveheart watched my preparations from the corner nearest the door and had the decency to remain silent throughout.

'Don't think you're off the hook,' I warned him, raising my finger. 'I might even take you with me. As evidence.'

He wagged his stumpy tail energetically, and sat down on my clean cardigan. Jonathan was surely impressed by Braveheart's new tricks, I told myself. At least there was one area I'd triumphed where Cindy had failed miserably.

As I was toying with the idea of a page-dog Braveheart

meekly trotting down the aisle at my bridal heel, he launched himself against the window in a fury of barking, and the two pigeons on the windowsill flew off vertically, leaving streaks of very obvious distress all over the window.

I sighed. That'd teach me to get ahead of myself.

We set off through Greenwich Village towards Paige's office – Braveheart on a very tight leash, and me taking care to walk in the shade so I didn't arrive feeling any more flustered than I already felt. The chess players were out in the park already, ignoring the NYU students streaming past, and the old lady who read tarot cards in a booth on Sullivan Street had one customer in, and one reading the paper outside.

I kept telling myself that I hadn't done anything wrong, but if I was being completely honest, there was a new small voice in my head, and it was more cross than anything else – cross that I hadn't contained the situation as well as I'd have liked. I hated that feeling of leaving a job half done.

Particularly when I knew I *could* have done it so much better. Had I been properly assigned to it. In my professional Honey Blennerhesket capacity.

I stopped outside Dean & Deluca's and looked at myself sternly in the glass. I saw a tallish, dark-haired girl in a tight-around-the-bosom vintage frock, gripping her handbag and frowning. Without thinking, I put a hand to my hair, and, for a second, wished I had my blonde wig to slip on. I knew where I was when Honey . . .

Melissa, I reminded myself. You're perfectly capable of dealing with this as *Melissa*. Honey is just a state of mind. That wig does not have magic powers. And Jonathan's right. Maybe it is time to stop blurring the lines in your life.

I pushed the frown out of my forehead with my spare hand. And before Braveheart could follow his twitching black nose into the deli, I swept us both off to Paige's office.

To my surprise, Braveheart was ushered in with great cooing and fussing and given a bowl of water by the receptionist, while I sat on the black leather sofa and ran through my apology again in my head. Not too effusive, I told myself. Retain pride. You weren't actually *told* what to do here.

'Melissa,' said Paige, shortly, appearing from nowhere.

'Hello, Paige,' I said, pulling myself together.

'Come in.' She nodded her head towards her office and we sat down.

'I won't take up too much of your time, Paige,' I started. 'I've come to apologise for the fiasco yesterday. It was entirely my fault – well, the fault of Jonathan's dog, which I know I should have had under proper control, but even so, Ric—'

'Melissa,' said Paige, holding up both her forefingers, then moving them from side to side, as if she were playing with an invisible cat's cradle. Then she pointed them at me. 'Stop you there.'

'Sorry,' I said, rather thrown by the fact that Paige didn't seem as raging mad as I'd expected.

'*I* should be apologising to *you*,' she began. 'In fact, I thought that's what you were here for! Let me assure you right now, that New York is not like this at all! What must you think of us, getting you into a fight in your first week in the city! Oh, my God!' she laughed. 'Isn't that just the most awful thing? I hope you haven't put that on your postcards home! Hi, Mom! Today I was nearly beaten up in Central Park and was rescued by a film star! Well, hey, come to think of it – maybe you should!'

'Um, actually, no,' I said. In my immediate mortification at the bad publicity, I hadn't even considered that I should have been angry about it. Still, it had been sort of my fault . . .

Paige leaned forward in her seat, as if we were suddenly old friends again. 'Ric is a tricky customer,' she said. 'Don't you think? But, you know, he's a genius, and sometimes you have to cut them a little slack. *However,* I can see we've got a problem here, and I'm asking you, as a fellow Brit – what can we do? What's the best way to help him out?'

I looked at Paige carefully. Obviously Godric still hadn't told her exactly how we knew each other. And I wasn't going to put her straight.

'I can see how he comes across badly,' I agreed. 'But he's really not as rude as he makes out, not intentionally. I mean, I think he's more . . . shy than anything else? Lacking in social confidence?'

'Like a rough diamond, you mean?' Paige looked eager for my opinion. I felt quite flattered. I'd got rather used to second-guessing how I was getting things wrong over here.

'Yes! I mean, does he have a girlfriend, for instance?' I paused. 'I'm not totally stupid, Paige. I know that if he did have a wife and two kids you might not want to make a big deal of it, but does he *have* a girlfriend?'

She hesitated. 'I get the feeling there was one, quite recently, back in England. He refuses to discuss his private life? Says it's none of my effing business.' She laughed hollowly. 'Ric! So discreet! But you know, you're right, he does need to be seen out and about with a smart girl.'

'Well, then.' I sank back in my chair, feeling vindicated. 'You just need to get him one, and you're away. She'll knock all this flouncing and showing-off on the head. No decent girl wants to be seen out and about with a man who insults everyone he meets.'

Paige seemed to think for a moment.

'Not that I'm offering to do *that*!' I added, without thinking. 'I've completely given *that* up for Lent!'

At once her eyebrows shot up and she leaned back in her seat.

Oops. That was a stupid thing to say. Given that Paige didn't know about my secret agency past, it must have sounded plain bizarre.

'So, er, I can only apologise for the fracas in the park,' I said hurriedly, 'but, ah . . .'

Paige said nothing but carried on staring at me, a smile on her lips, as if she were thinking hard about what to say next.

I faltered. It was very unsettling.

'I really hope it hasn't spoiled anything for Ric, and, um, I can give him some really excellent arnica cream for the bruising . . .'

'Melissa. Can I level with you?'

'Please do,' I said, already suspecting that this wouldn't be so much a levelling as a full-scale bulldozing.

'No, the incident in the park wasn't ideal. I mean, I can't pitch Ric as a charming English gentleman if he's got a black eye and a reputation for brawling, now, can I?'

She said this with a fabulously warm smile, as if she just couldn't stop seeing the funny side, and I found myself smiling back with relief.

'Well, no,' I agreed. 'But it does prove he didn't fib about any stage-fighting qualifications on his CV!'

Paige laughed. 'That's true!'

I didn't want to come straight out and say, 'So, you're not mad?' like a character in a Nancy Drew novel, because that was generally the point where my father dropped the bonhomie smokescreen and revealed his true frothing at the mouth. But I did sense that an early departure would be in my best interests.

'I mean, if there's anything I can do,' I said, with some relief, seeing the finishing line in sight, 'just let me know. I'll give you my number back in England.'

'Ah,' said Paige, sitting back up again. She jutted her lower lip cutely. 'Oh, no, we can't really leave a situation like this so long. Gotta move fast, know what I mean?' she said with an 'atta-girl!' thrust of her fist. 'I was kind of hoping you might be able to help me recoup a little ground now.'

'Now?'

'*Now*. The trick to being an agent is to work out what people want then give it to them,' she said. 'And if that fails, work out what you want them to want, then give them that.'

'Right . . .' I *really* wasn't following this.

'Listen, between you and me, Melissa, I've had two calls already this morning from casting directors who've never shown any interest in Ric whatsoever – until now. Go figure, huh? So, hey! Let's turn this negative into a positive!'

Light began to dawn, and I was fascinated, despite myself, by how pragmatically Paige was rebranding Ric before my very eyes. 'You want him to come across as a sort of *extreme* Mr Knightley?' I asked. 'Like, full-on chivalry – with fists?'

Paige paused. 'That might be kind of complex to get across. I'm thinking more . . . plain dangerous.'

'*What?*'

'Yup! Dangerous! Like one of those poets. A real actor, uncompromising, passionate, fiery . . .'

'Rude?' I suggested sarcastically.

'Yup, rude,' agreed Paige. 'Rude, surly, mean, a guy who's seen it all, the mean streets of London, England. Like – ah, Guy Ritchie!'

'Paige,' I said, trying to think of a nice way to put it. 'Guy Ritchie isn't exactly from the wrong side of the tracks. His mother goes to the same hairdresser as mine.'

'Chuch!' Paige flapped her hands. 'We don't need to know that! I just want Ric to be dangerous, but mannerly at the same time!'

I racked my brains for a comparison. 'Like . . . um . . .'

'Yeah . . . like . . . um . . .' Paige pressed her lips together, then pointed at me. 'Like no one! He's a one-off. That's the whole point. He's Colin Farrell meets . . .'

'Harold Shipman?'

'Excuse me?'

I sighed. 'English joke. Look, Paige, that sounds amazing. Best of luck!'

'Melissa, I need you.' She looked at me with serious eyes. 'I need you to help me with this.'

'No, no,' I said, but already she was reeling me in. I could feel it.

'Wouldn't you love to be involved with something so exciting? I mean, you know this guy! Don't you think you're already invested? And, God, don't you want to help out a . . . *friend* at a really crucial time in his career?' Paige had dropped her voice to a sort of hypnotic sing-song monotone, and although she was asking questions, she wasn't exactly leaving space for answers.

'Oh, I barely know Ric, really,' I tried, but she was rolling on, eyes sparkling.

'Hey, I know you're on *vacation* and everything, but what kind of agent would I be if I didn't grab skills like yours when they come along? I mean, wouldn't you say you have a great understanding of how men should present themselves? And isn't this just a once-in-a-life-time challenge for you? And we can make it totally worth your while in terms of financial compensation, if you know what I'm saying here. Melissa, I have to tell you, on a purely personal note, I just love the way you behave with those cute old-fashioned manners' – she wagged her finger at me jokily – 'I hear all your thank-you letters are right up to date with Bonnie and the girls!'

I gaped. How did she know that? And if she knew, did Cindy know too?

'You have so much to share with Ric on that score. So what I'm saying, I guess, is that, just for a little while, if you could just be there with him when I can't be, just steer him round. I mean, I can tell how great you are with tricky situations!'

'But, Paige, I'm only here for—'

She opened her eyes, until they were huge and babyish. 'It's only for when I can't make it. I may never have to call! Can we just play it by ear?'

Jonathan would freak out.

'Jonathan will freak out,' I said firmly.

'Is he in *charge* of you?' she scoffed. 'I know what men can be like! And Jonathan's bark's much worse than his bite. Why not just tell him you're seeing a friend? Come *on*! He's probably secretly really proud of what you can do. He's always telling people what a star you are.'

'You think?' I said uncertainly. I couldn't quite get used to the fact that these people had all known Jonathan much longer than I had. Besides, the teeny amount I was seeing of him during the day meant that I could practically rehearse the Ring Cycle with Godric and he'd never know.

'Sure!' The waggy finger again. 'He *loves* women who can do their own thing. Independence, you know? It's the secret of healthy relationships. But to be serious a second, Melissa, you know what? I think it was fate that we bumped into each other at that party? Let's not laugh in the face of fate. Ric needs you right now. I need you. And it could really be the start of something for you too.'

Finally she stopped, tilting her head to one side, like a little bird, to let me respond.

Oh, *God.* Maybe I did owe Godric a favour for getting me out of that awful fight in the park. And I did feel a certain patriotic responsibility to arm him with at least a few useful social hints and tips. I really should have sorted him out when I had the chance, backstage at St Cathal's Bicentennial Memorial Hall.

'OK,' I said firmly. 'But you must understand that Jonathan's privacy comes way before Godric's reputation.' I paused to let it sink in, and gave her a diluted version of the Look. 'Way before.'

'I understand completely,' she said, and gave me a smile that reminded me uncomfortably of Allegra.

13

As the week went on, I had more and more calls at random hours from Gabi and Allegra, both bitching about each other, or asking disturbingly obvious questions. 'Is a waxing voucher an acceptable wedding gift?' 'Can step-cousins marry?' 'Who refills the petty cash box?' That sort of thing. Despite my repeated promises to Jonathan that, yes, I was keeping the office at arm's length, I found myself breaking my resolve to step away from the drama.

If I'm being completely honest, one morning I snuck out of bed at 4.30 a.m., just to phone the office to see if they were there – at 9.30 a.m. English time.

They weren't.

They weren't there at 5 a.m/10 a.m., either, but I couldn't keep checking after that, because Jonathan got up at 5.30 a.m. most mornings, and I didn't want him to find me snoring over my mobile at the kitchen table, listening to my own outgoing message.

I also didn't mention to Jonathan that I'd done a couple of discreet trips around Banana Republic for one Ollie Ross, a client who claimed normal shirts gave him 'gibbon shoulders', and that I'd Fedexed a whole box of dental hygiene products back to the office for tactful distribution. However, in the interests of making Jonathan's friends my friends, a task I was setting my mind to, no matter how awkward it made me feel, I did tell him I'd spent a fascinating hour pumping Bonnie for American business etiquette advice for my father.

Naturally, Jonathan was happy enough for me to be doing *that*, even if he did sound rather dubious.

'You sure this isn't just . . . busy work?' he asked one morning, looking over my notes. 'Your dad really needs to know how to greet an . . .' He peered at the paper. 'An Uzbeki divorcee?'

'Of course he does,' I replied, snatching it off him. 'Don't be so cynical.'

I wasn't sure what busy work was, but it sounded like one of Jonathan's technical office terms, and I didn't want to appear any less professional than I already did in New York. Anyway, it *was* keeping me busy. I'd emailed Daddy several reams of notes, but so far he hadn't got back to me on them, merely reminding me to invoice him so he could clear it with the Olympic people

I had plenty of time to be busy on my own, since Jonathan's insane schedule seemed to have redoubled even since I'd arrived. He'd stopped promising to try to make lunch, and since the day I'd turned up at his office, having teetered up Fifth Avenue in peep-toe sandals, weaving under the weight of a full picnic basket (inc. glasses and linen), only to have Lori confess guiltily that he was 'out with a client' when he'd promised he'd be free, I'd stopped hoping he'd offer.

Though I didn't like to say anything, I also had the distinct impression that some of the furrows on his brow were being caused by his own personal sale – his and Cindy's old apartment. He brushed off any polite enquiries about how it was going with a 'let's not bring that problem into *this* house', but I'd heard him outside one evening on his mobile, yelling and kicking the iron railings in a most un-Jonathan-like fashion.

So, no, all in all, I wasn't getting quite the 'us time' I'd hoped for. But I couldn't help being touched by the ways Jonathan tried to make up for it. He tried to stay awake long enough in the evenings to take me on romantic evening sightseeing buses, but fell asleep on my shoulder halfway round. He sent me texts, reminding me he was thinking about me with complete punctuation. Every morning at about ten thirty Lori would phone up, and ask if there was anything she could arrange for me, and every day I'd feel terrible about saying, no, I was fine. Then, when I put the phone down, I'd worry what sort of gift I should send her when I left. The American etiquette guides were turning me very paranoid.

'Darling, are you sure you're doing everything you want to?' he asked one night, while we were eating spaghetti in some little Italian place down the road. 'Can I get you into any museums? I'm arranging a fundraiser at the Met right now – you'd love that place.'

I didn't want to tell him that I was just as happy absorbing New York through the medium of coffee and eavesdropping. It made me sound rather shallow. 'The Met's next on my list, honest. But, you know,' I said hesitantly, 'it's so much nicer when you're with me.'

'Really?' A surprised sort of pleasure spread across his weary face, and the worry lines faded around his mouth. In the dim light, he suddenly looked about ten years younger.

I fought an instinct to lean over and press his head maternally to my comforting bosom.

'Course.' I smiled. 'I'd be happy just to sit in the park

and feed the ducks as long as you were with me. You'd
have to bring the bread, mind you. A girl has standards.'

He reached across the table and took my hands,
sending shivers up my wrists and into my heart. I stroked
the calloused patches from where he went on the rowing
machine at the gym. Hand cream. I could get some from
Kiehl's that wouldn't look girlie.

'Melissa,' he began. 'I'm sorry I've not been around.
It's just that work . . . it's crazy at the moment. And then
there's . . .'

I slid my fingers between his so our hands criss-crossed
tightly. 'Don't. You're here now. We're having a lovely
dinner, candles, wine . . .' I nodded my head towards the
room in general. I'd picked this place over the more fashionable suggestions Lori had made, just so we could hold
hands and not spend an hour getting ready to go out. 'I
flew over to be with you. I'm not so bothered about anything else.' I dropped my voice. 'And I like places where
I can slip my shoes off.'

There was a brief scuffling beneath the table, and then
I felt something nudge my toes. It was Jonathan's foot.
I could feel his silk socks against my bare skin.

Mmm.

'Well, OK,' he said, his face giving no hint of the
journey my foot was now making up his inner calf. 'In
that case, let me make some arrangements.'

Two days later, he brought me breakfast in bed, and
announced he had Big News.

'Now, I hope you don't have any plans set for today,
because I'm taking the afternoon off,' said Jonathan, and
raised his eyebrows to indicate that I should make some
appreciative gesture.

'I should think so too. What's the point of being in charge if you can't take the afternoon off?' I glared at Braveheart, who was trying to slink onto the bed, and he scuttled off to his basket in the corner of the room.

'Now, *there* you've got the difference between English managers and American ones,' he sighed. 'Unhappily, I don't have a PA like Gabi to make up dental appointments in Harley Street that take three and a half hours of Friday afternoon. After lunch.'

I gasped on her behalf. 'I'm sure she doesn't . . .'

'Oh, Melissa.' He wagged his spoon at me. 'That's why I put Patrice in charge of that office. Nothing gets past her. She is a New Yorker. She doesn't give a damn about test matches but she knows exactly when they are.'

'Well, I'm glad you're taking time off,' I said, moving on swiftly. 'What do you have planned?'

'It's a surprise!' Jonathan beamed with pleasure. 'You have to meet me outside the Met at one thirty.'

'We're going to the Met?'

'No! Much better than that. Although nothing is nicer than the Met,' he added quickly.

'Oh no,' I agreed, so as not to look ignorant. 'Should I wear anything in particular?'

'Nope.' He finished off his strong coffee, then winked. 'Just your very nicest . . .' He opened his mouth then stopped himself. 'Summer dress,' he finished instead.

'Well, of course I'll wear a summer dress,' I said, confused. Sometimes it felt like there was a whole other FM station of innuendo that I simply couldn't pick up with my poor AM brain. 'What else would I wear?'

Jonathan flashed me a wicked look and shoved a stack of papers into his briefcase. 'It's not so much the dress as the . . . Oh, never mind.' He dropped a kiss on my head. 'Don't get into trouble, and I'll see you later.'

I spent the morning in the deli on the corner, dutifully writing my postcards. They were pretty much the same to everyone: 'Having a fantastic time! Seen the Empire State Building and been personally shopped at Bloomingdales. Am meeting lots of Jonathan's friends, who are all very interesting!'

On Emery's card, I added that I'd bumped into Godric, who was now a real actor; on my granny's card, I added that we'd had cocktails at the Algonquin.

I waggled my fountain pen and frowned. The morning coffee hadn't worked its usual magic on me, and an odd sense of malaise was hanging over my chest. A sort of . . . flatness. I shook myself. It was probably jet-lag catching up with me.

And a spot of loneliness. Braveheart was with the walker this morning, and he was my only real daytime companion. It wasn't like I'd expected to be swept off into a cheery round of *Desperate Housewives*-style coffee mornings with Jonathan's female friends, but even so . . .

I grabbed my mobile off the table, and dialled the office. Nothing like some displacement worries to get rid of pretend ones.

It rang a disconcerting twelve times before they answered.

'Hello, the Little Ladies?' gabbled someone eating a croissant or similar.

'The Little Lady *Agency*, Gabi,' I reminded her tersely.

'What? Oh, er, hello, Mel.' There was the sound of shuffling and hasty throat-clearing. The faint hum of Radio One also vanished. 'How are you?'

'Oh, fine. Fine! I'm just having an iced latte in a lovely deli in Greenwich Village,' I said airily. 'Just . . . writing my postcards and . . . relaxing.'

'God, you are *so* lucky,' said Gabi enviously. 'And I suppose Dr No's going to be taking you out for dinner later and generally lavishing you with gifts?'

'Um, yes.' I beamed. Coming from Gabi it sounded much better than it had on my postcards. 'He is, actually. We're having a surprise this afternoon.'

'Has he had your wardrobe restyled for New York yet?' she enquired. 'Has he put a GPS on your handbag so you can't get lost in the big city?'

'What?' Was *that* how Jonathan knew about Hughy's dental appointments?

'He's done that on the London agents, you know. Put GPS on their briefcases so Patrice knows when they're working and when they're in the Slug & Lettuce. Came in handy when Hughy left his briefcase on the train. We watched it go all the way back to Pershore on Patrice's little screen.'

'Gabi, he hasn't put GPS on me,' I said, ignoring the bit about the wardrobe revamping. That had been a gift, hadn't it? 'He's . . . very busy, though.'

'Busier than he is in London?'

'Yes,' I said, and was surprised to hear how small my voice went.

'Blimey. Still, I suppose he doesn't have the expert back-up that he does here.'

I bit my lip. That wasn't what I'd wanted her to say.

'How are things in the office?' I asked quickly.

'Oh, fine.'

'Just fine?'

'When Allegra's not here, things are fine,' said Gabi

tightly. 'When she's here, things are . . . less fine, but fortunately she's only here about ten minutes a day, so it's surprisingly manageable.'

Before I could probe that worrying statement more carefully, Gabi went on, 'Listen, Mel, don't mean to be rude, but I'm expecting a call, so can I get back to you?'

'Ship to shore, is it?' I joked, but a lead weight plummeted in my stomach at the thought of Gabi and Nelson. That was seriously romantic. At least it was an ocean keeping them apart, not an appointments diary. I shoved that thought aside as totally unworthy.

'Sorry?'

'Nelson? How's he getting on? Have you spoken to him recently?'

'Oh, er. No. I haven't. He told me not to ring him unless something burned down or blew up.' She sighed. 'It's historically accurate, apparently. I can write to him if I want to, but he's not sure when he'd get the letter.'

'Oh,' I said, mindful of the mobile number he'd given me. Thinking about Nelson really made me want to talk to him. He'd blow away this funny mood with some of his patented Dial-a-dad ranting. 'And the flat? How's that going?'

'It's fine. They've got the carpets up. Listen, Mel, can I call you back? I, um, I don't want to miss this call. It's about . . . the, er, weekend.'

'Right-o,' I said, somewhat bemused, but she'd put the phone down before I could move onto pleasantries.

I checked my watch. Quarter to twelve. What time would it be with Nelson? I opened my diary to the page where I'd written down his secret mobile number, but before I could dial it, something stopped me.

I told myself it was because I didn't want to disturb

him in the middle of a reef-knot masterclass, but I wasn't so sure I was being completely honest with myself.

It felt wrong, calling him if Gabi didn't even know about his mobile number. And there was something else too.

I started forlornly at my empty iced latte glass. I didn't even like iced lattes. That was another blow. They looked so yummy in Dean & Deluca.

My mobile buzzed on the table, and I picked it up with a rush of delight, spotting the New York number on the display. I did have friends here!

'Hello, Ms Romney-Jones?'

'Yes, it is!' I said. 'Hello!'

'This is Yolanda at Park Avenue Pooches. We have Braveheart washed, walked and ready for collection!'

'Thanks!' I said hollowly. 'I'm on my way.'

A gleaming Braveheart and I arrived at the steps of the Met at one thirty on the dot, but there was no sign of Jonathan among the crowds of tourists milling around.

The sun was scorching hot, so I sat down on the steps in a small patch of shade, arranged my full cotton skirt so my knickers weren't on show, and waited for him. Braveheart sat at my feet and panted, lolling his big white fluffy head. I scratched him behind the ears and he made an appreciative growling noise.

Jonathan still hadn't appeared by quarter to. It was very unlike him to be so late and not call, I thought, checking my phone in case he'd left a message. But he hadn't.

As I was looking at it, a text arrived with an incongruously English doorbell noise. A couple of tourists looked round, startled.

'Where best place emergency lawyer?'

It was from Allegra. Since she was already lawyered up to the gills with the finest nitpickers money could buy, I assumed it was a query on behalf of a client, possibly one who'd done something too humiliating to run past the family solicitor. I texted her the details of a friend of Nelson's, who specialised in getting dodgy solicitors off the hook, then resumed my scanning of the crowd for Jonathan's red hair.

The phone ding-donged again.

'Not big enough. Need QC.'

Crikey. It must be serious. I was texting Allegra with firm instructions that it wasn't her job to start initiating legal proceedings or egging anyone else on into complicated libel suits, when the phone rang.

'Hello, Melissa? It's Lori? From Mr Riley's office?'

'Hello, Lori,' I said. 'Are you calling to tell me Jonathan's in a meeting?'

'How did you know?' she asked, very seriously. 'I am. He's in conference with . . .' She hesitated. 'With a client, and he's just called me to say he can't get away? He's very sorry, and has asked me to send you a car? It should be with you . . . now.'

I looked up, and indeed there was a black Lincoln Continental on the other side of the road, complete with driver looking up and down the pavement.

'I can see it.' I hauled myself to my feet. Braveheart woke up with a snort of disgust and started truffling about in my bag for food.

'Ah-ah!' I said sharply.

'I'm sorry?'

'Just the dog, sorry. Not you.' After a moment's token resistance, Braveheart followed me on his lead and we both trotted down the steps. 'When does Jonathan think he'll be finished?'

'He'll be there as soon as he can? He's really sorry? I've given the driver directions and a map for you?'

I established that it was in fact my car and got into the back as the driver held the door for me. Braveheart initially refused to get in, and when the man tried to lift him up, he went to nip his hand.

'No!' I said, with a firm glare. 'Bad!' Honestly, up until now he'd been so good. Then again, I was pretty foul in hot weather myself. If it wasn't for the fact that I knew Jonathan loved me in this huge-skirted frock, I'd have resorted to my faithful linen trousers, and hang the fact that they made my bum look the size of a wide-screen telly.

'I'm sorry?' Lori sounded shocked. 'It's an unavoidable delay, I'm afraid, and he really is making every effort to be with you as soon as he can.'

'No, no,' I apologised. 'Just the dog again!' I made it clear to Braveheart that he wouldn't be joining me on the leather seats. 'Um, well, if you could thank Jonathan for the car, and let him know that I'm happy to wait, that would be kind.'

'I certainly will,' said Lori. 'Please call me if you need anything.'

Is he with Cindy? I wanted to ask, but I bit my tongue, and sat back so I could gaze out of the window. I wondered where we were going – Jonathan hadn't said.

If he was with her, then he really *wouldn't* want to tell me where he was then. And yet she was getting priority over our lunch date . . .

Now, come on, I tried to tell myself. She's a *client*.

Like Jonathan used to be *your* client? the idle voices went on.

'No!' I said aloud, so forcefully that Braveheart looked up, unaware of what he'd done now.

I scratched his ears in apology. These idle voices weren't so idle today. They were positively queueing up with unpleasant thoughts.

We'd only gone a few blocks when the car pulled up and the driver got out to open my door again.

'Central Park, ma'am,' he said. 'I was told to direct you to the boathouse?'

Jonathan had sent a car to drive me just a few blocks to Central Park? I got out, feeling embarrassed.

'I could have walked!' I said to the driver. 'Honestly!'

But he just smiled politely and gave me a map of the park, prepared by Lori, with directions printed out to the Loeb Boathouse.

Choosing as much shade as we could, Braveheart and I strolled through the park to the beautiful boathouse, where I ordered a pot of tea for myself in the restaurant, and a bowl of water for him. And we waited for Jonathan.

And waited.

And waited.

We waited so long that I'd made a fresh list of to-dos, jotted down some new ideas for the agency, filed my nails, sent three texts to Gabi insisting that she find out what on earth Allegra needed legal recommendations for, drunk two pots of tea and made so many notes in my little book that the waiting staff were probably starting to mutter among themselves about restaurant inspectors.

Every thirty minutes or so, I'd get a call from poor Lori, apologising for the delay and even though I assured her that I was having a lovely time just people-watching,

I couldn't help feeling tetchy. Then cross, then hurt, then plain worried.

In the end, I caved in and phoned Gabi.

'Is it, er, unreasonable to call the police if your date is two and a half hours late?' I asked.

'Depends where your date's meant to be,' she said. From the sound of the background noise, she was in a bar. A bar where people were laughing and getting drunk.

'He's out with a client,' I quavered. 'Lori won't tell me anything more than that.'

'Cindy?' said Gabi immediately.

'I don't know!' I felt sick.

'You think she's stabbed him in their empty apartment and set fire to the evidence? Or that he's stabbed *her* and is clinically dismembering the corpse and constructing a watertight alibi based on train times?'

'Gabi! That's not helping!'

I could hear her giggling. And I could also hear *male* giggling. I heard her say, muffled, 'It's Mel. Yeah, he's stood her up. I *know*!'

'Who are you with?' I demanded. 'And where are you?'

'I'm in Hush,' she giggled, then went as serious as she could after, I estimated, three cocktails. 'Look, take Auntie Gabi's advice and go home. That'll teach him to leave you hanging around. He's an idiot. No man should keep you waiting, Mel, specially one as lucky to have you as he is. Dr No needs to learn to get his priorities straight.'

Her voice was rising in a bit of a tirade, but at that point I spotted Jonathan's red hair glinting in the sun as he jogged rather awkwardly down the path, and I rose to make sure it was him.

'Gabi! It's OK! I can see him. Call you later!' I said, hanging up as quickly as I could.

Braveheart confirmed that it was Jonathan with an attention-seeking volley of yapping.

'Shh!' I hissed to him, as heads turned. 'Don't look so *keen.*'

Jonathan bounded up to my table and leaned on it, breathing heavily. It only took him a few moments to get his breath back; he did, after all, play competitive racquet sports three times a week.

'Hello, darling,' I said, biting back the urge to say, 'Have you been with Cindy?'

'Melissa, I can't apologise enough,' he said, wiping the back of his hand across his pale brow, now flushed with heat and exertion. Possibly a touch of mortification too. 'You must be seriously razzed. I've been trying to get away for the last ninety minutes, but it was just impossible. I am *so* sorry.'

'It's fine,' I said, surprised at how calm I sounded. 'Lori kept me up to date with your progress. She might as well have played "Greensleeves" at me, and told me my call was important to her, though.'

'I'm sorry?'

'Forget it. You're here now.'

I was smiling sunnily, but my panic was simmering into crossness. If I'd kept him waiting because I was at work, he'd probably have played his 'who comes first?' hurt card and cancelled me until I was ready. In fact, hadn't he made a huge deal about how I couldn't work while I was in New York, because I was here to see *him*?

'You brought the dog?' he asked quizzically. 'Thought we established that he wasn't safe in parks?'

'Of course.' I fondled Braveheart's white ears. 'A dog isn't an *accessory*. It's a part of the family. If you want him to behave well, you have to show him, not just bring him out of the doggy nursery when you feel like looking like a dog-owner.'

'OK, OK,' he said, regarding Braveheart with suspicion. 'But tell him to behave.'

'You tell him.'

'I don't think he gets my accent,' said Jonathan. 'That or he just doesn't like sharing you with me.'

I looked up, straight into Jonathan's eyes. 'Well, these days I see much more of him than I do of you.'

Jonathan bit his lower lip and looked guilty. He shoved a hand through his hair, messing up the neatly gelled waves. 'Guess I deserved that.'

'Kind of. But you're here now, so let's enjoy this glorious afternoon,' I said, getting to my feet. 'Where are we going?'

He offered his arm for me to take. 'The plan was to walk romantically through the park until we chanced upon the boating lake, then you were going to be all amazed at the beautiful lake in the middle of the city, and I was going to suggest going for a row in one of the boats.' He smiled wryly. 'That was the plan, anyway.'

Poor Jonathan. I knew how he felt about his plans.

I'm arm-in-arm with the man of my dreams, the sun is shining and getting less hot by the moment, and I'm wearing a dress that makes me feel like Gina Lollobrigida, I told myself. There is no point in spoiling that combination of positive things by being moody. None at all.

'Oh, look!' I gasped, turning in pretend surprise at the lake, then turning back to him. 'Jonathan! I never knew there was this great big *pond* in the middle of New York City!'

'No?' he replied, playing along. 'Do you want to go for a turn around the lake?'

'I certainly would,' I said, allowing him to lead off towards the hiring hut.

Jonathan let me pick out the boat, helped me and Braveheart in, then rowed us out into the middle of the lake with long, sure strokes.

'I used to row at Princeton,' he explained unnecessarily as we cruised past less professionally manned craft. 'Made the first boat for a season.'

I made appreciative noises. Rowers, in my experience, were disturbing. They had a bloody-mindedness rarely achieved by rugby players, and barely even understood by cricketers. Cricket might be a little complicated, but at least it had the virtue of being arranged around food and drink breaks. Rowing was just shouting and pain barriers and eight men thinking as one.

'I can row too,' I said, not wanting to sound weedy. 'Not like, *boat race* rowing, though. Dinghies, like these. Nelson taught me to row his inflatable, when we were out sailing.'

'Really?' Jonathan feathered a little, to manoeuvre round another couple, then let us drift gently to a halt.

'Mmm. Mainly so he could stay aboard and shout while Roger and I went ashore for supplies, I think.'

'Well, you can row us back.'

'Erm . . . OK.' We should probably set off in about ten minutes then, I thought, but didn't say anything.

With an easy gesture, Jonathan pulled in his oars, and reached for his briefcase. He gave Braveheart a nervous glance. 'Do I have to tell you how nervous I am about that hell-hound being in this boat with us, on a lake, when I'm trying to impress you with my casual native New Yorker thing?'

Braveheart looked up from the wooden floor, where he was lying as if butter wouldn't melt.

'He'll be fine.' Actually, I had the feeling he was scared. I stroked his ears again and felt him trembling slightly. 'He's not so naughty these days, are you? No. You're Melissa's little chap.'

'If you say so. Now then.' Jonathan triumphantly produced two champagne flutes, and a chilled bottle of champagne and set them on the spare seat. 'Somewhere, in the middle of town, there is a Zabar's hamper, in a taxi, going round and round trying to find me. I hope Lori's caught up with it and taken it home. This is all I could fit in my briefcase. I hope you don't mind drinking on an empty stomach?'

I was charmed. 'Not in the slightest! That's just lovely.'

And it was lovely too. The sun was fading gently in the sky and dancing on the ripples made by other, distant boats. It felt a little cooler in the park, and I could see the very tops of the ornate apartment buildings on the Upper West Side rising gracefully above the green trees, but there were no grating sounds of traffic, just faint splashes and birdsong.

'Thank you,' I said, as Jonathan handed me a flute. It was still so cold that beads of moisture clung around the glass.

'Flutes, yes?' he said, with a raised eyebrow. 'You see? I listen to your improving words.'

I smiled, as a warm glow spread through me. God, it was so nice to have in-jokes that didn't involve me falling over something or being shown up by a family member. He was talking about the party where we met: the welcome party I threw at Dean & Daniels. I told him his fountain of champagne saucers was tacky, and amazingly, from that choice piece of snobbery, he decided to hire me as his pretend girlfriend.

'You know, it's exactly fifteen months since we met,' he said, gently chinking his glass against mine. 'That was the first thing you taught me, and I haven't stopped learning since. To you.'

'Oh, no . . .' I demurred, chinking my glass and leaning forward to let him tip up my chin with his finger, and kiss me very gently on the lips. He couldn't really kiss me any more energetically anyway, on account of the boat and the glasses, but it was quite a sexy kiss all the same.

'What have I got to teach you?' I sighed, leaning back and admiring him in his neatly rolled shirt-sleeves. 'You don't need fixing up. You don't need telling where to buy decent shoes. You don't need to be told not to take a girl to an all-you-can-eat restaurant.' I smiled, drunk on a moment of pure happiness. 'I mean, look at you. You don't need someone holding your hand while you buy a fabulous suit like that, do you?'

'Well, I do have a good tailor.' Jonathan sipped his champagne. 'And I get help from the shopper when I go to Saks.'

'But that's the point,' I said euphorically. 'You go to Saks! You don't just go to TK Maxx and pull out things at random! Besides,' I added, 'you always look immaculate. Even Gabi can't fault your wardrobe.'

'Well, if *Gabi* says so . . .' Jonathan's mouth twitched in amusement. 'If she spends half the time shopping at weekends as she does online from the office she ought to know.'

I blanched.

'But honestly,' he went on, 'it's all an elaborate screen

for my inner slob. I mean, I'd be happy for you to come shopping with me, pick out a few things you think I'd look good in.'

'Oh no!' I said, scrunching up my nose. 'You don't need me for that! You just carry on with your own marvellous taste.'

He pulled a face. 'I mean it, Melissa. I'm not really as organised as you think, honey. You're the organiser.'

'Darling, if you want to think that, it's fine with me,' I said, stretching out my white legs in the last of the sunshine. My 'organisation' was born from panic and an addiction to Smythson's delicious leather-bound planners. Jonathan's was too precise to be anything other than pure instinct.

Braveheart was asleep, his nose on his paws, worn out by his walk through the park. His granddad-white eyebrows flickered as he slept, as if he were chasing other dogs in his sleep, now I'd almost stopped him doing it in real life.

'There's a dog who knows how to relax,' observed Jonathan.

'Yes, well, you should take some tips.' I looked up at Jonathan before he could set off apologising again. 'I'm not cross about waiting, Jonathan, but you had the afternoon off. You *have* to take time off. How else will they understand how much they really need you?'

He sighed. 'Look, I know. I *know*. You don't need to tell me. You think I'd rather be at work when I could be here with you? Huh? But things are really frantic at work right now, and I need to prove myself, what with the promotion and everything.'

'But you did!' I goggled at him. 'You flew back from London, you're working all hours. What more do they need you to do?'

'Justify my salary, I guess.' He raked a hand through his hair. 'We're a big firm, sure, but real estate is a small pool at the top. I know Lisa is lining me up to take over, not now, maybe not for five years, but there's only one other guy between me and her. And she owns the whole business, all sixty offices. *And* the ones in London. *And* Chicago. *And* LA. And between you and me, we're looking into buying a Parisian operation too, so . . .' He shrugged again, but there was a flash of panic behind his studied nonchalance. 'I can't screw up.'

'You won't,' I said, patting his leg reassuringly. 'But, honestly, darling, you need the odd afternoon off. I don't want you having a heart attack or getting high blood pressure.' I looked at him with my mock-stern expression. 'I've seen what stress can do to estate agents, don't forget.'

'Melissa, don't look at me like that. Not if you want to keep this boat stable.' He loosened his collar. 'If anything's messing with my blood pressure it's you.'

I blushed, and tried not to let him see how flattered I was. 'Oh, Jonathan, you're a workaholic,' I said. 'Admit it.'

'Well, actually, no. I'm not, really. It hasn't always been like this,' he replied, topping up our glasses. We were drifting a little now, but with nothing to bump into, I didn't mind. 'I mean, I've always been a hard worker, always wanted to get on, have security. But to tell you the God's honest truth, when things started going . . . a little *awry* with Cindy, that was when I put in serious hours at work. And I mean serious hours. Getting in before seven, staying until eleven.'

I felt the familiar prickling of curiosity and intimidation that Cindy inspired. Sixteen-hour days? Blimey.

'Just because of . . . problems at home?' I ventured, unable to resist. What was she doing? Throwing plates?

He nodded. 'Kind of stupid really, since she wasn't getting in until eleven herself. Now, Cindy – she *is* a workaholic. She was the youngest director her company ever had, internationally. She was literally running her department before she was twenty-six.'

My stomach crept a little as the perfectly coiffed Ghost of Cindy materialised in the boat between us. Her hair, unlike mine, was not frizzing in the humidity. Neither was she perspiring beneath her cardigan. Still, I needed to grasp the nettle here. I needed to show him I wasn't afraid to talk about her.

Even though I . . . *was*, rather.

'What exactly does she do again?' I asked casually.

'Oh God, Cindy works in *advertising*,' Jonathan groaned, as if it were a technicality that he'd argued over too many times to bear contradicting. 'The sales side, not the creative, but she goes on about it like she's Van Gogh crossed with Donald Trump. She runs international marketing campaigns, really big money operations. She's good at what she does, but it's a very unpleasant industry. If you're not in by seven, you might find someone else sitting at your desk tomorrow morning, you know? They want complete commitment, especially from women.'

I could imagine. Just getting groomed to that sort of level in the mornings required a good hour, and that was even before you got to the office and launched into your daily ball-busting. And I thought wearing stockings for work was pushing the boat out.

'You don't mind me telling you this?' he asked suddenly. 'You don't mind hearing . . . ?'

'No, no!' I said quickly. 'I want to know.'

'I'd understand if you wanted to, you know . . .' He made a walling-off gesture with his hand.

I shook my head. As my mother was wont to mutter, better to know all than to guess half. 'No, honestly. Go ahead.'

'OK.' Jonathan coughed self-consciously, as if he were working out how best to present things. 'Well, um, at first, it wasn't too bad,' he began. 'We were both working hard to pay the bills, meeting our goals. All our friends are kind of *driven*, as you've no doubt noticed, so it wasn't like we were any different. But after a few years it got to be like a competition: who was spending least time at home. She was out all the time because she was working, and I was out . . .' He hesitated. 'I was out because when Cindy was in, she was such a four-door bitch that I'd rather have been anywhere else than sharing a take-out with her. It was always take-outs, by the way. She doesn't do cooking.'

'Oh,' I said. The way he said it was rather sad, not bitter. No wonder the poor man got so excited the one time I offered to roast a chicken. 'Stress can make people say things they don't mean, though. That's why you have to relax.'

'Yeah, well, I kind of put the arguing down to the stress of work, but then we argued on holiday too. When we ever got to go on holiday. No,' he corrected himself. 'That's not fair. Cindy didn't mind scheduling holidays, but they were competitive too – safaris and skiing and God knows what else. I just wanted to go back to my parents' place in Boston, you know, kick back with a few beers but . . .' He rolled his eyes. 'Cindy didn't *do* kicking back. Unless it was some kind of new gym class. And my mother never forgave her for the time she gave my entire family dental work for Christmas.'

I flinched. 'So your mother must be thrilled she's lost a daughter-in-law and gained a daughter-in-law right back.'

That raised a raw smile. 'Yeah. If it were anyone else, I'd laugh. The only good thing is that Cindy refused to leave New York for Thanksgiving so it'll be Brendan missing out on Mom's turkey this year, and not me.'

'Oh, Jonathan,' I said, taking his hand. It was easy to be generous to Cindy from a distance, but inside I felt very jumbled up. I felt nervous, and out of my depth, and very, very sorry for him. Suddenly I wasn't sure this was something I could fix. Far from being the hard-done-by divorcee, he sounded sad, as if he'd lost something precious. I wondered why he'd never told me these things before. Maybe he did prefer to keep things neatly boxed away.

The rowing boat drifted on peacefully. Even though I knew we were in the heart of the city, I felt completely alone with him, sheltered by the trees and the glittering water. I searched my mind for the right thing to say, found nothing, and squeezed his hand tighter between mine.

Eventually, Jonathan lifted his head and looked me straight in the eye. 'What I'm trying to say, is that even if we both ended up workaholics, I think only Cindy was *born* one. I was made into one.' He paused. 'So there's an outside chance you can *un*make me.'

'But she'll have to slow down now she's had Parker, surely?' I said. 'I mean, on a biological level at least.'

'Melissa, she was back in the office *five days* after the birth.'

'And Brendan?'

Jonathan nodded. 'He's looking after Parker. He writes screenplays, freelance. I know it's pointless to torment yourself with "what ifs" but I do sometimes wonder why she insisted that she couldn't find time in her schedule for childbirth when she was married to me, then . . .' He didn't finish but stared hard at a duck paddling past with three ducklings in a line behind.

If Gabi could see him now, I thought fiercely, she'd never call him Dr No again. He didn't look so executive now in his bespoke shirt – he looked heart-breakingly vulnerable. Who in their right mind wouldn't want to have children with this handsome, successful, caring man?

'Don't!' I said. 'Whatever you're thinking, stop it! Because I bet it had nothing to do with you at all!'

I had to bite my tongue to stop myself saying that Cindy, in my opinion, was exactly the sort of premier league cow who thought she could get away with seeing both Brendan and Jonathan just so long as she kept her diary straight. Getting pregnant by Brendan probably wasn't so much a romantic decision to celebrate their love as a scheduling slip-up that forced her into an emergency merger.

I supposed, grudgingly, that at least she hadn't tried to pass Parker off as Jonathan's. Whether that was noble or just doubly cowish, I didn't know.

Or maybe, added a prurient voice, it said more than I wanted to know about the regularity of their sex life.

It says everything you want to know, I reminded myself. If you were being honest.

'Well, all I can say is that I'm glad she's moved on,' I said firmly. 'She obviously had no idea what she had.'

I looked at him closely when he didn't reply at once. In fact, he was staring at Braveheart a bit too hard.

My heart was hammering in my chest. Frankly, I could have done without Cindy popping up in our lovely romantic rowing boat, like a stingray with perfect teeth, but I had to know.

'Jonathan?' I prompted him.

He sighed. 'Yes. Yes, she's moved on. But she's . . . It was OK when I was in London, because she literally couldn't get hold of me there, except by phone. And you don't always have to answer the phone. Now, though . . .' He pressed his lips together. 'I'm telling you this because I don't want you to get the idea that I'm hiding anything. I haven't told you *before*, because I saw how you acted when we visited the old apartment. I thought I could contain her. Which was pretty dumb. Cindy is not easily containable.'

'Like small house fires?'

He laughed mirthlessly and tipped back the rest of his champagne. 'Like small house fires. Well, no, more like those raging savannah fires that destroy all in their path. She blows hot and cold: first, she wants me to sell the flat, then I can't get hold of her to sign documents. She makes a big deal about changing her will so I'm not even mentioned, then phones me five times in a day to check I've got the number of the best interior designer for Jane Street.'

I swallowed. Well, you did ask to hear this, I reminded myself.

'She's a control freak,' I said flatly.

'You got it. Look at Braveheart. She moved heaven and earth to get that dog and now she's dumped him on me, just at a time when I *really* don't need a puppy

around the house, you know? With the decorators, and
you here.' He fiddled with his glass. 'And the constant
calls to check I'm meeting her care guidelines. I mean,
Jesus.'

'Calm down, Jonathan. I'm dealing with the dog,' I
said firmly.

*How often had she been ringing him? And why hadn't he
said so? And why was he still so wound up about her – one
minute sad, the next livid?*

'I know. I know.' He sighed. 'But if we could just make
a clean break . . . You know, when you've been together
as long as we were, the hardest things to divide up are
your friends? I can hardly ask her to stop seeing Bonnie
and Kurt, and God knows it's pretty petty to start bickering over who's known who the longest. Or make a rota
of parties we can go to.'

'Oh, I know,' I sympathised. This I *did* know about.
'Whenever Daddy threatens to divorce my mother, she
reminds him that she'd get the accountant, the wine mer-
chant and the cleaning lady. And he soon backs off.'

Oops. Their anniversary. I'd nearly forgotten. I only
just stopped myself mentioning it out loud. Not a good
moment.

I looked at the empty bottle. I'd drunk half and didn't
feel in the least bit puddled. Ex-wives had a very sobering
effect. I wasn't sure I really wanted to hear much more.
But I'd opened the can of worms, so I'd just have to
square up my shoulders and finish them.

'Of course, she's very curious about *you*,' he went on.
'She pretends not to be, but I know she's pumping
everyone for details.'

'Let her think whatever she likes. If I meet your friends
they'll make up their own minds.' I screwed up the last

of my courage, and tried to make it sound casual. 'Listen, should I meet her? Would that not get it out of the way? For all of us?'

'That's very sweet of you,' said Jonathan. 'But you're only here for a little while and I don't want to spoil your visit by letting Cindy create her own mini-series. Besides, you're so right – let her stew.' He smiled. 'Whatever they're telling her is only half the story.'

I smiled at the compliment, but inside I was less certain.

'I just don't want you to feel . . . I don't know, intimidated by her,' he went on.

'I'm not!'

Ding!

The truth was that International Ad Queen Cindy was so far out of my orbit that I wasn't even jealous, merely awe-struck.

He fiddled with his watch, as if he were searching for the right words. 'Believe me, I have moved on.' He looked up so I could see the sincerity in his grey eyes. 'And I hope – for Brendan's sake, for Parker's sake – that she has. But I can't help worrying that she'll just carry on meddling in my life – *our* life – because she can. She's that sort of woman. So what I guess I'm saying is . . . Melissa?'

I was still tingling at the way he'd said, 'our life'. *Our* life.

'Mmm?'

He opened his mouth to speak, then closed it again, and smiled. When Jonathan smiled, the worry lines vanished and his eyes glittered with boyish mischief. They would still look boyish when he was seventy. I melted inside, and temporarily forgot about Cindy.

'Melissa,' he said. 'Here we are in Central Park, talking about my nightmare of an ex-wife, when all I want to do is sit here and look at you. Maybe get you to say something every now and again, in your sexy accent.' He took my hand again, turned it over and traced the lines on my palm with a ticklish-light touch. 'Sometimes I look at you, and I can't believe you're really mine.' He raised my hand so he could press my palm against his lips, and looked over the top of it. 'Lucky me.'

'That's funny,' I said in a wobbly voice, 'because I frequently have the same thought.'

We smiled, and the bright light made us both squint.

'Don't fly away when your job here is done, Mary Poppins,' he said unexpectedly, in a very bad Dick Van Dyke cockney accent.

'Gor blimey no, guv'nor.' I kissed the tip of his nose. 'Plenty of work still to do here. Now, shall I row us back, or would you like me to summon some cartoon animals to take the oars?'

Jonathan sat back with a laugh. 'I am more than happy to watch you, Miss Mary.'

'Fine!' I said. 'Prepare to be impressed.'

We went round in one huge circle for about twenty minutes, during which time Braveheart deigned to wake up and started getting feisty with the ducks, so Jonathan took one oar, while I took the other, and together we rowed the boat back.

It took a long, long time, but I think it was the happiest hour's exercise I've ever taken.

14

My parents' wedding anniversary was in three days' time, which I reckoned was close enough to risk buying a card. I was in Kate's Paperie, a vast temple to stationery-based politeness, staring at a 'Wow! You Made it to Your 35th Anniversary, Parents!' card and wondering if it was sarcastic enough, when my phone rang, and I discovered I needn't worry about posting it in time. I could deliver it by hand.

'I need you back here in London,' announced my father, without bothering to enquire about the weather or the state of the exchange rate. 'Tout suite.'

'Daddy, I might be busy,' I tried.

He snorted rudely in response. 'I'm not asking as your father, I am summoning you *as your employer*.'

I wrinkled my brow, trying to work out what he meant, then I remembered about the Olympic etiquette stuff.

'I thought you'd forgotten about that,' I protested. 'I mean, I haven't had any acknowledgement from your secretary that you even *got* it.'

'My secretaries are very . . . busy,' he said evasively. 'They don't have time to waste on trivialities.'

I stared longingly at a huge display of thank-you notes. Manners were so much easier when you could just buy a year's worth of polite sentiments, and despatch them at intervals. I wondered if I could place bulk orders for my family.

'I need you back here for Friday lunchtime,' Daddy bellowed. 'So you'd better get cracking.'

'But that's the day after tomorrow! I can't just—'

'For Pete's sake, Melissa, you're on holiday! What have you got to rush away from? An urgent appointment with a bagel? If you weren't prepared to take this assignment seriously, you should never have taken it on,' he reminded me censoriously.

I didn't remember being given much of a choice. Besides, why did he need me there at all? Surely I just had to do the research for him?

'I didn't budget for two sets of return tickets,' I countered, as a last-ditch effort. 'I don't know if I have enough money in my account.'

He tutted, as if I were attempting some audacious street robbery, then said, 'I might be able to arrange something. But get yourself back here. And make sure you're wearing something smart.'

'I always look smart,' I objected.

Daddy made another derisive noise, then added, as an afterthought, 'Oh, and fetch something nice back from Duty Free for your mother. It's our anniversary at the weekend. Fifty quid, preferably under, and don't try to smuggle anything back through the wrong channel. We've only just got your sister away from the rozzers.'

'Oh, that's good news!' I said, relieved. 'And Lars?'

'I can't talk about this now,' he said abruptly. 'I will see you on Friday.'

And he hung up.

★   ★   ★

When I explained this turn of events to Jonathan, he took it with his customary sangfroid. In his line of business, jetting hither and thither wasn't such a big deal. He was also inspecting the latest missive from his bathroom designers, so I only had about forty per cent of his attention anyway.

'Have you checked he's booked your ticket?' he asked.

I nodded. 'The lovely Claudia emailed the details. Business-class return.'

'Hey. That's nice of the old man.'

'I very much doubt he'll be paying for it,' I said heavily. I'd got my mother a huge bag of multicoloured wools and fancy needles from a shop I'd found on Sullivan Street; I doubted very much that I'd get the money back for that either, but at least Mummy wouldn't be unwrapping another silk negligee in the wrong size. With someone else's monogram on the breast.

'I'm just sorry I can't be coming with you.' Jonathan gave me a rueful grimace. 'Would have been quite fun to test out those new business-class beds BA does. Still, I'll get some of this out of the way, so when you get back, I can give you my full attention.'

That made me feel slightly better.

Thanks to the luxurious seat on the plane and the lavish toiletries bag supplied therein, not to mention the use of the business-class spa on arrival, I caught a taxi to Victoria feeling positively refreshed. I just had time to fit in a quick visit before the afternoon meeting with Daddy – and, actually, when you put it like that, I felt like I almost deserved my business-class luggage tag.

I felt a rush of affection for London as I walked down the street, noticing all the things I'd missed without realising: parking meters, discarded copies of *Metro*, Pret a Manger. Maybe a touch of trepidation too, though, in case I ran into a queue of disgruntled clients hammering on the door and demanding their money back. Still, I reminded myself nervously, I shouldn't be too mean to Gabi and Allegra. There was a lot to pick up, and they'd probably been trying their best.

I waved at the beauty therapists in the discreet salon on the ground and first floors, and checked my bag for the presents I'd brought from Bloomingdales. I hoped Gabi was in before Allegra, not just because her present was significantly nicer, but because I could at least get a reasonably accurate version of the previous fortnight's events. If I encountered Allegra first, it would take at least half an hour of intense chat about herself before she'd even consider getting round to what she'd been up to at work.

In the event, I needn't have worried because when I reached the second floor I found the agency door locked, a stack of post on the table outside, and no sign of either of them.

Frowning, I checked my watch. Ten past ten. Where were they? I could hear the telephone ringing, and I let myself in as fast as I could get the key in the lock.

Once inside, I nearly dropped my post in shock and had to steady myself against the leather couch.

For a start, the leather couch wasn't where I'd left it. It was on the other side of the room, where the desk had been. The desk was up against the opposite wall and looked as if a small but savage land battle had been fought on it recently. All my lovely pictures had been taken down and there were shopping bags and discarded coffee cups everywhere. Worst of all, the dressmaker's dummy was wearing some kind of rugby kit.

My knees felt like buckling, but the phone was still ringing, so I pulled myself together and answered it.

'The Little Lady Agency. How can I help you?' I said smoothly, running my eyes around the office. Thank God I'd come back!

'This is Thomasina Kendall,' said a clipped voice. 'Can I speak to whoever organised my son's christening present on behalf of Patrick Gough?'

Patrick Gough? The name didn't ring any bells. It must have been something the girls had sorted out while I was away.

Oh, *God*.

'I'm terribly sorry,' I apologised, searching around for the absent desk diary, 'but I think one of my assistants was looking after that for Patrick, and they're not in the office at the moment. Was there a problem? Is there something I can deal with for you?'

'No,' said Thomasina Kendall. 'I need to speak to whomever it was *directly*.'

I fervently hoped it had been something simple, like Gabi leaving the price tag on a silver rattle, rather than Allegra giving a newborn baby a replica Aztec sacrificial knife.

I opened the drawer, saw a pair of boxer shorts draped over everything from the desk top, and closed it again. Then I closed my eyes too, for good measure.

'I am *so* sorry, Mrs Kendall. If you give me a contact number I'll ask her to call you the instant she comes in.'

'If you could.' She rattled off a series of numbers on which she could be contacted throughout the day. Whatever it was she needed to talk to them about, clearly it couldn't wait.

I put down the phone, feeling ill. A band around my

forehead, coaxed into existence by incipient jet-lag and the sight of traffic wardens in a ticketing frenzy around Ebury Street, tightened.

Calm down, I told myself, trying to find three positive aspects of the gloomy situation facing me. Three positive things and the rest wouldn't look half so bad.

One, the phone hadn't been cut off.

Two, they'd clearly been doing *something*.

And, three, I could always tidy up. Everything would look a hundred times better after thirty minutes' intensive tidying up.

I opened my eyes, sank back into my familiar carved oak office chair and surveyed the confusion: no biscuits in the glass barrel, five dying bunches of flowers on the shelves, magazines ditched everywhere, and, bafflingly, one small red stiletto discarded on top of the filing cabinet. There was a lingering smell in the air that I couldn't quite pinpoint. It smelled like . . . gunpowder.

In twelve days, Gabi and Allegra had turned my office into a fifth-form common room. And that was only the mess I could *see*. A shudder ran through my blood.

I couldn't stand it any longer. I yanked open my desk drawer and rummaged around until I found the photograph of me and Jonathan, absent from its pride of place by the phone, then placed it firmly on the desk. Then, as my momentum picked up, I pushed back my chair, grabbed the nearest three magazines and dumped them in the bin, followed by all the paper coffee cups, plastic bags and discarded bits of clothing. Breathing deeply, I hung the pictures back on the wall – I could already hear Allegra snotting about having to look at such low-level art – and started to retidy the book shelves with cross, jerky movements.

And, honestly, I *hate* tidying up. I really wasn't tidying it out of a neat freak inability to endure a badly stacked pile of books (as Nelson would have confirmed, had he been there) but until the office was back to the way I'd left it, I felt unsettled. As if I'd been burgled.

Just as I was tottering unsteadily about the place with the Dyson, like one of those unhinged sitcom house-wives hoovering in high heels at 3 a.m., the door opened and Gabi rushed in, with two big Hamleys bags balancing her small frame. She wasn't, as I'd carefully hinted in my instruction file, wearing a skirt and pretty heels, but her jeans, a black cotton shirt, and a pair of gold trainers.

'Oh, my God, you're back!' she gasped. Then she rearranged her face into an unconvincingly confident smile, and exclaimed, 'Oh, my God! You're *back*!'

I turned off the vacuum cleaner. We both watched as a red casino chip whirled and then sank back into the grey dust of the transparent chamber. Somewhere in my head, I registered that it was for five hundred pounds.

'When did you fly in?' asked Gabi quickly. 'You must be really jet-lagged. Can I make you a coffee? I've got some more biscuits in here somewhere . . . Not telling tales, but I've been here and out again already this morning, because I had to collect a present that Allegra was supposed to have sorted out yesterday, before she felt tired and had to go to Calmia to have her chakras rebalanced. Oh, I see you've . . . Er . . .' She trailed off and looked at me, Dyson in hand. 'Sorry,' she said con-tritely. 'I was planning to do the cleaning today. Honest.'

I took a deep breath. Much better to know the whole story than to guess half. Why was I thinking that so much these days?

'Just tell me,' I said, 'without any exaggeration *or* explanation, what's been going on while I've been away?'

'With what?' Gabi hedged.

'Well, you could start with why the desk is on the other side of the room? Why there's a shoe on the filing cabinet? Why there are sixteen messages on the answering machine? What you've done to Thomasina Kendall's son? Why no one was here when . . .' I stopped, hearing my voice rising with each question, and pressed my lips together, breathing into my stomach to calm myself down. It wasn't like me to be so shouty, either. Tidying up *and* shouting. Blimey, I was turning into an office manager.

I let out all the pent-up breath in a big sigh, and felt marginally better. But not much. 'Maybe I will have that cup of coffee.'

'God, Mel,' said Gabi, turning on the coffee machine, 'you've only been in New York two weeks and already you're barking orders at me like Jonathan. Take a chill pill. Sit down, will you? Have you had a good time?'

'I've had a fantastic time,' I said, but I wasn't going to be sidetracked just yet. Not with my desk drawers full of men's underwear. 'Come on, give me the bad news. Before Allegra gets in.'

Gabi tossed her head dismissively. 'Chuh. In that case, we've got time for a minute-by-minute account of the past twelve days for both of us. And I thought I had a bad attitude to time-keeping. It's her fault the place is in this mess.'

'Really?' I gave Gabi my best 'now, is that the whole truth?' look.

'It is!' she insisted. 'The police were here yesterday! She claimed she was too traumatised to tidy up after they'd searched it, and—'

I held up my hand, as my heart sank into my stomach-flattening pants. 'Stop there. Slowly, please. The *police* were here?'

Gabi nodded. 'They've done searching her place, and your mum's place, and they still haven't found whatever it is they're looking for, so when they found out Allegra was here, suddenly we had the boys in blue knocking on the door. They fingerprinted everything, even your dress-making dummy.' She sniffed. 'You can still smell it, can't you?'

I sank my head onto my forearms on the desk.

Police! In my office.

No. I couldn't think of three positive things to say about that.

In fact, I couldn't think of one.

A grim thought occurred to me and I sat bolt upright. 'God in heaven. Tell me they didn't—'

'Nope, they didn't find anything here, either,' added Gabi cheerfully. 'But they had a good laugh watching your home movies of Tristram Hart-Mossop leching at you in Selfridges. And I got some very interesting gossip about one of them who knows the protection officers at Downing Street. Apparently, Cherie likes to—'

'Don't tell me,' I yelped. 'Just tell me some nice encouraging things, until I get my composure back.'

'OK,' said Gabi, heaping ground coffee into the filter. She took a look at me, and added an extra scoop. 'I've spoken to some awfully worried young posh blokes, who are all having hernias because you're in New York.' She put her head on one side curiously. 'What is it you do to these people? Some of them sound desperate. You can tell me, Allegra's not here.'

'Nothing, really,' I said, feeling mollified. 'I just . . .

Well, it's not all just shopping, you know. It's the talking, and, er, listening.'

Gabi looked baffled. 'But half of them never say anything.'

'Oh, it's all about giving them a bosom to cry on. I mean, a shoulder. To cry on.'

'Well, that might be closer to the truth than you know,' said Gabi, and turned the coffee machine on. 'Your bosom could bring a grown man to tears.'

'And what exactly do you mean by that?' I demanded.

'Oh . . . Never mind. If you look on the desk, there's a list of messages. Do you mind having your coffee black? We're out of milk.'

'That's all right.' I moved the invoice files and the post file to one side. So I could see Gabi better over the desk, I also moved the large cardboard box that had been dumped there.

'What's this?' I asked, peering in. 'Is it those breath fresheners I sent over? I thought we could slip some in with each invoice. Then no one can take it personally.'

'Ah, no, they're in the store room. You don't need to see that,' said Gabi quickly, bouncing off the sofa as if propelled by an ejector seat. 'That's just . . . just a nothing.'

She swooped to take the box away, but I swooped it in the opposite direction first and held the box away from her.

'Is it for Nelson?' I asked teasingly. 'Are you sending him special rations?'

'No,' she said. 'But listen, Mel, it's not important. Look! Here are some letters from your editor at that magazine, for your column.' She waved them at me, as if to get me to let go of the box to take them. 'Some very juicy ones here, one from a chap who's got a thing about kilts.'

But my curiosity was piqued. 'So what's in here then?' I asked, reaching inside. My hand made contact with a whole load of soft things. 'Don't tell me you've taken up knitting socks for Nelson?' I asked, pulling one out.

When I saw what it was, I nearly hurled it straight back in. 'Argh!'

Gabi sighed.

'What in the name of all that's holy is this?' I shook it at her then peered more closely. It seemed to be a knitted toy dog, except it had six legs and one ear much longer than the other, and was knitted from a strange green mohair which gave it a fuzzy halo. There was also a tumour on its back, bulging obscenely, but not quite as obscenely as its red tongue, which lolled out at some length. The whole thing looked radioactive.

'Is it a dog?' I asked incredulously. 'A camel? An . . . anteater? I mean, *what*?'

I dropped it onto the desk with a shudder and looked at Gabi for some explanation.

She opened her mouth, then closed it again and shrugged.

Silently, I reached into the box, and pulled out a cat, created in a luminous rainbow stripe, sporting a tail that was three times as long as its body and massive ears that bent in different directions. For some reason, there were three of them. It also had terrifying human-shaped eyes sewn onto its head in green wool, complete with *Clockwork Orange* eyelashes and staring pupils.

I put it next to the dog. They made a fearsome couple. In fact, just looking at them brought back vague stirrings of childhood nightmares.

I giggled nervously. 'Gabi, did my mother send these?'

She nodded. 'There are lots.'

I peered into the box and vaguely made out a tangle of legs, heads, tails and torsos, all in different colours. It was the lucky dip from hell. A child could end up with lifelong issues if they woke up with something like that next to them on the pillow.

'Mummy must have been very busy,' I said, trying to think of a positive observation to make.

'She's knitting away her stress,' explained Gabi. 'I had a very interesting chat with her on the phone. Apparently, there's been a bit of bother with—'

'Gabi,' I said firmly, 'one catastrophe at a time.'

She rolled her eyes in a manner that Nelson would hardly have recognised. 'Look, it hasn't been a total disaster while you've been swanning round New York,' she snapped. 'If you look in the invoice file, you'll see that it hasn't all been police raids and shopping. Some of us have been doing some work.'

I bit my tongue and opened the box file. 'I know,' I apologised. I had no right to yell at Gabi. Coping with Allegra was a full-time job for her, let alone doing anything else. Just because Allegra's entanglements with the police had started to swish airily over my head didn't mean Gabi had had time to get used to the constant drama. 'I'm sorry. I know you've been working hard and I do appreciate it.'

'We have. Well, I have.' Gabi poured me some coffee and brought it over to the desk. I noticed, as she put the cup and saucer down, she surreptitiously moved the box of mutant toys to somewhere out of my eye-line.

'Oh, come here and give me a hug,' I said, pushing my chair back and going over to embrace her. 'I've really missed you.'

'I've missed you too,' she said, hugging me back, and

I was relieved. It was horrible being cross with Gabi – I wasn't cut out for ball-breaking, and, to be honest, I was quite glad about that.

'So,' I said, 'what's in the Hamleys bags?' I peered but couldn't see inside. 'I love Hamleys. I could spend all day in there!'

Gabi looked shifty, and at that moment the door swung open and Allegra shimmered in. When she saw me, a ghost of a double-take flitted across her face, then vanished behind her usual expression of barely concealed impatience.

'Hello, Melissa,' she said. 'Ah, splendid, you've made coffee, Gabi. Black, three sugars, please.'

'I made coffee for *Melissa*,' said Gabi through gritted teeth.

'Biscuits?' Allegra held out her hand towards Gabi expectantly.

'Allegra, this isn't a café!' I protested. 'And Gabi isn't here to furnish you with *elevenses*.' I took a deliberate look at my watch. 'As it now is.'

Allegra shot Gabi a filthy look. 'Well, she's keen enough to provide—'

'In my bag,' snapped Gabi quickly. 'There are some Bahlsen chocolate wafers.'

'Excellent,' said Allegra with a vulpine smile.

I looked between the pair of them. They were fixing each other with the sort of death-looks I'd last seen in the St Cathal's Junior Common Room circa 1987.

'So,' I said, trying to keep the atmosphere non-combative for as long as possible, 'Gabi was just telling me about the presents she'd got in Hamleys this morning. Isn't it just the most fun place to shop for other people? Did you find my christening present checklist?'

'I did, thank you. It was most helpful,' said Gabi point-
edly. 'I bought a train set, after *looking around* for *half
an hour* and reading your notes really carefully.'

Allegra tossed her head and helped herself to another
biscuit.

I looked first at Gabi, then at Allegra, but couldn't for
the life of me work out what was going on. Honestly, it
was like being at a tennis match, only with an invisible
ball. Not only could you not see what was going on, but
it was impossible to tell who was winning.

I pulled myself together. After all, I was the one in
charge here.

'Anyway, getting back to business,' I said briskly,
'maybe one of you can tell me what the problem is with
Thomasina Kendall?'

'You little snitch!' hissed Allegra, at the same time as
Gabi snapped, 'I said nothing, so don't even think of
blaming me!'

I banged my hands on the desk to get their attention.
'Stop it! Stop it right now! Allegra! Tell me what you sent
that poor child!'

Allegra heaved in a long breath through her long nose.
'Did Gabi tell you that the police have been here,
harassing me?'

'She did, yes, but that's—'

'And that I've been incredibly stressed and busy, com-
plying with their impertinent demands? I've had to provide bank statements and—'

'Allegra!' I said fiercely, trying to ignore the fact that
her job, for which she was being paid more than *me*,
clearly came some way down her list of must-dos. 'Get
to the point. Police. Why?'

Gabi looked impressed. Then a bit scared.

'I, unlike some people, have been too busy with personal tragedy to trail around Hamleys looking at tacky gee-gaws for over-indulged brats,' Allegra informed me. 'And since I was anxious to meet the deadline for posting the present to this ridiculous child—'

'Who has two minor royals for godparents,' added Gabi.

'Is that kind of thing impressive in Mill Hill?' sneered Allegra. 'I wouldn't know.'

I closed my eyes and placed my palms over my eyelids. Tea bags would only ruin my eyeliner and I needed that in place for Daddy's meeting.

'Because I *knew* he would inundated with exactly that sort of boring, mass-produced tat, I sent him a beautiful, unique piece of art, which any child of taste would treasure for ever,' she finished, with a distinct note of smugness. 'I fail to see the problem. Gabi and I will have to agree to differ about what constitutes a thoughtful gift.'

'Well, in that case you should have got him some therapy sessions, for when he's able to talk!' interrupted Gabi furiously. 'If he ever manages to gain the power of speech!'

A ghastly idea was beginning to solidify in my head.

'Allegra,' I said, trying to keep the panic out of my voice, 'just tell me. What did you send?'

She made a dismissive gesture towards my desk. 'A couple of those toys Mummy's been knitting. A cat, I think, and a giraffe.' She paused. 'Or it could have just been a leopard with a long neck. Whatever. The child'll adore it.'

The blood drained from my face, as I saw my reputation as a telepathic gift-giver evaporate in a hot gust of nanny gossip. 'Allegra, please tell me this is your idea of a joke.'

'I've got the train set right here,' Gabi put in quickly. 'We can wrap it up now, and courier it over there, and say there's been an awful mistake, and—'

'No, it's too late for that,' I groaned. 'The child's traumatised mother is already on the warpath.'

'Oh, how preposterous!' Allegra waved her hand. 'Silly woman probably prefers those dreadful silver teething rings.'

'Allegra!' I howled. 'How many times do I have to say this? It isn't about what *you* think is the right thing to do, it's about listening to the client and helping *them* decide!'

'I did try to stop her,' said Gabi. 'But she flounced out.'

'Oh, shut up, Gabi,' snapped Allegra. 'I suppose you haven't told her about your little outing last weekend?'

Gabi shot Allegra a dirty look. 'That's hardly the same thing.'

Allegra arched her plucked eyebrow. 'No?'

The phone rang, interrupting this ghastly double act, and I picked it up crossly.

'Good morning, the Little Lady Agency.'

There was a familiar nasal squelch. 'Ah, the lovely Mel! Wasn't expecting to hear your dulcet tones.'

'Hello, Roger,' I said. This was all I needed.

Allegra gave Gabi a triumphant smirk, and Gabi scowled back so hard her mascara smudged onto her cheeks.

'Can I speak to Gabi, please?' he said. 'If she's there.'

'She is here, Roger,' I said, gesturing to Gabi. 'We're just in the middle of a meeting, actually . . .'

'I won't keep you then. Anyway, how are you?' he enquired suavely. 'Enjoying New York?'

'Very much,' I said, confused by his cordiality. Last time we'd spoken, he'd been virtually Neanderthal. 'Listen, I'm sure we'll catch up soon, Roger, but in the meantime here's Gabi.'

I mouthed 'keep it brief' at her as I handed over the phone, then leaned over to Allegra.

'You will phone Mrs Kendall and apologise for sending those revolting toys,' I hissed. 'I know Mummy's very stressed right now, and I'm sure when she gets less tense she'll make lovely creatures with the right number of appendages, but those things would scare an experienced adult, let alone a child who probably won't even venture beyond the confines of SW3 until he's eighteen!'

'Shh!' said Allegra, pointing at Gabi.

I turned back, bewildered, to see Gabi looking most discomfited, twisting the phone cord around her finger and keeping her eyes fixed on me.

'No, that's fine,' she said carefully. 'I'm glad it went well.'

'*What* went well, I wonder?' muttered Allegra, with malicious glee.

'No, I don't think there's any need to speak to . . . Well, I don't know, Roger. I thought we agreed that . . .'

I looked at Gabi. Panic and guilt were written all over her face.

I held out my hand for the telephone.

'If that's all you called about, Roger, we're in the middle of a meeting right now,' she said quickly. 'So maybe we can talk about this later.'

'Give me the phone,' I said. 'I'd like a word.'

Gabi continued to gaze at me. 'Here's Melissa,' she said, and handed me the receiver.

'Roger,' I said heavily.

'Hello again! Jolly decent of Gabi to leap into the breach, if you ask me,' Roger chuckled. 'I can quite see why you might not be up to it, but in the humble opinion of R. Trumpet, Esq., Gabi makes quite the blonde bombshell too!'

I said nothing, but from Gabi's reaction, my face was probably speaking for me.

'Have to say, there was quite an awkward moment when Gabs got a bit carried away in the Gay Gordons and brought the whole set down, arse over tip,' he went on, less jovially. 'I didn't realise that Moira Sutton really did have a false leg, but, generally, you know, no one noticed. And, mmm, I should probably tell you that the aged mama was a bit narky about your comments about Celia's get-up – well, I say "*your*" . . .' He chortled at the memory, which was obviously tickling him no end.

I glared at Gabi. I'd spent hours buttering up Lady Trumpet, that weekend at Trumpet Manor. *Hours*. That was the whole point about the pretend girlfriend dates: it wasn't just about the dress and the wig. It was about talking to the datee's friends, bolstering their confidence, probing delicately, then laying subtle foundations for them to springboard into better things.

Allegra and Gabi were bickering again, under their breath. It seemed to be about the biscuits.

'So what were you calling about, Roger?' I enquired. 'Because, sadly, I don't think Gabi will be making any more outings in that capacity.'

'Shame,' said Roger. 'We got on rather well. Anyway, I was ringing to ask about whether she was going to invoice me through the office, or whether she'd do it for cash. You know, freelance.'

I glared at Gabi. 'I think she'll be invoicing through the office,' I said. 'And perhaps making a charity donation.'

'Rarely?' exclaimed Roger. He meant 'really' but his inner Sloane mangled his vowels in moments of extreme surprise.

'Yes, rarely,' I said. 'The RNLI, I should think. Would you excuse me, Roger? I'm right in the middle of a debriefing.'

I hung up the phone on Roger's snorts. It rang again immediately, but I sent the call to the answering machine.

Gabi looked shocked. It went totally against my office efficiency grain to let a phone call go unanswered.

Instead, I folded my arms, and glared at the pair of them in silence until the bickering petered out.

'I'm terribly disappointed in you two,' I said, drawing up my spine until the suspenders on my stockings stretched. I was reminded of Mrs McKinnon, my fearsome Home Ec teacher, and since she used to make me quail with the fearsome power of her disappointment, that was no bad thing. 'I didn't ask you to do very much. I didn't make any outrageous demands. In fact, I only asked you to follow some very simple instructions, and you deliberately ignored them. I'm especially disappointed in you, Gabi,' I said, turning to her.

She bowed her dark head contritely.

'Bring me the wig, please,' I said.

She got to her feet, and went over to the filing cabinet. I swallowed my distress that she'd just stuffed it in under 'w' for wig. The wig held a sacred place in my heart. I'd built up my business with the help of that wig and, whatever Nelson might say in teasing, I remained in awe of its powers.

Honestly, I thought, this was almost more than I could stand. Between these two running riot with my reputation, and Jonathan intimating that I should be organising tea party classes, and Paige Drogan playing me like a cheap fiddle, I was hardly the Honey Blennerhesket who'd waltzed around London in this very wig, charming all in her path with verve and elan.

Honey, I knew, would not be putting up with this. But then, Honey didn't have to live with any of these people, whereas I did.

Gabi put the wig in front of me on the desk, and sat down.

I smoothed out the soft hair until it was shiny and sleek again, then opened my big handbag and put it safely inside.

'I'm taking this back with me,' I informed them. 'If you can't be trusted.'

'Oh, for heaven's sake, Melissa, stop acting like some religious martyr,' snapped Allegra. 'No one's impressed.'

I turned on her, furious. 'Don't talk to me about being impressed! If you think you're getting paid for the rest of this month, you can start by turning up before eleven o'clock in the morning! I am sick and tired of people underestimating how hard it is to do this job,' I fumed. 'And I thought you two might understand. But you don't, and that makes me really rather *sad*.'

I realised that tears were rising in my throat and I stopped, mid-rant. Obviously the flight had affected me more than I'd thought. Or maybe it was something else. I blinked rapidly.

The phone rang again, and this time I picked it up as a reflex reaction.

'The Little Lady Agency?'

Allegra and Gabi both flinched this time, in guilty anticipation.

There was a nervous cough. 'Ees Franco? The father of Inez, the daily cleeeaner of Meester Ralph Waterstone? Plis inforrrrm Allegra that my daughter ees being investigated by the DHSS. I hope she ees happy! But we haf frrriends, and we knows wherrre you leeve! Mother of God!' Then the phone slammed down.

'She was an illegal immigrant,' whined Allegra, before I'd even opened my mouth. 'What was I meant to do?'

'You were only meant to tell her to clean the loo with a different cloth to the one she uses on the bath!' snapped Gabi.

'Shut up!' I yelled, raising my hands. 'Shut up! Shut up! Shut up!'

That finally shut them up. They probably thought I was about to have a seizure. It certainly felt like that from where I was sitting.

'I need to have a look through the diary, and the post,' I went on, after a pregnant pause. 'Gabi, would you walk round to Baker & Spice and get us some cake. Allegra, kindly call Mrs Kendall, explain about the mix-up, apologise like you've never apologised before, send that train set, and then . . .' I hesitated. 'Then just go and do something else for the rest of the day, please. I'm sure you've got plenty to occupy you.'

She gave me a pitying look, as if I were the one causing trouble. 'Those of us with full lives do, Melissa. I'll call you later.' And she swept out. I was surprised not to hear a clap of thunder and lightning as she left the building, although we did hear the front door slam with a ferocity that probably ruined several relaxing treatments in the salon below.

'Mel?' asked Gabi tentatively.

'Can you give me ten minutes?' I said, trying a brave smile. 'I just need a moment to see the funny side. I mean, I know there is a funny side. But I'm just having a temporary sense of humour failure.'

'Sure,' she said. 'I'll go and get those cakes.'

And she spun on her heel and scurried out, without even asking for petty cash.

15

I couldn't stay mad at Gabi for long. She knew me too well, for one thing, and, besides, there was something about my office that always calmed me down. The lilac walls, I think, and the fact that only I knew about the emergency stash of Dairy Milk in the secret compartment at the back of the desk. In the sensible hour Gabi took to walk to Elizabeth Street and back again, I'd made eight brisk phone calls of apology for services rendered (or not, in three instances), replied to five letters and opened all the post, while taking deep breaths and listening to Ella Fitzgerald.

I also allowed myself to try on the wig. Just seeing myself in the bathroom mirror with that long caramel fringe falling into my eyes made me feel more in control of everything. A strange peace fell over my shoulders, along with the additional hair, and I knew I could tackle anything. Hadn't I conquered my own shyness, and built up a successful business, all on my own? In this very wig?

Then I took it off, in case one of them came back.

Smoothing out a few knotty problems was actually rather invigorating after kicking my heels in New York, and the jet-lag soon fell away as my brain negotiated the familiar steps of London social routines once more. It wasn't exactly cheering to find out what the girls had been up to, but at least now I knew for certain, instead of extrapolating wild conclusions from their random phone messages.

For instance, I spoke to poor Toby Henderson *before* he'd had time to give his entire wardrobe to Oxfam, as advised by Gabi and Allegra, and managed to soothe his shell-shocked ego back to semi-operational state. In a stroke of genius, I looked up his measurements, still on his file card from our trip to Austin Reed last year, and suggested doing some shopping for him, online, when I was back in New York.

At half twelve the office door edged open, and Gabi's dark curls appeared nervously round it; she found me in a surprisingly good mood, considering the horrors I was unearthing.

'Just think,' I said down the phone to Toby, motioning for her to sit, 'you won't have to go into a changing room and I know how much you hate that. I know. I *know* – *not* the most hygienic places . . . No, you won't have to deal with Allegra again. I promise. Ever. Yes, on my honour.'

Gabi made some fresh coffee, rather self-consciously.

'Or Gabi,' I added, in response to Toby's question. 'Actually, she *does* have a boyfriend. No, I don't think she talks to him quite like that though.'

Gabi started to make an outraged face, then remembered she was meant to be being contrite, and stopped.

'Toby, I'm terribly sorry, but I have to go,' I said, as he began to unload his new hair loss agony. 'But I think I saw something exactly for that kind of problem in Duane Reade, this super American chemist place, so why don't you write me a nice long email, and I'll sort it all out for you by the end of the week?'

That seemed to cheer him up, and I crossed his name

off my list with some relief. It was the last one. Apart from Roger Trumpet, with whom I intended to have a *very* long chat, but not over the phone.

'Well,' I said, as Gabi put a cup of coffee and a slice of chocolate cake in front of me. 'That's that cleared up. And you might like to know that Piers Saunders isn't going to sue us, after all.'

'Sorry,' she said immediately. 'But he should have known Allegra wasn't a real skin specialist—'

I held up a 'stop!' hand. 'Gabi, come on – if these people had *any* idea what they were doing, they wouldn't be calling us in the first place.' I gave her my best impression of Nelson's 'charitable works' face. 'I know you and Allegra don't have much sympathy for dithering men, but, for my sake, can you try? This is my livelihood you're dealing with, not to mention their feelings.'

Gabi cast her eyes down in an expression I recognised as my own 'pretending to indulge Nelson's charitable works' face, then looked up, unable to disguise her unquenchable thirst for gossip.

'So, you *are* coming back then? Jonathan hasn't proposed now he's finally lured you out there?'

I blushed. 'Yes! And no. He hasn't. Come on, Gabi, it's only been a *fortnight.*'

'But it's going all right?' She added a meaningful look. 'He's OK with your snoring? He's seen you first thing in the morning?'

'Yes,' I said, busying myself with my desk tidy. We weren't exactly at the manky foot-rub stage. I got the impression that Jonathan liked the finished version of womanhood, but didn't want to see the workings, as it were. Face-packs, he said, were for spas, not sitting rooms.

'He's making more time for you now?'

I hesitated. 'Um, yes. Sort of. And the house is amazing! The master bedroom has two bathrooms.'

Gabi kicked off her shoes and tucked her feet under her on the sofa, balancing her cup and saucer on the arm until she saw my expression, and replaced it carefully on the side table next to her.

'Well, go on then,' she said encouragingly. 'Spill. What kind of house has the King of Realtors chosen for his domain? Does he have a walk-in tie wardrobe? Does he let you sleep on whichever side of the bed you like, or has he drawn up a rota so you don't dent the mattress unequally? No, no!' she cackled, delighted by her own imagination. 'Don't tell me. He's worked out some kind of spreadsheet to allocate you space in his flat, and time in his schedule, depending on whether the pair of you hit pre-agreed targets.'

Honestly, she was so dreadful about Jonathan. If she had any sort of imagination, she'd realise that what was stern in the boardroom could be quite different in the bedroom . . .

I made myself blush at that. But, you know.

'Gabi!' I protested. 'He's actually quite messy, you know. His cleaner comes four times a week.'

'Huh?' said Gabi. 'Really? But, be honest, has he synchronised your diary with his? The ultimate gesture?'

'Even if I tell you that he's been the very model of a romantic host, would you believe me?'

'Honestly?' She screwed up her face. 'No. You've already told me his scheduling shortcomings. And frankly I don't understand what you see in starchy, buttoned-up workaholics in any case.'

'Good,' I said, cutting my cake into slices. I was only

going to eat two bits. Out of five. That made it sixty per cent less fat, which was almost a diet cake. 'More for those of us who do.'

'And is his apartment as minimalist as his social skills?'

'Will you pack it in?' I said. 'As a matter of fact, Jonathan doesn't have an apartment, he has a whole house. In Greenwich Village, which has trees and cobbled streets and neighbours and everything.'

'So he's sold the huge apartment on Park Avenue that he had with . . . Cindy . . .' Gabi's voice trailed off. 'Not that I've got a dossier, or anything,' she added defensively.

'Yes,' I said to spare her blushes. Gabi was the sort of PA who made her job interesting by raiding the HR files like she was on an MI5 intelligence mission. 'He's selling it right now.'

'He's selling it? You mean, as in *he's* . . .'

I nodded.

Gabi widened her eyes. 'That's so typical! And you tell me he's not a control freak? Jonathan,' she said, raising her hand like a lollipop lady, 'step away from the marital breakdown drama!'

'No, Gabi, it's not like that — Cindy made him! She's always on his case about it. She's driving him round the bend . . .' I stopped. We were getting onto quite thin ice now.

Gabi's eyes narrowed again. 'I see. How convenient for her. To have her ex over a barrel and on the end of a string. No wonder you're paranoid. Did you find out if that's where he was the other day, when he was late for your lunch meeting?'

Suddenly I didn't really want to talk about it any more.

'Um, he didn't say where he was.' I forked some cake

in half, trying to ignore her very perceptive observation. 'Ooh! Are those new shoes you've got on?'

Gabi, though, was not so easily thrown off the scent when it came to gossip. 'Hobbs sale. Half price. So she hasn't engineered a dramatic meeting then?'

Any minute now, I would stop glowing about the boat trip and the romantic dinners, and my lurking fears about Cindy and the Coven of Blonde Friends would spill out. Then there'd be no packing them away again. In desperation, I tried the distraction technique that worked so well on Braveheart. 'Did you know in New York they say "I don't care" instead of "I don't mind"? I couldn't work out why people were being so rude to me when I was trying to be nice.'

'Really?' Gabi looked distracted at the mention of shops. 'Did you get my Kiehl's stuff? Because if you haven't I've just been reading about a new cleanser you can only get in New York . . .'

For a good ten minutes, every time Gabi's mouth opened to ask another question about Cindy I told her about the enormous trucks on the streets, and how breathtaking Grand Central Station was, and the super-cheap OPI nail varnish, and the bus maps that you needed to have A-level maths to figure out, and how weirdly hard it was to buy stamps. For variation, I also filled her in on Braveheart, Jonathan's romantic meal on the river, our boating expedition, and the frosting-tastic Magnolia Bakery on Bleeker Street.

'And do they love your accent?' she demanded. 'Do you tell them your gran is an Hon?'

'No! I do not.' I paused. 'I'm not telling anyone very much about me, to be honest.'

'Not even about your agency?'

'Especially not that.' I hesitated. This wasn't going to play well in Gabi's eyes either, I knew it. 'Jonathan wants me to softpedal the whole agency thing. Because it comes over wrong to Americans,' I added, seeing the outrage on her face. 'The fact that it's *men*, and me, and you know. And I don't want to show him up or anything. Everyone's so easily offended over there – they keep asking me if I mind them smoking, or drinking wine, or talking about religion.' I stopped, as a positive thing occurred to me. 'The good thing is, I never miss any of their jokes, not like I do here. You always know when to get your hearty laugh ready, because they check first that you won't be offended by the punchline.'

'Thoughtful,' said Gabi drily. 'So, come on – you *haven't* met Cindy?'

'No,' I admitted. I pressed my lips against each other. Even though I didn't really want to talk about it, something inside was urging me to get it off my chest. 'Jonathan and I had a really good talk about her, and he doesn't want me to spoil my trip by meeting her.'

'How thoughtful of him,' said Gabi sarcastically.

'Don't say it like you don't believe me. Plus, he doesn't want to see her any more than he has to. Apparently, she's acting up about their apartment. It's been on the market for ages, because she's being so difficult.'

I met Gabi's 'for heaven's *sake*' look, and she sighed. 'And not just because his new girlfriend is in town?'

I bit my lip, but it was too late. The floodgates were opening, sweeping away all the lovely things I wanted to remember. 'Oh, Gabi, I feel like she's there all the time, but in a negative way. Like, when we meet people, I can see them looking me over, to see if I've got anything in common with her. And Jonathan's always telling me how he loves the fact that I'm *not* pushy, and *not* plastered in make-up, and *not* this, that or the other. I mean, even his new house – and it's *so* gorgeous, honestly – is *not* on the Upper East Side, and it's *not* full of her awful paintings, and it's *not* somewhere that her father had to call in nine favours to get past the co-op board.'

'But I thought it was all done and dusted, with the divorce. You told me last *year* that he—'

'I don't think it's that simple,' I said unhappily. And I *was* shocked at how unhappy I felt, now I thought about it. 'I know she's been calling him about the apartment sale. And then she's having Parker christened, or unspecifically named or something, and he's still Jonathan's nephew—'

'For a posh family, that's *very* trailer park,' observed Gabi.

'Quite.' I looked into my coffee cup. I knew I should tell Gabi about what that Jennifer woman had said at Kurt and Bonnie's party, about the 'rebound girl'. But suddenly, a familiar old mortification started to creep back into my stomach and I wondered if that's what they were *all* saying. Maybe even saying to him *right now*, over well-meaning cocktails in Bemelman's, while I was away.

'Mel?' said Gabi. 'You're . . . you're not crying, are you?'

I shook my head. 'I was really excited when I flew in,' I said sadly. 'Now . . . I'm not so much.'

She got up and came to sit on the edge of the desk, so she could put her arms round me. 'Listen,' she said firmly. 'Cindy sounds like a nightmare. But you've known that for ages. And Jonathan is very clearly nuts about you. Who wouldn't be? You're beautiful, and clever, you run your own business, and you can sew bias-cut skirts. You could be on *The Apprentice* and *The Apprentice: Martha!*. What more could a corporate weasel like Jonathan want?'

'So why does he want me to run poxy baby showers?' I exploded.

There was a pause, then Gabi said, 'No. Back up. You've lost me.'

'Oh, it's just a conversation we had over dinner. He thinks I could set up another Little Lady Agency in New York, but organising tea parties for brides, and new mothers, and sweet sixteens, so vast quantities of presents can be handed over. Showers, they call them.' I pursed my lips. 'Emotional blackmail, more like. You should see the lists they make.'

'But, Mel, more weddings?' asked Gabi anxiously. 'I mean, Emery's wedding was fab, but it nearly killed you.'

I shrugged. 'I don't *want* to do weddings. But I get the feeling that's what Jonathan thinks I should be doing. I mean, I could certainly make a lot of money out of it. His friends are obsessed with etiquette, and they think I'm some kind of expert.'

'Well, you are. To be fair,' said Gabi, 'I don't know anyone else with their own set of strawberry forks.'

I gazed helplessly at her. 'But is it really awful of me not to want to do that *all the time*? Even if Jonathan wants me to? Be honest. I don't like brides. I don't like what all that white does to women's brains. And I prefer dealing with men. They're just so much more straightforward.'

Gabi gave me a 'well, duh' look. 'Which is probably exactly why Jonathan doesn't want you doing it. He's scared you'll run off with someone better. Running off with a groom would *really* wreck your business.'

'Don't be ridiculous!' I scoffed. 'The whole *point* is that Little Lady men need help buying their own socks, and he's already perfect!'

'Maybe he doesn't see it like that.' Gabi paused. 'I mean, not being funny or anything, but maybe he's still sore about Cindy running off with his less thrusting and dynamic brother? That's got to hurt, when you're Mr Perfect.'

I considered. Jonathan was obviously still sore about his marriage breakdown, but that only proved how much he still felt about Cindy. Not good.

'Well, yes, but I just don't understand why he's being like this when he's always been so gung-ho about my so-called "business savvy".' I put bunny ears around it, in case Gabi thought I'd lost all remaining traces of irony.

'Has he come straight out and told you to pack in the agency here?'

I wriggled. 'No. But we haven't really discussed what's going to happen next. I didn't want to look pushy. I've only been in New York ten minutes. But he has told me, quite specifically, that I'm not supposed to do anything, you know, agency-ish, while I'm out there, and he's been a bit, well, funny . . .'

Gabi peered at me closely. 'And you have, haven't you?'

Honestly, she could read me like a book. I really had to learn how to be more poker-faced. 'Sort of. Actually, no. No! Well, yes.'

Gabi giggled. 'Oh dear, Mel. Dr No doesn't like being disobeyed. It's not programmed into his circuitry.'

'I didn't do it on purpose!' I protested. 'I just got . . . niced into it.'

She wagged her finger. 'And that, Melissa, is your

Achilles heel. The *nice*. God almighty. And it was a man, too, wasn't it? Go on, tell Auntie Gabi. I have this odd feeling that Jonathan's funny moods are about to fall into place.'

With a growing sense of panic, I confessed all about Godric, and Paige manoeuvring me into looking after him, and the photo in the paper, and how I was meant to be turning him into Mr Knightley Extreme. Back in London the whole thing suddenly looked like a disaster waiting to happen. No. A disaster that was actually *happening*.

'I don't even know what she *wants me to do*!' I wailed. 'How on earth am I meant to make him look *dangerous*, Gabi? I'm used to smoothing down rough edges, not roughing them up. I don't even know what bad boys are like. I mean, the only bad boys I've been out with were bad in the "I didn't pay my congestion charge and some-times don't brush my teeth for three days" kind of bad.'

Gabi tapped her fingers against her jawline. 'Well, Orlando von Borsch was bad. He had slip-on shoes. And he broke your heart.'

'I don't think that's quite what Paige's after.'

'Isn't it? Getting a gullible MP's daughter to arrange his tax investigation while he tops up his alligator-handbag tan on board HMS *Saucy Sue* or wherever he was, using the pneumatic Lady Tiziana Buckeridge as a human sunlounger—'

'Gabi! Stop it!'

She wagged her finger again. 'And was it not the action of a solid gold bad boy to advertise this outrageous behav-iour in *OK!* magazine? Orlando niced you good and proper, Mel. Just because he sometimes told you that you were jolly good *fun*.'

I glared at her. 'Thank you for your sage advice, Auntie

Gabi. But had you met Godric Ponsonby, you'd realise how he isn't even in Orlando's league. Anyway,' I added, 'Orlando is all in the past for me. I am no longer that kind of girl. I have more self-respect these days.'

'And how did Jonathan take the news that you and this Godric were once an item? Hmm? Doesn't a film star rather put Cindy the Fireman's Friend in the shade, ex-wise? You know, the more you tell me, the more I'm starting to feel sorry for Dr No.' She clapped a hand to her mouth. 'Did I just say that?'

'Gabi! We *weren't* an item. It was just one of those school things. Years ago. I'm surprised he can remember. Anyway, you know more about bad boys than me. What can I do with him to keep Paige happy? Just so I can get out of this mess before Jonathan really kicks off.'

She pulled her lower lip sternly over her top one. 'I think you should tell this agent that your boyfriend has instructed you, in no uncertain terms, that your ingenuity is strictly off limits, and that you can have no more to do with this project of deception.'

'You think?' I sighed. 'I mean, you're right. I should. But Paige's kind of scary and—'

'Of *course* I don't think you should tell her that!' roared Gabi. 'Jesus! I know you never had much of a sense of irony, Mel, but are they draining it out of you, or something?' She slid off the desk and refilled our coffee cups. 'If you prove to Jonathan how well you can handle this, he won't have a leg to stand on about making you do boring wedding parties. Much better that you just do it, then pretend that it took you so little effort you didn't even remember to tell him about it.'

'Exactly!' I said, relieved that it had been Gabi who'd said that.

'Right. OK, you want that kind of upmarket living, downtown connections bad boy thing, yeah? Well . . .' She thought. 'Get him a BMW from somewhere, one of those classic old-school ones, and some really English suits, from Oliver James or someone like that. As English as possible. Does he watch *EastEnders* out there?'

'I don't know.'

'Well, just get him to drop a few "lor' luvva duck!" type things into conversation – Americans love that sort of stuff. "You're 'avin' a laaaaarrrrrfff, incha?" You know, retro cockneyism. Get him to wipe his nose on the back of his hand a lot like he's got a coke problem, and, oh yeah, have his nose broken while you're at it. Tell everyone he did it boxing in that East End pub where the Krays used to hang out; no, actually, *say* that, but say it in such a way that it sounds like he *really* got it broken in a fight. About his mother.'

I boggled at her. Where was this flight of fancy coming from? Or, indeed, going? So much for the shy, missing-Nelson, period Gabi.

I wondered dubiously if this had anything to do with that nightclub she'd been in the other evening when I called. Oh dear.

'What else?' Her brown eyes were glittering. 'Tell him to pay for everything in cash – it looks good and secretive. Has he got a ring? Great. Get a bigger one. One really big diamond ring on his little finger, and one of those big camel coats he can wear over his shoulders.'

'It's still summer, Gabi,' I said faintly. 'Are you thinking of the Mafia? Because I don't think—'

'He needs some personal pain and suffering in his past,' she steamed on. 'And some women who've broken his heart, but who he'd do anything for, even now. No kids though,' she added, 'that just looks careless. What's his girlfriend history?'

'Paige thinks there was one girl a while ago who dumped him,' I admitted, my mind filling with Godric's pasty gloom. 'But apart from that I don't know. It's hard to imagine him with a woman.'

'Hmm. Well, find out. Then make some up.'

'Gabi, I don't know if Godric can pull this off! He really hates interviews and photographs and dealing with people. He's just not that confident. He comes across arsey, but I know he's just shy. You know, like Roger. I can't even see him wearing *jewellery*.'

Gabi looked disbelieving, as if strutting around London with a camel-hair coat over one's shoulders, peeling off fifties from a grimy roll, was something we all did most days. 'He's an actor, isn't he?'

'Well, yes, but you can only really make out what he's saying when he's on stage, or on the telly or something.' I stopped as light belatedly dawned on my thick head. 'But this is perfect, because he can just *act* someone else. Ace!' I bounced up off my seat and gave her a big hug. 'God, I knew you'd work it out for me! I *knew* it was a good idea to come back!'

Gabi squeezed me. 'Well, if you're anything like you were first thing today, then you should be flying back for weekends. Jeez.' She held me at arm's length. 'Talk about stroppy. It was like Gordon Ramsay rocking up to bollock us.'

'Was it? Sorry. But, you know . . .' I didn't want to admit how much better I felt, after just a few hours in the office. In my own office. Being me. Not Jonathan's girlfriend, or Cindy's replacement, or even Braveheart's wrangler.

'I know,' said Gabi. 'But listen, don't let Jonathan make

you give up what you love doing best. And don't let anyone make you think you're not blonde enough or skinny enough or over-achieving enough. Because you're perfect as you are.'

I hadn't said any of that. So how on earth did she know that was what I was thinking?

Gabi's face softened. 'You know, I do want things to work out for you and Jonathan. Really I do. You've been there for me so many times in the past – you'd tell me if something serious was up, wouldn't you?'

I nodded slowly. But it wasn't anything serious. Nothing I couldn't sort out. Nothing I wanted to . . . make real by telling Gabi.

We looked at each other for a long moment, and then she rubbed her hands together expectantly.

'So, have you got a picture of this Godric, then?' she asked. 'If you're hanging out with film stars I need to know what they look like.'

I turned on the office computer to find Godric's official website. The desktop picture had been changed to a miserable Nordic icescape, with the words, 'Death is not the end', swirling back and forth in sinister cycles.

'Allegra,' Gabi explained unnecessarily. 'I'll change it back.'

'Would you?' I said faintly.

I found RicSpencer.com, complete with his new head-shots, that conveyed all the emotional range of a punch-up without actually revealing the full, unpleasant picture. While Gabi was swooning over them, I realised, to my shock, that it was almost time for me to leave for Daddy's meeting.

'Mel, he's gorgeous!' she said. 'Why did you never introduce me?'

'Because I haven't seen him since I was seventeen. And even then I'm not sure I'd have introduced you. He threw up in my car, you know.'

'You are the jammiest person I know,' she said lustfully. 'He is a fox.'

'A sloth, more like. Anyway, stop it. You've got your own fox to be considering.'

'My fox who never writes, who never phones, not even a carrier pigeon,' replied Gabi mournfully. Then, in more robust tones, she added, 'A girl has to keep her options open.'

I shoved some Rescue Remedy into my handbag. One crisis at a time. I didn't feel up to tackling the Nelson/Gabi issue just yet. 'Why don't you email Godric your ideas?' I suggested. 'Saves me time, and you can have a nice little correspondence.'

And, I thought privately, it'll start weaning him and Paige off my influence. Jonathan can hardly be cross if the advice has apparently come from Gabi and Allegra, the Bad Boy experts.

'Can I?' she asked, eyes lighting up.

'Yes, but let me see your email first, OK?' I insisted. 'Now I don't expect Allegra to apologise to me, but I want that apology to Mrs Kendall out of her, if it's the last thing I do.'

'Leave it with me,' said Gabi. 'Where are you off to in such a smart skirt, anyway?'

'To see my father. He wants to talk to me about this etiquette research he's commissioned me to do.'

Gabi gave me a patient look. 'Melissa. Think. Are you sure he's not stringing you along for something else? There's no scam in it anywhere?'

'No! It's for his Olympic committee. I'm rather

touched he's asked me to help, actually. We're working together.' I knitted my brows. 'Honestly, I've thought about it from every possible scam angle, and I can't see what's in it for him. Maybe he just wants to include me. Out of family feeling.'

Gabi snorted, and I left before she could make free with her suggestions to the contrary.

Crossing London after New York felt rather odd. The streets were winding, for a start, and weren't *logical.* The meeting was taking place at the antediluvian members' club my father belonged to, and as I walked down Piccadilly, en route to Pall Mall, I was struck as never before by the sheer elaboration on the building façades. Fortnum and Mason nearly brought me out in a proud patriotic rash. It was all so . . . old!

Daddy was lurking in the fusty reception area, ready to pluck me from the disapproving eyes of the doorman. It was not an establishment that readily welcomed women, or indeed any aspect of the twenty-first century, which was why my father liked it so much.

'She's my secretary,' he explained, hustling me past the front desk.

'You could just have said I was your daughter,' I protested, under my breath. 'There's no shame in that!'

'For the purposes of today, you are my secretary. Got that?' he hissed, as he propelled me past an oak door and into a panelled meeting room, where two besuited men were sitting in stunned silence in front of a presentation plate of cheese in various shades of orange, while Allegra regarded them with her steeliest gaze. She had changed, I noticed, into a very sharp black pencil skirt and matching jacket, accessorised with a lapel brooch that looked like a stainless-steel chrysanthemum. She looked like a wildly sexed-up, big-budget, Goth version of Honey.

The anti-Honey.

I shuddered, as the thunder clapped in my head.

Before I could say, 'What are you doing here?' Daddy moved swiftly to cut me off.

'Always late, eh? These women! What *can* one do?' he tutted blokeishly to the first of the two men, and Allegra snarled something in what might have been Swedish, but could easily have been her clearing her throat.

'Anyway, now my assistant has finally laid her hands on that vital paperwork, let's get down to business! As you know, gentlemen, there will be a significant tender for cheese at the Games; we'll need that plastic stuff for the continental breakfasts, plus regional specialities for lunch buffets, as well as a selection of quality cheeses for the formal dinners,' he rolled on.

Then he paused, while Allegra cackled away in tongues. 'Melissa, take it down, take it down!'

'But my shorthand is rubbish!' I hissed. 'I failed my exams twice.'

He leaned very close to me, so close I could smell the Jahlsberg on his breath. 'Just pretend then. And do try to smile. You might at least *look* authentic.'

And so this bizarre meeting passed. Since Daddy had spent the best part of his parliamentary life chasing various EU cheese freebies round the five-star hotels of Europe, I should have known he'd find a way to shoe-horn his cheese interests into his new line of work. Sadly, the delights of Cheddar weren't enough to stave off the jet-lag creeping up on me. I literally had roughly three functioning minutes left on my brain meter when Daddy abruptly drew things to a close, swept Sven and Ullick off to a boys-only drinking session and unceremoniously booted me and Allegra out into Pall Mall. It was drizzling, but warm at the same time – a seasonal treat only London could offer. Like a monsoon without the excitement factor.

'What was that about?' I demanded, as we walked in the direction of Green Park Tube.

'Oh, I don't ask,' said Allegra. 'I think we had to make an appearance at some point. For the sake of his invoices.'

I stopped walking and stared at her. 'What do you mean?'

Allegra didn't stop. 'Oh, I expect he's claiming us on expenses. Two secretaries, three secretaries . . . every little counts.'

Was this a scam, after all? That cash going into my account for Allegra's salary – *was* that Daddy's money? But surely I'd be getting more than twenty per cent of it, if that were true. I batted the thought away.

Allegra was some way off now, and I had to hurry to catch up with her.

'How's Lars?' I asked, panting slightly. 'I hear things are moving on with the investigation? I meant to ask earlier, but . . .'

Allegra turned to me with a disgusted expression. 'Do you think I *care*? That little shit. He sent me flowers, you know. From the police station! Like I would be impressed!'

I decided I didn't want to go down that road either. Allegra didn't offer many conversational avenues in this sort of mood. 'Well, just so long as you know what you're doing. And you're OK.'

She didn't even dignify that with a response.

I steeled myself. 'Allegra, you will speak to Mrs

Kendall, won't you? Those toys were most unsuitable for the poor little chap.'

'Are you going home for the weekend?' she demanded, ignoring me.

'Um, yes, I suppose so. It's Mummy and Daddy's—'

'I know! Give them this from me,' she said, reaching into her bag and shoving a small giftbox at me. I recognised it as one of the emergency scented candles I kept in my office present-drawer. 'If they're still together by the weekend. I've seen Daddy's *real* secretary.' She pulled a very descriptive face. 'Apparently, Claudia used to be a Rhythmic Gymnast. Still is, by the look of her.'

And she stalked off towards Cork Street without a backward glance.

16

Jonathan met me at JFK on Sunday night, and drove me back to Jane Street.

'How was home?' he asked, as we crossed the bridge back into Manhattan. I was still transfixed by the glittering, metropolis skyline.

'Oh, er, quite pleasant, actually.'

'Parents on drugs?'

'Parents not there.'

'But I thought . . .'

'Yes, well, I thought too. I only saw them for a few hours. Emery had booked them on a mini-break to Venice six months ago, and forgotten to tell them. William called while we were having dinner, to tell them a cab was on its way. They only made the plane on the final call.'

'What a shame,' said Jonathan.

'Not really,' I said. 'Two hours goes a long way with my family.' My parents had an up and down relationship, but the ups tended to be as dramatic and vocal as the downs, which didn't make 'home on an anniversary weekend' an ideal place for a child reluctant to end up in therapy.

'Anything happen while I was away?' I asked to push that lurid thought away.

'Braveheart's been foul. He's furious with me for letting you leave the country. He bit Yolanda? The dogwalker? Bonnie needs you to help her with some bridal shower gift she has to buy. Paige wants us to go and see that idiot Godric in whatever play he's in off-off-off-Broadway.'

Jonathan took his eyes off the driving for a moment. 'You want to go?' he asked, as though we'd been offered front-row seats at an autopsy.

'I'd quite like to see Godric act,' I said. 'And maybe you should too? It might improve your opinion of him.'

Jonathan leaned out of the window to pay the bridge toll. 'Unless he's acting his pants off in the part of a civilised intelligent human being, I doubt that. What else?'

'Sold your apartment?' I asked. I tried to sound casual, but it was much easier to promise Gabi I'd be tough about Cindy than it was to do it, now I was back in New York without a safety net.

'Almost,' he said.

'Problems with the buyers?'

Jonathan's face turned stony, and I knew he was concealing extreme annoyance. His voice remained light, though, which only made me more edgy. 'Problems with the co-vendor, I regret to say. I'm going to have to get lawyers involved if she doesn't stop messing about.'

'Oh,' I said, sinking back into my seat. 'You think she will?'

'I intend to make her,' replied Jonathan grimly, and I let the subject drop.

The next day, I got up to walk Braveheart and pick up some groceries. Jonathan had most of his food and drink delivered, but never seemed to have enough milk. I was beginning to realise just how many people were involved in the smooth running of his life: Concetta the cleaner, Yolanda the dogwalker, the grocery man, the dry-cleaner's, the squash coach, the shopper . . . Apparently, he assured me, this was completely normal for a Manhattan professional. I hoped he'd leave enough space in there for me to do something. My offers to start picking out decorating materials had been gently squashed, even though I felt like I knew his house better than he did, given the amount of time I spent in it.

'Now,' he said, standing on the doorstep, so our heads were at the same height. 'Do nothing today, OK? Go shopping or something. Visit a cathedral.' He leaned forward to kiss me, quickly in case anyone was watching.

'I will,' I promised.

'Great,' he said. 'I might be late because of my fundraiser meeting, but don't forget we're having dinner at the Grammercy Tavern tonight with some people?'

'Lovely!'

More people? Were we ever going to get dinner on our *own* again?

Jonathan must have sensed my flicker of reluctance because he touched my nose. 'Can you blame me for wanting to show you off? Everyone wants to meet you, and I can hardly say no, when you're making me seem like the luckiest guy in town.'

'But—'

He moved his finger from my nose to my lips. 'Come on. This is the most exciting I've looked for years. Give a ginger guy a break, OK?'

There was something about Jonathan's natural authority that really was awfully sexy, when you weren't on the office end of it.

Maybe I should see if Lori needed some extra temp

staff, I thought sadly, watching his athletic frame vanish around the corner.

When I'd fed Braveheart, and read the papers, and looked at my guidebooks, despite my best tourist intentions I found my thoughts straying back to work. The trouble was, I wasn't all that keen on being a lady of leisure, particularly when all Jonathan's female friends – more of whom I'd be meeting that evening – were such high-flyers, and also, since I'd just seen how much damage Gabi and Allegra could wreak on my business in a matter of days.

Besides, I told myself, I needed to talk to Gabi about some problems I'd spotted with Nelson's flat when I'd popped in to check up on the builders. I poured myself another cup of coffee from Jonathan's drip machine, and dialled the agency number.

Again, there was no reply. Where were these two? Was Allegra translating something for Daddy somewhere else? And was she getting paid twice? The more I thought about it, the fishier it got. Honestly, they were all such shameless scammers.

I turned on my mobile phone, and accessed the new voicemails. From the extended bleeping there seemed to be quite a few.

'What ho, Gabs, Roger here. Lunch today OK for you? I've booked at Foxtrot Oscar. Hope Mel isn't too cut up. Got a bit of an ear-bashing from her at the weekend. Think living with Remington's gone to her head a bit. So, um, probably best not to tell her about the other night, eh?'

What?

Roger blethered on some more, in an unrecognisably chummy manner, then rang off, obviously blithely unaware that he'd left a message on the wrong office number.

My brow creased. Surely Gabi couldn't have been drinking in Hush the other night with *Roger*? *Could* she?

The next message was from Tristram Hart-Mossop's mother, Olympia. 'Good morning. This is Olympia Hart-Mossop, Tristram Hart-Mossop's mother,' she announced, in case I couldn't make the connection myself. 'I need to make an appointment with you to, am, discuss certain new developments regarding my son. He's very, am, anxious to ascertain when the transmission date of his makeover show will be, as his schoolfriends intend to organise some kind of party around it.'

Oops.

'So if you could call me back,' she wound up nervously, 'that would put all our minds at rest. He's hectoring me about buying a new outfit for the event. A new outfit,' she repeated, in wonderment. 'Apparently several young ladies are keen to attend. Am, yes. Thank you. Goodbye!'

I picked at a left-over mini muffin. Transmission dates. I should have thought of that. Maybe Paige would have a good explanation I could borrow for shows that didn't get made. I made a note to ring her back – I didn't want Tristram to lose face, not now he was on the road to super-studdom.

'Hello, Mel,' said a familiar voice, backed with what sounded like seagulls. 'It's Nelson. I knew you'd be checking your voicemail, even though you're not meant to be, so I thought I'd say hello. We're having a great time, weather's pretty grim, but that just makes it more fun. Not that I'm letting anyone put themselves at risk,' he added predictably. 'That would be silly. Well. Not unless they've really annoyed me.' I could hear clanking and swooshing in the background. For an engine-less ship it was very noisy. 'Anyway, just ringing to remind you not to buy any of those knock-off handbags, like the one you got in Turin that gave you a rash, and don't forget my deli list. GET OFF THAT MAST, TARIQ! AND WHERE IS YOUR REGULATION JACKET? So, yes, some granola and—'

A piercing emergency whistle ended Nelson's call, presumably the one around his own neck, and I felt a little bit bereft. Although I wouldn't have admitted it, especially not to him, I did worry. Awful things happened at sea, even to capable sailors like Nelson – storms, leaks, bits falling off the boat. I mean, look at Simon Le Bon. And Captain Bligh! He wasn't expecting that, was he? Nelson's leadership qualities did verge on a sort of militant Jesus.

Besides, I thought, in a small voice, it would have been kind of nice to have him scoff rudely, in his inimitable fashion, at my worries about Cindy.

I bit my lip. But what if he didn't scoff? I couldn't hide anything from Nelson. He could winkle out things I didn't even know I felt. Between him and Gabi I had no secrets whatsoever.

Braveheart pushed his china dish towards me across the floor with his black leathery nose, as if to say, 'Fill her up, lady.'

'You've eaten once this morning,' I pointed out.

He fixed me with his liquorice eyes and quivered with apparent starvation.

I buckled. 'OK. I suppose you are getting twice as much exercise as normal.'

He wagged his whole body with pleasure as I shook out a few dog biscuits, and then shoved his nose into the dish. I have to confess I took a certain pleasure in weaning him off Cindy's ridiculous Dog Zone diet and onto more traditional fare. Like Bonios.

The florist I booked my 'Year of Flowers' gifts with called to inform me that some miscreant had bounced a cheque with her; a client from Fulham was worried about how he could book a massage for his sister without looking like a pervert; a nervous, muffled call, possibly made from inside a stair cupboard, came from a client in an enviably smart house in Chelsea, who wanted to know how he could get his new mother-in-law to leave after her 'flying visit to the Harrods summer sale' had extended into a three-week nightmare.

And the final message was from Daddy. I knew that just from the first breath he took before launching into his message. It was short and to the point.

'Melissa. I've called the agency three times now and Allegra hasn't answered the phone. I need to get hold of her. The silly mare phoned your mother, talking about applying for a mortgage, and we don't want that, do we?'

Why not? I wondered. The rest of us had to.

But Daddy was frothing on. 'The last thing that silly girl needs – and the last thing I bloody need, come to that – is some nosey parker bank clerk poking through sensitive financial documents. Good God! I swear you three do these things just to bring on my early demise. Do I need to tell you I am on holiday, with your poor mother, and I'm still forced to deal with the cretinous shenanigans of her children? Hmm?'

With an odd, almost euphorically drug-like detachment, I watched Braveheart stuffing his face, and getting crumbs over his freshly groomed beard. None of the above was actually my problem for once. Allegra, Daddy, Lars . . .

Then I remembered that Allegra's salary went through my books, and normal service was resumed.

I had equally bad luck in getting hold of Allegra, and was lying down on Jonathan's big brass bed, flicking through a New York recipe book I'd bought for Nelson, when my mobile rang again.

I grabbed it, in case Allegra had deigned to return my call.

'Hey, Melissa,' grunted a familiar voice. 'You about?'

It was Godric. I hadn't actually spoken to him since I'd got back. I hadn't liked to, with Jonathan making transparent excuses not to see his play. Godric, though, was one of the few people I knew in New York who didn't view me through Cindy-tinted specs, and I was sort of getting used to his grumpy company. He reminded me, in some ways, of a very hung-over Nelson.

'Speak up, Godric,' I said. I could barely hear him for the sound of a car revving in the street below. 'I'm . . .' I flipped the book shut. 'I'm working.'

'Right,' he said, not sounding remotely bothered. 'Well, I got your list of suggestions.'

'Did you?' I'd asked Gabi to forward them to my email account so I could approve them, but so far she hadn't . . .

'You've *read* them?' I repeated, more fiercely.

'Yeah, your partner sent them to me.'

Partner, was it now?

'Right, well, I didn't have time to, um, conference with my *partner*, so maybe we should just have a quick run through them before you actually—'

'I'm not doing anything right now,' he said with something approaching eagerness. 'If you're about. You know.'

'Um . . .' No matter what Jonathan said, I couldn't just

drop Godric. That would be rude *and* unprofessional. And it wasn't like I was doing anything.

The engine continued revving in the street. I gave in and peered out of the window. A huge black car, the size of two king-size beds, was blocking the street, much to the annoyance of a couple of dogwalkers and an old lady who was trying to get past on her bicycle. I wasn't totally au fait with cars, but this one looked as if it did about three miles to the gallon. The driver was getting through a gallon or two now, just in show-off revving. Honestly.

'You'll have to speak up, Godric, I can hardly hear you. Some idiot outside . . .' I put a finger in my ear. 'Where are you?'

'I said, you want to go out for a coffee? I've got something to show you.'

I checked my watch. I wasn't meeting Jonathan until six, so I had plenty of time. I supposed I should at least find out what Gabi had told him to do.

'Well, all right,' I said. 'But I have to be back by three. I'm going out for dinner tonight.'

'Aces. Come on down.'

'What?'

'I'm outside.'

I went back to the window. I couldn't see inside the car since it had those 'look at me! No, *don't* look at me!' celebrity tinted windows, but Godric obviously saw me, because he started honking the horn. The woman on the bicycle looked up at the window, and I ducked down in shame.

'I'll be right there,' I said, grabbing my bag.

Outside, I avoided the gaze of passers-by and slid gratefully into the cavernous interior of Godric's car, horrifying myself by noticing, yet again, how delightfully powerful the air-con was. Nelson would have three environmentally inspired fits if he knew how many natural resources I was wasting on keeping cool in this sweaty city.

I looked round. Godric, in the driver's seat, seemed a long way away.

I didn't like to say, 'This is yours?' because wherever I placed the stress in the sentence it sounded faintly insulting. It felt as if I were sitting inside a very pricey black handbag: there was more leather than I'd ever seen outside a DFS showroom. Quite astonishing. Things glittered at me, and the bits that weren't leather or glittering were sort of dull black. It all smelled wildly expensive.

'So, you've—' I started to say, but he lifted a silencing hand.

I found that with men and cars. They seemed to acquire a whole new personality as soon as they were installed behind the wheel of something with an engine bigger than a lawnmower – a personality borrowed largely from films. Whereas Nelson turned into one of the camp stunt drivers from *The Italian Job*, Godric seemed to be channelling Tom Cruise in *Days of Thunder*. Or was it some kind of gangsta rapper? Whatever it was, he'd donned a new pair of black sunglasses. They were somehow . . . blingier than his usual ones.

'Put your seat belt on and don't touch nuttin',' he instructed me, in a strange combination of Brooklyn gangsta and Tufty Club safety drill.

'I have no intention of—'

'OK, let's go,' mumbled Godric and floored the accelerator. I was jerked forward then flung back in my seat so hard that my head actually hit the headrest, and from the cavalcade of horns around us I guessed we were lucky not to have collided with anything else.

I swallowed as Godric made appreciative noises over the sound of the engine. The trick was not to let them feel your fear. I'd learned that with horses at Pony Club.

'So, er, where d'you want to go?' asked Godric, running out of attitude.

'Don't mind!' I managed to squeak.

With a cautious stab in the direction of the matt black controls, he buzzed down the windows and turned on the stereo in one movement. Europe blasted out at tooth-rattling volume, mid-synth solo. It wasn't what you'd call street.

'It's the finaaal countdoooooowwwn! Top Gear Driving Anthems!' he yelled, making a death metal horn symbol with a broad smile. 'Rockin'!'

I hesitated, then smiled back. It was kind of endearing.

'I took your advice,' he went on. 'You did say an M6, didn't you?'

'Well, yes!' I said. Gabi was the expert, not me. Buildings flashed back at a worrying rate. 'It's, er . . . It's very impressive. Do you want to slow down a little?'

'Nope!' Godric straightened his arms against the multi-function steering wheel. I'd rarely seen him look so animated. It seemed unfair to spoil it for him.

I slid down into the leather sports seat and slipped off my shoes, the better to brace my stockinged feet against the nearest reinforced structure. It would be an experience, at least.

We roared through the streets, leaving a trail of soft metal and exhaust fumes behind us. Once I'd got over the initial stomach-lurch every time Godric changed lanes, I started to enjoy myself – after all, it wasn't often one was swept through New York by a film star, albeit a rather unfinished one.

We left the brownstones behind us, and I think we started approaching Central Park. The buildings got taller, anyway, and I could see green through the smoked glass.

'Where are we going?' I asked Godric.

'Don't know,' he yelled back, then added solicitously, 'you OK there? Comfortable? Not scared?'

I smiled, pleased to see him enjoying himself. He was quite a good driver, to be fair to him, and it was a pretty fantastic car. 'I feel perfectly safe in your hands, Godric!'

A strange look crossed his face and he reverted to his usual round-shouldered self. 'Uh, thanks, Mel.'

'Quite capable hands they seem to be too!' I added cheerfully. 'Are you going to take me on a bit of a joy-ride? Scream if you want to go faster, and all that?' I pushed a random button and felt my seat move in on me, gripping my waist in a surprisingly intimate way, for a car. 'Oooh! Godric!' I giggled. 'Something's vibrating! I'm getting all . . . tingly! Wow! What else can this car do?'

Godric made a choking noise, and I looked over. He'd gone very pink and seemed to be fidgeting suddenly with his trousers.

'Oh, God, sorry!' I exclaimed, jabbing at the buttons. 'Have I made your seat vibrate too?'

'No,' he croaked. 'It's just that . . . I, um . . .' He looked at me, and I noticed that despite the air-con he was perspiring. I made a mental note to introduce some natural fibres to his wardrobe. 'Thanks for coming out with me it was jolly decent of you know how busy you are and everything and—'

I patted his knee jovially. 'Eyes on the road, Godric.

You don't want to be a James Dean kind of film star, now, do you?'

That seemed to snap him back into his mean and moody actor mode and after a few blocks, I noticed that he was speeding up and getting quite chancy with the red lights. I hoped he wasn't doing it to impress me.

'Godric, don't you think you should keep an eye on the speedo?' I asked. 'I mean, it would be awful to get a ticket on your maiden voyage.'

He grunted in response and looked in the rear-view mirror for what seemed like the first time.

'What's the matter?' I asked. 'Is there something . . . ?'

When he didn't reply, I looked round myself – it wasn't the sort of car that had easy-to-check mirrors – and saw that someone was following us, very close.

'Gosh, they should back off,' I said, turning back in my seat. 'American drivers are so inconsiderate, don't you find? The cars are so huge they don't even think what a shunt would feel like.'

Godric didn't take my hint, though. His mind seemed elsewhere. 'So, you think this is a sexy car, then?'

'Oh, absolutely,' I agreed. 'A girl could really imagine being swept off her feet in one of these. It's very . . . James Bond.'

Godric flicked an eyebrow and, I think, tried to look like Jeremy Clarkson. 'The . . . *ride* is very smooth with the M series *models*. They're quite . . . *powerful*. If this car was a man, it would be . . . *Pierce Brosnan*. Eating a *steak*. In *Claridges*.'

I smiled politely. God knows I wasn't trying to encourage him, but there was a fine line between reining a chap in and destroying his confidence completely. Poor Godric needed lots of practice, Lord love him.

'Like the look of the back seat?' he added.

I twisted round. A broad expanse of leather gleamed luxuriously. 'Ooh, yes,' I exclaimed. 'You could practically lie down back there!'

When I twisted back, Godric snapped his head round very quickly, almost as if he'd been trying to look down my top. I tugged my cardigan together where it had started to gape.

'Did you know, you can see right down your—' Godric began conversationally.

'That doesn't mean you have to *look*,' I snapped. 'So, did you get your first pay cheque for the film, then?'

'Er, sort of.'

The other car was getting very near. I hoped they weren't car-jackers. I'd read about that sort of thing.

'Why don't you just let him past?' I suggested. 'Pull over?'

'Melissa, I have a British driving licence,' Godric informed me darkly. 'If he wants to get past, he can indicate. That's the way it works. Fair's fair.'

I looked round again. The car behind was now so close that I could see there were two men in the front seats, both wearing rather sinister-looking shades. If they got any closer, they'd be able to change the CD in the player. As I looked, one smiled at me, and it wasn't nice. At all.

My skin went cold. Could they be something to do with Allegra? Could they somehow have found out I was here? Could Allegra be mixed up, somehow, with . . . the Mafia?

I grabbed Godric's arm. 'For Pete's sake, this isn't the time for your ridiculous right and wrong games! Pull over, just pull over.'

'No way!' he snarled. Clearly he wasn't just driving a

Bond car. He *was* James Bond. Usually, I'd be perfectly happy as a Bond girl, but not like this.

'Please!'

Then belatedly, the passenger in the car behind slammed a revolving light on top of the car and turned on the siren.

I swivelled as far as my seat belt would allow. 'Godric!' I roared. 'It's the police! I am *telling* you now – pull over!'

A broad smile broke across his face. 'Excellent! Let's go!'

I couldn't believe this. We were in a car chase. Godric really did only galvanise himself in make-believe situations.

As we roared through the streets, my mind raced equally quickly, trying to establish some kind of defence. Paige would go insane when she found out I'd let Godric get himself into this much trouble. Or maybe she wouldn't. We'd never quite established just how dangerous she wanted him to appear.

A thought occurred to me. 'Godric, tell me honestly,' I said, in my very firmest tone. 'Do you have any idea why the police would have been following us? Before you started jumping lights.'

The CD shuffled Europe off, and the Smiths on. Morrissey didn't fit with the gangsta car any better than Joey Tempest had.

'Godric!' I snapped, as he squirmed pleasurably. This wasn't the time to discover his supernanny fixation. 'Quickly!'

He huffed and reslumped his shoulders. 'Ngh. Dunno. Oh, wait – it might be something to do with the dealer bloke.'

My heart sank. 'You are talking about *car* dealers here?'

'Yes!'

'Well, what about him?'

Godric gave sullen 'Why are you *bothering* me? Eugh! You're so *unfair*!' shrug, and any residual vestiges of film star vanished as the more familiar overgrown adolescent reappeared. 'I think I might have left him at the petrol station.'

The police car was now trying to overtake us, to head us off.

'What?' I shrieked. 'You *left* him?'

'Yeah,' grunted Godric. 'He was boring the pants off me, with his boring car dealer spiel, so when he stopped to put some petrol in it, I thought I'd just take it round the block a few times on my own, see what you thought, then take it back.' He paused. 'Only I got lost.'

I covered my face with my hands for a few seconds, but when I removed them, everything was still there. Including the siren.

'Pull over!' I said firmly. 'Pull over now!'

'I'm not very good with left-hand-drive cars,' he whined.

'Do it, or I'll do it for you!'

Godric lurched to a halt, nearly taking out a street sweeper.

'Right,' I said, thinking quickly. I had maybe thirty seconds. 'Don't say a word. Leave this to me.'

'What are you going to say?'

'I don't know yet. Let's see how mad they are.'

We got a rough idea of how mad they were when both policemen leaped out of the car and started yelling at us through a loudhailer.

'Get out of the car and put your hands on the roof! Don't try any sudden movements! We are armed, repeat armed.'

Godric and I stared at each other.

Then to my absolute horror, he frowned. The same

affronted English gent frown that I'd seen before he punched the man in Central Park. 'This is really not on!' he said. 'Armed police? How unnecessary is that? And you've done nothing wrong!'

Before I could stop him, he swung the door open, shouting, 'This is police harassment, you barbarians!'

'Noooo!' I yelled, jumping out as fast as I could. How much worse could this get?

The nearest officer made a grab for Godric and started to cuff him. 'Thought you could just stroll into a car dealership with your fancy British accent and steal a two-hundred-thousand-dollar car, huh? I am arresting you—'

'No, wait!' I protested, wilting slightly under the unexpected humidity. 'Do you know who he is?'

'Nope,' said the other policeman with supreme lack of interest. 'Hugh Laurie? Tony Blair? Don't make no difference – it's still theft.'

'I am going to get my agent on to you,' Godric was fulminating, his face turning red and white with rage. 'And she is going to sue your *arse* off!'

'Go right ahead, sir. We look forward to receiving her call. In the meantime—'

'But this is Ric Spencer, the actor! The Hollywood actor? And he didn't steal the car,' I insisted, as the other one started to approach me with a pair of cuffs. 'He was, um, taking it for a test drive.'

'We know that, miss. We received the call from the car-jackee.'

I swallowed. 'Yes, well, he was taking it for a test drive as part of his research for a new role he's playing in an upcoming movie with, er, Keira Knightley, in which Ric here—'

'Still theft.'

'Yes, but I was getting to that . . .' I stalled, as the cuffs got nearer and my mind got blanker.

'Would you hold out your hands for me, please, miss?' enquired the second policeman. I couldn't help but notice how nicely he asked.

However, with Gabi's words about being niced into things still fresh in my mind, I absently lifted my wrists out of reach, and went on, 'When he saw me walking down the road.'

I paused and raised my eyebrows with a big smile, as if I were about to begin the most hilarious cocktail party anecdote.

To my amazement, it seemed to work. Both policemen, and Godric, tipped their heads in lovely 'do go on' encouragement.

'Right, well, um, I was walking down Fifth Avenue, just, you know, looking at the shops, when I realised I was being followed! By a, um, by a big man. I could see him in the shop windows behind me, and I'm sure he followed me into the Gap. Anyway, I was just walking along, and I'd got to about, er, Thirty-Ninth Street,' I elaborated randomly, 'when I saw Godric in the car, so I waved at him, and at that exact moment, I felt someone try to steal my handbag!'

I clapped a hand on my maidenly chest for emphasis.

'I didn't know what to do! I mean, I'd read all your very helpful New York guidelines about what to do if you think you're being mugged—'

'We do advise you to hand over your bag, miss,' the policeman reminded me. 'Not steal a car to chase the offender.'

'Oh, well, normally I would have let him have it!' I

improvised. 'But I have some very confidential documents in here, pertaining to some work I'm doing on behalf of my father, who is, um, a key figure in the British Olympic committee. And so, you see, I was concerned about letting my bag go.'

I cannot tell you how much it pained me to use my father as a bargaining tool. But it had suddenly occurred to me that being arrested in the company of the man he'd forbidden me to get involved with looked bad on any front. If I was with Godric socially, Jonathan would be jealous; if I was with him professionally, he'd be livid.

And Jonathan took priority. I did not want to be arrested. I did not want Jonathan to know about this *ever*, even if that meant using my father to wriggle out of it.

The first policeman removed his sunglasses and rubbed his forehead, as if he were having trouble working out if I were lying, or merely insane. 'So you're saying you were being trailed because your father is some kind of British . . . politician? And this guy is a Hollywood actor? Anything else we should know?'

I opened my eyes very wide and tried to look disarming. 'I know it seems rather far-fetched, officer, but yes. I've had to have special police training at home, to avoid kidnap.'

The other policeman looked less convinced, although, actually, that much was true. I have an excellent kick to the shins, especially in the sort of shoes I generally wear for work.

'And you're saying you just ran into this guy?' he went on, suspiciously. 'On the street? How do you two know each other again?'

'Friend of a friend,' I said, at the same time as Godric said, 'She's my *girlfriend*!'

I glared at him. 'Godric, I'm not your girlfriend. That isn't going to help.'

He looked back at me, guiltily. 'OK, then, an *ex*-girlfriend.'

I smiled at him sympathetically. He couldn't have had that many exes if he was counting a hopeless fumble in a cupboard as one. 'Darling, it was very nice and everything, and of course it's awfully exciting to say I snogged a famous Hollywood star, but I don't think—'

'Can it,' snapped the second, still shaded officer. 'I don't need to know your romantic arrangements.'

'There's no need for that!' said Godric testily.

I think I was beginning to see his Achilles heel. He was one of those men who couldn't be told. The apparent gallantry towards women was just an offshoot of not wanting them to be ordered about either.

'Now, come on, Godric,' I said, with a 'he's *so* dreadful!' glance to the more understanding officer, 'I really don't think—'

But too late. Godric had the manners bit between his teeth. To my horror, I saw a human version of Braveheart: not interested in the shoe until you want it, then unable to release it from his jaws for rage.

'You simply *cannot* harass us like this!' fumed Godric, Englishly. 'How were we to know that you operate test drives as if perfectly innocent customers were potential thieves? I'll have you know that in London, the dealers are decent enough people to let you take the car around the block yourself without ringing the police to—'

'That's enough! Get in the car!'

'—have you hauled in like a common criminal. And another thing, this car did not have cruise control as advertised!'

The loudhailer came out again and I felt cold steel snap around my wrists. 'Get in the car! Do not attempt to escape!'

For the first time, I became aware of the people stopping and staring on the pavement, and I began to die inside, very slowly.

As I was shoved into the police car, I saw Godric attempt to take a swing at the officer, only to lose his balance, at which point the other policeman neatly tipped him into the other side.

'Do you think they bought it?' demanded Godric in a not-very-hushed undertone.

I glared at him, temporarily too cross to speak.

'Excellent,' he said, settling back into his seat as we roared off. 'I've always wanted to be a political prisoner.'

I hope you won't mind if I draw a veil over the intervening three hours at the police station, in which Godric and I went over 'our' story about nine times, including my fascinating description of my stalker. I tried to make it as vague as possible; the last thing I wanted was some innocent six-foot hunchback being arrested for trying to snatch my handbag.

We were allowed to make calls, and while the police were checking out our ludicrous-but-true details, I called home. The last thing I wanted was Daddy getting a call to inform him that I was under arrest for assisting a car theft.

The phone rang and rang, and suddenly I remembered that there was no one there! They were on Emery's anniversary mini-break.

Cold sweat prickled my skin.

Just as I thought I was about to burst into tears, the phone was picked up at the other end.

'Hello,' husked a heavily accented voice, 'I'm really just burgling this house, so I'm afraid I can't help you with any enquiries you might have.'

'Granny!' I almost sobbed with relief.

'Melissa! Darling!' she cried, in her more familiar Park Lane tones. 'How lovely to hear from you! Where are you calling from?'

'A police station in New York.'

'Gracious, how racy!'

'Listen,' I dropped my voice. 'I need you to cover for me. I can't explain now, but there's been an awful mis-understanding.' I gabbled the story.

' . . . And so I've told them he saved me from a stalker, and . . .'

'And?' said Granny. 'What do you need me to do? Sounds like you've got it covered. Jolly well done, dar-ling. Your father would be proud. Your very first inter-national lie.'

'I don't think they believe me!' I wailed. 'I mean, who would?'

'Let me speak to someone, Melissa,' she said calmly. 'We'll soon have this cleared up.'

I had some misgivings about letting Granny take the reins, since she was even more imaginative than Daddy, but she must have said something, because half an hour later Godric and I were chucked out of the cells, without even having our fingerprints taken.

'I understand you've had some trouble in the past, ma'am,' said the arresting office. 'You should have said. We take press intrusion very seriously in New York.'

'Um, well, quite,' I mumbled.

He cut me a cheeky glance. 'So, off the record, you got any good stories?'

I looked bewildered. 'About . . . ?'

'About dating Wills?'

Godric stared at me. 'You dated Prince William? I never knew that.' He gawped, then added, rather unnecessarily, in my opinion, 'You dirty cradlesnatcher!'

'Um, I don't talk about it. All in the past,' I muttered. *Granny*. Honestly.

After a brief lecture about wasting police time, and the etiquette of testing new cars in New York, we were free to go.

'God, I should tell Paige about your brush with royalty,' said Godric. 'She'll be—'

I stopped walking and grabbed him by the hands.

'Please, Godric,' I said. 'Can this be our little secret? Please?'

He looked down at me, with a noble glint in his dark eyes. 'If that's what you want, Melissa,' he said gruffly, 'then it's our secret. On my honour.'

Our eyes met, and we shared a solemn moment amidst the clattering hallway. I knew that Godric, with his dramatic fixations, would take it as a matter of principle not to tell. Flooded with relief, I leaned up and planted a kiss on his stubbly cheek. 'Thanks!' I said. 'You're a real friend!'

'Nngh,' choked Godric, and opened his mouth to say something but I put a finger over his lips to stop him.

'Say no more!' I shh'ed. I was wiping my lipstick off his cheek when I caught sight of a familiar form in the grimy waiting room, where various dishevelled and confused customers were congregating. A smart, besuited form with very square shoulders and shiny shoes I could see from twenty feet away.

'Oh, bollocks,' I murmured, as panic returned to my bloodstream.

'So, what are you up to tonight?' asked Godric con-versationally.

Any chances of covering this up vanished like steam off a latte.

'Do you want to come and see my play?' he blethered on. 'It's not very good, but, you know, it passes the time. And there's a party next week, actually, that you could come to? Paige wants me to take you. Ungh!' He pulled a face. 'Seriously! It's like she doesn't trust me out on my own or something. But I'd still quite like you to come anyway. If you wanted to,' Godric finished, in a smaller voice, but I wasn't listening.

'Jonathan!' I said, trying to sound as if I got arrested all the time. Well, it was worth making one small attempt to bluff it out. The adrenalin of talking my way out of the crisis, seasoned with the sheer horror of brushing with the law, was making my voice frightfully English.

'Melissa,' said Jonathan, through very tight lips. 'I realise you've got some kind of television fixation going on, but could you not have limited your research to *The Kids from Fame*, and skipped *NYPD Blue*?'

I let out a tinkly social laugh, but knew that this show of levity from Jonathan was for Godric's benefit. Underneath his polite smile, he looked seriously rattled. Rattlingly serious, even.

'I'm glad to see you've found the funny side to all this, but I still need to speak to the officer in charge,' he said. 'Would you excuse me, Mr Spencer?' And he moved away, towards the enquiry desk, ignoring the queue building up.

'No, honestly, there's no need!' I said, grabbing his arm.

'There most certainly is.' He disengaged me firmly.

'While I admire your grace in adversity, Melissa, might I remind you that you've just suffered both an abduction attempt and a false arrest? There may be consequences, legal consequences, actually. Not to mention security issues.' He banged on the desk. 'Hello?'

'But Jonathan, really . . .' I chewed my lip. Oh, God. This was why I tried not to tell fibs. I just couldn't handle them once they were out of the bag. 'How did you know about the, er, abduction attempt?'

He turned back, concern drawing deep lines around his mouth. 'Paige called me. She explained how Ric here got you out of a tight spot with some man who'd been following you and . . .' Jonathan ran a hand through his hair. 'Jesus Christ, Melissa! You really shouldn't be carrying politically sensitive documents! What was your father thinking? It's not your job, you don't have protection, and, you're on holiday! The cops had no right to cuff you. Absolutely no right whatsoever.' He turned back to the desk. 'Can I get some goddamn attention here?'

Godric opened his mouth and I glared at him. A cold chill ran over my skin, and for once it was nothing to do with the air-conditioning.

'If I don't talk to someone in the next thirty seconds, I am calling my lawyer!' barked Jonathan.

'Jonathan,' I said, pulling at his arm. 'Please? Can we just go home? I don't want to make any more of this than is absolutely necessary. I feel an utter fool. I should have been more careful with my bag. Handbag strap *firmly* across my body from now on.'

Jonathan paused in his slamming of the desk to give me a patient look. 'Honey, we're not in Parsons Green now, you know. You're telling me that someone was following you? And you're happy just to go home and forget all about it?'

I inspected my feet. 'Well, that's the thing . . . I might just have been paranoid. And I'd really rather not make a big deal about it, you know. The newspapers and everything?'

'Melissa! Get your priorities sorted out! I don't care about your stupid father, but I do care if you're being intimidated on the streets of this city!'

'Jonathan, I might have been wrong!' I insisted. 'And I just want to *go home!*'

'But . . .' He saw the pleading look in my eyes, and gave up. 'Fine. Let's get you home. I can deal with this later.'

Part of me bridled a little at the fact that he felt obliged to deal with it at any time, when it was dealt with already, but that part was more than swamped by the relief I felt as he ushered me out of there, back onto the street, his strong arm protectively around my shoulders.

'I'll, er, get a cab,' said Godric, who, deprived of his car, had shed his gangsta swagger and reverted to his usual dank Latin teacher persona.

'Thank you,' said Jonathan stiffly. 'I appreciate your taking care of Melissa.' And he shook his hand twice, then gave him an equally awkward slap on the back. 'Call me if you decide to take any further action about the arrest situation. I can recommend an attorney.'

'Oh, er, cheers,' mumbled Godric. 'I'll, er, see you around, Mel.'

'Oh, I shouldn't think so!' I said brightly. 'Maybe at that premiere of yours!'

A gloomy look passed over his face. 'Yeah. Right. I'll get Paige to call you.'

'No!' I said, with a sideways look at Jonathan. 'No, she can call Jonathan. If she wants to invite us *both*.'

Jonathan looked very weary at the mention of Paige's name, but was too well mannered to do anything more than smile in polite agreement.

Spotting a vacant taxi approaching, I managed to make it stop, for the first time since I'd been in New York. The tension must have made me look positively native.

17

Jonathan said nothing for several blocks. And that was worse than being yelled at by Officer Dibble.

Eventually, I could bear the silence no longer. 'Jonathan,' I burst out, 'please believe me, I honestly didn't know that . . .'

He ran a finger around his collar and loosened his tie. 'What?'

'Godric,' I said. 'I really did just bump into him. I wasn't, you know, *improving* him or anything.'

Jonathan looked at me strangely. 'Did I even suggest that you were? Interesting that you're more concerned about that than about being arrested. Or stalked! Look, I can see there was . . . an element of confusion about the whole incident, but as long as you're all right, that's all I care about.'

I bit my lip. 'But I wouldn't have—'

'Let's drop it, OK?' He patted my hand. 'You're safe and that's all that matters. We need to get home and get changed before Jennifer's party.'

I didn't like the feeling that he was forgiving me, when I hadn't done something that needed forgiving. For once. And he shouldn't feel embarrassed – *I* was the one who should be feeling mortified, and I was just about keeping it all in check.

'It's not like it's going to end up in the papers this

time,' I gabbled on, unable to stop myself. 'I spoke to Paige when, er, Godric got his one call, and I explained everything. She promised me that it wouldn't go any further. She gave me her word.'

'I wouldn't set too much store by that,' said Jonathan. 'She's an agent. Would you excuse me for a second while I pick up my calls? I had to run out on a meeting.' He got his mobile out of his jacket and started to speed-dial. As he listened to his messages, a pained look spread over his face, tightening the lines around his mouth. From the expression, I wondered if it was Cindy.

It certainly sounded like a woman's voice.

I stared out of the window while he jotted notes down in his diary, not even looking at the landmarks flashing by. This wasn't how it was meant to be turning out. Shouldn't we be ice-skating hand-in-hand on the community rink, or whatever the late summer equivalent was? Not sitting in silence in a taxi. While Jonathan called his office *again*? A terrible thought struck me. Had this just been a holiday romance for him?

Jonathan clicked his phone shut and turned to me, putting his finger on my chin to turn my face gently to his. 'Melissa, honey,' he said, more quietly. 'I was just really worried about you.'

I shook myself. It hadn't properly occurred to me how serious it must have looked from the outside. Blimey. I was getting sucked into Godric's egocentric world.

'Honestly, Jonathan, Godric borrowed the car for a test drive, he did what you can sometimes do in England, and drove around on his own for a bit, and the dealer called the police. I mean, I can understand why they freaked out . . .'

Jonathan drew in a deep breath. 'Whatever. Tell me about this stalker.'

I hesitated. Why had it been so much easier to lie to the police than it was to tell Jonathan the truth? 'I tried to explain that there'd been a misunderstanding. They wouldn't listen. And Godric wasn't helping. He got aggressive, and they must have got the wrong idea. So I . . . I tried to use my initiative.'

His face clouded. 'Don't tell me. You *invented* the stalker?'

'Yes,' I said quickly, to get it over with. 'But I didn't invent Prince William. Granny did that, to make it look like the man following me was a press photographer, I think. I should really check that with her. She has a fertile imagination.' I paused. 'I suppose at least she didn't say it was Kate Moss I was dating.'

Jonathan blew out the breath in his cheeks and sank back into his seat.

'Don't be mad with me!' I begged. 'I didn't know what else to do! I'd never normally . . . lie to a policeman,' I finished, in a smaller voice.

Lying to authority figures was something everyone else in my family did, not me. Oh, God. I was reverting to type. It would be chain-smoking and cheese-backhanders before I knew it.

'I'm not mad at you,' he said carefully. 'I could never be mad at you. Not even for . . . lying to a policeman.'

Was I imagining a hint of a laugh there? Surely not.

'But . . .' He exhaled again. 'This stepping in to fix Ric's little theft problem – it's *working*, Melissa. This is what I meant! You made up the story to get this guy off the hook! Why couldn't you just have said he'd picked you up in the car, you had no idea it wasn't his, and let him talk his way out of it?'

'I couldn't! I couldn't just stand by and let him—'

'Deal with it himself?'

That was a good point.

Jonathan pressed on. 'Or let his agent deal with it? The agent who gets paid to look after him? Who is more than equipped to—'

'All right!' I flustered. 'You've made your point. But I owed him a favour! He got *me* out of trouble in the park when Braveheart attacked that other dog and that ghastly man went ballistic with me.'

'And I guess he's a friend,' said Jonathan obliquely.

I turned to look at him. 'Yes. He's a friend.'

There was an awkward pause, where I wasn't sure what to say.

'Melissa, you have a big heart and it's one of the things I love about you,' sighed Jonathan. 'But . . .' He raised his eyebrows then dropped them. 'Enough with the fixing, already. Leave it. Please. I'm really not going to tell you again. Just concentrate on relaxing. Enjoying New York. Being with me.' He gave me his serious look, the one that seemed to see straight through to my lingerie. 'Next time I catch you Honey-ing, you're on the first plane back. I mean it, Miss Romney-Jones.'

'OK.'

'OK,' he said and made a 'drawing a line' gesture with his hands. 'End of afternoon. Let's start again with this evening.'

I felt marginally better.

'It should be a really nice evening tonight,' he went on. 'I haven't seen Steve and Diana in ages, and they're so keen to meet you. And the Grammercy Tavern is a great place to eat. You'll love it.'

'I'm sure I will,' I said, trying to inject as much enthu-siasm into my voice as possible.

To be honest, I was actually pretty shattered. Being arrested really took it out of you. I had no idea how Pete Doherty managed it so often. Secretly, I was yearning for a long bath, some amazing take-out from Jonathan's encyclopedia of take-out menus, and the remote control of the cinema-size television, not another round of meeting his amazing friends, all of whom made me feel as if I were being interviewed for a senior position in a very friendly blue-chip investment bank.

I shot a sideways glance at his lovely chiselled pro-file, currently directing the cab driver round a more effi-cient route. Jonathan was bound to know some kind of foot massage. He was extremely good at, well, other types of massage. He'd studied it in some detail, appar-ently, to the point where he sometimes came out with some disconcertingly physio-type commentary, which rather took the shine off the experience, if you know what I mean.

Then I remembered that we weren't quite at the smelly-feet-massage stage of things, and felt a terrible pang of homesickness for Nelson and his lumpy sofa. With Jonathan on it, of course. In his Ralph Lauren deck trousers.

The two images weren't really mixing in my head.

I pulled myself together. I had a reputation to uphold here. Think. Party. New people. More names, and jobs, and addresses full of numbers. 'Lovely!' I said, in a voice that sounded eerily like my mother's. 'What time do we have to be there?'

'Seven for seven thirty. So you've got time for a bath and a pot of that tea and . . .' Jonathan ran a finger along my damp hairline, making my skin tingle underneath. 'A quick lie-down?'

'Great,' I said. 'Um, Jonathan,' I added, 'my feet are in shreds with all this walking. Any chance of a, er, a quick massage?'

He looked at me seriously. 'Why didn't you say, honey? I'll get Lori right on it.'

One and a half blocks later I had a Milk and Almond Pedicure booked at Bliss Spa, for ten o'clock the following day.

Awfully nice, but not really what I had in mind.

Jonathan and I arrived at the Grammercy Tavern on the dot of seven fifteen. He was looking dashing in a cream linen suit, and I was wearing one of my slinky Honey silk dresses, which had returned from Jonathan's dry-cleaner looking newer than when I'd bought it in the Selfridges sale and about four times more expensive.

He caught me drawing a deep breath as we got out of the cab and almost laughed.

'Hey! Relax!' he said, slipping his arm round my waist. 'It's just dinner with a few friends.'

'It's easy for you to say that,' I said, though I didn't object to his steering me confidently past the intimidating doorman. 'I haven't met this many new people since freshers' week.'

'What can I say?' he said, giving my wrap to the receptionist. 'Everyone's dying to meet you. Listen, before you meet your adoring public, did I tell you how beautiful you're looking this evening? In fact,' he added in an undertone as we made our way towards the bar, 'I will be pleasantly haunted by the last time I saw you in that dress all through dinner.'

I nudged him to shut up, but playfully. I remembered too: it had been our three-month anniversary – which was quite an evening, put it like that. Oysters had been involved, as had dirty martinis and a ride on the London Eye.

'Jonathan! Hey, man!'

Another man in a suit, sitting next to another man in a suit, sitting next to two women, also in suits, sitting next to Kurt and Bonnie Hegel, waved at us, and Jonathan steered me towards them with a discreet hand on the back.

They all looked like they'd come straight from work, and suddenly I felt overdressed, not underdressed. God. Was I ever going to get this right?

I smiled and got ready to concentrate on remembering their names. When I got nearer, I realised to my horror that one of the women in suits was Jennifer with the Flapping Tongue from Bonnie's party.

OK. Rise above it, rise above it, I told myself frantically. She's more embarrassed than you.

'Melissa! Hi!' gushed Bonnie, engulfing me in her usual embrace of bones. 'You look absolutely stunning! You look like Catherine Zeta Jones!' Much as I liked Bonnie, it was like being hugged by something from the Natural History Museum. I wondered if I felt all squelchy by comparison.

'Hello, Bonnie,' I said when she released me. 'What a gorgeous jacket.'

'You see!' she stage-whispered to the two women next to her, directing a huge smile my way. 'You see? Isn't she a darling?'

I wasn't sure what they saw, but concentrated anyway as Kurt introduced everyone: he and Bonnie we knew;

I certainly did remember Jennifer, yes; Wentworth was another university friend of Jonathan's, as was Steve.

'And this is my wife, Diana,' Steve added. 'We're all set to give birth in eleven and a half weeks' time!'

'Hello, Melissa,' cooed Diana, flicking back her coppery fringe to see me better. She had one of those precision-cut messy bobs that fell back into place perfectly every time she moved her head.

I gulped. I'd barely even noticed she was pregnant. Everyone here was so *fit*.

'So you're back in New York!' observed Wentworth.

'Seems so,' said Jonathan.

'Oh, you are *so* London these days!' shrieked Bonnie. '"Seems so,"' she repeated in deadpan tones. 'Come *on!*'

'Jonathan, I need to drag you aside for a moment,' said Wentworth. 'Yeah, yeah, OK, I know!' He raised his hands against the barrage of *Friends*-style barracking that ensued. 'But I'm looking at this apartment and I need the inside line from the man here about the board.'

'Oh, God, if it's where I'm thinking, you may as well not bother,' said Steve, rolling his eyes. 'You are a dead man walking. We tried that, didn't we, honey? You have to have a Nobel Prize or a direct line to George Bush Senior to get past those guys.'

Diana nodded. 'We made donations to every charity you can think of, we put the freaking dog on a macrobiotic diet to get him under the pet weight limit, and we still didn't get invited back.'

'Melissa, I refuse to have you listen to that awful property talk,' said Bonnie, taking me by the arm and patting the spare seat next to her. 'Let's get you a drink. Champagne, isn't it?'

She signalled to the waiter, then turned back to me.

'So, tell me, how are you finding everything?'

Everyone asked me that, all the time, as if I were the first English person to set foot in Manhattan since the *Mayflower* landed, and I was never sure what to say: 'It's all so big!' was clichéd but true. And they were being nice, and I wanted to be nice back, so I could hardly say, 'Why are you all so obsessed with dental products?' or 'What's with the sales tax on coffee?'

Bonnie and Diana were looking at me eagerly.

'It's all so big!' I carolled. 'And the subway map makes no sense whatsoever.'

'Oh, you are funny. Let me come with you one morning,' said Bonnie indulgently. 'I'll show you how it works.'

'Not that you need to take the subway, with Jonathan's car service?' added Diana.

'Oh, I prefer public transport,' I said and when she looked stunned, I added, 'I like to see people? See where I'm going? That sort of thing.'

My flute of champagne arrived with about seven different dishes of nuts and nibbles. About two seconds later, the black-clad form of Jennifer materialised and placed itself on the seat next to mine. The breasts did not move during this manoeuvre.

Bonnie and Diana exchanged glances.

'Hello, Jennifer,' I said, to show there were no hard feelings.

'I'm so sorry,' said Jennifer in a big rush. 'I have to apologise. I've been carrying around this . . . this awful tumour of guilt.' And she scrunched up her hands to demonstrate the tumour-ness of her guilt. 'My thoughtlessness must have made you feel insecure and humiliated, and you must believe me when I assure you that *no one* was in any way discussing you, or you and Jonathan, or you, Jonathan and Cindy—'

'Or Jonathan, Cindy and Brendan,' put in Diana.

'Or *any* combination of the above,' said Bonnie firmly.

'I am so mortified.' Jennifer put a hand to her string-of-pearls area. 'Can you forgive me? I so want us to be friends. Jonathan is a wonderful, dear old friend of mine, and any woman he chooses to spend his life with is a woman I really want to get to know.'

'Well . . .' started Diana, but Bonnie shut her down with a look.

Good going, Bonnie, I thought approvingly.

Jennifer now had a Hand of Appeal on my knee, which was taking it a little far. Call me old-fashioned, but there's a time and a place for a hand on the knee, and this wasn't it. But she looked genuinely mortified, and something about her reminded me of Gabi. The Botkier handbag, maybe.

'Really, there's no need,' I said. 'Please let's just wipe it from our minds. I'm always putting my foot in it. And now you've met me you know I'm not blonde – and not even that young!'

'Really? How old are you?' she asked, rather directly.

'Oh, er, twenty-eight?' I stammered.

Jennifer put her head on one side. 'Really.'

'So, let me just get this straight in my head, was that someone else?' Diana butted in. 'I definitely heard Jonathan dated a blonde girl.'

'I think wires were crossed,' I said firmly, before Bonnie could start complicating matters.

'Well, I appreciate your graciousness,' said Jennifer. 'I don't think I could be so kind.' She sighed. 'The British have beautiful manners. It's like . . . they're just born with a natural grasp of etiquette.'

I thought of Godric. And Roger. And Gabi. And Prince Philip.

Though he was, of course, technically Greek.

'I wouldn't go that far,' I demurred. 'The accent covers a multitude of sins. And it doesn't wash at home, sadly.'

'But you do have great manners,' said Bonnie. 'I noticed that when we were over there. All the little kids say please and thank you. It's adorable.'

I wondered where Kurt and Bonnie had been staying. 'Well, I suppose we do get it drilled into us,' I said. 'Thank you for saying so.'

'Oh. My. God!' exclaimed Jennifer, as if she'd just had a marvellous idea. 'You could run classes in it here! I've seen things like that on the internet. You get to spend a week in a stately home in the UK, and learn all about flower arranging, and the aristocracy, and how to curtsey properly.'

'Really?' I hoped my father never stumbled on that website. My mother would be teaching port-passing before she could say 'bilk', along with everything else.

She nodded. 'Oh, yah. The HR department at the agency I work for? The head of PR went on a course, so she'd know how to deal with some of our British clients? She can make scones now.' Her brow furrowed. 'Scoones? Scones? Scornes?'

'Whichever you like. Lovely!' I said, because I honestly couldn't think of anything else to add, apart from, 'Did Jonathan tell you to tell me this?'

'So, Melissa!' cooed Diana. 'Are you shopping it up like crazy?' She winked at me conspiratorially. 'You can tell us. It's just girls together! We won't tell Jonathan!'

I laughed along with them, despite the fact that (a) Jonathan didn't seem to care what I spent on clothes, and (b) I wasn't really what you'd call a shopaholic, not compared with Gabi.

'Well, I've got a suitcase full of those plastic bleach things you stick on your teeth, what do you call them? White Strips,' I said. 'We don't have them at home. And I found the most amazing thank-you notes in that nice Crane's store, but apart from that . . .'

A cacophony of tinkly laughs drowned out my other admissions, which were going to be: nasty American chocolate that tasted of earwax (to try to break my own mid-afternoon snacking habits); several insane books on etiquette that would make the Queen freak out with social inadequacy (to be put on the office shelves to reassure clients); giant-size tubs of Palmers Cocoa Butter (my rule being that if you're going to have lots of surface area, you should keep it nice and soft); and breath fresheners. Americans seemed crazy about them. There were whole aisles full of them in pharmacies and I'd laid in a stock for the office. I might as well have had shares in Tic-tacs, the number of boxes I pressed onto clients.

'Listen,' said Bonnie, touching my arm, 'heaven knows Jonathan's no stranger to mad shopping, but if you want to hide any bags over at our apartment until you go home, we won't let on!'

And off they went again, laughing through their perfect noses and casting knowing nods at each other.

'I hide my emergency Bendel's card in my ante-natal bag!' hooted Diana. 'It's the last place Steve'd look!'

'Nooo! Sherman thinks I cut up my Bloomie's plastic but it was really his donor card!'

'You can tell us,' said Diana, wiping her eye. 'You're among friends. How much've you spent?'

'No, really,' I insisted. 'I don't really ever find much

in the shops. I usually make my own clothes. You know, nothing much fits when you've got, um, my curves' – I waved a hand at my ample bosom and swooping hips – 'so I prefer to run something up myself. Or convert some of my granny's clothes.'

I realised they were all looking at me with strange expressions. 'She did some modelling when she was younger,' I added defensively, in case they thought I wandered around in M&S cardies and slacks. 'Um, Lanvin, I think. She knows all about darts and letting out seams, anyway.'

'Vintage!' breathed Diana, stroking my cardigan reverently. I tried not to back off, but it was quite weird. I felt like a donkey in a petting zoo. 'Oh, my God. I should have guessed that cashmere wasn't new. And you do it yourself?'

'Oh, yes,' I said. 'We learned. At school.'

Bonnie, who had ordered more drinks and about a gallon of mineral water, looked shocked. 'At school?'

'I know!' I said, with a self-deprecating laugh. 'Ridiculously behind the times. I should have been doing business studies or something, not learning how to greet a duchess at a ceilidh. Still—'

'Pardon me,' interrupted Diana. 'A duchess? At a what?'

'A Scottish country dance?' I elaborated. 'We did that too, for gym when it was too wet to play hockey. Lace-up pumps and everything! Gay Gordons, Strip the Willow. Sounds quite racy, doesn't it? Only it absolutely isn't. Not with the boys we had to dance with. Some of them acted like they'd never seen girls before.'

Come to think of it, most of them hadn't. And if there weren't boys available the taller girls had to 'volunteer'. As if being a foot taller than everyone else wasn't complex-making enough. I still habitually led and bowed, much to Jonathan's chagrin. I didn't tell them that though. I didn't want them thinking I went to some kind of Victorian institution.

Bonnie was shaking her head in amazed fascination. 'Oh, my God! Oh. My. God! I had no idea! So, were you, like, at school with anyone royal?'

They were all looking at me now, and I wasn't quite sure what they wanted to hear. But at least I was on firmer ground than with cross-media advertising budgets or apartment boards.

'I don't think so. Oh, um.' I paused. I should really wind this conversation up soon, I thought. Very soon. 'There was some talk about Muffy Churchill and Lord Freddie Windsor, but I think that was just idle rumour!'

'You've never met Prince William?' swooned Diana.

'No!' I said quickly. 'No, never!'

But at the mere mention of Prince William, these three highly groomed professional women started giggling like teenagers, and squeaking stuff about Prince Harry and royal prerogative and lovely manners and how beautiful his teeth were for an Englishman.

'He *will* go bald, though,' I pointed out quickly, before we got on to how many people would fit into Westminster Abbey for the ceremony. 'I mean, look at his dad . . .'

That just made things worse, as it turned out Kurt's firm had had some kind of royal visit from Prince Charles who had charmed everyone by eating a digestive biscuit *right there in front of them.*

'Oh, Melissa, you know what would be so cool?' demanded Diana, shooting a quick look across at Bonnie.

'What?' I played along, emboldened by the second glass of champagne.

'If you could organise my baby shower!'

Now I *knew* Jonathan must have put them up to it.

'Oh, I don't think I *could*, sorry. I mean, I don't know what they are,' I said apologetically. 'We don't have them in England. A pipe of port for a boy, and a charm bracelet for a girl, and that's your lot, really.'

Diana wrinkled her brow as far as it would wrinkle, which wasn't far. 'A pipe? Of port? That sounds kind of . . . ew. But, no, the shower – that's just a lovely, lovely afternoon where the mom-to-be gets together with her closest friends and spends some quality time with them, and receives beautiful gifts for the baby.'

Bonnie nodded. 'It's a lovely moment. The grand-mothers-to-be attend too? And it's a lovely bonding time for everyone, in the dizzy whirlwind of the whole birth experience!' She waved her hands around to demonstrate the whirlwind effect, and Diana rolled her eyes about too, in simulation of the dizziness she was feeling.

'And it would be so fabulous if you could do it like a traditional British tea party!' added Diana. 'You know, like one of those nursery teas you read about in books!'

'Well, yes, that would be lovely,' I said, feeling hemmed in. 'But I'm sure there's a tradition about who arranges it? Isn't it meant to be your best friend, or your chief bridesmaid or something?'

Jennifer, Diana and Bonnie all drew in a sharp breath and cast their eyes down at the cocktail nibbles.

'Oh, sorry,' I said quickly. 'Have I . . . ?'

Honestly, this was the trouble with Jonathan intro-ducing me to all his friends without bothering to fill me in on where the bodies were buried.

Bonnie glanced quickly at the others, and assumed the

mantle of responsibility. 'Diana's matron of honour was *Cindy*,' she said.

'Don't get me wrong, I love Cindy,' Diana added, a little too quickly. 'But – ha, ha! – I don't want her round my baby!'

'Not without supervision! And a fire extinguisher!' Jennifer chimed in.

'And of course she's run off her feet with Parker, so I doubt if she could anyway,' Bonnie explained. A nanosecond too late.

'Oh,' I said.

All four of us looked at our empty glasses.

The abrupt silence allowed the conversation from the other end of the table to cut in.

'So what are the home-owning differences over there, Jonathan?' Kurt had his earnest interviewing voice on. He did sound as if he were perpetually auditioning for a job on breakfast television. 'Would you say that the UK property market would be affected by the introduction of a co-op board arrangement in state-owned blocks?'

Jonathan's eyes were glazed like a week-old cod, but he was still making polite nodding gestures as Kurt moved condiments around to illustrate his points. When he caught me looking in his direction, Jonathan moved his eyebrow in his familiar, near-imperceptible 'it's just you and me in this room and no one else' way, and my heart melted.

I knew nothing about baby showers. I didn't even like babies all that much. But if it would get me some brownie points with Jonathan, when he was making such an effort for me, then, fine, I'd do it. I really wanted this to work. I really, *really* did.

And if it would show Cindy up in the process, well . . . that was just coincidental.

'Oh, I'm honoured that you've asked me!' I said brightly. 'What a lovely way to get to know New York better. I'd love to help out. Let's get together over coffee this week and I can give you some ideas, Diana.'

'Oh, my God! Oh, my God!' she said, clapping her hands together so hard her bob bounced. And then fell back into perfect place.

'Really, it's a pleasure,' I said, as Jennifer and Bonnie joined in the raptures so genuinely that I did start to feel that maybe I could turn things around. Maybe, if I just tried really hard, I could fit in with Jonathan's friends. Maybe . . .

'Melissa?' said Diana, suddenly very serious.

'Yes?'

She smiled angelically. 'Baby says thank you.'

If I hadn't grabbed my wineglass, I honestly think she would have placed my hand on her tiny pregnant stomach for confirmation.

I smiled nervously. 'Brilliant!'

'Ahh,' said Bonnie, as if she'd just match-made us. 'Cute!'

18

Immersing myself in Diana's plans, however, wasn't enough to save me from an excruciating scene when the news about Godric's 'felony' became public knowledge.

Ironically – or perhaps not – it was my father who broke it.

He called me on my mobile as Jonathan and I were having a rare conversation about what he could do to the house, over an early cup of coffee before Jonathan went off to work. We were sharing a box of fresh blueberry muffins. The flowers he'd brought me home the previous evening were on the table between us. Even Braveheart was behaving himself. I should have known it couldn't last.

'Melissa!' Daddy roared. 'You sly dog!'

'What?'

'Dating Prince William! I'd never have guessed! He doesn't seem the type to go for older women.'

Jonathan raised his eyebrows enquiringly.

'Wrong number,' I lied.

'It's in the papers, you know,' Daddy went on, less gleefully.

'What?' I demanded, turning cold. 'How?'

'Oh, Melissa . . . Anyway, what were you doing with that film star chap? And in a *BMW*, for heaven's sake. Have you ditched that stuffed-shirt Yank?'

I glanced over at Jonathan to see if he'd heard. The expression on his face suggested he had. Daddy was certainly bellowing loud enough. He sounded quite refreshed.

'My father,' I mouthed apologetically.

But Jonathan was getting up from the table.

'Don't leave yet,' I said, panicking.

'I'm not leaving. I'm just going out for the papers,' he replied.

'If you're going to nick a car, you might at least have found an Aston,' Daddy went on. 'Buy British and all that.'

I pressed the phone to my chest. 'No! No, don't go!'

Jonathan looked impassive. 'I don't want to interrupt your family call. Anyway, I'll be late.'

I slumped in my chair as the front door slammed behind him.

'Why are you ringing?' I asked Daddy tetchily. 'Just to have a laugh at me? And before you ask, I didn't tell them that. Granny did. She seemed to think it would help.'

'Your mother's very upset. It's shocking for her image to have a daughter who gets involved with police chases.'

I stared out of the window. It had come to something when New York felt more normal than London. '*Which* image?'

'You haven't seen *Country Life*?'

'No, funnily enough, I haven't been to the dentist recently.' But even as I said it, Mummy's words about lavishing Mrs Armstrong's prize-winning lemon curd on journalists floated ominously into my mind. I pushed them aside. One family press crisis at a time.

'Ah, well, you'll see soon enough. Now listen, if you get a call today from anyone from London, as a result of your carryings-on, I want you to tell them that Red

Leicester makes your hair shine, and you eat three ounces every day. Got that?'

'Fine,' I said dully, and hung up.

Braveheart and I looked at each other, and waited for Jonathan to get back.

Jonathan was not pleased. His irritation was well masked by polite amusement, but I could tell he was furious underneath.

'Ex-girlfriend of the heir to the throne, current girl-friend of a Hollywood film star – I should be flattered you're having breakfast with me at all,' he said, sounding a bit too much like Alan Rickman for my liking as he slapped the papers down on the table.

'But—'

'Melissa, this isn't like you.' He looked at me, his eyes now the colour of steel.

'It isn't!' I wailed. 'It's . . .'

My voice trailed away, as we both stared at the evidence to the contrary.

Nothing – and I mean, nothing – I said could make him see it was just wild press exaggeration. It didn't even stop him sweeping off to work on time. If only he'd been mad, I could have dealt with it. Biblical disappointment was so much worse.

And that wasn't the half of it. I still had to tackle Paige. She was meant to have contained all this. She *promised* me she would!

With a very heavy heart, I went upstairs to dress myself into some kind of dignity. Despite the September heatwave, I pulled on stockings and suspenders, a smart summer dress and heels, then applied my most serious make-up.

I gazed at my finished reflection in the round

dressing-table mirror, rehearsing my disappointment. Stern disappointment. 'How *could* you, Paige?' I started.

No, not firm enough.

'Paige, you've let me down, you've let Ric down and, most of all, you've let yourself down.'

I stared at myself. There was something missing. I just looked too guilty.

I sank onto the bed. Other people would have probably snorted some cocaine or something at this point. Or had a drink. Or . . .

My eyes moved towards my overnight bag.

No. I shook myself. No, that was a very slippery slope. *Just quickly. Just for a moment or two.*

No!

But I was already halfway across the room, sliding back the zip, feeling about feverishly for the forbidden bag.

And then, before I knew it, the wig was on my head, the blonde fringe was falling into my eyes, and staring out of the mirror was Honey, her eyes positively gleaming with ire.

'Paige.' I paused and gave myself a devastating glare of dismay. 'Darling, what happened? I'm simply bewildered! I thought you knew everyone and could do anything!' Rueful shake of the fringe. 'Oh dear . . .'

Without warning, a deafening volley of outraged barking broke my attention, and I was horrified to see that not only was Braveheart on the bed, now strictly forbidden, but that he was preparing to launch himself at my head.

'No!' I roared as he and I tussled in a very undignified manner, his sharp little teeth locked firmly around a thick hank of real hair. 'Braveheart! Get off!'

Breathlessly, I managed to remove him from my hair, real and fake, and stowed the wig well out of sight under my spare evening petticoat. Braveheart retreated suspiciously to the corner, where he set up a defensive growling towards the wardrobe.

'You're quite right,' I said to him, brushing myself down, 'I don't need the wig, now, do I? No,' I repeated, more to myself, though, than him. 'No, I don't.'

Erupting at Paige Drogan mightn't change the fact that my picture was right there next to Godric's more animated headshot, plus illustrative, insinuating copy, but it would make me feel as if it wasn't all my fault.

'Ms Drogan is unavailable this morning,' Tiffany informed me, without moving her telephone headset.

'Then I'll wait,' I said, settling myself into the uncomfortable chair. I ignored the tempting range of glossy periodicals on offer, choosing instead to stare straight ahead at Tiffany, until she was unnerved enough to make a few discreet calls.

Paige came hopping out of her office, beaming with delight.

'Melissa! Just the person I wanted to see! Come on in!'

I stalked in after her and closed the door.

'I can't stay long,' I said, trying to summon up the imperious tone I'd found when I was be-wigged. 'But I needed to see you about this awful business in the papers.'

'Hey, it's not so awful, Melissa,' said Paige, tipping her head to one side. 'In fact, it's exactly what I asked you to do! You made him look like a real knight on a white charger, rescuing you like that!'

'Paige, he was about to be arrested for car theft!'

'Well, even that wouldn't have been totally bad news,' she conceded happily. 'Ric Spencer is impulsive! He's gotta-have-it!' She looked over her glasses. 'I tell you, in six months' time, BMW will be begging him to steal their cars. So well done, honey!'

'Listen,' I said furiously, 'it might be great for Ric, but it's not great for *me*. I told you Jonathan wasn't keen on me seeing Ric at all, and now the papers are making out I'm his girlfriend! I thought we had an understanding that *nothing of that nature* would happen. I thought you'd be able to keep details like that *out* of the papers.'

Paige looked surprised. 'What can I say? People draw their own conclusions.'

'Yes, that I'm cheating on my boyfriend with some actor!'

'With some film star,' she corrected me. 'Anyway, Ric dating a beautiful politician's daughter – it just adds to the mystique, don't you think?'

'No,' I said firmly. 'I'm sorry, Paige, but this simply isn't on. I can't have anything more to do with Godric. Jonathan means an awful lot to me, and I won't risk hurting him, not for anything.' I paused. 'I'm surprised you don't care about how he feels. He's your friend, isn't he?'

Paige's surprise turned slightly patronising. 'Melissa, Jonathan's a professional. We're all professionals here. Maybe it's different in London' – she pronounced London as if she really meant Carlisle – 'but I think he understands that I need to work for my client. I thought *you* understood that too, in your line of work?'

'Obviously not,' I said, with a smile I didn't feel. She had no idea what my line of work was, not really. 'Never mind! It's been a fascinating experience.' I stood up and

offered her my hand to shake. 'Let me know when the
retraction runs, won't you, so I can show Jonathan?'

'What?'

'The correction that Godric and I *aren't* dating.'

Paige shook her head sadly at me. 'Honey, you have
a lot to learn about the ways of the world.'

I was so furious with Paige, but proud of myself for
actually losing my temper, that I took myself down to
the Magnolia Bakery and bought the biggest, sickliest
cupcake they had. I'd had smaller birthday cakes as a
child.

I was licking the last of the blue icing off the paper,
when my phone rang.

'Melissa, it's Godric.'

Oh, great.

'Hello, Godric,' I said heavily. 'How are you?'

'Shit. Do you want to have a cup of tea?'

'I'm kind of busy,' I fibbed, then paused, feeling a
sudden twinge of sneakiness. It was all very well yelling
at Paige, but she wasn't the one saddled with a hermit's
personality in an actor's body. Godric sounded even
glummer than usual, which was saying something. It was
only fair to say goodbye in person. And if I was completely honest with myself, being with Godric meant I
could just be me. Melissa 'Melons' Romney-Jones. That
was quite a big temptation right now.

'Go on. Please,' he said unexpectedly. 'I'll pay.'

'Are you *feeling* all right?' I asked.

Godric sighed and made strange noises down the
phone, which I assumed was nose-clearing. I sincerely
hoped it wasn't manly sniffling. 'Just feeling a bit . . . I'm
fine. Shut *up*, all right?'

No, then.

'Listen, I know where we can get a nice cup of tea,' I said. 'And some treacle tart.' No one, but no one, can feel miserable in front of a plate of treacle tart and a pot of tea, and I knew just where to get some full-on English tuck.

Godric phlegmed again, and when he'd finished, I gave him directions to Tea and Sympathy on Greenwich Avenue. If I was going to remove Godric's one English crutch in New York – and my own last remaining friend, albeit in the loosest sense of the word – I needed a strong cup of tea to do it with.

'Godric, I have to ask, is there something up?' I asked, once we were installed in a corner table with a pot of Tetley's (three bags) between us. I insisted on a corner table and kept my shades and sunhat on, just in case anyone could be bothered to recognise us.

He paused momentarily in his gradual transference of the contents of the sugar bowl into his teacup and looked up at me. He had no need of a disguise, looking, as he did, about as far from Hollywood heart-throb as it was possible to be. The bags under his eyes had tipped from 'moody' to 'ill' and his skin was the colour of wallpaper paste. If you went in for consumptives, he would have been a real pin-up. If not, you'd have been struck by his more-than-passing resemblance to the Just Say No poster-boy.

'No,' he lied, with a foul glare. 'Eff off. Didn't anyone tell you not to be so nosey?'

'Frequently,' I replied briskly. 'But you look ill. And I don't want to catch anything, not with my schedule. Does Paige know? I'm sure she has a doctor you could see.

I'm sure she won't want your upcoming promotion plans ruined.'

That got the cat out of the bag. At the mention of his big film, Godric flaked visibly.

'Shut up,' he whined, then looked hopeful. 'Do you think I look ill? You know, now you mention it, I haven't had a dump in a few days. Maybe I'm sickening for something. Maybe I need the care and attention of, um, someone to nurse me?'

'Stop that right now,' I said, topping up his tea. 'There's no point malingering. It's part of your job, all that schmoozing and dressing up. That's why they pay you so much money. You have to go and put the glad hand about.'

'But it's a load of bullshit!' he moaned. 'Those bloody awful pretend people, with their shiny faces and their tedious bloody coke habits.'

'Godric.' I pointed the teaspoon at him. 'Cut it out. We all have to do things we don't want to, from time to time. It's called having a job.'

'But I'm an *actor*!'

'That's still a job, last time I checked. Now, what's the problem?'

He heaved a sigh. 'You know that play I was in? Well, I've got to go to some bloody awful circle jerk party on Friday night. I really don't fancy going. Paige says I have to. Something to do with brown-nosing the corporate sponsors.' He looked up at me hopefully. 'I don't suppose . . . ?'

'Not on your life,' I said. 'Godric, you have to understand, I really can't risk that sort of thing happening again, even if it's totally innocent. I have to think of Jonathan here.'

He looked at me with his big sad eyes, and I felt a twinge of something, possibly remorse.

'I'm awfully sorry,' I repeated. 'But come on, Godric, you have to get over it. There'll be lots of compulsory parties in your career.'

'It wouldn't be so bad if I had someone to *go with* to these effing awful wank-fests,' he whined. 'At least I'd have someone to *talk* to. About something other than *everyone else there.*'

God, this shyness masquerading as misanthropy was wearing.

'Well,' I said practically, 'can't you call someone? A friend? Someone from your acting classes?'

'Don't have any friends here. Specially not at my classes.'

'What about someone in London, then?' I suggested, knowing rather how he felt. 'Surely Paige can arrange for them to come over. No . . . old girlfriends, perhaps?'

Godric looked agonised. 'Shut up.'

'Well, what about your parents, then? Wouldn't they love a glamorous weekend in New York?'

Godric fixed me with his most sarcastic glower. 'My parents? Hardly. Paige's already told me that they don't fit in with this image she's building. Not windswept and aristocratic enough. She asked me if I had any better-looking relatives who could step in for the premiere.'

'No!' I was shocked.

He nodded. 'That's nothing. You know what she wanted me to be called to begin with?'

I shook my head.

'God. God Spencer. I really had to put my foot down about that.'

I pursed my lips. *God?* Paige Drogan clearly wasn't

quite the person I thought she was. Maybe I should rethink this benefit of the doubt thing.

'How's Jonathan, you know, about the car . . . incident?' asked Godric.

'He's not as mad as I would be if it were me,' I said carefully. 'I tried to explain about Granny being a bit, you know, melodramatic. I think he saw the funny side.'

'It wouldn't surprise me if Paige fed them all that information herself,' he grumbled. 'I mean, the police can't release details like that, can they, if there's no arrest made?'

I looked up at him. 'No.' I frowned. 'That's right. It must have been her.'

'The sly cow,' said Godric. 'I felt bad about that, you know. And we were really starting to have a good time together, weren't we?'

'Um, yes. Yes, I suppose we were.'

Godric stared into his teacup. 'I haven't had such a good time with . . . with anyone for ages. Cheers. For bailing me out. Appreciate it.'

He gave me an awkward pat on the arm. There was something about his expression that I found oddly touching. Even if he was socially prehensile, I felt like Godric and I had started to get to know each other, and, more than that, I'd helped him. Sad to say, it was quite heart-warming.

Then of course, he had to go and spoil it by saying something bloke-ish.

'You know, Melissa,' said Godric, leaning over the tablecloth so I could see his chest hair poking out of his Aertex shirt, 'you're a game girl.'

I shrank back as if he'd scalded me. The last time someone had called me game, I'd been in the dining room of the Savoy, wearing my wig and suspenders and my dining companion had erroneously assumed I was the pudding course. He'd also been over sixty with some kind of circulation problem, but I'd had no compunction about putting him straight.

'Don't say that,' I said, and my voice came out rather snappy.

'Why not?' Godric raised his eyebrows. 'It's about as good as it gets, being a game girl!' He nodded. 'You should be flattered!'

You know, sometimes I think men and women share a vocabulary, but not the same language.

'Godric,' I said firmly. 'To a woman, being called game is . . . well, it's practically short for being *on* the game.'

'I disagree!' he said. 'Being game means you're up for it, you know, not too high-maintenance. You don't care what people think.'

I stared at him in mild horror. 'And that's a *good* thing?'

'Men *love* game girls,' he went on, warming to his theme. 'They're great fun! You know, resourceful. Like you were when we got nicked. Honestly, that really knocked my socks off, the way you got us out of that tight spot. Shows a bit of spirit!'

And on he went: drinking games, shenanigans in parks, reckless driving, cross-dressing . . .

All of a sudden, I could see exactly why Jonathan didn't want me hanging out with Godric, or indeed standing in for anyone else's girlfriend.

It made me look *game*.

The cold fingers of fear gripped me around the neck, where my nice-girl pearls should have been. Why had I never seen it like this before?

I didn't want to be a 'game' girl. Game girls never got married. Game girls ended up alone at fifty-five with nine 'boisterous' Labradors, running the Pony Club trials with red noses and hearty handshakes, always being invited to other people's Christmas lunches and never coming 'because of the dogs', then spending the day swilling back a bottle of Baileys and weeping over a Michael Palin travelography. No one, in short, ever fell in love with a game girl.

They were nice girls. But they were still 'girls' when they were slapping HRT patches on themselves, and that wasn't quite right.

I wanted to be resourceful, yes. Amusing company, sure. But not *game.*

I sat speechless as my future unfolded before me in the tearoom like some hideous Charles Dickens vision, while Godric worked himself up into a froth about some up-for-it lass who'd once mounted one of the lions in Trafalgar Square while wearing only a policeman's helmet. I was willing to bet the price of a Greenwich Village cappuccino that he'd once had a crush on some blowsy elder sister.

'. . . and of course, all that is just. Incredibly. Sexy.' Godric finished with a slurp of tea to disguise the fact that he'd just said the word sexy.

'Listen, Godric,' I said. 'It's one thing to think of a girl as game *in your head*, but don't ever say it aloud unless you want to split up with her. I once . . .' I hesitated, but then steeled myself. 'I once had a boyfriend who thought it was the height of compliments to tell me I was game. He used to wear Gucci loafers, and get me to pick up his dry-cleaning too.'

'Really?' Godric looked as if he wasn't sure whether to disapprove of that or not. 'And what happened?'

'Well, we split up when he ran off with someone else.

But that's not the point,' I added. 'I should have known from the moment that Orlando told me that "all boys love a game girl" that he was only after one thing.'

Godric's brow had darkened.

'I mean, I did adore him,' I went on, encouraged by his apparent shock. 'He was awfully charming. Very handsome, and frightfully good at . . .' I shook myself. Now wasn't the time to be thinking about *that*. 'But now I realise that a man like Jonathan . . . what? What are you looking at me like that for?'

'Orlando?' Godric demanded. 'Orlando what?'

'Oh, you won't know him,' I said. 'He's not an actor.'

'I'm not just an actor,' huffed Godric. 'Orlando *what*?'

'Orlando who?' I corrected him. 'Orlando von Borsch. His father's one of the stuffed olive von Borsches. He's one hundred per cent cast-iron Euro-trash. Well, one hundred per cent gold-plated Euro-trash, actually. You might have seen him in—'

'I know exactly who he is.' Godric's face looked like thunder. 'He copped off with Kirst—With my girlfriend at Crazy Larry's before I flew out to do this stupid film, and that was the last I saw of her.'

Talk about small world!

'Really? Is Crazy Larry's still going?' I asked curiously. 'I thought it had . . . Oh, I mean, that's terrible! Poor you! What was her name?'

'Kirsty,' he said reluctantly. 'Kirsty Carruthers. Do you know her?'

I shook my head. 'No, sorry.'

Godric turned his head away like a wounded animal. 'I'm over it now. I mean, if she's seriously impressed by someone so creepy he virtually slithers into the room on his stomach, she's welcome.'

I slipped my hand across the table and squeezed his thumb. So this was the girlfriend that Paige had meant. No wonder Godric was such a miserable sod. Despite his stroppy behaviour, I knew Godric was rather like Braveheart: all snap and no bite.

Well, OK, Braveheart had a nasty nip. And I'd seen Godric's left hook fell a passer-by, *and* get us arrested.

But *apart* from that, I realised in an unexpected flash of insight, they both just did it to avoid being nice to people because they were scared of being hurt again. Braveheart didn't ask to be a brattish, tug-of-love latchkey pet. Godric was obviously resorting to the tactics he'd used when he was last dumped, whenever that was.

I blinked at my own ghastly Oprah-style psychoanalysis. Two more weeks in New York, and I'd have my own chat show.

'I'm not saying we were in *love* or anything,' mumbled Godric. 'But I was, erm, pretty keen on Kirsty. And I thought she liked me. Just goes to show.' He hesitated, then raised his puppydog eyes. 'Um, you're a woman, Mel – I mean, just between us, you know, it wouldn't be because I asked her to . . . ?'

'Asked her to what?' I prompted, my mind filling with lurid possibilities as he flushed painfully. 'What? Spit it out.'

Godric stared at me, horrified. 'No! I didn't ask her *that*! Christ almighty!'

I blinked. I really had no idea what he was talking about. 'Then what?' I prompted.

'Iron my shirt,' he mumbled into his chest.

I sighed. If that was the most outrageous thing he'd suggested then no wonder Orlando had slimed her off her feet. 'No, Godric. I don't think that'll be it. But, chin up!

You're about to be a big film star!' I said encouragingly. 'Stupid old Kirsty, eh? Nelson reckons the only films Orlando's in are the ones he shoots himself on his yacht in . . .' I stopped. That probably wasn't the best thing to say either. 'Forget the whole sorry affair. This time next month, you'll have women beating down your door.'

Godric flinched.

'Most men would love that,' I pointed out. 'Beautiful model types with long legs and perfect teeth. You don't get that in west London.'

'I'd rather have a game girl with fat legs and a nice smile,' he muttered under his breath. 'Like you.'

'Don't be silly,' I said briskly. 'Now, do you want some more crumpets? I think these are better than the ones we get at home.'

'Melissa,' said Godric suddenly, grabbing my other hand. 'Please come to the party with me! You have no idea what it's like! Everyone coming up to you, and saying how much shorter you look in real life, and offering you drugs you have no idea how to take, and asking about people you're meant to know, and then you get drunk to try to get through the sheer hell of it, and everyone round here tuts at you if you so much as light up inside, and . . .' His eyes were wild and staring. I wondered if he really was ill. 'Please come. Just for half an hour. Please.'

'But Godric, no. I *can't*. I promised.'

'It's not for work,' he pleaded. 'It's a favour. For me. You don't have to stay long. I'll bail out once I've done the rounds.'

I was pinioned to the table, as Godric gripped both my wrists with a feverish strength. A waitress looked over and made an 'oh, bless you!' face. She probably thought he was proposing.

Inside my head a terrible struggle was raging between my conscience, which was now painfully aware of exactly why Jonathan didn't want me pretending to be other people's girlfriends, and my other conscience which couldn't let a fellow shy Brit down in his hour of need. I felt a certain kinship with Godric, even more so now I knew we were both victims of the Orlando von Borsch charm-Panzer.

'It's the photographers I hate the most,' Godric went on. 'I don't have one of those stupid photograph faces. They always make me look like I'm Special Needs.'

'Why don't I call Dwight?' I asked desperately. 'The chap who did your *Spotlight* pics? You can spend an afternoon with him, and work out what your best expression is, and get used to being photographed unexpectedly. I'll ask him to pop out from behind trees.'

But Godric had tightened his grip on my arms as a new thought struck him. 'If you come with me, they won't bother to photograph *me* at all,' he babbled. 'Paige's really excited about all the coverage there's been about me dating an MP's daughter. She reckons it makes me look Establishment-cool. Like Mick Jagger.'

'Well, there you go, Godric. There's a very good reason I can't come with you.' I shrugged apologetically. 'I refuse to be manipulated by Paige Drogan's publicity machine. They'll know it's me. And Jonathan would be enraged and embarrassed, because everyone thinks I'm his girlfriend. I mean,' I added hastily, 'I *am* his girlfriend.'

'Please, Melissa,' he said, and for once, his voice sounded genuinely pleading. It had the authentic note of gruff, English-bloke embarrassment at having to ask his mate's sister for a date. 'I need you to.'

I wavered. Even as I was being stern with him, some-

thing about Godric's slumped shoulders was melting my
heart. It reminded me of how I sometimes used to feel
when I had to start yet another new school in the middle
of a term: desperate to make a good impression, but
already seeing the cliques clamming up in my eager face.
I'm not naturally good at parties, you know. It's just something you learn to do, like cooking, or driving. Learning
to enjoy it is like taking it to degree level. But no one
had ever taught Godric, and it was awfully tough for him
to start now.

'Please,' he said. 'I'll have a talk with Paige.' He swallowed, and I could see this was a grand gesture coming
up. 'I'll persuade her to make it clear that it was all a
mistake. That you're just a friend.' He paused. 'You know,'
he said awkwardly, 'you're the only real friend I have in
New York. So it's not a lie.'

'Don't over-egg it, Godric,' I said, not unkindly.

Wheels were starting to turn in my head, albeit very
slowly. There was a way round this – a way that would
kill a few birds with the one stone. It was rather a riskily
chucked stone though.

'Before I decide anything, have you got Kirsty's phone
number?'

Godric started to pretend that he'd discarded it straight
away but I raised a commanding finger and he dug about
in his jacket pocket for his mobile.

'You're not going to phone her, are you?' he said, as
I wrote it down in my notebook.

'I don't know,' I said, and snapped it shut. 'I haven't
decided. Now, how about a crumpet?'

Godric gave me a baleful look, opened his mouth, then
to my surprise, closed it without speaking.

19

Sometimes, it feels as though fate is right on your side, blowing wind into your sails and generally speeding your plans through as a personal priority. Frequently, however, just as the harbour's hoving into view you discover that actually the reason you're speeding along was because fate has cut your anchor and the harbour wall is heading up fast, but I'm getting a little ahead of myself here.

Three things happened that made me believe that, for once, I'd come up with a seriously clever little plan, with side benefits all round. I phoned Kirsty, I spoke to Paige, and Emery invited me for dinner.

First things first.

Kirsty, when I got hold of her, could not have been more thrilled to hear from me, especially when I told her I was a friend of Godric's, trying to arrange a surprise for him.

(True! No ding!)

'He's in New York? I've been desperate to get hold of him for months!' she squealed. 'But his phone isn't working and he won't answer his emails.' Then the bubbles dropped out of her voice. 'Has he . . . ? You're not organising . . . an *engagement* party or something?'

'Good heavens, no,' I said. 'Not at all. Between you and me, I think he's still completely nuts about some girl in London, but of course he's far too gentlemanly to name names.'

Then it all came tumbling out: the happy six months of spag bol and Italian cinema, then the row about her skirt being too tight for 'a lady', her snogging Orlando out of drunken pique, and Godric seeing it as the biggest betrayal since Samson and Delilah, and him refusing to take her calls, and her regretting it almost immediately (but not that immediately, because I seem to recall some mention of antibiotics), and then him going off to the States 'on some job' and not leaving any details.

'And I wish I knew where he was, just so I can say sorry,' she finished up miserably. 'Is he still acting? Did he get any work over there?'

It was rather sweet, I thought, that she still wanted him even without knowing he was about to be a huge film star. If she wanted Godric in his original state then it must be love.

'Yes, he's doing rather well,' I said. 'So, do you think you could come? It's awfully short notice, sorry.'

'I'd clear my diary for Godders,' she said fervently. 'Um, I'm not sure about flights though.' She paused discreetly. 'I'll have to check my, er, my diary.'

'Oh, if you can come, I can arrange the tickets from this end,' I assured her.

'You can?'

'Yes,' I said, feeling like a fairy godmother. 'I can.'

Well, maybe a fairy godmother in the vengeful, unpredictable Allegra Svensson sense.

The weather had cooled off sufficiently for me to button myself into a new fitted suit I'd bought from Saks, which had just the right amount of sauce, coupled with just the right amount of nanny-ness. Finished off with a new pair of black leather pumps, I felt far more like myself than I'd done in ages, wig or no wig. As I strode through the jostling crowds on Broome Street towards Paige's office, I smiled at everyone I passed, even the weird staring people.

Tiffany didn't bother to pretend Paige was busy when I walked in. She couldn't, since I'd called to make an appointment, and refused, in a very polite way, of course, to get off the line till I got one.

'Melissa,' said Paige coolly, as I sat down. 'What can I do for you?'

'I have a great story for you, Paige,' I said. 'For Godric.'

She put her fingers together. 'I'm listening.'

'I think I can reunite Godric with his very sweet English girlfriend,' I said. 'I don't know anything about her, but she knows my flatmate's brother from some real tennis club or other, and Woolfe's frightfully picky about who he hangs out with.'

'Is she pretty?'

'That doesn't matter,' I said sternly. 'What matters is that she and Godric sound very star-crossed, and having her around might make him less of a growling dog and more of a malleable charmer-in-the-making.'

Paige tipped her head to one side, and pressed a button on her phone set. 'Tell me more.'

I explained how I could arrange for Miss X and Godric to 'bump into each other' at a party and leave the rest up to fate and cocktails, having laid the groundwork personally.

'But,' I added, 'I'll do this on the following conditions. One, you pay for her tickets over here, plus a decent hotel, and two, you do not, under any circumstances, tell anyone from the press until they're sure it'll work out. If it doesn't work out, you are not allowed to sell some Ric Spencer Heartbreak story, either.'

Paige squinted at me. 'And why should I? Huh? If they're so in love, can't they sort it out themselves?'

I looked at her firmly, and wished I had my tortoise-shell-winged Honey glasses to peer over. 'Paige, Jonathan thinks so highly of you. You're a very tight-knit group of friends, too. Honestly, you lot are so lucky to have a social circle like that, even now.'

'And?'

'And . . .' I sighed. 'It would be really *awkward* if Jonathan found out that you were the person behind all the stories in the papers about me and Godric. I mean, he'd wonder what sort of friend would make his girl-friend look like a two-timing slapper!'

Paige looked shifty. 'I don't know where he'd get that idea from.'

'I know! Fancy the police passing on all those details!' I shook my head. 'He might even wonder if you were doing it on purpose to drive some kind of wedge between me and him – and I know you'd hate the very idea of that!' I added gaily. 'Putting your client before your friends. Crikey!'

We sat there in silence for a moment, the atmosphere balanced precariously on a knife-edge.

For one heart-stopping second it occurred to me that maybe Cindy *had* told Paige to do all this – wasn't she her friend from college, not Jonathan's? I battled down the rising panic, and told myself to get a grip. I could hardly make a go of things here if I kept being so paranoid.

But then Paige obviously weighed up the benefits against the blackmail, and sprang back to life. 'Melissa, that's a charming plan you've come up with!' she cooed. 'It would be an awesome thing for us to do for Ric. But, ah, I don't see quite why we should have to stand tickets for this girl?'

I pretended to pause, then beamed as if an idea had just occurred to me. 'We never did agree a fee, did we, for the time I spent with Ric? Why don't you get the tickets and we'll call it quits?' I waited a beat. 'Better make them business class, actually. I daren't tell you what my day rates are in London!'

Paige managed a smile. 'I'll get Tiffany straight onto it. Can she call you for details?'

'Absolutely,' I said, allowing myself to smile. It was a nice thing to do.

And that balanced the books in my head, as far as Paige Drogan went.

When I got home from all this machinating, I had a call from Emery.

I took a moment to establish it was her, as usual. When I answered the phone there was a protracted pause, as if between her dialling and me picking up she'd forgotten who she'd called. Emery always made calls as if she were on ring-back, and it was her phone that had rung, not mine.

Emery the Memory, Granny sometimes called her.

'Melissa?' she murmured uncertainly.

'Hello, Emery,' I said. 'How are you?'

'Mmm,' she said. 'I'm in New York on Friday and I was wondering whether you were about for a spot of dinner? And I do mean a spot. I've found an amazing new macrobiotic place where they bring you all your food in tiny paint palettes and syringes. Doesn't that sound fabulous?'

My heart skipped. Perfect! I could tell Jonathan I was meeting Emery for dinner, leave an hour earlier, prep Godric for his big moment at the party, then leave in time to meet her.

'Just you,' she added. 'William's not coming – he's away in Europe on business, so I thought I'd have a weekend shopping and so on. We could have a girls' night! Without Allegra!'

If Emery had any idea how perfectly she was fitting into the plans, she'd be astonished. I don't think any member of my family had ever been so unwittingly accommodating.

'That sounds brilliant,' I said. 'I'm putting it in my diary right now.'

We were still chatting – or rather she was telling me at long and gusting length about her new yoga teacher (I think), and I was trying to get off the phone, when the door opened and Jonathan wandered in.

'Emery,' I mouthed, and he pulled a face.

'Give her my love,' he mouthed, backing away so I couldn't put him on.

I wrapped up the conversation as quickly as was polite, made arrangements to meet her on Friday, then went to find him, going through the post with a frown on his pale forehead.

'To what do I owe this unexpected pleasure?' I asked, putting my arms round him happily.

'Client cancelled on me. Wanted to rearrange. So I thought I'd pop back and see you.' He took a step back, and regarded me with a critical eye. 'And I'm glad I did. New suit?'

I nodded, and twirled, so he could see my seamed stockings.

'I like it,' he said, hooking his eyebrow sexily. 'Makes me feel . . . kind of nostalgic. What did Emery want?'

'Dinner on Friday. She's in town for the weekend.'

Jonathan paused, and for a second I thought I caught a glimpse of furtiveness about him, which was most out of character. 'Sorry, sweetie, but I can't make it. I have to meet with a client, and Friday evening's the only time . . . they can do.'

I batted him with a gourmet pizza leaflet. 'You weren't invited! It was just me and her. Sisters only.'

He looked relieved. 'I won't expect you back early then.'

'Well, I wouldn't go that far,' I said. 'But I appreciate the thought! Anyway, enough about Emery. What shall we do now?' I slid my arms under his jacket and pressed myself up against the fine fabric of his shirt. 'How about a backwards evening? Start in bed, then get dressed and go out to eat?'

Jonathan grinned, pushed the hair out of my eyes, tipped me backwards and kissed me, holding my head in the palm of his hand as if we were swing dancers.

I giggled. That was another side of Jonathan Gabi didn't know: the old romantic who loved Hollywood musicals as much as I did. Who could dance, properly.

This was more like it, I thought happily, returning his kiss with upside-down enthusiasm.

Then he swung me upwards again. 'Much as I'd love to take you upstairs and unpeel you out of that delicious suit, I can't stay. I've got another client in an hour, then I might be late.'

My heart sank. 'But we were going to go out for dinner tonight, weren't we? Just the two of us!' We'd only been out on our own three times since I'd arrived, though I managed to bite my tongue on that.

Jonathan sighed, and scratched his ear. 'I'm sorry, honey. Really I am. That's why I came all the way over town now, so I could see you for half an hour.' He stroked my jaw ruefully with his finger, circling around my lips. 'I'll try to get back as soon as I can. You appreciate how much I'd rather be with you, don't you? Listen, instead of going out, how about we phone out for sushi, and watch *Singing in the Rain*? Hey?'

I looked at him, trying hard not to listen to the screechy 'Cindy! Cindy!' voices in my head.

'I didn't get that huge TV just for decoration,' he added. 'You're the only one who's watched anything on it.'

'OK,' I said. He was trying. I knew he was. 'But don't be late.'

I passed the rest of the afternoon drifting listlessly through Bloomingdales, but I didn't buy anything, then at half five I wandered back to Greenwich Village, taking even more time than normal to inspect all the wrought-iron porches and overflowing window-boxes.

As I washed my hair in Jonathan's huge roll-top bath, and soaked in deep bubbles, I came up with positive after positive after positive about my situation, but somehow I just couldn't bounce myself into a better mood.

Even reading through the comprehensive stack of exotic food delivery leaflets didn't cheer me up. Nor did dancing round the house with my iPod plugged into Jonathan's minute but powerful stereo system. Even television, my friend and secret life coach, didn't work. I'd flicked through all the channels at least twice, including one showing nothing but court cases, without finding anything that I really wanted to watch and it was still only half seven.

I looked around the room and wondered what the hell was wrong with me. Here I was, in this fabulous Greenwich Village town house, surrounded by beautiful objects, drinking Jonathan's Fine Wine. And yet, it didn't feel *right*. Why?

I stared at the bottle of wine. It was nearly empty. How had that happened?

Ah, I thought, as a familiar sense of morbid doom settled about my shoulders like a fusty mink cape: the wine trap. One glass of wine takes the edge off my shyness nicely, two glasses turn me into a hilarious social commentator, but three glasses and I hit a troublesome seam of melancholy. Usually Nelson or Gabi manage to spot my eyes filling with unshed tears for the poor donkeys of the Sudan, or the sheer unfairness of the congestion charge, but here, on my own, there was only Braveheart, and he wasn't helping. He wasn't even awake.

My hand reached for the bottle to pour myself the all-important fourth glass, but the thought of Braveheart made me hesitate. Drunk, in charge of an animal that needed me! An animal that had been shoved from pillar to post by two selfish parents who didn't love him. An animal that, let's face it, was my only company this evening, while Jonathan put his clients way before our relationship. Clients who may or may not be his glamorous ex-wife who probably didn't even *drink* and definitely didn't haul herself onto tables to do the twist, only to have them collapse under her.

'Braveheart!' I called, stretching out my arms.

A vague skittering came through from the kitchen. Then a pause, while he did something I didn't want to think about, then, eventually, he shuffled up.

I patted the sofa next to me. I was trying to train him

not to get up on the sofas, but right now I needed a bit of a cuddle.

His solid little body was comforting, like a hot-water bottle.

'You're glad I'm here, aren't you?' I demanded woefully.

Braveheart stared at me, and I thought I could detect some disgust in his black button eyes.

'If you were a proper film dog, you would lick my nose now,' I heard my voice quaver on. 'In an endearing fashion.'

Braveheart wriggled himself off my knee, and vanished behind a packing case, but I could hardly blame him.

Take yourself in hand, I told myself. For God's sake!

I grabbed the phone off the coffee table. I just wasn't seeing things properly. What I needed was to tell someone what a great time I was having. That would soon put things in perspective.

My fingers hesitated over the keypad. But who would be up at this hour? It would be . . . half twelve. Half twelve. Hmm.

Gabi. But she might be out – with someone. I didn't want to negotiate that minefield. That required total sobriety.

I couldn't phone my family, not unless I wanted to hear how much worse things could be.

That left one person. Who would have no qualms about putting me straight about how lucky I was. I pulled out my diary and started dialling the number Nelson had given me. OK, he'd said emergencies, but it was typical of him to be all headmasterly about it. I knew he'd love a call.

I listened to the phone ring. Technology was amazing, I thought, sloshing the last of the wine into the huge glass. Somewhere out in the ocean, Nelson was bobbing around in his hammock, probably taking a night watch right now, steering the ship with one of those great big wheels . . . I'd seen *A Night to Remember*. I knew how these things went. I wondered if he'd got a nice thick white polo-neck to keep warm. Maybe I should look for thermal undies in—

'What?' barked a familiar voice down the line. 'What's happened? Are you OK?'

The alcohol, I think, triggered a warm rush of happiness at the sound of his voice. 'Nelson!' I cried, stretching out my pedicured toes. 'It's *me*!'

'I know it's you,' he said. 'No one else has this number DON'T YANK IT ABOUT! TREAT IT WITH RESPECT!'

I blinked. 'What are you doing?'

'I'm supervising the night watch. Yannick is steering the course and Leah is DON'T PLAY WITH THAT IT'S NOT A TOY!'

'Oh. I see. Are you busy?'

Either Nelson heaved a huge sarcastic sigh down the phone or there was some serious interference at that point. 'I'm in charge of an eight-hundred-tonne square rigger, Melissa, but apart from that, not really. So, I take it this is a social call and not some "get me out of jail" panic?'

I looked around the room. Just talking to Nelson seemed to bring a little bit of my London life into the room. He sounded like home. Evening had started to fall and was casting shadows over the chairs and packing boxes. I'd made some efforts to tidy up, but since it wasn't really my house I hadn't liked to unpack too much. Partly because I wasn't sure I wanted to see what was in all the boxes. And partly because Jonathan was never here to make a fun game of doing it together.

'Melissa? Are you still there? Having a good time?'

'Um, yes!' I hauled myself back, feeling a slight dizziness. Maybe I was drunker than I thought. 'I'm having a *great* time! Jonathan's been taking me round the city, introducing me to all his friends, and he's put his secretary totally at my disposal, so Lori's been booking me into spas and tearooms and what have you.'

'Lovely!' said Nelson. 'ARE YOU CHEWING?'

'No!' I replied, startled.

'Not you, YOU,' he roared. 'NO GUM ON THIS SHIP, YANNICK!' There was a slight pause in which I thought I could hear a seagull. 'OR TOBACCO, NO! I DON'T CARE IF IT IS HISTORICALLY ACCURATE!'

'Nelson, there's really no need to shout quite so—'

'IF YOU WANT HISTORICAL ACCURACY I CAN LASH YOU TO THE YARDARM FOR A FEW HOURS, IF YOU WANT? So, have you been shopping then?'

'God, yes, I've been to Macy's, Bloomingdales, Henri Bendel's, where I met a gorgeous denim adviser called Seth who told me I had a cute ass, can you believe that?'

'Yes.'

'And I've had a cupcake at the Magnolia Bakery, which wasn't as nice as your sponge, you'll be pleased to hear, and I've been to the street where that Led Zeppelin album cover was photographed, and . . .'

My voice cracked and I stopped. To my surprise, tears were bulging along my eyelids. 'I . . .'

'I'M GOING BELOW DECK NOW SO YOU'D
BETTER CONCENTRATE, THE PAIR OF YOU.
I THINK YOU'VE BOTH SEEN *TITANIC*, YES?'
bellowed Nelson. 'Hang on, Mel, I'll be right with you.
I SAW THAT, YANNICK!'

I wiped away the tears quickly, with the back of my
hand. 'I'm having a great time, Nelson, really.'

There was a pause, the sound of non-marking-sole
shoes on wooden floors, and I could tell he was now
inside.

'Ding!' he said gently.

A huge lump rose up in my throat as I imagined his
big blond bearhug engulfing me.

'Come on. What's up?' he said.

'I don't know!' I sobbed. 'I . . . don't know!'

'Melissa, you know I love you and your funny ways,
but can we keep the am-dram to a minimum? International
mobile rates are outrageous, for both of us. Now, what's
happened? Things not working out with Remington?'

'Things are working out,' I gulped. 'I just . . . he's
never here. He's working *all the time*, and I think he's
spending most of that overtime with Cindy.'

'Why would he be with Cindy, for crying out loud?'

'He's selling their apartment. Didn't Gabi tell you?'

'Gabi? I haven't spoken to her recently. Listen, have
you told him any of this? How you feel?'

I shook my head. 'No.'

Nelson made a familiar 'ungh!' noise of despair that
made homesickness bloom in my stomach like a bright
red flower. 'Well, why not, for crying out loud? I did flick
through all those stupid magazines you left in the loo –
even *Roger* knows talking is meant to be the solution to
all relationship ills!'

'I don't want him to think I'm being whiny!' I whined. 'I don't want him to think I'm not enjoying myself!'

'But it doesn't sound like you are.'

'I *am*.' I paused. 'It's just . . . not quite turning out the way I thought it would.'

Nelson paused too. Then he put into words what I was thinking. 'New York, or Jonathan?'

'Both,' I said, in a small voice.

'Oh,' said Nelson. He coughed. 'Why do I get the feeling you're not telling me the whole story?'

'Because you'd probably shout at me?'

He laughed, and over the shifting, whistling air between us, he suddenly felt very close. 'Go on then, you stupid woman. In no more than two hundred words, please.'

So I told him. Godric, Paige, the police, Cindy, Bonnie, everything. Even Braveheart.

'Right,' he said, when I'd forced out the last agonising word. 'I think you need to talk to him about this Cindy business. But that's all it'll be – business.'

'You think?' It was easy for him to say that.

'Mel, I don't know Jonathan as well as you do, but he doesn't seem the type to treat his new girlfriend the way his wife treated him, now does he?'

'No.'

'I'm not saying she might not be trying to wind him up, but the man adores you. The best thing you can do is just be yourself. The woman he fell in love with.' There was a painful grinding noise.

'Was that the ship?' I asked urgently. 'Nelson? Are you sinking?'

'No, that was me. I can't believe you're making me say these things.'

'I feel so much better for talking to you, Nelson,' I said, and I meant it.

'Good, because you know how much I THIS IS THE OFFICERS' MESS! GET BACK ON DECK! WHAT DO YOU MEAN THE CAPSTAN CAME OFF IN YOUR HANDS? IT'S TITANIUM!'

I sensed our conversation had drawn to a natural close, an impression reinforced, worryingly, by the connection being lost.

I sat back on the sofa in the warm darkness, and digested Nelson's pearls of wisdom.

Be the woman Jonathan fell in love with.

But that woman had been an organiser, a fixer, a stitcher-up of people's problems. A woman he didn't seem to want in New York.

But that was who I *was*. And I was starting to wonder if, despite his protestations to the contrary, Jonathan really was in love with Honey, the beautifully constructed end result, and not Melissa, the woman paddling furiously beneath Honey's swan-like elegance.

I pushed that thought to one side. I wasn't sure if the wine wasn't giving me a worrying insight into the dark and melodramatic workings of Allegra's head.

But I'd sworn, from now on, I'd be myself. Not hide behind Honey. Maybe between them, Gabi and Nelson were right. If I stitched Godric's problems up, Jonathan would see that that was where my strengths lay. He'd be proud of me.

Just thinking about taking an active stance made me feel better. That was what was bringing me down, I told myself, leaping up to turn on the table lamps: passivity. Tomorrow I would finalise my plans, go and buy some material and make a really cute summer dress.

The Romney-Jones New York collection, part I.

Then I knocked over the side table with the wine on, and was scrubbing at the hand-woven rug with table salt when Jonathan finally arrived home, bearing sushi and a very small La Perla bag.

20

Godric's party was being held in one of those trendy bars that are so small and in-the-know that you can't find them the first three times you walk past, and then when you manage to remember to take a friend back there, hoping to wow them with your connections, it's closed down and moved on.

I wasn't at all sure I had the right clothes with me for a party involving media types and actors. Trendy was never part of my wardrobe repertoire at the best of times, and anything I'd bought so far in New York (on the advice of the nice sales girls who understood about dressing to impress) was designed to look expensively understated, or understatedly expensive. In other words, everything I had was awfully Upper East Side, and I needed something a little more Meat Packing. As it were.

In the end I opted for my simplest black dress and a pair of polka dot *Roman Holiday* sandals. That looked pretty good on its own, as I let myself out of the house into the early evening warmth. But in my handbag I had my own special magic wand, which I knew would transform everything.

Believe me, I *agonised* about whether to wear the wig. I knew Jonathan had a huge problem with it, but, I reasoned, surely it was better to disguise myself completely, just in case there were any photographers around? They'd already snapped me with Godric as myself, so more pictures of brunette Melissa-the-MP's-daughter would just add fuel to the fire. Some random blonde, on the other hand, would be merely another party guest.

In addition to this, I'd been turning over my plan to reunite Godric and Kirsty, and decided that it needed a little something extra, just to add some pretend drama. Kirsty didn't know what I looked like, so wouldn't it make Godric's reaction to her arrival more romantic, from her point of view, if he abandoned the fabulous glamour-puss he was talking to, just like that, as she walked into the room?

As he would have to, since I'd be legging it off to supper with my sister.

Theoretically, I could see how Jonathan probably wouldn't agree with it, but he never need know. It wasn't as though I was really passing myself off as *anything*. I was just disguising myself. For half an hour, and – specifically – for his benefit.

I stood in the loo at the Starbucks on Sixth and Waverley, gazing at myself as I adjusted my illicit blonde hair so the fringe hung into my eyes, and a shiver of guilt, heavily laced with excitement, ran through me. The blonde hair was like a gorgeous gilt picture frame around my face, casting a sexy glow over my skin. My eyes seemed to darken and open up, seeming more black than dark brown. There was an element of shock in there, too.

Honey.

I was Honey again.

I fluttered my eyelashes at myself, then reached for my make-up bag. There was something about that curtain of light-reflecting hair that demanded more drama in my face. Carefully, I traced another layer of dark liner along my upper lids, then a touch more mascara. Then a quick flush of pink shimmer along my cheekbones. Then another final round of mascara.

I stood back to admire the effect. Suddenly the dress looked effortlessly chic, almost don't-care-ish. Maybe it was the way I was standing differently. With my dark eyes smouldering out from beneath my fringe, and my lips barely glossed, I looked like Brigitte Bardot.

'Wow,' I said, without thinking. How on earth could Jonathan prefer Melissa to this?

Thinking about Jonathan brought me round very quickly and I checked my watch.

I'd promised Godric I would stay for exactly forty minutes at the party, including that bit at the beginning when no one's arrived, and the five minutes it takes to get away. I absolutely *had* to be out of there by eight thirty, even if the party had barely got going by then. The shrieky little voices of my conscience were scarcely allowing this as it was.

Since the restaurant she wanted to try was only a few blocks away, I'd told Emery to meet me outside at eight, to be on the safe side. I'd never known her be less than an hour late for anything. I'd told her I was having a drink with a friend, but as it was Godric, I hadn't invited her to join us. I didn't want my plans for Kirsty to be screwed up by him falling for a married woman he'd probably had a crush on ten years earlier. She still looked pretty much as she had done at school, damn her huge blue eyes.

When Godric shuffled into Starbucks ten minutes later, he walked straight past my table, then failed to spot me when he turned round and scanned the place with a surly eye.

I raised a discreet hand, not wanting to draw too much attention to myself.

Godric's boggling reaction, however, did that for me. 'Hai carumba!' he bellowed. 'Melissa!'

I gestured for him to sit and to stop his adolescent thrusting gestures.

'Quick tip,' I hissed. 'Don't walk into a date venue and scan the room like that. Makes you look stood up before you've even *been* stood up. And don't forget – you're a film star now.'

He was still gawping at me as if I were a two-headed calf. 'Effing hell, Mel,' he gurgled. 'You look . . . you look like a model. Not a skinny model, you know, one of those decent-sized ones. Like Sophie Dahl or something. Before she got scrawny.'

'Thank you,' I said. 'I'd stop there if I were you.'

'Can we go?' he said, leaping to his feet. 'Let's go now.'

He tugged my chair out for me, while I was still on it. While I admired his strength, it probably wasn't a habit he ought to develop.

'I thought you didn't want to go to this do,' I protested. Honestly, I'd never seen him so enthusiastic.

'I do now,' he said, and smiled. It was the first time I'd seen Godric smile, and, really, the effect was transformational. His entire face changed from that of a constipated teddy bear, to that of a, well, quite an attractive teddy bear.

'OK then,' I said. 'Let's go.'

The enthusiasm lasted until we got to the club, and then it wavered, at the sight of three extraordinarily cool people sloping wearily down the stairs, as if they were en route to a haemorrhoid clinic.

Godric stopped. 'I'm wearing all the wrong things,' he grunted forlornly. 'I look like a geek.'

'You look fine,' I said. If Kirsty had fancied him in

London, she was definitely going to go for it here. I checked no one was about, then undid one button on his shirt, dug around in my bag for my grooming creme, ran some through his hair so it looked glossed rather than greased, and, for a final touch, I pulled off one of my green glass cocktail rings and shoved it onto his little finger, as a tribute to Gabi's Urban Gangsta advice more than anything.

'What the hell is that?' demanded Godric, staring at it as if it were some kind of obscenity.

'It's a talking point,' I said. 'Right, you've got thirty-nine minutes remaining. For the next thirty-nine minutes, you absolutely *can't* refer to me as Melissa. Not even when you're talking to me. You don't know who's listening. And if you see a camera, you *have* to tell me.'

'What should I call you then?' he asked.

'Honey,' I said firmly.

Well, it was too late now to make up a whole new identity. At least I'd remember to answer to Honey.

I pushed aside a flutter of misgiving. This was about giving Ric a boost. After I'd zhouzed up his personality and introduced him to my surprise guest, he'd be fine on his own, I knew it.

'Let's go, Ric Spencer,' I said.

The funny thing about that wig was that it let me saunter into places I'd normally feel awkward in, even with my usual breezy attitude to social events. The shoes I was wearing also helped with the sauntering. Walking is so much easier in high heels, I find. It makes you use your whole body.

Downstairs, the room was very dark, made even darker by blood-red wall-hangings and the red light bulbs glowing inside huge paper shades above us. I blinked, trying to make out where the bar was. Adding to the

Stygian effect were the hordes of black-clad people packing the side tables, and what I now realised was underfloor lighting beneath maroon glass tiles. It was like being in a kidney, if kidneys had very loud sound systems and a free bar.

As I hovered, looking for a seat, a waitress passed with a huge tray of vodka shots of various colours in one hand, and another tray of empty glasses in the other. Without even breaking chat, people grabbed fresh glasses and replaced old ones as she passed. When I turned back to Godric, he was throwing one blue drink down his neck and preparing a yellow one to follow it.

'Actors,' he explained, with a gasp. 'You need a couple too.'

'No, thanks.' As a sop to my conscience, I'd made a vow not to let a drop past my lips. Besides, I needed to concentrate. People were already starting to look our way, in a sort of Mexican wave of nosiness.

'See?' grunted Godric. 'They're looking at us, wondering who you are.' For once, though, he sounded almost pleased.

'Godric, they're looking at you, you idiot. You've just been in a play here. They know your film's coming out. Honestly . . .'

His eyes were scanning the place and before he could toss back his urine-coloured shot, a short dark man in a black vest sidled up.

'Ric! How you doing?'

'Er, fine. Um, Ivan, this is Honey – Honey, this is Ivan Mueller.'

'Hi! Hi!' Ivan was shaking my hand before I knew it. 'Don't you have a second name?'

'No,' I said, 'just Honey.'

'Cute!' he exclaimed and paused significantly.

'Ivan was the stage manager for a production of *Three Sisters* I was in last year,' Godric supplied, in the manner of someone having their teeth pulled.

'And I *loved* working with him!' exclaimed Ivan theatrically. 'We had a ball, didn't we, Ric?'

Godric shrugged.

'We did.' Ivan confirmed. 'Sooooo . . . What are you doing at the moment?'

'Just finished a short run of *The Real Inspector Hound*,' grunted Godric. 'Was OK.'

'It was marvellous,' I added, in a deep coo. 'Ric was splendid. He got some rather good reviews, didn't you, darling?'

Godric straightened up a bit. 'Well, yeah. S'pose so.'

Ivan pulled a face that suggested profound internal excitement.

'Are you working on something right now?' I asked politely.

'Am I? Oh, my Lord!' he exclaimed with a flourish of the shoulders, and launched into a long-winded litany of dismay and lack of professionalism, illuminated by unsubtle glances around the room at various miscreants seated in distant and not-so-distant corners.

Godric looked nauseous throughout, but I was rather intrigued. I even recognised some of the names Ivan was throwing about like so much indiscreet confetti. It was, as Ivan assured me, a disgustingly incestuous business.

'. . . and my partner Raj is a make-up artist, and what he sees, let me tell you, Honey, certain ladies would not want to be made common knowledge,' he said, finally pausing for breath with an arch look over my shoulder. 'Ooh, look who's just walked in! The poor thing! I have to fly. So nice to meet you, darling!' He gave me one of those showbiz air kisses, then bestowed another one on Godric who flinched. 'And look at you, all sexed up!' he added, as if noticing him for the first time. He nodded at me, 'You suit him, Honey! See you soon!'

And Ivan vanished back into the crowd. I realised the room had filled up with people in the intervening minutes, like sea water running into a sandcastle. Godric and I were marooned at the edge of the room.

I checked my watch nervously. Where was Kirsty? I'd given her very specific instructions but as she'd only flown in that afternoon, I hadn't been able to pick her up and sort her out myself. I hoped Paige hadn't somehow managed to intercept her.

'See what I mean?' snotted Godric. 'It's insufferable.' But he looked quietly pleased around the gills at the same time. 'I mean, he knows exactly what I'm doing right now. I know exactly what he's doing. But everyone always effing asks. It happens at all these parties – I hate actors.'

'But you're doing really well!' I said encouragingly.

'Only cos you're here.' He gave me another intense look. 'I really appreciate you coming. I've been—'

'You're going to have to learn how to do this on your own, you know, Godric,' I said quickly. 'Just pretend to be one of the characters you play, um, like . . .' My mind went blank. 'What was the last play you were in where you had to be someone sociable?'

Godric looked pained. 'Potiphar. In my prep school's Christmas production of *Joseph and the Amazing Technicolor Dreamcoat.*'

'Well, there you are!' I said, while working out just how many years poor Godric had spent playing antisocial psychos. 'Be like that. Elvis-ish.'

'Can we sit down?' he said suddenly. 'I feel a bit . . . seasick. It's these effing walls.'

I steered him towards a table that had conveniently just become vacant and he sank into a red velvet chair, long legs buckling beneath him.

'It's not easy when you're shy,' I said, determined to get at least one useful lesson across. 'But you just have to pretend to be someone else. It works, I promise you. And then when you realise you can do it as yourself, you're away.'

I did mean all this, honestly. But there was a little voice at the back of my head, reminding me that I did it so much better when I was Honey. She didn't worry about what people thought, or whether she was living up to expectations.

'It's funny, isn't it?' said Godric. He sounded quite pissed already.

'What is?'

'We're both here, pretending to be other people. You're a blonde woman called Honey, and I'm a film actor called Ric.'

I snapped my attention back to the evening, and checked my watch surreptitiously. We only had fifteen minutes left.

'Yes. That's very true.'

'And yet . . .' Godric waggled a finger. 'And yet, only we know that underneath it, you're Melons the wardrobe mistress, and I'm Godric the geek.' His face fell. 'But in real life, you're still pretty gorgeous, albeit not quite as sexy as you are right now, whereas I'm just the sort of guy who does A-level Latin. And gets dumped.'

Men, in my experience, are far, far worse at fishing for compliments than women.

'Oh, nonsense!' I said. 'You're a *very* talented actor. My friend Gabi thinks you're sex on a stick.' I paused. 'That's a direct quote, by the way. It's not a term I'd normally use to describe men.'

Godric looked at me with huge, tipsy, baby-seal eyes. 'And how *would* you describe me?'

'I'd say you were . . . a very handsome, talented actor.' Where was Kirsty? I searched the room for a tallish, thinish, English-ish girl. Argh. I could have done with her emailing me another photograph. Presumably she wouldn't be wearing dressage clothes when she arrived in the bar.

'You said the talented actor bit before,' pouted Godric.

'I know,' I stalled. 'But personally, I find the talented bit as sexy as the . . . as anything else.' God, this was a delicate one. Godric was staring at me, but swaying gently. I tried not to notice how much sexier he did look this evening.

'I mean, Jonathan is gorgeous,' I went on, 'but I find the way he's so professional and clever, and good at ordering wine, just as sexy as his lovely strong hands. And you're such a versatile actor – women love men who can *do* things. Believe it, Godric. And stop being so grumpy with people. I know you're shy, but it's not coming over.'

'Jonathan's not here, though, is he?'

I met Godric's dark-lashed eyes. I don't think he'd meant to be so perceptive, but he'd really managed to hit a nerve. I swallowed. Jonathan *wasn't* here.

Godric did have quite a Rufus Sewell'esque gaze, now I looked properly.

'No,' I said. 'He isn't. But that's not the point.'

Godric looked deep into his drink, then downed it, grabbed two more from a passing tray. Without thinking, I grabbed one too and tossed it back.

We both gasped, then stared at each other.

Godric broke the spell by burping.

'How many of those have you had?' I asked anxiously.

'Five.' He looked shifty. 'But I had a couple of quick ones before I came. Dutch courage, you know.'

Great. This was *all* I needed. Godric, loose in a social situation, tanked up, and me in an illicit wig and high heels. I didn't fancy my chances if I had to carry him up those stairs, either.

'Well, steady on,' I said, trying not to sound nannyish. 'There isn't much by way of canapés going round to soak it up.'

'Don't care,' he said, tossing a green shot back. He took the opportunity to shift a little closer to me. 'Mel, I mean, Honey,' he said with a hint of a slur, 'there's something I need to tell you.'

'Ah, well, no, there's something I need to tell *you*!' I said quickly. There was no point making it a surprise. He'd recognise her far quicker than I would. 'Mind if I go first?'

'I always like a lady to go first,' he said with a leer. Then he looked confused, then went back to the leer.

I ignored all of it.

'I've phoned Kirsty and had a little chat about Orlando, and about you!' I said. 'Are you cross?'

He was staring at me. He was actually staring at my chest, so I clapped my hands loudly in front of his face, at which point he rather blearily transferred his gaze to my eyes.

'You phoned Kirsty?'

'I did. I told her I was ringing because I needed to get something back from Orlando, and someone had given me this number. Bit of a fib, but, anyway, it turns out they split up ages and ages ago!' I beamed. 'Isn't that great? She's too ashamed to call you, because of what happened. But I said you weren't bothered.'

'I'm not bothered,' he said.

'Well, no, of course you're not, because you've been so busy with your career and . . . What do you mean, you're not bothered?'

'I'm over Kirsty,' said Godric loftily. 'She means nothing to me any more.'

'Oh, Godric, don't say that,' I cried. 'She sounds lovely! We had such a nice chat, and she says she misses you, and feels awful about falling for a . . . Godric.' I looked at him sharply. 'Your hand's on my knee.'

'I know,' he said, with an Elvis-like curl of the lip. 'For the time being.'

I removed it and replaced it where we could both see it, on the table. Godric stared at it, as if it belonged to someone else.

'So I got chatting to Kirsty,' I went on quickly. 'And it turns out she's in New York at the moment! Isn't that a coincidence! She's come all the way . . . Godric! Are you listening to me?'

'Melissa,' said Godric. 'I have fallen, in love, with you.'

I stared at him in shock.

'You're what I need in this stupid, pretenshss, world of wankers,' he slurred, his eyes suddenly full of emotion. 'A good, solid game girl with proper tits. And nice strong legs.'

'Well, I'm awfully flattered,' I gabbled, 'but really, I think you're just transferring your feelings for—'

He tried to put a finger sexily on my lips, but it went into my eye instead. With some effort, he placed it correctly. 'Don't think,' he said. 'Jus' feel.'

And then he lunged.

I would love to be able to say, snootily, that being kissed by Godric Ponsonby was like being assaulted by a dishwasher on economy cycle, or like having my face scoured by one of those super-absorbent magi-mops, but to my acute surprise, it was actually not an unpleasant experience.

He smelled very clean, underneath the rubbing alcohol aroma of the vodka, which is a trait I've always found rather sweet in overgrown public schoolboys: big date equals comprehensive bath. And his lips were soft, he'd shaved, and he didn't attempt to lick the inside of my mouth.

All in all, it was about nine hundred per cent better than our previous encounter in the wardrobe cupboard.

But it was completely and utterly inappropriate, and after a few, um, seconds, I fought him off.

'*No*, Godric,' I said firmly, as if I were talking to Braveheart.

'But why? Isn't it meant to be? Us meeting again after all these years?' he demanded. 'Don't you think it's fate?'

I looked deep into his eyes. I hated saying no, especially when I'd just realised how fond I was of the surly brute, and how I'd hate to hurt his feelings, but . . . 'No! Godric, it's not,' I said. 'I love Jonathan. I do. I love him.'

He said nothing, but widened his eyes fearfully, and when I followed his gaze, I realised why.

'Kirsty?' I said, recovering as fast as I could.

Kirsty, as indeed it was, was standing right next to our table, the living embodiment of what Gabi derisively called the 'Sloane Square Ski, Surf and Sand Club'. She had long, ruler-straight blonde hair parted in the middle, a fur gilet, straight-leg jeans and a pair of wide, pale eyes that were gazing at us and filling up with water faster than a leaky dinghy.

'Kirsty? Is it you?' I cried with joy. 'Hello! It's Melissa!' I leaped up from my seat and shook her limp, somewhat damp hand.

Her lip, frosted with pink gloss, wobbled. 'What were you . . .'

'Did you know Godric's in a simply *enormous* film? No? Well, he was talking me through his big romantic scene at the end – look, I'm sure he'll show you too. Apparently, there's a special way you have to kiss on camera, so you don't actually have to *kiss* the actress, if you know what I mean,' I improvised wildly. 'Godric?'

Godric and Kirsty were staring at each other. I couldn't work out quite what the stares were leading up to: tears, a fight, a reconciliation? I looked from one to the other.

Nope. No idea. That was the trouble with certain types of posh people, I'd found. Too much stiff upper lip eventually freezes your entire face. Aristocratic Botox.

'Shall I get you a drink, Kirsty?' I enquired. 'I'm just about to leave for dinner.'

At this point, Godric seemed to regalvanise himself. 'Is he going to join us?' he demanded.

'Who?'

'Jonathan?'

'I'm not having dinner with Jonathan,' I began. 'I'm seeing my sister. You remember Emery, don't you?'

Godric's brow creased. 'So what's he doing here?'

I spun round.

Sure enough, standing at the top of the stairs leading down into the main bar area was Jonathan. And he wasn't alone. Standing next to him, mouth opening and closing in mid-yap, was a beanpole of a blonde woman in a silver sheath dress, the spitting image of one of the super-ball-busters off *The Apprentice*.

Cindy.

My blood froze.

Honestly, it really did. It felt like it had set, thick and sluggish, like jelly in my veins.

Before I could move, Jonathan's eyes, rolling in annoyance at whatever Cindy was ranting about, met mine. He was standing beneath one of the only illuminated areas of the whole venue, all the better for me to make out the look of surprise, then extreme annoyance, then disgust that crossed his face.

I felt physically sick.

'Oh, *Christ*,' I moaned. Had he seen Godric fall on my neck? That must have looked so incriminating from a distance.

'What?' demanded Godric. 'What now?'

I opened my mouth to tell him, but the words wouldn't come. It was as if I were seeing the whole thing from Jonathan's perspective: the deliberate disobeying of his request, the lying about where I was, worst of all, the wearing of the wig.

I put my hand to my head to yank it off, but stopped. What was the point? I was so busted. The best I could do was to stick to the truth: that this was a last favour for Godric, and I was only wearing the wig so as *not* to embarrass Jonathan.

Then again, rallied a voice in my head, what the hell was he doing here with Cindy, when he was meant to be with a client?

I felt even more sick, and if I hadn't been clinging onto the table, I think my legs would have buckled entirely.

But rather than let them come to me, I decided to face the problem head-on.

'Would you excuse me?' I said to Godric and Kirsty, took a deep breath, and walked over to meet them by an aggressive display of black thistles.

'Hello, Jonathan,' I said. 'Shh! I'm in disguise.'

'Melissa,' he replied, his face a study in granite. 'Melissa, this is Cindy. Cindy, this is Melissa Romney-Jones.'

Cindy up close was no less smooth and hard than Cindy at a distance. She was, however, very difficult to describe: she looked air-brushed from blow-dried head to pedicured toe. She certainly didn't look like someone who'd recently seen a baby, let alone given birth.

'So you're Melissa?' she drawled, as if it would never have dawned on her that it could be me. 'They <i>said</i> you were . . . a blonde.'

I dragged up all the pride I could, under the circumstances.

'I'm not usually,' I said in a friendly tone, 'but I'm right in the middle of a secret operation right now. I'm acting Cupid for my old friend Godric and his estranged girlfriend, and I don't want anyone to know it's me. Hence the wig.'

Oh shit, I thought instantly, as Jonathan's face turned grey with anger. So plan A hadn't worked.

'You are?' Cindy looked frankly sceptical. 'How . . . accommodating. And is it working, Godric?' she added. 'Are you reconciled?'

Godric, in full parfit gentil knight mode, had stomped up behind me and was glowering at Jonathan. He favoured Cindy with an extreme scowl. 'We were about to leave, actually.'

Kirsty wisely said nothing. Her saucer-sized eyes were

widening into dinner plates. She was probably wondering if she'd been flown out to be in some reality TV show.

'I'd take that as a yes, Melissa!' said Cindy. 'Congrats! Is it one of your specialties, reuniting estranged lovers?'

She said this with a significant glance at Jonathan.

My stomach turned. 'No, this was just a one-off. And I was about to leave myself, to meet my sister for dinner,' I gabbled. 'She's probably outside right now.'

'Really?' said Jonathan, his voice dripping with sarcasm. 'Will she recognise you? Or is she in disguise too?'

I tried a tinkly laugh. 'Oh, Jonathan. Didn't you see her outside?'

Bloody hell. It would have to be Emery I was meeting, the woman so vague she couldn't remember her PIN number, even when it was the year of her own birth. The chances of her being in the right area, let alone on time, were slim.

'No,' said Jonathan. 'We didn't.'

'Emery?' demanded Godric, who wasn't quick at the best of times. 'You're meeting Emery?'

'Yes!' I insisted. Godric's vocal tic of habitual disbelief was hardly helping my case. 'I didn't mention it in case you still . . . in case you still had feelings, or something.' I held up a hand before he could say anything.

'But why would I have feelings for *Emery*?' demanded Godric. 'I only ever fancied *you!*'

'Ten years ago!' I added, as Kirsty looked aghast. 'Ten years ago! Ah ha ha ha!'

Godric opened his mouth, but I glared so hard at him, I swear pictures fell off the wall.

Cindy smirked. 'Well, they do say true love never dies. Don't they, Jon?'

'I wouldn't know,' he said through tight lips.

She nudged him, flashing me a 'men!' eyebrow-hike. 'Come on, honey. You're the romantic. Remember Antigua?'

I felt an odd cocktail of emotions churn in my stomach: fear, depression, inadequacy, but also rage. Why hadn't Jonathan told me he was seeing *her* this evening? How many other times had he seen her without saying?

And what were they going to talk about when I left? Antigua?

I drew myself up to my full height.

'Anyway, I can see you're fully occupied this evening, Jonathan,' I said. 'Is Cindy your client, or . . .' I swallowed. 'Or is this a social occasion?'

Cindy glanced at Jonathan. 'Business or pleasure, Jon? Huh?' She looked back at me. 'Let's say a bit of both.'

'Cindy's company is sponsoring the production,' Jonathan explained tightly.

'Yuh, I had to come along this evening, and since Jonathan wanted to . . .' She paused just long enough for me to think she was making up an excuse. '. . . meet to discuss the apartment sale, I thought we might as well meet here.'

I turned to him.

'That's right,' he said tonelessly.

Something snapped inside me, and sank like a stone, deep into the pit of my stomach.

'Well, in that case, I won't keep you from your discussions,' I said. 'Goodnight, Godric, Kirsty. I hope you have a lovely evening. I made a reservation for you at Cipriani's. So nice to meet you, Cindy.'

And I swept out.

21

Of course, who should I run into at the top of the steps but Emery, a mere ten minutes late for the first time ever.

I resisted the temptation to drag her downstairs and show her off as evidence. It was too late for that.

'Melissa?' she said, peering at me on the street. 'Melissa?'

'Yes, it's me,' I said, 'it's just a wig.'

'Suits you,' she said. 'You look like Mummy would have done. If she was younger, and a bit fatter. And sort of . . . crosser.'

'That's not the wig,' I said. 'Come on, I need a drink.'

We ended up, not in the fancy restaurant Emery had booked – since she hadn't remembered to write down the address – but in a simple Italian place where we ordered large bowls of pasta and some red wine.

I let everything tumble out, and Emery listened with a wise expression on her face. I knew it didn't necessarily mean she'd come out with anything wise, but Em had always been very good at sympathy. Years of weeping over orphaned lambs and First World War poets had seen to that.

'How do you manage?' I asked her. 'With William's ex?'

'Oh, it's very simple,' she said. 'I never see her. Well,

of course, Veronica's dead, which helps, but you mean Gwendolyn?'

I nodded. I didn't have the energy to do much else.

'I just pretend she doesn't exist,' said Emery serenely. 'I tell myself she's a fictional character, who sends us Christmas cards.'

'But what about Valentino?' Valentino was William's five-year-old son.

Emery widened her eyes. 'William won't let me meet him. He doesn't want lines to be crossed.'

I paused, my spaghetti dripping on my napkin. 'You're telling me that *William* wants you to pretend Gwendolyn and Valentino don't exist?'

'Mmm. His therapist says it's easier for him to keep things in boxes than it would be to try to make us all into a collage. Separate pages, you see. I think it's rather a good idea. I find it much easier to put Daddy on a separate page since he's in another country from me.' She smiled pensively. 'Actually, I've just about put him in a different book.'

'Em, I don't think that's so healthy.'

'You want to have this other woman floating in and out of your life, *for ever*?' asked Emery with unusual sharpness.

I thought. 'I'd rather have her where I can see her, than go mad wondering where she's hiding,' I said.

Emery kicked me affectionately under the table. 'Poor Mel,' she said. 'Have you thought about going blonde permanently? It rather suits you.'

I sighed, and pushed my pasta away.

Emery had to leave to get back to her hotel in time for her late-night meditation routine, so I wandered slowly back through the streets of the West Village to Jonathan's house, my wig curled up in my bag like a dirty secret, my own hair lank and dark. Like I felt.

When I reached Washington Square, I sat on the steps of one of the elegant town houses, and sank my head into my hands. The lamps were all lit in the park, and people were still playing chess, walking their dogs for the last time, and strolling back from their nights out, full and happy.

An awful heaviness filled my chest, pinning me to the spot. Nothing could feel worse than this. I'd had some pretty grim moments in the past, but nothing that paralysed me so completely. It was like being trapped in quicksand; the more I tried to explain, the more guilty I looked, and the more Jonathan would realise he'd made a mistake. And the more he'd turn his back on me – quite rightly too. I'd let him down. Even if it was for a very good reason, I'd still let him down.

No matter how wrong he'd been for seeing Cindy without telling me, I was the one who'd deliberately gone against his feelings.

My eyes filled with tears, and I wished I was sitting on my own front door steps. More than anything I wished I was at home.

And so I called the one person I knew who'd tell me what I should do, or else tell me to snap out of it.

The phone rang three times, and was then answered very abruptly.

'What now?' sighed Nelson. 'THAT'S NOT WHAT I CALL A SHEET KNOT, LEANNE! DO YOU WANT THIS SHIP TO CRASH INTO ROCKS AND SPLINTER INTO MATCHSTICKS BE-CAUSE OF YOUR NAILS? AGAIN, PLEASE!'

'You were wrong!' I wailed. 'I took your advice and I've really messed things up with Jonathan. I think . . . I think I'll have to come home!'

Nelson sighed again, and I heard him order some minion to take over. I think I even heard the minion say, 'Aye, aye, Cap'n,' but that might have been underprivileged urchin cheek.

'Right, quickly, please, and don't leave anything out,' he said, but his voice was more gentle than his words.

I tried to explain as quickly and as simply as I could. Nelson's clicking and whistling put me off rather, but I forced the words out, even though I winced inside at each one.

'Right,' he said eventually, 'I assume you did all this out of your usual misguided desire to help everyone apart from yourself? And to prove to Remington Steele that you were just as capable in New York as you are here?'

'Yes! I don't humiliate myself for *fun*, you know!'

'God, you're dim,' he sighed. 'Adorable, but dim. OK, first of all, don't come home.'

My heart sank. 'Ever?'

'No! Don't come home *now*, like you've done something wrong. You're not having an affair, you're not working on the side, and you're not lying to him. If you come home it'll be like admitting you are. You'll just have to wait for him to calm down, then explain that you weren't doing the pretend girlfriend stuff as a job, you were helping out a friend. OK, you should have told him, but, you know, control freakery and all that. Pretty bad show.'

'You think?' I said doubtfully. 'But it'll be unbearable. He's furious.'

'Melissa,' said Nelson. 'If this paragon of estate agency

ends up marrying you, it won't be the last time you'll do something so daft that he'll be speechless with fury. But if he has anything about him, he'll also realise that you did it for the very best reasons, and if he loves you, he'll see why that's far more important than some wifey who just follows orders.'

Tears started to slide down my cheeks again, but I managed a weak smile through them.

'Thank you,' I said. 'I know you don't like him very much.'

'It's not that. I, er, don't really think I'm . . .' Nelson decided not to go on with whatever he had in mind, but instead said, 'Look, Melissa, it's really very simple: ask yourself, what would your granny do? She's bound to have been in a similar situation. Why don't you phone her?'

'No,' I said, looking out over the park railings. 'No, I don't need to do that. I just wanted to . . . talk to you.'

'Jolly good,' he said gruffly. 'Flat OK?'

For some reason, that little question was more comforting than an hour of soothing noises. 'Yes, I called in while I was back in London, and it seemed to be going to schedule.' I hesitated. 'I'm not sure Gabi's being all that strict with the builders though. She seems to be, um, out quite a lot.'

'Yes,' said Nelson. 'I hear she's been out keeping Roger company.'

'Really?' I hedged. How much did he know?

'Indeed so.' Nelson sounded quite amused. 'So we'd both better hurry back and save them from a social fate worse than death, eh?'

He didn't seem very concerned, and I wondered whether I ought to warn him that his weeping dockside girlfriend wasn't acting quite so weepy in his absence.

Not that it was any of my business, but Roger was his best friend. And Gabi was my best friend. And the consequences for our mutual social lives could be vile.

'Look, much as I'd love to sit and hear you snivel transatlantically, I have a deck inspection to supervise and you have a boyfriend to make up with. Am I going to see you in a few weeks?'

'I'll be on the dockside with my hanky, Cap'n,' I assured him.

'Yes, well, make sure you have your adoring American there too,' he replied, and was then cut off amidst clanking background noises.

I hoped the urchins hadn't decided to punish him for unauthorised use of a mobile phone. Those cabin-boys in Hornblower novels could be vicious.

I put my phone back in my bag and sat for a moment, pulling myself together. I had to go back and try to fix what I'd broken, even if it turned out to be unfixable. Never let it be said that I ran away from my own problems, or tried to pretend that someone else's didn't exist. At least then I'd know.

I was still fighting the temptation to phone British Airways and get on the first flight home when I walked up the front steps. Maybe Jonathan had been right; I didn't have the same understanding of New York that I did in London. It was like hearing a familiar song sung in a different language; when you tried to join in, it didn't sound in tune.

But I kept Nelson's words in the forefront of my mind, and made myself walk back into the house where Jonathan sat on the leather sofa, staring blankly into space. The room was dark, with only the street light filtering through the trees outside, dappling the faded walls. He still hadn't made a wallpaper/paint decision.

I went to turn on the main light, then stopped.

Braveheart saw me walk in, and launched himself through the room, his claws skittering on the wooden floorboards. I picked him up as he tried to lick my face.

This wasn't helping my dignified speech, but it gave me something to hold onto.

'Jonathan, I'm sorry,' I began. 'I know I've done something you didn't want me to do. I had no intention of hurting you, or embarrassing you – that's why I wore the wig. So no one would know it was me.'

He turned round, and I was shocked at the stoniness of his face, which made the presidents on Mount Rushmore seem positively festive. It was the expression he wore when he didn't want anyone to see what he was feeling; the last time I'd seen him look this grim was when he was telling me about his divorce from Cindy, way back before we started dating properly.

'It's not *about* the damn wig,' he snapped. 'Although why you think no one would recognise you in it is yet another manifestation of this weird lack of esteem thing you have and . . . Oh, I can't be bothered having that conversation again. You just don't get it, do you?'

'I do!' I protested. 'I understand *perfectly*. You don't want me to show you up! You didn't want me to be working in New York! And I swear to you, I *wasn't* – I was honestly just doing a favour for a friend who—'

'Happened to be in love with you?'

I went crimson. 'Oh, he's not. That was the vodka talking. Anyway, not all exes are mad and out for revenge. I'm good friends with, well, nearly all of my exes. He's just—'

Jonathan raised an eyebrow. 'How are you still so naïve?' he demanded.

'I'd rather be naïve than cynical!' I protested hotly. 'And at least I *told* you about Godric. How many times have you been meeting up with Cindy without telling me? Eh? How many phone calls have you two had? What else has she been doing?'

'That's not the point!'

'It is!'

'Fine, maybe it's *a* point, but let's deal with Godric first, OK?'

Braveheart wriggled and I put him down, seizing the opportunity to reorder my thoughts.

I couldn't believe it. This was our first big row.

When I stood up, I took a deep breath and put my hands on my hips. 'Jonathan, I *am* sorry. I really am. I had no intention of showing you up. I was simply doing what I thought was an easy, helpful favour for a friend in need.' I looked at him stoutly. 'I have so many chances to make you happy, and only had to do this one small thing for Godric. I was *only there* to make sure he met up with *Kirsty*, his ex, so they could reconcile, and . . . all right, maybe it wasn't the best idea to use the wig, but at the time it seemed like the best way of *not* showing you up. You have so much confidence, so much . . . aplomb, and he has none. And I know how he feels.'

'Melissa, Ric is a film star,' said Jonathan patiently. 'If he can't walk into a party on his own, he's going to have something of a career problem.'

'But he's *not* a film star! He's just a normal man, a chap who did some acting at school, then some acting for money, and now he's just an actor who happens to have got famous . . .' I trailed off, realising how weak that sounded.

Jonathan shook his head. 'But *why* can't you see how that makes me feel? Arriving at a party, only to find my girlfriend wrapped around some pin-up?'

'I wasn't wrapped . . . You're not jealous of Godric, are you?' I asked, shocked. 'I mean, there's nothing to be jealous *of*!'

'No?' A flash of vulnerability broke through the chiselled granite for a second. 'When he was hanging off your neck, was that just acting?'

'I'm not going to dignify that with a response,' I retorted. 'Have I made a big deal about you selling your flat for Cindy? Letting her carry on interfering in your life?'

Jonathan's head whipped up. 'Hey! That was uncalled for.'

'I don't think so,' I said. 'Some girls might have stamped their feet over it, but I haven't. Because I trust you. And I thought you trusted me.'

A terrible silence fell.

'I thought I could,' said Jonathan quietly, his face suddenly very sad. My heart cracked. 'Maybe you're not the one with the problem.'

'Jonathan!' I said, hurling myself across the room like Braveheart, and kneeling on the sofa next to him. 'Don't be silly! Of course you can trust me!'

For an awful second, I thought he was going to push me away, but he slid an arm around my waist so I fell against him, then hugged me hard for a few minutes, while neither of us spoke.

Finally, he drew a deep breath. 'From now on I'll tell you whenever Cindy calls. You can see all the cell phone bills. I didn't mention it, because I didn't want you worrying.'

'I'm not a little girl,' I replied. 'I can cope with the idea that she's around.'

'Yeah, well, maybe I can't.' He looked at me. 'If it makes you feel better, I'll ask her not to come to the fundraiser at the Met next week.'

Jonathan had been working on this fundraiser for months now; apparently charitable volunteering was a significant element of his new role. From the papers I'd seen, it was something between a state opening of Parliament and the New Year's Ball in Vienna.

'She's hosting a table,' he went on, pained, 'but if it makes you feel better . . .'

'No,' I said. I wasn't running scared of her. I was a St Cathal's girl. 'She's part of your past. But she doesn't have to be more than a bit player in your future.'

Jonathan looked at me with what I hoped was admiration, and I seized the moment.

'But, Jonathan, we're not going to *have* a future if you don't make some more time for me,' I said bravely. 'I've hardly seen you. I didn't fly all the way over here to hang out with your dog and your secretary, agreeable though they both are.'

'Honey, you know how busy I've—'

'I do know. But you're the boss. And I'm going to have to go back to London any minute.' I gazed up at him. 'Then you'll be wishing you'd spent the afternoon viewing *me* instead of chasing phone calls in the office. Even Bloomingdales gets kind of lonely when you're on your own all day.'

'I didn't realise you were lonely.' He sighed. 'Guess when you put it like that, it sounds so simple.'

'That's because it is.'

'Yes, well, your front elevations are a darn sight more attractive than most of my current portfolio.' Jonathan twisted my hair round his fingers, sliding them into the ringlets he'd made. 'It's not a case of choosing between you or work, Melissa. You should know that. Don't ask me for something you know I can't deliver.'

My throat tightened. That wasn't what I wanted to hear. But Jonathan hadn't finished.

'But, yeah, I take your point. I haven't made enough free time for you, and that's more my loss than yours. I'm going to fix that.' He lifted my chin so I could see from his serious grey eyes that he meant what he said. 'And if I do that for you, will you—'

I flinched, not wanting to hear him say it. 'Don't. I've learned my lesson. No more man management.'

'Don't look so whipped.' Jonathan traced the lines of my face, up over my cheeks, around my nose. 'There are plenty other ways you can do your thing in New York without wearing yourself out dealing with idiots like Ric, you know.'

'Like what?'

'Well, like this baby shower you're planning for Diana. You'll make an awesome job of that. She knows so many people in Manhattan, I'm sure you wouldn't have a minute to spare if you wanted to set yourself up advising on that type of event.'

Visions of endless grabby shopping lists filled my head, but right then I'd have agreed to become Braveheart's full-time PA if it meant halting the downward spiral to dumpsville.

'Let's enjoy the rest of your time here,' said Jonathan softly.

'Right,' I said. At least he wanted me to *stay*. He was even looking ahead to my working. Surely that was good? 'Well, I could certainly do that, I suppose. Yes. I could definitely do that.'

'Melissa, you make me so happy.' With one strong movement, Jonathan lifted me up into his lap and snuggled me into his chest.

I relaxed completely, as powerful relief chemicals flooded my system, sweeping away any awkward little protesting voices in my head. I felt as though I'd slid right to the edge of the precipice, seen the terrifying drop at the edge, and somehow managed to cling on.

'We're good then?' he murmured into my hair.

'Yes,' I said, inhaling his familiar warm smell. 'We're good.'

22

For the next few days I threw myself into being the perfect girlfriend with a vigour that would have winded Martha Stewart. I chased up the designers and the builders and all the other teams of people working on Jonathan's dream house, and had the conversations he hadn't had time to have, including some tough talking about deadlines.

I taught Braveheart to fetch without destroying the item being fetched.

I made sure the bits of the house not being worked on were tidy and clean, and put flowers on the kitchen table, and read the instructions for all the appliances.

I even made my phone calls to the agency in the dead of night, or under the guise of walking Braveheart, and never even referred to the problems that Allegra and Gabi were stirring up between them at home.

And, armed with a couple of new American etiquette books for reference, I made arrangements to meet up with Diana Stuyvesant to talk about her baby shower.

The summit meeting took place in Diana's airy Upper West Side condo, and featured the contributions of Indiscreet Jennifer and Bonnie, as well as my own suggestions.

Cindy, for me at least, was more conspicuous by her absence than she would have been had she turned up. I spotted a couple of spaces on the grand piano where photographs had been swiftly whisked out of sight, and not rearranged to cover the gaps.

Still, thinking of Jonathan, and wanting to be as helpful as I could, I fixed my smile and pretended not to notice.

'OK, I want you to make this as British as possible!' said Diana, clapping her hands with delight.

'Well, I can't make it totally British,' I replied patiently, 'because, as I said before, we don't really have baby showers.'

'Whyever not?' demanded Jennifer, as if it were the most barbaric thing she'd heard in her life. 'How does the poor mom get any *stuff*?'

'She buys it herself from John Lewis,' I said, with the merest hint of gritted teeth.

Honestly. We'd been here nearly an hour and so far all they'd discussed was where to lodge the registry. Between weddings, sweet sixteens, twenty-firsts, confirmations, birthdays, graduations, anniversaries, new pets and house-warmings, there didn't seem to be a single occasion that you couldn't issue a list of demands for in New York. Whereas I distinctly recalled getting my Christmas list back from Santa with various items crossed out and appended with the rather innocence-crushing note: 'Santa is not made of money.'

'Why don't you make it completely unique and instead of asking for gifts, ask for . . . advice?' I suggested, seizing on something I'd read in Emily Post's enormous Bible of Proper Behaviour. 'You could ask your guests to ask their mothers for the best piece of advice they learned when they had their first babies – you know, get a blackout curtain for the bedroom, or what have you. Then you can make a scrap book, with everyone writing in their ideas, and maybe sticking in a baby picture of their own?' I paused. 'I mean, I don't have children, so I don't know any specific examples, but I'm sure mothers will have some good practical ideas. And we could get a really gorgeous hand-bound book from somewhere.'

'I had a nanny,' said Jennifer. 'But I guess I could ask her?'

Diana nodded. 'I'll be having a day nurse when baby arrives. And a night nurse too, for the first six months at least. Steve was insistent.'

'You'll need her for longer than that,' warned Bonnie. 'How else are you going to have time to fit in moments for yourself . . . and Steve?' she added, with a knowing look.

'Well, why not ask all the nannies for ideas!' I said quickly. 'It can be like a Do-It-Yourself Supernanny manual!'

'Oh, that is so perfect!' squeaked Diana. 'Supernanny! Write that down at once! I love it!'

'You shouldn't even be here,' said Jennifer sternly. 'This is meant to be a surprise.'

Diana pulled a face. 'I had a *surprise* on my bridal shower, if you remember? A visit from that mad bitch feminist divorce lawyer to make sure we all had adequate pre-nups? Remember? Jacqueline got hysterical because she didn't have one at all? And Cindy got up in her grill about how she had a duty to protect herself, and my mother ended up leaving in tears? Not doing *surprises* again, thank you.'

Jennifer and Bonnie exchanged glances.

I smiled and clicked my pen. This was an opportune moment to go to the loo. 'Would you excuse me?' I said. 'Where's the . . . ?'

'Right down the corridor on your left,' said Diana.

'Toilet?' demanded Jennifer. 'Or lavatory?'

I stared at her. 'Sorry?'

'Toilet? Or lavatory?'

Oh, God. We'd been playing 'What would the Queen say?'

'Lavatory?' I guessed. 'Loo, probably. Where I live, anyway.'

'Loo!' hooted Jennifer and Diana in unison.

'Oh! Oh!' Bonnie flapped her hands. 'You could put it on the door, for the shower!'

I slipped out.

Diana's apartment was very elegant, with high white walls and lots of nooks and crannies, filled with fresh flowers. The main wall, running the length of the apartment, was filled with photographs from top to bottom, going from faded baby pictures through high school, graduation, university, weddings and parties and families. It was like an exhibition of her and Steve's life – a really clever idea.

I didn't mean to be nosey, but I couldn't help surfing through the images, looking for pictures of Jonathan.

It didn't take long. Here he was aged about twenty, looking kind of dorky in one of those college boy jackets. His hair, bright copper, was brushed up into a quiff, and he had a whole crop of spots, like angry red barnacles on his chin.

In fact, apart from the spots, and that he'd obviously just won some sporty trophy thing, he looked endearingly like Rick Astley.

Jonathan's hair made him pretty easy to pick out of the college photos. There he was a few years later, with a group of other tuxedo'd guests at Steve and Diana's wedding. It looked like a very smart do, very white flowers and gold chairs, but they seemed comfortable with each other, in the way only old, old friends can be, laughing and knocking back the champagne. There he was again, holding Diana up in her wedding dress, with five other ushers. She looked like a canoe.

I didn't want to admit it, but I knew subconsciously I was looking for a photograph of Jonathan with Cindy.

And suddenly my eye fell on it: both of them in a large group, on a manicured lawn behind a spacious, white-painted holiday house. I picked out Bonnie and Kurt, Steve and Diana, Jennifer – and Jonathan and Cindy.

My heart stopped and I held my breath as I looked at them together. Both of them were smiling and relaxed in their chinos, jumpers thrown over their shoulders. It could have been a page from a Ralph Lauren catalogue. Everyone looked sparkling clean.

Could I compete with that? Not only was everyone older than me, they were just more . . . finished than I was. The women had that no-make-up make-up look down pat. And as long as Jonathan was part of this group, Cindy would always be there in the background, like a ruler I was always being measured against. She would be Margaret Thatcher to my John Major.

Not a nice thought.

I took a pace away from the group shot and found another picture of Jonathan in his rowing eight at Princeton with Steve. It was, as he said, the First boat. Even at six two, Jonathan was a good few inches shorter than the rest of them, but he had a determined look on his face, even in the crew shot, that told me that he'd decided to be in the boat, had worked his socks off, and got there. God knew what he looked like when he was actually rowing.

I was admiring Jonathan's well-muscled legs when I realised that the conversation in the kitchen had risen back to normal levels, now they assumed I was safely ensconced in the bathroom. And what they were talking about froze me in my tracks.

'I saw Cindy the other day,' Jennifer was saying. 'She was pumping me for details about Melissa.'

There was an unspecific groan.

I held my breath.

'What did you tell her?' asked Bonnie.

Pause. In which I was willing to bet they were pulling faces. God, I wished I could have seen what those faces were.

'She said she'd seen her in some bar with some other guy! An actor? Some English guy Paige is representing.'

'Oh, my God! No!'

My thoughts exactly.

'And she was wearing a wig?' Jennifer went on excitedly. 'Like a blonde wig?'

'Really? No!' gasped Diana. 'Was she, like, being intimate with this guy?'

Long pause.

I felt ill.

'I'm sure Cindy got that wrong,' said Bonnie firmly, and I could have kissed her.

'She said Jonathan was pretty mad! He went home straight afterwards in a complete silent fit. Wouldn't even stay for a drink.'

Well, at least there was that, I told myself, hopefully. It wasn't like he'd stayed there all night, whooping it up with her.

'She was there with *Jonathan*?' demanded Diana. 'Oh, my God! What is going *on* with those two? Did Melissa know Cindy was going to turn up with Jonathan? That must have been a shock for her.'

Someone snorted. Jennifer? 'Listen, if *seeing* Cindy's a shock, can you imagine what's in store for that poor girl when she gets to *know* her?'

'Well, I spoke to Jonathan about it,' said Bonnie's firm voice, 'and he told me that Melissa was doing a favour for a friend. She was acting as a matchmaker, and she had to wear the wig so no one would recognise her in the bar.'

'And he believed that?' scoffed Jennifer. 'Like, duh!'

'*Jennifer*, the guy is just some old friend of hers from London, an actor. Paige had her doing some kind of work with him. Melissa's a good girl. Besides, Jon had no right to be there with Cindy without telling her.'

I had never realised how much I liked Bonnie. I took back every mean thing I'd ever thought about her bony ribs.

'Yeah, well, there is that,' conceded Diana. 'So what did you tell Cindy about Melissa?'

'I said she was super-polite,' said Jennifer. 'And charming and very cute.'

My heart lifted.

But unfortunately, Jennifer hadn't finished.

'Sure, a little, um . . . naïve, maybe. But she's British, and, I mean, kind of young? Compared with Jonathan.'

I seethed a little. I wasn't half as naïve as people seemed to think. In fact, if people could only recognise that looking for the best in others wasn't automatically a sign of mental frailty . . .

'You think she's up to all that social stuff Jonathan

has to do now? I mean, there's some serious heavy lifting there. And say what you like about Cindy, she certainly knew how to work a room. They were a team, you know? Remember those New Years parties they used to throw?'

Someone sighed. From the note of concern injected into the sigh, I guessed it was Bonnie. 'I know. I do worry about that. I mean, I think Melissa is so much better for him, but there was always such a *feistiness* about Jonathan and Cindy, you know? A real love-hate thing goin' on. You get into habits, in relationships . . . I just worry that maybe Melissa . . .'

'Men can be so dumb . . .'

I hated all these trailing offs.

'I know what you mean. A spark, mmm.'

Literally, sometimes, I observed to myself, but none of the three seemed to notice.

For a second, I was too distracted by the delicious novelty of getting a joke other people had missed that I almost didn't notice the implication of what they were saying: that there was no spark between me and Jonathan?

I begged to differ on that one.

But the other two were making concerned agreeing noises.

'And I don't think Cindy's over him, do you? They still seem to be in touch about the flat and such like.'

'You know what she's like – she can't let anything go. And Brendan's already rowing with her about Parker's day care.'

'You think they'll get back together?'

The breath seemed to stop in my body, as silence suggested that they were pulling faces again.

What were *those faces?* I agonised.

'Well, there's Parker to consider now,' said Bonnie finally.

What did that mean? That if it wasn't for Parker it would all still be to play for?

'Bonnie, I know she was a whole handful of trouble, but those two . . . It's a long time, you know? You don't just get over someone like that.'

'Unless you're already all over his brother,' noted Jennifer. 'Which she was. For a long time, I hear.'

You could have heard a pin drop. Well, you could have heard three coffee cups being refilled.

'Is Melissa all right, do you think? She's been a long time in the bathroom. You don't think she's sick?'

'Oh, no, she's probably just getting a good look at a proper shower!'

Tinkly laughter.

Feeling somewhat grubby, I crept back round the corner into the bathroom, which was the size of my bedroom back home, flushed the lavatory to warn them I was on my way, then cringed, wondering if the long delay between leaving and flushing had made it look as if I had some kind of digestive problem.

Too late to worry about that.

I breezed back into the kitchen, where three heads snapped round in a classic 'you caught us!' guilt fest.

'Melissa!' said Diana. 'We were just wondering where you'd got to!'

'Oh, there's so much to admire in your lovely house!' I said. 'I was looking at the old college pictures of Jonathan. He hasn't changed much, has he?'

Jennifer and Diana both laughed in agreement, but Bonnie fixed her eyes on me and I felt as if she were trying to look into my mind.

'You know something, Melissa? I haven't seen Jonathan like this since we were fresh out of college. I mean that. He seems really *happy*. Don't you think, girls?'

There was a murmur of agreement. I tried to tell myself that if Gabi found a new boyfriend, I'd try to be welcoming and fair to the new one, as well as carrying on liking Aaron just the same.

Then I remembered she did have a new boyfriend and it was Nelson, and I wasn't handling that very well at all. Out of love for both of them.

I looked round the table: Bonnie with her inquisitive eyes, looking straight through me; Diana with her immaculately messed-up auburn bob; Jennifer and her astonishing breasts.

Love Jonathan, love his friends.

'Good!' I said, taking a deep breath. 'Actually, I've just had rather a good idea for the cake!'

23

If Jonathan's office was keeping him in a state of hypertension, then the additional organisation he'd taken on for the charity fundraiser was stretching even his extraordinary powers of organisation to the limits.

He kept his promise, though, and carved out much more time for me than before, even calling himself when he was running late, instead of getting Lori to do it. Better than that, he did it graciously, without a hint of guilt-tripping. We went on a day trip to Long Island, and took a night-time Ghost Walk around Greenwich Village, and managed to grab lunches, teas or power breakfasts on days when his schedule was too tight for anything more. But even when we were sipping cocktails at the Carlyle, or strolling hand-in-hand through Central Park with Braveheart, I could tell his brain was always making lists, or working on logistical problems, and with only a few days to go until the big night, the little crease between his eyebrows deepened into a furrow.

I could hardly complain about Jonathan's preoccupation, though. I was pretty busy myself. Officially, I was consulting with Diana and her caterers, while unofficially sneaking out of the house to make check-up calls to the office at least once a day, sometimes very early in the morning indeed, just to catch Gabi and Allegra unawares. After their little performance last time I was home, I didn't want them thinking that they weren't under constant supervision. I wanted a business to go home to.

And that was the weight on my mind: going home. Somehow, Jonathan and I had managed to skirt around the small matter of my return to England, and, indeed, what would happen after that. I was meant to be flying back three days after the fundraiser, but it was impossible, of course, to think beyond *that* massive deadline. So now there were two elephants in our hallway: Cindy, and the Future.

Could you blame me for enjoying my lattes where I could?

The morning of the fundraiser rolled round all too soon, and it didn't get off to a great start for me.

I'd set my phone to vibrate at five thirty because I really, really wanted to catch Gabi and Allegra out. In the end I couldn't sleep anyway, running things I'd heard the girls say, and the stupid things I'd managed to get wrong, back and forth in my mind, until I got up at five, and went downstairs.

In his crate, Braveheart didn't even bother to wake up, but I slipped Jonathan's fine cashmere jumper on over my pyjamas and let myself out to sit.

To my astonishment, the office phone barely rang once.

'For Christ's sake, Gobby, I'm bloody well doing it!' bellowed Allegra, to an accompaniment of slamming drawers. 'Unless you're calling to apologise for that completely unnecessary—'

'Is that the Little Lady Agency?' I demanded in a hoity-toity voice. 'Have I mis-dialled?'

'No, this is the Little Lady Agency,' confirmed Allegra, in slightly sweeter tones. 'What's your problem?'

'To whom do I speak?' All right, I should have dropped it there, but it was too transfixing, hearing Allegra's public voice.

There was a brief pause. 'You're speaking to Melissa Romney-Jones,' said Allegra sweetly.

'I very much doubt that,' I said, in my own voice.

'Why's that?' she enquired.

Honestly. 'Because I'm Melissa Romney-Jones!' I exploded. 'Allegra. It's me.'

'Oh?' Allegra sounded vaguely surprised. 'You don't have a very distinctive voice, Melissa.'

For goodness' sake! She'd only had twenty-eight years to get familiar with it.

'How is everything?' I asked, watching a student cycling unsteadily down the cobbled street. 'Why aren't you telling people who you are?'

'Because I'd rather keep my whereabouts to myself, thank you,' she snotted. 'And everything's fine. Nothing we can't handle.'

I put aside my concerns about the truth of that for the moment. 'Everything OK?'

'Is there something in particular you want?' Allegra snapped. 'Because we're having a busy day here. Already. You have noted the time? Yes? Just gone ten?'

'What are you doing? Apart from giving cheek to potential clients.'

'I'm taking some bloke called Rupert Braithwaite out shopping for some kitchen equipment, and Gabi's meant to be sorting out a birthday present for some brat in Mayfair.'

Which reminded me. 'Allegra,' I said firmly, 'you *have*

spoken to that poor woman about the knitted toys you sent *by mistake*, haven't you?'

'Sorry, Melissa, something's just come up, got to go, will have Gabi phone you later,' gabbled Allegra and hung up on me.

I sat there, staring at the mobile in my hand. What on earth was that about?

I went back inside, and sat for a while in the kitchen, watching the light spread through the slatted shutters, over the wooden floor, as the sounds of the city waking up began to filter in along with the dawn. I hoped Jonathan wasn't going to let the designers plan the character out of this house. It had so much cobwebby charm in a city that seemed to be constantly cleaning and improving itself.

I wished, for a moment, that he'd let me do it for him. There had to be something I could do for him.

Then I felt a kiss on my hair.

'Couldn't sleep either, huh?' said Jonathan. He was already in his gym kit and looked disgustingly awake.

I shook my head. 'Darling, isn't it a bit early for a run?'

'No! Big day ahead! I thought I'd get my run in early, before I jog to work, then start with the arrangements by six. I need to make sure everyone's on track.'

I goggled. So this was the full Dr No mode. 'At six in the morning?'

He nodded, and started to pull on his trainers. 'We start early here, Melissa.' His head vanished beneath the table. 'You got your salon appointments booked?' floated up.

'Yup. Lori's done herself proud.' I was spending no fewer than four hours at Bliss Spa. 'I'll be a different woman by the time you see me at the Met tonight.'

He re-emerged. 'Don't be too different, please,' he said, kissing my forehead. 'I like the woman I've got just fine. You could go just as you are and still be the cutest one there.' He checked his watch. 'OK, gotta go. Don't call me if you need anything—'

'Call Lori,' I finished. 'I know.'

'Hey!' he said, as if it had just occurred to him. 'I can take the dog!'

'I don't think he'll like it,' I warned.

'No, it's a cool thing for us to do together,' said Jonathan, approaching Braveheart's crate. 'C'mon, little fella! Come for a jog with Daddy!'

A low growling emanated from the crate.

'OK!' said Jonathan, as if he were making an executive decision. 'Stay home and look after Mommy then!'

He clicked his fingers and pointed at me with a near-satanic energy for such an unearthly time of the morning, then jogged off.

I went back to bed, but didn't get much sleep.

I was woken at nine, just as I'd finally dropped off, by a man from the florist bearing a huge bunch of roses, and a smaller bunch of other flowers that on a normal day would have looked lavish. I tipped him the right money – having learned florist delivery tips as part of my never-ending research into American tipping – and staggered to the table with the floral tributes.

The huge bunch of velvety crimson roses was from Jonathan. The card, in his handwriting, simply read, 'Always'. I allowed myself a moment just to stand and quiver with romance. He was, undoubtedly, the classiest man I had ever met.

The second bunch of freesias and lilies contained a

card saying, 'Orlando von Borsch finally comes good! Love from Godric and Kirsty xx'.

And that really did send me into the power shower singing.

Once dressed and invigorated by such early morning efficiency, I called the builders at Nelson's house to check up on them. Gabi and Woolfe, predictably, hadn't been running the show with the necessary ferocity, so I told them I'd stupidly forgotten to unhook Nelson's hidden security webcams in the house – a handy trick I used to buck up slacking cleaners. Yes, I said, I could see Jason waving at me, and crikey! Would Dave please stop doing that?

I couldn't see them, of course. But builders are easy to second-guess.

Once I'd done that, even my usual to-do list was exhausted. I'd bought a new dress for the occasion and as I had nothing else to do but get ready to wear it, I gave up, and spent the rest of the morning browsing round the little vintage shops in the Village, buying presents to take home. I even called in at a bookstore and was flicking through the English magazines, when I suddenly caught sight of *Country Life*.

Or rather, I caught sight of my mother – *Country Life* cover girl and the new face of the Women's Institute.

Dumbstruck, I flipped through to the feature, where Mummy sat looking twenty years younger than she really was on her chaise-longue, wearing a silky pair of Indian trousers, surrounded by pots and pots and pots of jam, gleaming like jewels on every available surface.

I squinted. Was that Allegra scowling in the background? She looked as if she'd been made over by a seriously determined stylist, in a pretty red dress and – heaven forfend – blusher. The caption read, 'Belinda

Romney-Jones, at home with just some of her year's pro-
duce, with etiquette expert daughter, Melissa'.

Melissa?

Well, if Allegra was still under Swedish Mafia surveil-
lance it was cheaper than plastic surgery, I guessed.

My eye skimmed the article with a mixture of pride
and dread. 'Mrs Romney-Jones, wife of long-serving Tory
MP, Martin . . . Keen home-maker . . . knitting . . . supporter of WI markets . . . "I've always loved making jam,
ever since I planted our first quince tree!"'

Pride, horror and bewilderment swirled up in me, and
I couldn't read any more. I still bought the magazine
though.

By two, I was in Bliss on the very last lap of my pam-
pering, when the phone rang.

That was very bad in itself, I knew, as phones were
verboten, but what made it worse was that it was Daddy.

Nobody knew how to puncture a relaxing mood like
Daddy.

As usual, he didn't bother with 'Hello! How are you?
We miss you' or anything like that. He went straight in
with, 'I need to get time sheets off you for that research
you're doing for me, in the next twenty-four hours. And
don't bother adding extra hours onto them because I've
got to get them past those bottom-feeders at Customs
and Excise.'

The Russian lady pummelling the dead skin off my
feet glowered upwards. I felt got at from both ends.

'Yes, well, of course, I'd do that,' I began, 'but I don't
have the—'

'Well, get them!' he squawked. 'You have been putting
all this through the agency accounts, haven't you?'

'Yes!'

'Don't say yes like that! Your sister, it seems, has set up her own company to process her salary!'

'What?'

'Indeed! What? That's not what I need to hear when I've got Simon round here with some missive from the bank, your grandmother wafting around as if she's in a second-rate touring production of *Blithe Spirit*, and bloody Lars hanging about the place, cluttering up the drawing room with spearheads!'

'Oh, is Lars back?'

'He's *just going*!' Daddy bellowed, I think towards Lars.

'And Mummy?' I tried, longing for one nice image to close the conversation on. 'I saw her feature in *Country Life*. Happy anniversary, by the way. Did you have a nice time on your mini-break?'

Daddy took a long breath. 'Melissa, your mother has barely stopped knitting for seven months now. When we plighted our troth, thirty-five years ago, I got Madame Butterfly. I did not marry your mother for her to turn into Madame bloody Defarge. And I resent the way she is constantly *armed.*'

'She's the face of the WI!' I added hopefully.

'Yes,' he said. 'Quite.'

I wished he could be nicer about her. It was never too late to traumatise a child.

Then either he was cut off by a poor Manhattan signal (charitable explanation) or he hung up on me (usual explanation).

I sighed.

'Sorry,' I said to Svetlana.

She glared at me. 'Forty minutes it take, to get strrrress out of your feet.'

We both looked down. They were jutting out of the water like two very tense rocks.

'Sorry,' I said again.

It would have been nice to sweep into the Met on Jonathan's arm, but he was too busy attending to last-minute details to take me in. Lori had organised me a very swish limo, though, which sort of made up for it a little bit, especially when I found a red rose corsage on the back seat.

I wished he'd seen me as I left the house, though. Yolanda the dogwalker called round to collect Braveheart for his overnight and nearly wept when I opened the door.

'You look like an angel!' she howled, hugging me as closely as she could given my voluminous dress and big up-do. 'An angel . . . with lipstick!'

I took that as a compliment, and promised to tell her if I saw anyone famous in the loos.

At the bottom of the long sweep of steps I took a deep breath, suddenly struck with nerves. Still, I'd told Godric to get on and do this sort of thing, hadn't I?

One, I told myself, arriving on my own means I can take my time and look at everything without being rushed past.

Two, no one will be looking at me with Jonathan and wondering why I'm not Cindy.

Three.

I took small steps up the red carpet, my stomach fluttering, staring at my new gold shoes, aware I was being observed all round.

I really wished Jonathan was here, just so I could tell him how speechless I was at the glamour of it all.

Three . . .

There was no three. I wished he was here at my side.

Tiny lanterns lit the way up the steps into the splendid marble hall, where huge sprays of lilies and roses sat like giant peacocks, throwing their musky night-time fragrance into the echoing air. Red ropes marked off the area for the party, and, even though I was early, black-tied guests were already gathering, removing coats and cashmere shawls, taking a glass of champagne from huge trays, before being ushered discreetly towards the Temple of Dendur, where the main event was taking place.

I handed in Granny's little fake fur jacket, and followed the flow of people, letting my spine lengthen and my walk swing. With no one watching me, I was revelling in the feeling of walking on my high heels through the empty halls. Beyond the ropes, the museum was empty, and I felt a delicious giddiness at the idea of the silent halls and darkened rooms, waiting, deserted, while the glitzy and glamorous ate and drank below.

The Temple of Dendur was a curious room: an ancient arch, with the stone temple behind it, dwarfed by a swooping modern glass ceiling. It glowed with a strange light, and I felt rather self-conscious about mingling in such a dignified setting. It was rather like having a wine and cheese evening in a church, say. On a much smaller scale, of course.

But mingling was on the menu, so I took a glass of champagne from a passing waiter, and looked round for someone to mingle with.

I'd made conversation with two or three friendly people without managing to catch sight of Jonathan, until suddenly I spotted him in the crowd, talking animatedly to an elderly couple in very fancy black tie.

Jonathan was born to wear black tie. He looked dignified, and yet comfortable in his dinner jacket; his hair
was neat without being overdone, his long hands were
elegant without being manicured, and he carried the
whole thing off with understated confidence. I felt so
proud to be with him that my chest swelled in my
corset.

While he talked, he turned his head discreetly, as if he
were looking for something, and when he caught sight
of me, looking for him, a smile broke across his face, like
sunshine.

He excused himself from the conversation, and made
his way through the crowds of guests, gliding around the
waiters with their broad trays of sparkling glasses. My
lips tingled with excitement as he approached, and when
he finally put his fingers on my bare arm, the hairs stood
up on my skin.

'Melissa, you look astonishing,' he murmured into my
ear. 'You're the most spectacular exhibit in here.'

'Too kind,' I said.

'I can see you're busy working your famous charm on
the guests, but could I beg a quick word?'

'Of course you can!' I murmured back. 'As many as
you like!'

'Oh, I only need a few,' he said, and my heart skipped.

Jonathan put his hand on the small of my back and
guided me away from the main crowd of guests, out of
the temple area and past a couple of dark-suited guards,
who went to stop us, then, realising it was Jonathan,
nodded us through.

'The museum is meant to be closed,' he whispered,
as he took my hand to lead me quickly down the corridors. 'We're not meant to be sneaking out like this,

but I, ah . . . I spoke to some people. We don't have long,' he added, 'but there's something I want you to see.'

Given that his to-do list ran into several pages, I was amazed he could even spare two minutes to admire my hair-do, much less slip off for a private moment among the sarcophagi. My heart-rate quickened, and not just because we were walking through the marble-floored halls so briskly that my high heels were only just keeping up with Jonathan's long strides.

Eventually, we passed through an area of what seemed like fairly standard cases of china, and emerged, unexpectedly, in a drawing room.

An English drawing room, complete with wooden floorboards, mahogany sideboards, and three of those old mirrors, half covered in tarnish, so the casual preener looks like she's got leprosy. It even smelled like a National Trust property. All it needed was a few bowls of very old pot-pourri and a retired lady sitting on a chair glowering at my stilettos, and I could have been in Great Chigley Manor House or some such.

Come to that, if there were two dogs, a lingering air of tension and cigar smoke, plus some distant shouting, it could be chez Romney-Jones. The instant homesickness was startling.

'Good heavens,' I said faintly. 'It's like . . . being at home.'

'I knew you'd like it!' beamed Jonathan. 'Come on, we're not done yet!'

The thing was, I thought, as I followed him, I wasn't sure I *did* like it. What was this perfectly nice drawing room doing here, in New York? I had a sudden flash of how the Greeks must feel when they turn up at the British

Museum and see great chunks of their own stuff displayed wholesale.

Barely able to contain his delight, Jonathan beckoned me through to a darker room, containing a huge, draped four-poster bed, with gorgeous old woven bedspreads falling in pleats around the base. It couldn't have been more English if it had had Union Jack curtains. Patriotism started to swell in my breast. Now that was what I called a bed of state.

'Wow!' I said. 'How splendid!'

'Isn't it?' said Jonathan. He stood behind me and wrapped his arms around my waist so we could both admire the good solid bed. 'I came here before Christmas last year, while I was going through all that . . . business with Cindy and the divorce. I love the Met for that. Whenever I feel tense, I like to come here, and I always see something that puts all the rest into perspective. Something beautiful, or peaceful, or just . . . special.'

'I know just what you mean!' I said. 'I like to go and look at the wrought ironwork at the V&A. Sturdy but beautiful.' I wondered if he was going to suggest some kind of romp. That would be taking risky sex to terrible extremes. Surely it was all alarmed?

'Well, when I came here, last December, I was very, very conflicted,' Jonathan went on. He squeezed me. 'But I'm not so conflicted now, I'm happy to say.'

I couldn't help reading the label on the side of the bed. It had come from a stately home just down the road from Roger's mother's place! I felt a sharp pang of national pride. So it might have been given away fair and square to the Met, but all the same . . .

'I came here,' Jonathan went on, 'wondering if I was

doing the right thing, and I saw this bed and you know what? I thought of you.'

'Steady on!' I exclaimed in pretend horror.

Jonathan squeezed. 'No, silly. I came here because I missed you, and London, and everything. The *comfort* of it made me think of you, and how comfortable you made me feel, like I wanted to tumble you into a bed like this, and close the curtains around us, and keep all the rest of the world out. It was totally English – solidly made, and honest, and such a thing of beauty. Like a fairy-tale bed, but made to last. And see? It's lasted five hundred years.'

I held my breath, not quite sure where he was going with this.

'Melissa,' said Jonathan, turning me round to face him. His expression was completely serious, and I thought I could detect a glimmer of nerves in his eyes. 'I didn't believe I could ever be this happy. I want to draw those curtains around us for ever, if you'll let me.'

Then he hitched up one leg of his dinner trousers, dropped to one knee and looked up at me from the floor. 'I appreciate that I should run this past your father first, but he's not answering his cell phone, and his secretary won't tell me where he is. Your grandmother gave me the go-ahead, though. So, Melissa . . .'

I swear I could not breathe, even if I wanted to.

'. . . would you do me the great honour of becoming my wife?'

I opened my mouth to speak, but nothing came out. The tears had already started to slide down my face with giddy, champagne-bubble joy. I couldn't believe it. Literally. I tried to absorb what Jonathan had just said, and I couldn't make my brain acknowledge it was real. He was asking me to marry him!

And if I needed physical evidence, he had a small ring-box in his hand, which he offered to me now.

'It's not the proper one,' he said as I took it with shaky fingers, 'because I know you'll want to go and pick out something together, but I thought you'd, you know, like to have something to show off tonight.'

I opened the old-fashioned blue leather box, and gasped when I saw the delicate little three-stone sapphire ring nestled in the worn red velvet. It glittered in the low light. It was beautiful.

'My grandmother's,' he explained. 'An eternity ring my grandfather gave her for their golden wedding.'

Kind of confident of him to have the ring right there, observed a detached voice in my head.

'Are you going to see if it fits?' he prompted. 'I can have it altered. That's not a problem.'

'But I haven't said yes yet,' I said with as much solemnity as I could muster.

Panic widened Jonathan's eyes.

'Oh, don't be ridiculous,' I said, dropping to my knees too with absolutely no regard for my sheer tights. 'Yes, of course, it's yes!'

'You don't know how happy that makes me!' he murmured as he cupped my face in his hands and kissed me.

We must have been the only couple in history to be just engaged, next to a four-poster bed, and end up kissing passionately on the floor.

I must admit, the way Jonathan kissed me, I didn't really mind. He kissed the way men do in films: long, slow, deep kisses, always with his eyes closed.

'Oh, Melissa,' said Jonathan, helping me up to my feet when we'd kissed long enough for pins and needles to be setting in. 'This is the best night of my life.' He put his arms round me and stroked my hair. The museum was so vast that we couldn't even hear the distant party noises. It was just us, and the great bed of state.

From that nice manor house down the road from Roger's.

I dragged my mind back to the present.

Jonathan nuzzled my neck, breathing in my perfume. 'This is the beginning of our life together! Isn't it a great place to start it?'

'It is,' I agreed. 'In an English room, in an American museum.'

What was wrong with me? I frowned at myself.

'You know,' he mused, 'I've thought about tonight so much, all the details . . .'

'You didn't think I'd say no, though, did you?' I said indulgently.

Jonathan looked blank for a second. 'I was really meaning the fundraiser, but, um . . .'

I stared at him, taken aback.

'But yeah, of course I've been thinking about proposing to you too. I wasn't sure, actually, that you'd say yes.' He recovered quickly, but not quite quickly enough.

'Well, I suppose tables and chairs are easier to arrange than people,' I said, trying to make it come out lightly, but maybe I didn't quite manage it.

'Sometimes that's easier on the nerves!' said Jonathan, apparently missing the irony in my voice. He hugged me to him, so my nose filled up with the heady mix of Creed and laundered shirts and his own indefinable man smell, then released me with a broad smile.

'Listen, we should be getting back to the party. They're going to start calling everyone in for dinner very soon and I want to . . . you know.' He grinned. 'Tell people. Shall we . . . ?'

He extended a hand towards the door, and, automatically, I led the way out.

'So, when can you get your things shipped?' he asked, putting his arm around my waist as we walked back through the drawing room. Our footsteps rang loudly on the wooden floor. 'Everything's in storage, right? You could just get it sent straight over from the holding company.'

'I . . . I don't know,' I said. 'I suppose I could.'

Not go back to Nelson's? At all?

'And then there's your agency to deal with, I guess,' he went on, now in full organisational flow. 'It seems to be running pretty well with Gabi and Allegra in charge, wouldn't you say? You feel happy letting those two carry on? Just keep an eye on them via email?'

'Jonathan, are you insane?' I laughed. 'I wouldn't let those two run a scouts' jumble sale! No, that's just temporary!'

'So you'll just close it down altogether? OK, I can see the sense in that.'

'I don't want to . . .' I stopped walking, as the reality of what I was saying dawned on me. 'I don't want to close it down, not just like that.'

Jonathan pulled a slightly impatient face, then smiled reasonably. 'But, honey, why not? You can't be flying back and forth every couple of days, now can you?'

'You fly back and forth!' I protested.

'Yes, but that's for business!'

'And what do you think my work is? People rely on me. I provide a service that people want! It's not so different from what you do.'

I was trying hard to keep it light, but something about the strained patience in Jonathan's eyes was starting to tick me off.

'Come on, Melissa, it's very different. Anyway, it's not like you're really doing the same things you started out offering now we're together, is it? Aren't you moving more into shopping advice and such like?'

'No, but it's not just about *shopping* . . .'

'Isn't it? Face it, Melissa, you're just acting like a glorified nanny to these guys, and, you know, I think that's kind of beneath your abilities. I mean, in terms of value for your time? I don't think so! I didn't want to say so before, because I know you're *loyal* and *kind*, and I love that about you, but guys like Godric? They need professional help, and they need to shape up. And, honey, I don't want to sound arrogant, but you won't *need* to work once we're married.' He took my hands. 'I mean, that's the point about being run off my feet – I'm pulling in a very decent salary now, and with bonuses . . .'

I stared at the ring on my finger, then looked up at Jonathan's face. I wanted to see the laughing boyfriend I'd rowed across the lake with, but in his dinner jacket, his hair smoothed neatly down, suddenly he looked much more grown-up than I felt. 'But I want to work. I enjoy helping people.'

'Then do what you've been doing for Diana!' he said, as if it were the most obvious answer in the world. 'Run showers! God knows they need a bit of help in the taste department! And she loves what you're doing for her baby shower. She can't stop telling everyone how cleverly you've arranged it all, and how sweet you've been with her mother, and Steve . . . I was so proud of you.' He shook my hands to emphasise his pride, but suddenly I felt babied.

'Jonathan, I think we need to talk about this some more,' I said, feeling the moment start to slide from under me.

'What's to talk about? You can't run your agency hands-on when you're living in New York, I don't want you to start up doing the same thing over here.' He lifted his shoulders, then dropped them. 'Anyway, I was meaning to tell you – I've had a rethink on the house plans?' He beamed, as if this was his trump card. 'Forget the conversion. I think we need to make it one house. For the two of us. Two of us . . . for now?'

I gaped. Why was it that this was everything I'd ever dreamed of, and yet it felt so wrong?

Jonathan took my silence for emotional speechlessness, and kissed me on the forehead. 'Don't want to let Steve and Diana get too far ahead of us, huh?' He checked his watch and grimaced in apology. 'Darling, I know this is an awful thing to say but I really do need to get back to the event.' He looked at me appealingly. 'We can announce it! Most of our friends are here!'

Most of our friends. *Our* friends? What about Nelson? And Gabi? And Roger? How would my friendships feel when I was living in New York? And how would it be when all my friends were also friends with Cindy?

I started to feel sick.

'But Jonathan, this is important to me! My agency isn't just about shopping! It's about working out what's missing in people's lives, seeing what I can help to fix! I mean, take Godric,' I said wildly. 'It wasn't so much that he was rude, or mean – he just didn't have enough confidence to be himself! And I'm not saying I've waved a magic wand, but he needed someone to talk it out with, and understand. And now look at him! He's got his girl-friend back, and everything!'

'Melissa, if you need men to fix, you can start with me,' said Jonathan, and to my amazement, he said it with a straight face. 'God knows I need someone to run my life for me, better than I do.'

'But that's the whole point!' I wailed. 'You *don't* need fixing! You're perfect just as you are! *Perfect!* And I can't be the sort of wife you need by your side at these things . . .'

'Well, maybe I'm just better at faking it than you think. Why else do you think I've got a cleaner four days a week, and I never buy my own clothes? You ask Lori how perfect I am.' He ran his hands through his hair impatiently. Clearly this wasn't going to plan. 'What sort of wife do you *think* I need?'

I searched Jonathan's face for some clue, but the stoniness had returned, shutting off any emotion.

I bit my lip, not wanting to give the answer I knew I had to, in all honesty. The reception was stuffed with immaculate, glossy women, working the room like a formation dance team of charm, devoting their whole lives to charity events, and networking, and having lunch with each other but not actually eating anything.

I thought of my mother, worn to a frazzle trying to maintain the social face of country Conservatism while the private face of knitting stress created deformed hippos. My father, driving her mad – driving *me* mad with his manipulations. I couldn't end up like that. Not with a man I loved as much as Jonathan.

But was Jonathan really the man I thought he was? Because he was glaring at me with an expression that seemed awfully Daddy-esque right now.

I wasn't just some *bed* he could ship out to New York, and put in a museum to be admired and never slept in. I had a purpose in life!

I controlled myself as best I could. 'You need a woman

who can stand at your side at these events, like a First Lady. A woman like one of the fundraisers in there, someone who knows how to work the room and look perfect all the time. And I can *pretend* to be like that, if that's what you want,' I said in a small voice, 'but it's not really me. I don't look perfect all the time. That's Honey. And I thought you didn't want Honey any more. I thought you wanted me.'

Jonathan stared at me for a long minute, then exhaled slowly.

'Melissa. I do want you. But I've had one wife who put her whole life into her career, at the expense of everything else,' he said, apparently ignoring what I'd just said. 'At the expense of me, of our home, our family. Are you really telling me that you're weighing me in one basket, and your damn agency in the other?'

I wanted to tell him that it wasn't about the agency, it was about me, and who I was. But if he couldn't see that – why should I have to tell him?

'Are you asking me to choose one or the other?' I demanded.

Because you asked him the very same question, and he couldn't choose.

We glared at each other, surrounded by cold marble statues. I was just glad that I was in my very best black tie dress, because the tight corset and stockings at least made me hold my spine up tall.

'I guess I am,' he said, and rubbed his chin.

My heart broke inside my chest. I could feel it leaking misery right through me. But I struggled to muster up all my dignity. The situation demanded that I keep my head held high, even if everything inside was shattering into little pieces.

'You're asking me to leave my family and my friends, and move halfway across the world, to be surrounded by *your* friends, *your* ex-wife, *your* ex-wife's dog, and all the . . . *baggage* that goes with that,' I said, in a voice that didn't sound like mine. 'And I would do that, Jonathan, because I love you. Even with the sort of schedule that means you never see me. But you're asking me to give up the one thing I've found in life that I do really well, and come here with nothing of *me*, and honestly, that's impossible. I wouldn't be the woman you fell in love with. You would get frustrated with me. And it wouldn't work.'

I made myself look at him, and the beautiful, familiar lines of his face made me ache, because I knew what I was saying was true, and it meant it was all ending. I'd walked across hot coals to get away from one controlling father in my life; I owed it to myself not to fall straight into being controlled again.

'I couldn't bear to have this turn sour,' I said, biting back the tears. 'It's been too wonderful. I've never been so happy in my life. But you're right – I don't know New York. Maybe you need someone who does.'

I struggled to remove the ring from my finger. It hurt as I dragged it over my knuckle, but not so much as it hurt inside.

'Here,' I said. 'I can't take this.'

'You're breaking off our engagement?' said Jonathan faintly.

I raised my eyes to his, and now they were filled with hot tears. It only added to my misery to see his were too. 'I have to,' I said. 'I couldn't bear to have you divorce me.' I gulped. 'I couldn't bear to have you realise you'd made another mistake.'

And before he could speak, I turned on my heel and

walked briskly down the corridor, leaving him standing there, as motionless as the marble statues.

I don't know how I found my way back, since the place was a maze of glass cases and roped-off areas, but somehow I was back at the coat-check, in a cloud of scented lilies and expensive ladies' perfume.

A steward tried to direct me towards the reception, but I mumbled that I didn't want to go in, and as I was stumbling out, my head down in case I saw Cindy, I bumped into a couple.

'Sorry,' I started to say, as they cooed, 'Melissa! Melissa!' at me.

Kurt and Bonnie Hegel.

Oh, God. Just what I didn't need.

'Melissa?' said Kurt, taking my arm. 'Are you all right? You don't look all right. You look as if you've had a terrible shock. Do you want to sit down? Bonnie, don't you think she should sit down?'

'I'm OK! Honest!' I managed.

'Kurt, go and get a glass of water for Melissa. Go on!' She flapped him away, and peered at me with a professional rigour. 'Are you *actually* OK?'

'Um, no, not really.' I shook my head. 'I've . . . I've had some bad news. I'm going to have to go home. Right away.'

'Home to Greenwich Village? Listen, let me call my car service, we can have you home in no time.' Bonnie got her tiny cell phone from her tiny clutch bag and had it to her ear before I could stop her. 'Hello, yeah, I need a car from the Met to . . .' She looked over at me, and whispered, 'Where to, honey? I forget Jonathan's new address?'

'To Kennedy Airport, please,' I said dully.

Bonnie's face registered such shock that I could see white all round her big green eyes. 'Hold the car, I'll call back,' she said, without taking her gaze off me, and clicked the phone shut. 'Where's Jonathan, does he know? Why isn't he taking you home? Jesus, he is so stupid about his priorities! Let me go and get him.'

'No, please,' I said, stopping her. 'He knows. He's busy with the fundraiser. It's going really well. I don't want to spoil it for him.' God knows how I was keeping all this together, but my voice was turning posher by the moment. It must have been the Stiff Upper Lip coming out. Much more stiff upper lip and I was going to look like Beaker from *The Muppet Show*. 'It's . . . a family matter. I have to fly back tonight. I should get to the airport.'

'But your cases?' Bonnie asked. 'Don't you need to go home and pick up your stuff?'

It would look too weird if I refused. Besides, I could hardly sit all the way back to London in a cocktail dress, fancy underwear and stockings. I mean, there were dramatic gestures, and there were dramatic gestures.

Oh, and I'd need my passport.

'Don't worry,' I said, dragging what remained of my self-control around me like the English royal armour that I'd just marched past. 'I'll get a cab home. Um, if you could tell Jonathan I'll be fine, and . . .' I gulped, as the self-control slipped. 'Tell him I'm sorry for messing up his seating plan for dinner. At such short notice.'

'Melissa, won't you let me help you?' Bonnie looked hard at me. 'Because if anyone's said anything to you . . . Even if it's Jonathan?' She pulled a face. 'He can be kind of dumb sometimes, I know. Don't be fooled by that poker face.'

I shook my head again as another little needle pricked my heart; they would always know him better than me. 'No. No, it's nothing like that.'

'I hear Cindy's here tonight,' Bonnie went on. 'Is that it? Is she being—'

I didn't let her finish. I didn't want to hear whatever it was she had to say, and I could see Kurt returning with a glass of water and a first-aid official.

'Bonnie, you've been very kind, but I really must go now.' I smiled at her. 'Thank you.'

And I took my fake fur jacket, ran down the beautiful steps and managed to hail a cab in seconds. I guess the dress might have helped.

Part of me hoped that Jonathan would leap into a cab and follow me, just like in an old-fashioned movie, but the other part of me knew he'd give me a gentlemanly distance to recover myself. He gave me such a gentlemanly distance that when I turned my phone on at JFK, surrounded by my bags, he still hadn't left a message.

24

I tried really hard to find three positive things about my early arrival back in London, where the skies were a dull elephant grey and a dank October chill hung in the air. I was in such a trance state that it actually wasn't so difficult to be objective about my situation; as soon as I stepped onto the tarmac at Heathrow and felt the rain soak through my open-toed sandals, it seemed as if the past few weeks, in all their Technicolor New York film set glory, had happened to someone else.

Whether I liked it or not, I was back, and the best remedy was manic busy-ness and a positive attitude that made Gabi demand to know what drugs you could buy in K-Mart. Never mind that I had to bite back tears every time I saw a small white dog. Leaving Braveheart stabbed my heart nearly as much as leaving Jonathan. He really did need me. Still, I'd made my choice. Doing the Right Thing would be heaps more popular if it wasn't such a monumental pain in the arse to live with.

The first positive thing was that I was able to chivvy along the decorators putting the final touches to Nelson's flat. Well, they weren't really *final* touches, as it turned out – more halfway-through touches. Gabi hadn't been supervising the various workmen with the sort of rigour that builders require, even with Nelson's alarmingly specific plan of action to hand, whereas I needed a place to sleep, and had nervous energy to spare. With Nelson due back in days and the new bath not yet plumbed in, let's just say that the project swiftly acquired an urgency usually seen in the latter stages of a television makeover programme.

And that was the second positive thing: I was able to meet Nelson at the quayside, to welcome him back off his voyage of charitable discovery.

Obviously, I had to drive Roger and Gabi there with me – with the accompanying emotional pea-souper that would suggest.

I'd offered Gabi the use of my car, on the noble assumption that she'd want to share a private moment with her long-lost sailor boy, but she wriggled and looked shifty.

'Wouldn't it be nicer if we *all* went tomorrow?' she suggested. 'I mean, Roger's missed him too, and so've you.'

We were sitting on the dust-sheeted sofa in Nelson's sitting room, waiting for the painters to come back off their lunch-break. I'd persuaded them to work Saturday in return for three follow-up jobs for clients who needed their flats de-bachelored, strictly cash-in-hand. As far as the office went, at least, I was firing on all cylinders. I had to be; if I stopped and thought how much I'd given up for my feckless clientele, I'd probably march round to their flats and make them do their own decorating.

I glanced at my mobile. Jonathan still hadn't called.

'Stop it,' said Gabi. 'A watched mobile never boils.'

I gave her a dark look. 'Gabi. Tell me the truth. Have you been seeing someone else while Nelson's been away?'

I didn't want to use the R word unless I absolutely had to.

She squirmed some more. 'Well, not exactly . . . Anyway,' she added, in a blatant subject change, 'I thought it would be kind of insensitive to have a big emotional reunion, in light of current events.'

I ignored that. Gabi had been hugely sympathetic, insisting that I'd done the right thing and that Jonathan's workaholism would only get worse, but it was totally unacceptable to use it as a sneaky way out of whatever she'd got herself into here. 'Have you been seeing someone else?' I repeated. 'Because if you've been messing Nelson about, then . . .'

We stared at each other, gripped by sudden fear. The consequences were too ghastly to speak aloud, and we both knew it.

'I haven't been messing Nelson about,' she said, fiddling with a set of paint cards. 'But, um, I think perhaps I'd better have a quiet word with him when he gets off, or whatever you call it.'

'Disembark. I think that would be a good idea,' I said firmly. I was horribly torn between wanting to help, but then again, since I was so close to them both, I wasn't sure I even wanted to know the gory details. 'Do you want to talk about it? I mean, you're sure? Nelson's . . .' I hesitated. Gabi had always maintained, erroneously, that I had a crush on Nelson myself, and I didn't want her to think I had vested interests in splitting them up now. I grabbed her hand. 'I want you both to be happy.'

She gave me an ambiguous half smile, half frown. 'Mel, I know what I'm doing. You of all people should know how hard it is sometimes.'

'It's not that I want everyone to be single, just because I am. I'd just hate to see him hurt,' I said quietly. 'Or see you hurt too.'

'I know,' said Gabi. She squeezed my hand back. 'I know.'

Then the builders came back and I had to use all the charm I had in reserve to stop them brewing up again.

We arrived at Portsmouth docks after an arduous journey during which Roger had provided a running commentary from the back seat, where I'd installed him with the map. I knew where I was going, and that way he got to feel in charge of operations, while I got to tune him out with the radio, since only the front speakers worked.

Even so, he still managed to poke his nose into the conversation Gabi and I were having about what still needed to be done on the flat.

'So are you in communication with Remington or what?' he bellowed as I was parking. 'What went wrong there? Been meaning to ask.'

'Shut up, Roger,' said Gabi. 'She doesn't want to talk about it.'

'No,' I said bravely. 'No, we're not currently in communication. I thought it would be best to give him some space. It's . . . we separated over a non-negotiable issue.'

Roger gave me a hideous knowing wink in the rear-view mirror that involved folding one half of his face into his neck. 'Like *that*, was it?'

'Shut *up*, Roger,' said Gabi testily. 'Are you deaf or just stupid?'

'Catch yourself on, girlfriend!' replied Roger, in the most appalling north London accent I'd ever heard. 'I'm only arksking!'

I looked at them suspiciously. This sort of familiar banter had all the hallmarks of emotional involvement. In so far as anyone could involve themselves emotionally with Roger Trumpet. Still, I thought, hadn't Gabi said she needed to be practical in relationships? And what could be more practical than the vast fortune Roger clearly wasn't spending on clothes and/or high living?

I locked the car, and strode across the quayside, leaving Gabi to upbraid Roger in her own time. Nelson's ship was already in dock and his diminutive crew were being welcomed back by crowds of cheering parents as if they'd been at sea for years.

I looked about but couldn't see Nelson. Then, as I got nearer, I spotted him by a pile of sail bags, haranguing some poor parents about their gangling teenager. He was still in his full ocean-going kit which, I was sorry to see, didn't include a parrot, a three-cornered hat or an eye-patch. As I watched, he finished whatever he was lecturing them about, and the teenager gave him a sudden, sprawling hug, and the father shook his hand in that hearty way you only see in black and white films.

I was very touched, on Nelson's behalf.

As they walked off, he spotted me, and waved.

'Melissa!' he yelled happily.

'Hello, Nelson,' I cried, throwing my arms around him. It was so nice to see him. At least some things in my life were where I'd left them. 'Still got the two arms, I see! And both eyes!'

'Touch of beer scurvy, though,' he said, picking me up, staggering slightly, then putting me down again almost at once. 'You might need to take me home via a pub.'

'Er, no. You're going straight home for a bath!' I said. 'Do you have any idea what you smell like?'

Roger and Gabi were now hoving into view, in full heated-discussion mode.

'And I don't know why you made us come in Mel's car when you could have driven us in that Audi TT,' he was moaning.

'Argh, *shut up*, Roger!' Gabi stopped when she saw us, straightened her shoulders, and tried to smile. 'Hello, Nelson,' she said. 'Welcome home! Um, can I have a word?'

'Ship to shore, we have a problem,' said Roger, holding his nose.

I grabbed his arm. If Gabi was dumping Nelson for this cretin, she really needed her head checking. 'Roger, we're going to get some coffee.'

Disregarding his gossip-hungry protests, I hauled him off to a mobile coffee wagon where we got four cappuccinos and waited at a safe distance for the conversation to draw to a close. The wind off the open water was pretty chilly as we sat on bollards, warming our hands round the paper cups.

'What do you think she's saying to him?' asked Roger, slurping his coffee.

Honestly. Had he no shame? 'I don't know. Didn't you discuss it with her first?'

'What? Why would she discuss it with me?'

I glared at him. 'So you could get your story straight, I'd imagine. When did it happen? That Hunt Ball that I wouldn't go to? Did you think that just because she was wearing a wig she wasn't someone else's girlfriend?'

Roger's face turned crimson.

'I wouldn't say so in front of Gabi, but I think you've behaved pretty shabbily,' I raged on. 'Nelson's your best friend! What were you thinking? I hope you and Gabi are really serious about each other because—'

'For the love of God, Melissa, what makes you think

I'm going out with Gabi?' roared Roger. 'I'm not deaf! Or *stupid*!'

We stared at each other. I didn't know whether to be outraged on behalf of one best friend, or awash with relief for the other. Or both.

'Well, we might have had a bite to eat in London after that ball affair,' he conceded guiltily. 'Took her to the Bluebird, you know. Cocktail or two. Three. She can certainly put them away, can't she? Talk about hollow legs.'

'So who *is* she seeing?' I demanded. 'Don't deny it – I called her in a bar the other night, and she wasn't on her own.'

Roger looked furtive, which gave him the air of a bloodhound that had done something it shouldn't, somewhere it shouldn't have been in the first place. 'I, ah, I . . . if she hasn't told you, then . . .'

I'm afraid to say I held my cappuccino threateningly over his trousers.

'Aaron! She's got back with Aaron,' he yelped.

Well, that made sense. Instead of the righteous anger I expected, I was surprised to feel a sudden warm glow of relief. I liked Aaron. He was funny, and sharp, and had the measure of Gabi. I hadn't entirely understood why they'd called off their engagement in the first place. Gabi and Aaron went together like Marks and Spencer. Or Boodle and Dunthorne. Or Fortnum and Mason.

Then I remembered Nelson's part in all this, and my heart jolted with sympathy. Poor Nelson! He'd come all the way back from sea to find he was dumped, before he'd even had a chance to get the kettle on.

'When did *that* happen?' I wailed.

'Oh, when Aaron called her to say that he'd decided not to carry on with the pathology degree, and go back to working in the City.' Roger sniffed. 'Apparently he sent her an entire car full of flowers, and got down on one knee and begged her to marry him.'

'She never said!'

'Well, she's still thinking about it.'

'Why did no one tell me?' I stared out into the dock. 'I can't believe she didn't tell me this.'

'Um, she thought you'd go mad. What with her being with Nelson and all that.'

'So she told *you*?'

'Yes? And what's wrong with that?' he huffed.

'Nothing,' I said, and felt a sad sort of happiness run through me, like the cold wind coming in off the sea. I tucked my warm jacket closer around me. 'Nothing wrong with that.'

'I thought you'd be pleased I'd made a new friend.' Roger sounded hurt. 'Nelson's always droning on about how nice it is having a good girl friend like you. And Gabi and I . . . we get on. I know you don't approve, but I'm bloody glad she came to that do with me. Top night.'

I put my arm through his and gave it a squeeze. That way I could show affection without having to look at whatever soppy face he was pulling. 'I'm glad, Roger,' I said. 'I'm really glad.'

As Nelson would have pointed out, there were strange and mysterious powers attached to the wig.

Over by the commemorative anchor, Nelson and Gabi seemed to have finished their little chat and now they walked over to where Roger and I were sitting. He did not have his arm around her shoulders, and she was clinging onto her Paddington bag like a life-raft.

I scanned Nelson's face for signs of distress, but he just seemed tanned and cheerful, as usual. Gabi, in fact, looked more churned up than he did.

'So,' said Nelson, rubbing his hands, 'who's for a pub lunch?'

'Is that it?' I hissed, as Gabi and Roger led the way to the nearest pub. 'It's all over and you're wondering whether you can get an organic steak and kidney pie?'

Nelson hung back a bit so we were well out of earshot. Then he slung one arm around my shoulders, as he was wont to do. 'Melissa, my darling child, there were many reasons for me going on that voyage. I mean, obviously I wanted to help some young people experience the joys of proper sailing—'

'Yes, yes,' I interrupted impatiently. 'I think we can take the sainthood as read.'

'And the flat did need tarting up. But . . .' He paused, and turned to face me. 'Promise you won't go off on one?'

'Of course I won't!'

He sighed. 'Gabi is a great girl, and I know she's your best mate, but God in heaven . . . She was driving me insane, Mel. I don't know whether it was some kind of phase she was going through, but honestly, she wanted me to be this Mr Darcy figure and boss her around and tell her what to do. It was *unnatural*. I didn't want to upset her, though, because I didn't want to cause trouble between you two. It could have been rather awkward.'

I stared at him, flabbergasted. Just how long had this ailing relationship been propped up, solely to spare my feelings?

'So you ran off to sea instead?' I said incredulously. 'That's very English of you. Was the Foreign Legion not recruiting?'

'It seemed like the best thing to do.' He shrugged his

shoulders. 'I mean, it played into her Jane Austen phase for a bit, the whole waving the hanky at the docks bit, but I knew the longer she was in London on her own, the more likely she was to get back with Aaron.'

'And now she has.'

'And now she has,' he agreed. 'Maybe it was just something she needed to do. Anyway, everyone's happy. She gets her Audi TT back, Aaron gets his soulmate back, I get my sofa to myself, and—'

'I get to share it with you,' I ended dully.

Nelson exhaled. 'Sorry, that was insensitive. Gabi mentioned—'

'The flat's lovely, though,' I said, in a voice that was a little too high. 'They put in all the plug sockets you asked for. And I've found you some new energy-saving light bulbs.'

He said nothing, but put his arm round me, kissed me affectionately on the bobble hat, and we carried on walking. 'You're the only girl for me, Mel,' he said. 'I'll make you whatever you want for supper, and I'll even rub your disgusting feet.'

Nelson might not have been much of a new man, but he knew how to make me feel better. And right now, my disgusting feet needed him more than ever.

The third positive aspect of my return to London was that I was able to attend my mother's private view.

I know! I was pretty bewildered to hear about it too.

I wouldn't even have known it was happening, had Allegra not chosen to grace the office with her presence shortly after my return.

'Oh, you're back,' she said, with scant interest, as she swanned in with two large Smythsons bags, and helped herself to a rum truffle from the huge box on the filing cabinet, sent as a thank you from a gratefully re-barbered client.

'Yes, I am. I've been back for three days.' I was in the middle of writing my etiquette column for *South West Now!*, specifically, a response to someone whose girlfriend had worse death breath than her cat. In my whirlwind of catching up, running the absent Allegra to earth had not been a priority. 'What on earth have you bought from Smythsons? What have they got that comes in bags that big?'

'I need guest books, for the private view.'

I rubbed my eyes gently, so as not to smudge my winged eyeliner. 'Allegra. You're not meant to be organising private views, unless it's for one of my clients. While Daddy's . . . While I'm paying you to work here, you work for *my* clients.'

I'd given up trying to disentangle my father's Olympic scammery. Ignorance wasn't just bliss, it was a whole legal defence.

'It's Mummy's private view,' she said disparagingly. 'Anyway, she said to charge it to your agency. She'll have her agent negotiate the fee later.'

'*What?*'

'Mummy is holding an exhibition,' said Allegra impatiently.

'Of *what?*'

'Oh, do stop saying "what", Melissa. It makes you sound very thick. Her work, if you must know, has been snapped up by a London art agent, who specialises in modern sculpture. Here, look at this.'

She dug about in her bag and thrust a thick laminated invitation at me.

It featured a grotesque creature in shocking-pink mohair. It could have been a cat, or a unicorn, but it had five legs, two and a half heads and either a horn, or a very pointy ear in the middle of its forehead. Underneath were the details of Belinda Blennerhesket's private view party, due to take place on 31 October.

Hallowe'en. How appropriate.

'Why's she doing it under Granny's maiden name?' I asked. This was some way down my list of questions, but it was the one least likely to throw Allegra into a froth of artistic outrage.

'She doesn't want Daddy taking the publicity spotlight for himself,' she replied. 'And I say, good on her. It's all her own work. Well, apart from the tenders she's put out to the local WI. They're rather confused, what with having to knit everything wrong and put in extra legs and so on, but if you ask me, Mummy's shown herself to be very enterprising. Fast as she knits them, I'm selling them. And not as *toys*, either,' she added snottily. 'As Art.'

'But how . . . ?' The mind boggled at the thought of Mummy doctoring knitting patterns, then handing them out at WI meetings. Mummy, more to the point, the WI poster girl! I sank my elbows onto the desk and rested my fuddled head.

Allegra smirked. 'That child I sent the toys to? The one you went berserk about? Well, his mother runs a gallery in Cork Street, and she positively demanded to know where she could get more.'

The smirk, already Daddy-like, increased as she said this, as if she'd known all along that the mother in question was connected to the art world's most fashionable players. I wished I knew for sure that this was untrue, but I didn't. Allegra was super-jammy like that. She didn't dress like the devil's handmaiden for nothing.

'I see,' I said. 'Well, that's marvellous news. I can't wait. What day is the 31st again?'

'Oh, you want to come?'

I stared at her. '*Yes*, Allegra. Since I was indirectly responsible for launching Mummy's new career.'

She raised her plucked eyebrows. 'Well, I'll have to see if I can get you on the guest list.'

She was so getting a pay cut.

'Anyway,' she said, as if she'd added telepathy to her list of spooky abilities, 'I don't need your job. I have a new one.'

'Really?'

'I'm acting as a marketing consultant to some very exclusive Scandinavian cheese importers.'

Allegra. Cheese. Importing. There were a lot of holes in those cheeses. I hoped she wasn't planning to do anything funny with them.

'Daddy negotiated it for me,' she went on, which only added to my suspicion. 'So between that and the gallery, I don't know if I'll have time to help you out any more.' She paused. 'Sorry!'

'No, Allegra,' I said, feeling the soothing rush of relief. 'Thank you.'

She swept out, snaffling another rum truffle, then paused at the door, and turned round with what I assumed was a sympathetic look. 'Still no news from what's-his-name?'

'No,' I said.

Allegra made a moue with her red lips. 'Poor you.'

'All for the best,' I said, and touch-typed fifteen lines of complete gibberish until she left.

Then I had a tearful moment, followed by four rum truffles in quick succession, and pulled myself together long enough to finish the article.

Mummy's private view was my first big social event since that awful last night in New York, and even getting ready for it opened up the festering wounds. I didn't want to wear anything that reminded me of the fundraiser of doom at the Met, and, as a result, I was still standing, snivelling, in my girdle when Nelson banged on the door and demanded to know if I was weaving my outfit from scratch.

All credit to him that he came into my room and virtually dressed me like a Barbie doll, in a not-at-all-awful outfit, while I moaned incoherently.

'Don't worry,' he said, buttoning up my circle skirt. 'It's Hallowe'en. Everyone will think you've come in costume.'

'Cheers, Nelson.'

'Can't have you letting the side down, can we?' Our gaze met in the mirror. Nelson's blond brows knit in brotherly concern. 'I think you made the right decision, Mel. You can't live your life under someone else's rules. Feminism and all that. And I'll keep telling you so until you believe me.'

'Suppose we're both dumped now,' I said morosely.

'No,' said Nelson, adding a jazzy scarf to my outfit. 'I'm dumped. You're the dumper. Big difference. Now, come on. Roger and Gabi say they're coming round later to do ghost stories and apple bobbing. Never tell me again that you don't have a rich and varied social life.'

Autumn was well under way now, and we had to tramp through crisp fallen leaves to get to the bus stop. The coppers and golds and bronzes were like delicate little works of beaten metal against the mundane pavement slabs, but, like a very bad song, they only reminded me of Jonathan's hair.

I leaned my nose against the scratched glass of the bus window and sighed, making the window mist up. My mind seemed to think in terms of very bad song lyrics these days. I'd never get to feel his breath against my neck in the morning again. Never get to touch the pale gold hairs on his forearms, or trace the freckles on his back. Never hear his lecture about using Factor 40 sun cream to prevent sun damage . . .

Nelson heard me sigh and gave me a half squeeze, half nudge.

We were probably the only guests at the view who had come by public transport: the room was rammed with glittery bat-people in Allegra's image, all smoking with their cigarettes at shoulder height, rubbing their noses and shrieking at their own jokes. I unwound my woolly scarf with some trepidation and handed it to the coat check girl, who looked at it as if I'd handed her a dead badger.

'If it's going to be one of those evenings, let's not stay long,' murmured Nelson, at the same moment that I leaned up to say exactly the same thing to him.

Around the perimeter of the gallery were glass cases containing Mummy's weird toys, illuminated with different-coloured spotlights, as if they needed any more freakish touches. I inspected the nearest tortoise/badger and recoiled in shock at how much they were asking for it. And according to the three red spots stuck on the caption, three people already wanted to buy it. Blimey.

'Don't look now, but someone's trying to get your attention,' Nelson muttered in my ear.

My hopeful heart leaped up irrationally into my chest,

in case, somehow, Jonathan had finally come for me. I spun round, smile already in place.

'Hello, darling!' said a familiar voice.

It wasn't Jonathan. It was Granny, looking regal in a floor-length silver velvet kaftan. A small diamond tiara nestled in her grey hair, managing to look offhand and deeply formal at the same time. She was also wearing a monocle, just for the sake of it. 'Aren't these people awful! But you look lovely.' She beamed.

'Hello,' I said, trying not to sound too disappointed.

'Hoping I was someone else?' she said, tipping her head to one side.

'Sort of.'

'Come with me, and let's get you a drink.' And she steered us through the gibbering masses, waving aside a waitress toting what looked like a giant peacock made up of different cubes of cheese.

'Your father,' said Granny, in a voice dripping with extreme distaste. 'Catering courtesy of his *cheese* friends. Have you seen his hedgehogs of many cheeses? They're meant to theme with the animals.'

'Er, they're quite retro, I suppose,' I said, pulling an oozing chunk of Stinking Bishop off a cheese jellyfish.

'And all *free*. Now then, what's this I hear about you calling things off with your young man?'

'Do we have to talk about it?' I dropped my cocktail stick into a passing tray. 'It's all anyone seems to ask me about these days.'

'Well, we're worried about you.' She pursed her lips.

'It's not helping. I can tell Mummy thinks I've lost my mind, and Gabi says she understands, but I don't think she does, and . . .' I raised my eyes to Granny's. 'I thought you'd understand, though. I just can't believe that

Jonathan, of all people, doesn't get the fact that what I do with the agency is about helping people, not selling myself to them! I don't *want* to spend my days making shopping lists for rich women who could buy anything they needed. I want to feel like I'm making a practical difference to people.'

'And you don't feel you can make a difference to him?'

'No,' I said sadly. 'He's perfect. From his perfect socks to his perfect scent.'

Granny let out an amused little huff through her nose. 'Darling, no one's perfect. Has it ever crossed your mind that he might be *trying* to be as perfect as possible so you don't feel you have to fix him too?'

'But I wouldn't mind—'

'Do think laterally, Melissa. You spend your days organising useless chaps. Jonathan probably thinks that's the last thing you want to do when you come home. In fact, he probably thinks that the more organising you have to do, the more you'll think of him as a client, not a boyfriend.' She gave me a knowing look. 'And he has his own very good reasons for not wanting you to think of him like that, now, doesn't he?'

I stared at her, while she signalled at a waiter for fresh drinks.

Well, I thought, when you put it like that . . .

'He's always struck me as being a little insecure, you know,' she went on, passing me a martini. 'All those lists, that endless twitching, the obsession with his hair. His ridiculous Dictaphone.' She gazed at me over her monocle. 'There was no need to bring a Dictaphone to that shoot your father gave at New Year, darling, was there? It wasn't as though he was going to see any property that needed selling.'

'No,' I conceded. 'And he's rather worried about doing enough at work . . .'

'And still quite cut up about his wife leaving him, I should imagine. Having to keep her under control and well away from you. Quite a juggle. I should know. And' – Granny gave me a friendly nudge – 'probably not all that happy about his beautiful girlfriend hanging around with a famous ex.'

I gave her a look. 'His girlfriend who used to go out with *Prince William*. And Godric wasn't my ex.'

She made a dismissive gesture with her free hand. 'Oh, call your solicitor.'

'Granny, I know what you're saying,' I sighed, 'but you're just making me feel as though I've made even more of a mistake.' I bit my lip as the truth of what she'd said sank in. 'Poor Jonathan. I was so busy feeling inadequate myself even to think he might be too.'

'Oh, darling, I'm not saying you made a mistake,' she replied. 'I think you did exactly the right thing – women who act like doormats to keep the peace only get chucked in the end for acting like doormats. No' – she patted my cheek – 'you did what you felt in your heart was right, and you'll never hear me tell you off for that. In fact,' she added, draining her glass, 'if he's got any sense he'll see that it's your spirit that makes you the girl you are. Besides, it's early days yet.'

I wasn't so sure.

'I know your mother and Allegra aren't exactly an advert for married bliss,' she said. 'But there's a difference between compromising your independence and compromising yourself.' She looked at me wisely. 'Love's about giving up a little independence, darling. But that doesn't mean you have to stop being you.'

'Well, that's fine,' I grumped. 'I suppose I'll know for next time. If there is a next time.'

'Darling,' said Granny, bestowing a kiss on my head. 'There's always a next time. Take it from one who knows. Now, where did that waiter go? These martinis are hopeless. I think I might have to have a word.'

Nelson and I sloped off by eight thirty, and as we turned the key in the front door, I felt the relief of being home sink into the very depths of my body. I eased off my shoes in readiness for a nice rub.

'Can't we cancel Roger and Gabi?' I asked as he pushed the door open. 'I don't think I can cope with those two on top of Art.'

'I can pretend you're dead drunk and miserable, if you want. That'll put Gabi off, but Roger's such a gossip-hound he'll probably insist on coming over. Oh, God, the lights have gone already,' he groaned, feeling about for the switch. 'Bloody cowboy electricians.'

Eventually, he found a switch that worked, and flicked it on, revealing Gabi and Roger sitting on the sofa wearing witch outfits and very convincing evil scowls.

'Surprise!' they said, without much enthusiasm.

Nelson and I shrieked in shock.

The room was bedecked in cobwebs and fake spiders, with a huge apple-bobbing bucket in the middle of the new rug, and plates of ghoulish blackcurrant jelly on the coffee table, and carved pumpkin heads on the television.

'Mwa ha ha ha ha!' added Roger, as an afterthought.

I clapped a hand to my racing heart. 'Oh, my God, you gave me a fright.'

'Give me that spare key,' said Nelson, holding out his

hand. 'Right now. And you'd better hope that those cobwebs come off my brand-new skirting boards.'

'You've had three trick or treaters already,' Gabi
informed him, peeling the keys reluctantly off her Tiffany
keyring. 'They wanted cash, or they were going to kick
the headlights in on your car.'

'Cash? What happened to sweets?'

'Inflation. You owe me fifteen quid.' She turned on a
table lamp and filled the room with a sinister red light.
'I know you're a misery-guts at the moment, but we
thought this might cheer you up.'

'And it will!' I pulled off my coat. 'I'm touched! Did
you get spooky films?'

'Many,' intoned Roger. 'And Nelson's got a casserole
in the oven.'

'Brains and eye of newt ragout,' said Nelson. 'Just a
little something I made earlier.'

I smiled. 'Then let the evil times commence!'

By eleven o'clock we'd bobbed for apples, drunk Nelson's
mulled wine, and freaked ourselves out with Gabi's tarot
cards, and now all four of us were curled up on the two
new sofas – my feet in Nelson's lap; Gabi and Roger's
heads at opposite ends of theirs. We'd finished watching
The Others, which Nelson and Roger spoiled by pointing
out the continuity errors, as was their wont, and now we
were watching the equally horrific Selfridges video of
Tristram Hart-Mossop quite blatantly ogling my cleavage
while I demonstrated how cufflinks worked. The shaky
camera angles suggested how amusing Gabi was finding
it, not to mention the salacious zooming in and out onto
my straining shirt buttons and Tristram's fidgeting
trousers.

'Oh, my God,' I gasped. 'Gabi! I look the size of a house! Why didn't you *tell* me!'

'Because you look bloody great,' she said, stuffing another handful of chocolate spiders in her mouth. 'You've ruined that poor lad for ordinary Sloanes.'

'Quite. We like women with a bit of meat on them, eh, Mel?' agreed Nelson, reaching over to wobble my stomach.

The doorbell rang downstairs as I was hauling myself up into a sitting position to protest. It carried on ringing, as if someone was leaning on the button.

Gabi and Roger groaned. 'If it's those kids from before, tell them your car's barely worth new headlights,' moaned Roger.

'What if it's my car?' demanded Nelson.

'Then *you* go down there,' said Gabi, looking far too comfortable to move. 'But take your cheque book.'

'In my day it was apples and toffees, *if you were lucky*. What's going to happen to this generation of bloody awful kids when they need to get jobs?' Nelson whinged, and I could tell this was the overture to a whole whinge opera. It had six acts and no interval. I'd sat through it several times. Spending time on a ship with kids clearly hadn't improved his opinion of them.

'Oh, I'm just about up, I'll go,' I said, heaving myself out of the sofa.

'Take this,' said Gabi, throwing me her black tinsel witch's wig. 'See if you can scare the little bastards off. Pretend you're Allegra.'

I shuffled off towards the stairs, grabbing a handful of chocolate spiders as I went, in case that might be enough. As a gesture to the evening, I was wearing my huge monster feet slippers I'd had since school, which made the stairs quite tricky, what with the wine and the lateness of the hour.

'I'm coming,' I yelled as the ringing continued. When I got to the hallway, I pulled Gabi's wig on – backwards, to make it look like my head was the wrong way round, then pulled open the door with a cackle. 'Ah ha ha ha ha har! A pox on you and all Satan's little wizards!'

I felt cold air, and a strange silence.

Oh, God, what if it was the police, about some damage to my car? Or Daddy?

I turned the wig round, and tried to compose myself. Really, Mel, I thought, leave the slapstick to Gabi and Roger.

But there was no one there at the door.

I tsked loudly. 'It's not big or clever, you know. Ringing the doorbell and running away!'

I leaned out to see if they were lurking by my car, and realised that there *was* someone on the doorstep.

Braveheart.

He was wearing a chic tartan coat, and gleaming brightly in the yellow street light. He was, to my amazement, sitting. And staying. And panting with his pink tongue out, a picture of self-satisfaction.

'New wig?' said a familiar voice. 'I don't think I've seen that one.'

I looked up, my heart pounding hard in my chest, and Jonathan stepped out of the shadows, wrapped up in a grey cashmere coat, and a green scarf. His coat was smart, but his jawline was rough with stubble and he looked a bit ropey.

'Hello,' he said with an uncertain smile.

'Hello,' I choked.

'Am I interrupting something?' He gestured towards my feet.

'Um, no. Just a little coven meeting,' I gabbled, kicking off my slippers and chucking Gabi's wig onto the post table. 'Smart casual, you know. Annual general meeting.'

Jonathan scooped up Braveheart before he could run off and stepped up onto the second doorstep, so we were standing at more or less the same height. Braveheart licked Jonathan's nose, which spoiled his dramatic effect somewhat.

'I had to come,' he explained. 'It was getting too much – the loss of appetite, the howling at night, the pining.'

He paused.

'And the mutt missed you too,' he added.

A broad smile split my face. Jonathan practically never did jokes. He must have thought about that one all the way across the Atlantic.

'Well, I'm very pleased to see you both,' I said, taking Braveheart out of his arms, so I could shoo him upstairs.

Jonathan coughed. 'Melissa, I'm afraid I have to do my speech now,' he said. 'Before I get distracted.' He lifted his hand so I couldn't interrupt. 'I made a mistake. You were right and I was wrong. It's not up to me what you do with your business. I should have known better than anyone how much it means to you to help people out. It wasn't that I didn't trust you . . .' He raised his eyes to mine, and they were bloodshot and weary. Somehow it only added a new edge to his good looks. 'I didn't trust myself. Not to be jealous, or insecure, or to drive you away with my stupid insecurities.'

'But you have no reason to be insecure,' I said, my heart rushing out to him 'Not with *me*.'

'I know that.' He took my hands in his, and they were cold. I rubbed them with mine to warm them up. 'I realise that now. That was the second apology. I shouldn't have tried to keep my communication with Cindy a secret. I got quite the ear-bashing on that score from Bonnie Hegel, I have to tell you. You have some serious fans in Manhattan. It wasn't that I didn't want you to know because something was going on. I was just scared, I guess, that somehow . . . she'd wreck things. Huh. I guess I did that on my own.'

'No,' I said. 'You didn't. You just . . . gave us both something to think about.'

Jonathan smiled wryly. 'I don't know about that. But . . .' He paused. 'Can't you understand how a guy like me might not quite believe his luck in having a girlfriend like you?'

'No.' I almost laughed. 'No, I can't!'

'Well, I'm telling you.'

We both looked at each other, and something lifted inside my chest! He'd flown across the world to apologise, and was doing it with such grace; he wasn't just too good to be true, he *was* true.

Jonathan raised an eyebrow. 'What if we just go for it – you think one of us might start believing it?'

'Maybe.' I put his hands around my waist and pulled him nearer to me, so close I could feel the chill of the night air on the cashmere. 'Maybe if we really concentrated on it. I might need some solid proof.'

Jonathan's serious face twisted up into a grin, but he straightened it quickly.

'I think that can be arranged. And I'm sorry for not making that clear enough. You're right. I need to scale back on the workaholism. You can keep your agency and I can keep my stupid stressy job?' he murmured, as his arms tightened around me, and his nose approached mine. 'I'm afraid we're both stuck with them, one way or another.'

'I'm sure we can talk about it,' I murmured back, tilting my head so my nose grazed his. 'There's bound to be a compromise somewhere. And aren't you the expert negotiator?'

'Oh, I think I can be quite flexible.' Jonathan's lips were touching mine, so lightly I could feel his breath on my mouth. 'When I want something as much as I want you.'

I let my body sink into his as our lips met, and our arms wrapped round each other, a warm spot in the cold draught of October wind. I didn't care about Nelson's yells to shut the front door to keep the heat in, or Braveheart's hysterical barking. I couldn't think about anything other than Jonathan.

We kissed until the moment was broken by Gabi screeching upstairs, and Roger bellowing, 'It's only a bloody dog with a wig on, Gabi!'

'I had to come back, in any case,' he said, disentangling himself. 'I needed to call in at the agency.'

'Did you?' I said uncertainly. 'What for?'

He was digging about in his pocket, then made a 'Found it!' face as he pulled out a ring box. 'Couple of things. First of all, I needed some advice on buying a ring . . . May I?' He looked up, with the ring in his hand and I was touched to see a brief hesitation in his eyes.

'Please do,' I said, and he slid it back onto my finger.

He looked at it critically. 'I mean, it'll do for now. But we Americans like to make sure a woman looks engaged from a distance, know what I mean?'

I smiled. 'This suits me fine, Jonathan. And the other thing?'

A satisfied sigh escaped from his lips as I turned the ring so the sapphires caught the light, as though he'd been tensed up until that moment. 'I need to buy a bed for this new house I've got in Greenwich Village. A great big, English, four-poster bed. Preferably old? With curtains I can close? It's a great big house, you see . . . Gets kind of lonely, just me and the dog?'

I smiled and slid my arms around his neck. I could hear the leaves rustling up and down the street in the wind. It would be even colder in Jane Street. Even more need to snuggle up. 'That sounds rather cosy. I'd be *more* than happy to help you find one.'

'Good,' he said, and kissed me again.

Hester Browne's Polite Thank You Notes

Obviously, one should always write thank you notes as soon as possible after the event. You can't blame the Post Office and your frightful handwriting indefinitely, and texting 'Thx 4 gr8 przzy!' is simply Not Done. These are a bit late, and not on Smythson's notecards, but they're heartfelt.

Thank you, Lizzy Kremer, for mixing patience and wit into a devastating agent cocktail, stirred with the swizzle stick of charming practicality, and spiked with something a bit kicky. And thanks to David Forrer and Kim Witherspoon for your equally potent Manhattan version (with a stack of nibbles on the side).

Thank you, Sara Kinsella and Isobel Akenhead at Hodder, for improving Honey no end, and Maggie Crawford and Mara Sorkin at Pocket, for my rough guide to New York and New Yorkers.

Finally, I'm indebted to the Jonathans, Rogers, Nelsons, and Godrics I know – so much so, in fact, that I won't thank them by name. Drinks all round, chaps. You're the best.